P9-CWE-014

Night Watch
Deep is the Night

Denise A. Agnew

ELLORA'S CAVE
ROMANTICA® PUBLISHING

An Ellora's Cave Romantica Publication

www.ellorascave.com

Night Watch

ISBN 9781419950827
ALL RIGHTS RESERVED.
Night Watch Copyright © 2004 Denise A. Agnew
Edited by Martha Punches.
Cover art by Syneca.

This book printed in the U.S.A. by Jasmine–Jade Enterprises, LLC.

Trade paperback Publication November 2004

With the exception of quotes used in reviews, this book may not be reproduced or used in whole or in part by any means existing without written permission from the publisher, Ellora's Cave Publishing, Inc.® 1056 Home Avenue, Akron OH 44310-3502.

Warning: The unauthorized reproduction or distribution of this copyrighted work is illegal. Criminal copyright infringement, including infringement without monetary gain, is investigated by the FBI and is punishable by up to 5 years in federal prison and a fine of $250,000.
(http://www.fbi.gov/ipr/)

This book is a work of fiction and any resemblance to persons, living or dead, or places, events or locales is purely coincidental. The characters are productions of the author's imagination and used fictitiously.

Also by Denise A. Agnew

∞

Deep is the Night: Dark Fire
Deep is the Night: Haunted Souls
Special Investigations Agency: Over the Line
Special Investigations Agency: Primordial
The Dare
Winter Warriors

About the Author

∞

Suspenseful, erotic, edgy, thrilling, romantic, adventurous. All these words describe Denise A. Agnew's award-winning novels. Romantic Times BookClub magazine called her romantic suspense novels "top-notch", and her erotic romance PRIMORDIAL received a Top Pick from them. With paranormal, time travel, romantic comedy, contemporary, historical, erotic romance, and romantic suspense novels under her belt, Denise enjoys writing about a diverse range of subjects. The fact she has lived in Colorado, Hawaii, and the United Kingdom has given her a lifetime of ideas. Her experiences with archaeology have crept into her work, as well as numerous travels through England, Ireland, Scotland, and Wales. Denise lives in Arizona with her real life hero, her husband.

Denise A. Agnew welcomes comments from readers. You can find her website and email address on her author bio page at www.ellorascave.com.

Tell Us What You Think

We appreciate hearing reader opinions about our books. You can email us at Comments@EllorasCave.com.

NIGHT WATCH

ৎ৩

Prologue
Pine Forest, Colorado
Tunnels beneath the Gunn Inn

ഔ

The ancient one lay on the dirt floor in his new hideaway, listening to the rhythmic moans and sighs of a young couple having sex upstairs in the inn.

More time to heal and he would have the strength to feed on the foolish, unsuspecting humans. The thousand year old vampire tasted opportunity not far from reach as it called to him with the scent of sweat and sex. He would break from his shelter and tear into the humans, glorying in their screams and the spurt of tasty blood. A craving built in his system, burning like fire along his veins.

Smells, like those of rotting death, called to him. These tunnels harbored more evil than just his own, and he planned to tap into that iniquity soon. Down in these depths, he felt regeneration of power. Those who had hunted him would rue the day they'd attacked him.

His body, dead but not dead, struggled to rid itself of damage inflicted by a silver bullet. His entire side throbbed with each breath. How long had it been? Two days since vampire hunters Ronan Kieran, Lachlan Tavish, and sweet Dasoria —

No. She called herself Erin Greenway, but she only inhabited the woman's body. Whether she would admit it to herself or not, she would again be Dasoria and belong to him.

He shifted, angered at the thought of his Dasoria turning on him. Revenge tore at his insides, urging him to leave this sanctuary and wreck havoc on her life. He could kill her current lover, Lachlan Tavish, then finish off her friend, Gilda.

She would be pliant then and willing to give herself to her true nature.

Some satisfaction could be obtained in blind, hateful vengeance. Then something stopped his escalating abhorrence.

Perhaps his mistake was in thinking Erin would realize she'd been reincarnated. He couldn't afford haste this time. That had been his mistake. Somehow he would force her to acknowledge her undead heritage.

Settling more easily into his curative state, he waited for the right time to resurrect from the darkness.

Ronan, Tavish, and Erin underestimated him. They didn't understand that once he regenerated he would arise more potent than before. Then all their machinations would come to nothing.

With a soft chuckle he settled into a vampire's deepest sleep.

* * * * *

Erin's breath came quickly, her chest on fire as she raced through the woods in pursuit of the bird of prey, the gargoyle flapping its horrid wings in the night. She aimed her weapon upward, hoping upon hope she would hit the creature and release its captive.

Red eyes like a demon turned to glance back at her. Fear rose like a violent ocean, threatening and unrelenting in its menace. Sweat broke out over her body as she tracked the animal threatening everything she knew.

The inhuman. The undead. The ancient one.

Sweetheart wake up.

She heard Lachlan's voice somewhere in her mind, urging her to awaken and leave behind the sinister dreams that often haunted her.

Branches reached out for her like skinny, naked arms. Dead limbs slapped her in the face, the sting sharp and angry as they scraped flesh. The trees hated her, as the gargoyle did, and they would do anything to keep her from reaching the only man she'd ever love. Fingers sprouted at the end of the branches and grasped at her.

"No! No!" She screamed the words, knowing if she gave up now she would be doomed and so would her beloved Lachlan.

The faster she ran, the quicker the gargoyle retreated, its hulking form sailing out of reach with Lachlan hanging from its hooked claws.

A feather light touch inside her brain said, *Erin, it's me. Come on now, you're having a nightmare.*

She wanted to break from the dream, but darkness held her in a tight grip.

It's a dream, lass. Only a dream. I'm safe and near you.

She reached out with her mind. *I know.*

Then come back to me. I love you. I want you.

Erin snapped from the dream with a gasp, her eyes dazzled by the mild glow of the bedside table lamp. Lachlan's powerful arms tightened around her, his naked chest pressing against her bare breasts as he murmured soothing words to her. Right away she recognized her bedroom and a sigh of relief flooded her. An emerald green paisley comforter lay over the bed, and she pulled it up over them.

His fingers caressed her hair and he pressed a kiss to her damp forehead. "It's all right. You're safe."

All around her familiar scents removed the last lingering horror. As she breathed deeply to calm her heart, the scent of sandalwood from an aromatherapy burner teased her nose. She kissed his shoulder and tasted the saltiness of his skin and recalled the wild time of lovemaking they experienced the night before.

Lachlan said, "Are you thinking about last night?"

"Of course. "

He smiled tenderly at her. "Good."

She snuggled against his naked body, relief moving through her like sweet wine as he kissed and caressed her into serenity. Warmth flooded the cold spots within her body and soul as he slipped his hands down to her ass. As he cupped her against his loins, his cock began to stiffen. Erin realized it wouldn't take much and she'd soon be under his ravenous lips and on her back with his cock tunneling deep and hard into her center. His thorough lovemaking would erase dreams for the rest of the night.

Erin touched his rock hard stomach muscles and smiled. "What is it about making love that takes the fear away?"

"Damned if I know, lass, but let's keep trying."

She knew raw sexual energy inside him thrummed and ticked. She licked her lips.

His mouth covered hers, tantalizing with his mint taste and the heated thrust of his tongue. Beyond all the pleasure, she knew he wanted to make her forget the nightmares that came since their battle with the ancient one. When gently she pushed on his shoulders, he released her from the passion-rich kiss.

His eyes blazed down at her with concern and arousal. "I'm sorry. I only wanted to comfort you, lass."

Erin reached up and touched his stubble-roughened jaw. His gaze held hers, warm and rich with love. She basked in the glow, aware few people found the staggering passion they did. "I know. But I wanted to say something first."

Small lines appeared between his dark brows. "Of course."

She slipped her fingers into the rich fall of his dark hair and savored the cool, silky smooth feeling. "The ancient one isn't dead. He's only hiding. Gilda and I won't be safe. None of us will."

Lachlan nodded. "I know."

"But he'll appear again soon. You know it, and I know it."

"The dreams are the same?"

"Yes. I'm chasing him again." Tears stung her eyes and she took a deep breath. "And I can't get to you."

Lachlan's arms tightened around her, as if he could protect her from anything and anyone if he kept her close enough. "Ronan and I will take care of you. We've got another friend coming who'll be able to help. A pesky Irish vampire by the name of Sorley. Ronan contacted him yesterday."

"Oh, lovely. A Scot and two Irishmen in my house. And guess what, two of them are vampires."

Lachlan grinned.

But even his smile couldn't erase her biggest concern. "The ancient one...he feels powerful, and he is coming back sooner than we think."

Lachlan caressed her arm, his eyes sad. When he didn't speak she knew he agreed.

She sighed, her eyelids drooping as the comfort and safety of being with this wonderful man eased her back into sleep.

Chapter One

℘

Micky Gunn didn't know if rabid paranoia and lurking insanity made her think something odd would happen tonight. Things—very frightening things—seemed to follow her, hiding in the bushes along the side of the road as she drove, and threatening to step out in front of her green Ford Escape.

What else is new?

Micky smirked, aware of her negative attitude and desperate to do something about it.

She'd left Colorado Springs earlier in the day, hoping if she moved away temporarily the shadow people would leave her alone.

She'd been wrong.

They haunted her thoughts, tormenting with doubts and a hunger to escape she couldn't shake. Did shadow people stay with a house or a place? Or did they cling to a person? Micky shook her head in denial and pressed on the accelerator the tiniest bit, unwilling to allow apprehension and panic stop her.

Perhaps she had lived with the shadows so long she would imagine them by her side forever, even if they left her alone in Pine Forest.

No. There must be a way. She would stop the shadow people once and for all, or die trying. Taking a shuddering breath, she envisioned in her mind's eye a light shielding her entire body against all negative influences. But something kept the image weak, a mere touch of white and gold at the edges.

"Damn it," she whispered.

She could blame her affinity for reading Edgar Allan Poe as a child for filling her head with nonsense. She remembered a creepy passage from *The Raven* that described her situation and feelings to the maximum. *And the silken, sad, uncertain rustling of each purple curtain thrilled me — filled me with fantastic terrors never felt before.*

Would she find her own purple curtain at the Gunn Inn?

She brought her musings back to arriving in Pine Forest in one piece. Snow threatened as little crystals of icy moisture touched the car and the surrounding wilderness. Amazing how such a pretty show of nature could become deadly. She drove cautiously, conscious of her impatience to arrive at her destination, but unwilling to risk a wreck. Moments later she saw the sparkling street lights of Pine Forest. She brought the car to a crawl as she rolled onto Main Street.

Micky scanned the street. Pine Forest used to be vital and thriving at night. At least that's what she recalled from visits when she was a kid clamoring for a new ghost story or two. Around Halloween the town went whole-hog with decorations and this year appeared to be no exception. Scarecrows made of corn husks and old clothes stood in many doorways along with their Jack o'lantern friends and filmy ghosts hanging from unseen threads. Not that this crazy town *needed* decorations to scare the life out of people.

In the fifteen years since she'd been here, the town's eerie atmosphere hadn't changed much. On the other hand, she'd always liked the weird ambiance of the place, even if she didn't believe the tales Uncle Carl once told her about the bed and breakfast. After all, a kid with her imagination should have been able to see ghosts at the inn if there had been any. What could she expect of this little town spread out below the Rocky Mountains, lush with critters, replete with ponderosa pines, and ghosts a-plenty?

Nosiness brought ghost hunters into town on a regular basis, people wanting to stay at one of the local inns and rub elbows with the neighborhood ghosts.

Then horrific murders brought the tourist trade almost to a dead stop a couple of weeks ago.

She could have allowed the knowledge that a serial killer prowled the streets delay her travel to Pine Forest, but what she left behind in Colorado Springs worried her at least as much as a serial killer. Maybe worse.

She thought back to her childhood days when she consumed H.P. Lovecraft stories as well as Edgar Allan Poe. She remembered yet another passage from a story, this one Lovecraft's, *The Whisperer in the Darkness.*

Most people simply knew that certain hilly regions were considered as highly unhealthy, unprofitable, and generally unlucky to live in, and that the farther one kept from them the better off one usually was.

She shivered, unnerved by her own thoughts.

Most of the shops looked deserted with a few exceptions, and she wondered if she should have scheduled her arrival in town for tomorrow morning.

But no, I had to get here tonight, didn't I? I had to outrun the snow.

I had to run, period.

The little devil on her right shoulder argued with the angel on the other, and tonight the devil and angel worked overtime. Second-guessing herself seemed to be the *crème de jour* lately. She imagined her stepmother's voice, long dead, harping in an accusatory tone.

You're always going off half-cocked, Micky. When are you going to learn to settle down? After all, you're thirty years old.

Thirty years old as of yesterday, as a matter of fact.

Big deal.

Emotional pain made her stumble back from the thought. So what if yesterday had been the most boring, uneventful birthday she'd experienced? She would get over it, if she put the day aside and concentrated on the future. She had a mission to accomplish with her uncle's old establishment.

Before long, restoring the place to its former glory would occupy all her thoughts.

No more shadow people. No more hurting birthdays in her past.

Self-doubt rambled in her head. *You want to run a big old guest house all on your own? Are you insane? You ought to take the money the old coot left you and invest it in something viable.*

No. She must find where she should be and where her life could blossom into something manageable and fulfilling.

Abruptly she realized she'd left the address for the Gunn Inn somewhere back at her apartment in Colorado Springs. From her memories of the place, the Gunn Inn nestled somewhere on the outskirts of town, hidden by tall trees and hedgerows. At the same time, she couldn't remember how to get there without the map.

Great. What to do now?

Her stomach growled.

Okay. Food first, directions afterwards.

She noted a dusty neon sign that spelled in red letters, *Poppa Joe's UFO Diner.* The sign featured a caricature of the stereotype alien head with large head, big black eyes, and almost nonexistent mouth.

"Quaint," she said, and parked across the street on the right. "Let's see what Poppa Joe's got to eat. Alien eyeballs, perhaps?"

Smiling, she grabbed her handbag and stepped out of the car. She waited for traffic to clear then crossed the street to the diner. A welcome blast of warm air hit her in the face as she opened the glass door. The place was almost obnoxiously bright, making her squint.

Light comforted her on most occasions. For the shadow people came in the dimness, hiding in corners and flickering in the corner of her vision. Still, they *could* appear in the most brilliant day, and she couldn't do a damn thing about it.

A waitress with curly black hair and a broad smile seated her in a booth. Micky ordered coffee and wrote down directions to the Gunn Inn. After the waitress left, she removed her navy fleece hat and waterproof fleece parka. She pivoted her head from side to side and groaned in relief when her neck cracked, releasing tension.

Feeling a little braver, she glanced around the room. A couple with three teenagers sat in a booth talking and smiling. An older man sat at the counter with a cup of coffee. A scruffy man with unkempt black hair sat there, too, munching on fries. His gritty, harsh expression sent a chill through her.

A man sat two booths away with a menu up so high it covered his face. He lowered the menu and their eyes locked.

Micky never believed in attraction at first sight. At least not the kind she felt when she saw this man. A wave of instant, burning attraction seared into her soul and claimed her.

My, oh my.

The man possessed a masculine face that could look boyish one instant, take-no-prisoners the next. With his thick, dark mocha hair trimmed close to his skull, she thought he might be in the military or maybe another occupation requiring similar discipline. His eyes looked hazel from this distance but she couldn't be sure. Intensely focused, he examined her with equal curiosity. His nose seemed almost perfect; not too small, not too large. And his mouth boosted kissable lips with a curve that begged exploration.

The intriguing man wore a toasty-looking navy cable turtleneck sweater. She wished she could see whether he was a causal slacks or jeans kinda guy.

More than individual physical features, he owned a look of know-a-lot without the arrogance some possessed; he'd been around the block without becoming jaded. Micky got the immediate impression of leashed power, a man who welded his physical skills with discipline. Danger crackled around him like a live wire, a part of his exterior, his force of personality for all to see.

Most of all, he didn't flinch from her blatant stare.

For a searing second she imagined his lips on hers, his touch exquisite and gentle. His cock would slide inside her, stirring into a steady pumping motion that reached every inch of her sopping wet channel.

As a wave of pure lust surged through her, she popped out of the high-intensity fantasy with a jolt.

The man continued his appraisal, and she inhaled sharply as heat filled her face. His steady gaze said he'd read her mind and liked what he saw.

I'm certifiable. I can't believe I'm gawking like this at a total stranger.

A strange noise jolted her attention back to the counter.

The guy who'd been consuming fries picked up his plate and threw it toward the waitress behind the counter. "Bitch!"

As the plate sailed toward the waitress, the woman let out a blood-freezing scream and ducked. Glass shattered as the plate crashed into the coffee machine. The enraged man stood, his hand going under his long dark coat. A big handgun emerged in his grip, and he pointed it dead on at the waitress.

Cold death gripped Micky, a sub-zero sensation that made her body seize in place.

Horrified, Micky managed a warning. "Look out!"

Before she could react in any other way, the man swung toward her and took a bead on her head.

I'm dead.

Instinct kicked in. She dropped, diving toward the guy's legs.

A blur whooshed by Micky, knocked the weapon out of the man's grip and slammed him into the counter with tremendous force. The madman slumped to the floor in an unconscious heap.

Menu man stood over the menace with feet spread wide and hands fisted at his sides. His chest rose and fell heavily.

Then he looked at her, sprawled on her belly like a fish out of water.

Seconds crawled as he kept his attention pinpointed on her. Her insides tensed, her muscles cramped.

"Call the cops and an ambulance," the man growled at the stunned waitress behind the counter.

Wide-eyed and trembling, the woman who'd been attacked rushed from behind the counter and toward the back room. Another server followed.

"You all right?" menu man asked as Micky got to her feet.

She stumbled back into the booth, sitting down with a thump. "Yes." She swallowed around the hard lump in her throat. "Thank you."

She watched the quick-thinking man in fascination. Now he was in plain view, she saw he stood maybe a hair less than six feet tall, with command radiating from every inch of him. Menu man wore jeans that curved over his muscled thighs with intimate closeness. He bristled with tensile strength, chained by the veneer of civilization.

His gaze flicked to her and the fire in those eyes caught her up once again. A dazzling combination of grey and green, his gaze stayed intent and blazing. With the assurance of a woman who followed her instincts, she knew he worked to serve and protect in some capacity. Either that or he loved to kick butt and take names. In any case, she'd seen he could be extremely dangerous in the right circumstances.

Just like Davy.

She'd dated too many men like long-gone Davy Benjamin. Cops often possessed a hard edge that couldn't be breeched, cynical and sometimes ruthless. They were often blinded by the horror they saw and the politics they might play to survive the system.

Davy had been an A-number one player. Handsome and impossible.

Until the day he died.

Micky jerked out of her memories, realizing she stared rudely at the man in front of her. She half expected him to ask why she gawked like a fool.

Davy would have said, *Whatcha lookin' at, girl?*

Instead it crossed her mind to fear this stranger. Any man who could move that fast and take out a person bent on destruction...well, he deserved respect.

Mumbled exclamations of relief and worry filtered into Micky's psyche, and she realized the family with teenagers sat huddled in their booth with alarm etched into their pale faces. On the other side of the room, the smattering of people seemed shell-shocked.

Quicker than she expected, sirens split the night and Pine Forest police officers arrived and took control. Questioning ensued. As she heard menu man's deep, resonant voice explaining what happened, she calmed. His voice held authority and assurance.

"I'm a cop." He showed his badge identification. "Denver police."

I was right.

"Jared Thornton," one uniform said as he looked at the ID. "You don't have a weapon on you?"

"Didn't think I'd need it. It's in my car."

The officer nodded. "What brings you here?"

"I'm here to solve my aunt's murder."

Menu man's words hung in the air for so long, Micky thought everyone waited for him to continue.

But he didn't and the officer spoke. "Your aunt was one of the people killed in this rash of serial killings?"

"Edith Pickles."

"I'm very sorry for your loss, but you're out of your jurisdiction."

One corner of menu man's mouth turned up, sarcastic before he replied. "I understand that."

19

When Thornton didn't elaborate, the uniformed officer handed the identification back to him.

Paramedics checked out the half-conscious criminal on the floor, and Micky moved to another booth farther away from the action. Her body trembled deep inside, a constant vibration she couldn't seem to stop. After a time the police reached Micky, and she gave her side of the story.

"I'm assuming you'll want to press charges. He did point the weapon right at you," one officer asked.

"Of course she will," Jared Thornton said.

Micky's mouth opened to protest Thornton's presumptuousness, but the policeman seemed to take his word. Anger slow-burned inside her. She couldn't let these men get away with treating her like an insignificant weed.

After signing the paperwork, she turned away and got ready to leave. Thornton took a step closer to her, and she felt his heat, a power thrumming and humming although he no longer needed it.

When he didn't speak, she drew her shoulders back and stood. "I didn't appreciate you taking over. I can speak for myself."

Challenge entered his expression and toughened his countenance. He stuffed his hands into his pockets. "You don't look like you're ready to handle anything without a little help right now."

So that's how it is. Disappointment warred with a desire to smack him. Her admiration for his physical form and take-charge personality started to fade as irritation arose inside her. So much for the wild fantasy she'd experienced when she first saw him.

So much for common sense. She'd allowed herself to become attracted to the same type of man again, something she couldn't afford at this point in her life.

"Like I said, I don't need your help."

"You can trust me." His voice held gathering impatience. "I'm a cop."

"I'm not questioning your ability as a police officer, Mr. Thornton, but I don't appreciate the domineering attitude."

Micky turned away before he could reply. Hot new resentment made her want to escape. A few deep breaths lowered her anger, but not all of it.

A few moments later the Pine Forest police officers told everyone they could depart.

Strange weakness hit her and her stomach protested with mild nausea. She pressed a hand to her midsection and took a deep breath.

As Thornton put on his thick parka he frowned. "You all right?"

"I'm fine."

He clasped her shoulder and his hand felt strong through her sweater. She twitched a little at the unexpected contact. "Everything's all right now."

"I know," she said softly.

Micky reached for her coat and the movement made him let her go. She wouldn't let weakness show. She didn't care if she had to crawl out to the car. After she shrugged into her coat, she reached for her handbag and slung it over her shoulder. Then she reached inside one pocket of her coat and retrieved her hat. She pushed it down over her hair and ears, grateful for the warmth.

"You're looking shaky," he said.

She tried a smile and failed. She leaned back against the side of the booth, weariness making her voice soft. "I won't ask if you've ever had a loaded gun pointed at you."

Without answering her question, he asked one of his own. "Do you have someone to pick you up, or did you drive here?"

"I've got my SUV." Suddenly he reached up and pressed his fingers to the side of her throat. She flinched. "What are you doing?"

He looked up and down her body, his inspection a professional surveying for injury. He took his hand away. "When was the last time you had something to eat? Your pulse is fast and you're pale as hell. You look like you're about ready to pass out."

"Around eleven o'clock this morning, I think. I was about to eat when that—that creep started…" What other explanation did she need?

"Your blood sugar is probably low. Come on. We'll get something to eat somewhere else."

Before she could protest, he took her upper arm in that proprietary grip. She stopped under the awning as they went outside. "You don't get it, do you, Mr. Thornton?"

"If you get in your car and have a wreck, I'll feel responsible, all right?"

"I'm *not* your responsibility."

Keeping his light grip on her upper arm, he stepped closer and looked down on her. Micky half expected him to ask her to call him by his first name. Instead he said nothing, a damnable silence she imagined unnerved everyone he encountered.

His eyes widened the tiniest bit. Caribbean sea-green and earthly gray combined in his penetrating gaze. Intrigued, she stilled and experienced Thornton, allowed his essence to fill her sensibilities for a lingering moment. She didn't let people this close often, and she didn't allow their emotions to pierce her. Again, she wondered what his carnal mouth would feel like on hers. Would all that seriousness etching his face soften and turn passionate? What would this hard-nosed, indomitable cop look like in the throes of making love? Wild and free, her imagination allowed a picture to form. She craved to know what his naked body would look like.

They stood under the awning in blowing snow simply staring at each other like two loons. Waves of unaccountable, strong attraction seemed to vibrate between them.

Or am I imagining it? Maybe it's just me that's attracted. God, I've got to try and maintain my sanity. After tonight, I'll probably never see him again.

"A lot of power in silence," she said without thinking.

His attention landed on her lips, as if he read her thoughts. "Silence is a technique I use in police work. Scaring the shit out of a suspect because they don't know what I'll say next. Gives them time to think."

She managed a smile as cold wind blasted under the awning. Instead of following his conversation, she sighed. "I'd better go if I'm going to make it to the Gunn Inn."

"Where is that?"

"Outside of town."

"In this weather?"

She nodded. "I'm a Coloradoan born and bred, Mr. Thornton."

"So am I, but I also use common sense."

Renewed irritation united with fatigue. "I'm not allowing a little snow to stop me."

Before he managed another word, she turned away and headed back to her car. But not before she caught his smile. His mouth curved into the most attractive, all-out-gorgeous grin, an amalgamation of wise-cracking and sweet.

Wise-cracking and sweet? One minute the guy glared at her like the hard-nosed cop, the next he flashed a smile more gorgeous than a movie star's.

After she started the car and headed down Main again, she decided not to think about the unusual Jared Thornton for the rest of the evening. Now that she'd survived the strange occurrence in the eatery, she no longer felt dizzy or uncertain.

Tonight's incident would be a weird event she could tell her friends about some day.

Right now Micky didn't want reality, because she knew if she thought about how her life might have ended this evening, she would start to shake. Instead, she would head to the one place she'd found sanctuary in her young life, the place where good things had happened.

Relaxing, she watched the snow covering the road and realized she didn't have long to check out her uncle's establishment, get back to town, then catch some sleep. If she explored the place now, she would sleep better tonight.

After reaching the west end of Main, she took a left on Mynah Bird Road and headed south toward the outskirts of Pine Forest. Ponderosa pines lined the dirt road, tall and intrusive. She'd always loved the forest, delighting in the sense of isolation. Tonight the trees didn't seem quite as comforting with snow falling and the fact she headed toward an empty house.

A few friends questioned why she'd come to Pine Forest now. While another murder hadn't been committed in a couple of days, that didn't mean the creep didn't still prowl the city.

A chill ran up her body and she reached over to turn up the heat. She wouldn't be here either if Uncle Carl hadn't decided to depart this world last month.

Old Uncle Carl hadn't said anything about Pine Forest hitting the skids, but then she also didn't speak much with him. Correction…used to speak with him.

That's why when the phone call came notifying her of his death, she'd been shocked and saddened all at once. Saddened because she felt she should have made more effort to keep in touch, and shocked because he'd left his rambling bed and breakfast to her. She still didn't believe it.

She would assess the inn's condition in the next week or so and have no difficulty deciding whether or not to restore it to the pleasant, popular place it had been ten years ago.

Micky watched for the weathered inn sign and it appeared on the right a few moments later. She turned down the long, narrow drive and soon three stories of rambling Queen Anne came into view. Memories bounced into her psyche of carefree days under her uncle's kindness. She couldn't have asked for a more attentive relative, a nicer heart. In a sense, he'd replaced the father her birth parent had never been.

Shame pierced her. *So why did you stay away for so long?*

She shook off the pain of guilt. Maybe all she could do now was to restore his inn.

One overriding question came back to her. She'd been safe against the shadow people here. Would she be safe again?

She parked the car in the circular drive rather than the small dirt parking lot to the right side of the house. Wind almost tore off her hat, but she dashed through the increasing snow and up the six steps to the porch. She'd have to make this exploration quick.

Once inside Micky reached for the light switch, going by instinct and memory. Uncle Carl's lawyer assured her the utilities had been left on. Light blazed from a crystal chandelier hanging from the high-ceiling of the foyer. A wide dark wood staircase wound up to the second floor. A large window at the top of the stairs gazed down at her like a dark, menacing eye. She shivered, shut the door, and made certain she locked it behind her. Quiet enveloped the big house, and for a second she considered retreating. What did she know about running an establishment like this? How could she expect to make a success of a venture her uncle ran for close to thirty years? Micky shook her head and decided she wouldn't make snap decisions or let the size of the place intimidate.

Exploring the first floor went fast. Everything remained much as she remembered it, although Uncle Carl had replaced some worn furniture and repainted in recent months.

She traipsed through a formal dining room, decorated with royal blue velvet curtains, beautiful dark wood paneling and matching highboy and sideboard. An updated gourmet kitchen dominated the left side of the house. A sizable office, huge front living area, and enormous library covered the right side. Everything looked clean and undisturbed. Thank goodness for her uncle's lawyer and his contacts. Feeling better about the entire situation, she breathed a sigh of relief and started toward the second floor.

That's when she saw the shadowy form flicker by the corner of her right eye.

Micky shivered with real fear as realization poured over her.

They'd followed her here.

Chapter Two

ॐ

Instant tears sprang to Micky's eyes as she stopped with one hand on the banister and one foot on a tread. *No. This can't happen here.*

But it was. She'd seen the shadows and knew without a doubt they'd followed her.

How naïve she'd been to believe she could escape.

Her breathing increased and her heart rate jumped. She fought the urge to panic, to run from the house without another thought.

She knew if she attempted to look directly at them they would flit away. New fear arose as she tried to manage her rising emotions. Trepidation mixed with genuine desire to press forward. Maybe her fate in life was to live with the ever-looming presence of shadow people. Whatever she did, she couldn't allow her fears to overwhelm. If they did, she would find no relief here or anywhere else. Although Micky hated the fact the shadow people had followed her to the one place she assumed she could be safe, she took a deep breath and proceeded up the stairs to explore her inn.

Despite the light feeling in her stomach, she pushed forward with renewed confidence. She reached the top of the steps and started down the hallway. She'd inherited this house and by God, she would explore no matter what specters haunted her.

As Micky opened the first room on her right and flicked on the light, she ignored two more flashes of dark shadows at the corners of her eyes. They would show themselves to her again and again if they thought they could frighten her. At least it seemed that way to her.

The Victorian decorated room, wallpapered with a fading blue rose print and adorned with dark blue brocades and shimmering green velvet, seemed clean of insects and dust. The lawyer specified that a cleaning crew had been in couple of days ago. He also mentioned they'd interrupted a young couple "doing it" out in the garden in back.

"Doing it," she whispered into the quiet house. "There's a concept."

She couldn't recall the last time a man held her in his arms, much less made love to her. *Going on six years, I think.* Six long, sexually dry years. Not that she'd enjoyed the act in the long run.

No. There was always *that* illusive big O. The one thing two lovers hadn't been able to help her achieve, no matter how hard they tried. In the end, her sexual inability made her feel like a freak, and her boyfriends turned away. Davy had been one of those men. The last in fact.

She again thought of Jared Thornton, and how his authoritative masculinity drew her. She'd always liked alpha men, although her relationship with Davy had proved some men took it too far.

Deciding now shouldn't be the time to ponder Jared Thornton's seething sexuality, she checked a few more rooms. As she looked into the last room, a board creaked behind her. All the hairs on her body seemed to stand on end, and with a gasp she whirled around.

The semi-dark hall, illuminated by the light of the bedroom and the light at the top of the stairs, hid the shadows and maybe something else. She strained to see but detected nothing unusual. Her breathing came harder as she turned off the light in the room and headed down the hallway at a quick pace. Deciding she'd check the basement and top floor tomorrow, she took the stairs at a clip.

She reached the bottom of the steps when the doorbell rang. Micky let out a squeak. Her heart hammered, and she wanted to scream with frustration at the way fear jolted her body in reaction to each unexpected event.

"Who is it?" she asked.

"Jared Thornton."

Her breath seemed to freeze up and at the same time overwhelming relief made her sag against the banister just a little.

"Miss Gunn?"

Rich and strong, his voice resonated with safety and comfort in the darkness. A shadow passed near her left peripheral vision. She gasped, startled. Propelled by the sight of yet another shadowy being, she headed for the door. Who cared if she let in a stranger at this point? A human presence would be preferable to the unwanted creepiness that stalked her now.

"Miss Gunn, are you all right?"

She opened the door as he spoke. His gaze scanned passed her, taking in the surroundings.

She stepped back from the door and waved him inside. "Come in."

A cold breeze followed, and she shivered as she closed and locked the door.

Snow dusted the shoulders of his parka and his hair. "Is everything okay?"

"Of course." Her voice sounded raspy, and she cleared her throat. "Why wouldn't it be?"

He walked toward the staircase and peered up, almost as if he expected someone or something to jump him. "You drove through a blizzard to an isolated house by yourself. That's what's wrong. It's not very smart."

Irritated, she opened the door and let the elements blow inside. Wind shrieked like a banshee in the worst pain imaginable. "And you're rude. If you've come here to insult me, you can get out."

Surprise popped into his expression a second before he cloaked it with hard-bitten authority.

He let her stew in his resolute gaze awhile before he spoke. "Sorry. That didn't come out like I meant it."

She made a soft noise of disbelief and closed the door again. She leaned against the door as if it might be her last defense. "Then how did you mean it?"

"I was concerned about you, that's all."

His gracious, if indirect apology should have appeased her, yet she felt too on edge to acknowledge the smallest gesture.

Feral intensity built in his gaze like a beast centering on his next meal. A surge of anticipation, unprecedented and exhilarating ran through Micky with liquid heat. Attraction pushed aside animosity as he moved nearer and stared without remorse at her mouth. For a foolish moment she thought he might lean over and kiss her without another word. She'd seen that expression before on a man, but not often and not lately. A thrill dipped into her stomach, lightning quick and just as shocking. She saw hunger in his eyes, a longing to sample her once.

You don't know him. Take it easy on the lust.

Lust, as she well knew, could hit like a sucker punch and disappear like a fire drowned by water.

She had to speak or be caught up in the net. "Why are you here, Mr. Thornton?"

"Call me Jared."

She nodded and crossed her arms. "All right, Jared. Why are you here?"

"Because I was concerned after what happened tonight. Like I said, it wasn't safe for you to come out here."

Amused a little around the edges, she absorbed the easier emotion. "Do you always rescue women?"

"Yeah, sometimes."

"Is it because you think they can't take care of themselves?"

"Of course not."

"You're protective."

"Yeah. So sue me."

His deep voice started a coil of heat in her stomach, and she pondered the veiled suggestion in his actions. "Why me?"

The directness in her question appeared to take him off guard, and she found it intriguing. She'd never peg this man as easy to surprise.

He cleared his throat. "Instinct. To serve and protect is my motto."

His impersonal suggestion dowsed her arousal the tiniest micron. "I see."

"There's a killer out there, Miss Gunn, and he isn't picky about who he murders. You could be a target right now and not even know it."

Chills replaced any heat she'd felt in his presence. Her entire body went on alert, and she almost considered running for her car and speeding away.

Sanity reasserted itself. "Why would I be a target?"

"The killer hasn't established much of a pattern other than cornering any female who is alone."

"And draining their blood," she whispered.

"So you've heard."

"It's been all over the papers in Colorado. I'm surprised it hasn't turned into a national story yet."

"If the death toll goes up, you can be sure the media is going to swarm this place like flies on carrion."

Her imagination, primed by the night and the knowledge shadow people lurked nearby, kicked into overdrive. She visualized the scene he mentioned, a slab of rotting beef being attacked by hundreds of ravenous insects. Again a rippling shiver went through her body.

"Why don't we get out of here? We can have a hot drink and get some food into you," he said as he edged a little nearer.

She smiled even though his nearness started a strange flutter in her stomach. "My stomach is feeling pretty hollow now. I forget to eat when I'm having a crisis."

One of his dark eyebrows went up. "Which crisis? The incident at the diner, this house, or something else?"

Damn him, he'd gone straight into cop mode, or maybe he'd never let up. "I guess the diner and the house."

Again Jared gave her an intense stare that probably made criminals freeze in their boots. "Nothing else?"

"You wouldn't believe me if I told you anyway."

Oh, damn it, Micky. Why can't you just leave your mouth shut? What was it about this cop that made her want to confess like a death row prisoner?

"What do you mean?" he asked.

"Nothing."

"Are you in some sort of trouble?"

"Are you always a cop?"

She tensed as he moved closer to her.

He drew in a deep breath. "Yeah. Down to the last bone."

"How disappointing."

She meant what she said because she felt it without remorse. A man who never left his job behind would be doomed sooner or later, especially if he dealt with scum of the earth every day.

Consequences often came in big packages, and from the growing irritation on his face she might regret her words. As she knew, not every cop was honorable or even likable. No doubt in a few seconds she'd find out which brand of peace officer he represented.

"Answer me." Steel-edged softness touched his words. "Are you running from something?"

Startled by his insight, Micky found her mouth open on a syllable of surprise. She pressed her lips together for control. He couldn't know about the shadow people, but somehow he'd picked up her desire to get away from them and everything else unsatisfactory in her life.

"You could say that. But don't worry, detective, it's nothing illegal."

"That's what they all say."

"At the risk of sounding like I care whether you believe me or not, what would I have to do to convince you?"

"Tell me the truth. That always works."

He placed one hand on the wall beside her. *Hadn't this guy ever heard of personal space requirements?* She inhaled deeply, far too aware of him for her liking.

"Are you a mind reader?" she asked.

"Of course not."

"Then how do you know whether someone is telling you the truth?"

"Cop's gut feeling."

Micky ached deep inside with the sudden need to explain all the reasons why she'd left Colorado Springs for Pine Forest. She was dying to tell him of her fears and her wishes for a safer, saner tomorrow. But how could she? This man would turn away from her and laugh.

The same way Davy did all those years ago.

Why do you care? Davy was your lover. This man is a stranger and confession is often easier to someone you don't know, right? If he turns away, so be it. There is no emotional investment required.

With all his male brawn so near, she felt hyperaware of Thornton. His wide shoulders and chest drew her, and she craved to feel power against her fingers. He might not be particularly tall, but he still looked down on her. The force of his personality matched his physical brawn, and that made him devastatingly attractive.

Micky drew in his hot scent, a subtle mix of sage and sandalwood that teased her down to the toes. Stubble grew on his upper lip and jaw, a testimony to a day without shaving. His gaze, the clearest peridot and topaz mixed together, penetrated her defenses. Heat shimmered below the surface, a banked fire she didn't understand and yet craved to know.

In defense, she decided she wouldn't let him get away with intimidation.

"Why are you standing so close to me?" she asked.

Surprise flickered through his face, laced with unrest.

She smiled, satisfied with taking this clever man off guard. "Didn't expect me to ask that, did you?"

Renewed interest made his gaze turn melting hot. "Damn."

His other hand dropped onto the wall beside her.

Caged, she tensed. Excitement melded with fear.

Everything inside her coiled, ready for a fight. Not an altercation based on fists and harm, but a struggle to maintain her head when this man made her want things she shouldn't. Heat rushed straight up her neck, over her throat and into her face. She felt her vagina clench and release with an immediate craving to hold something hard, long, and thick deep inside. Her nipples hardened, tightening to little points that he could feel if he reached up and cupped her breasts in his hands. Her wild reaction to him startled her like nothing before.

"You could be in big trouble right now." His voice went rough and husky. "Serious trouble."

"How?" She sounded breathless to her own ears.

"If I was intent on harming you, you wouldn't stand a chance in hell."

His words had the intended effect, and she hated it. Her sensual arousal almost departed...would have left if the fire in his eyes hadn't kept her in place, trapped her in a sexual undertow.

She threw him a bone. "Do you intend to hurt me?"

"Of course not. You're messing with fire, Micky. It's not a smart thing to do."

"And you're the fire, I suppose?"

"Push me too far, and I could be."

She didn't know whether his statement qualified as innuendo, but it came in a close second. Insatiable curiosity made her want to know what would happen if she *did* shove him that last inch.

"You're trying to prove a point to me, I think." With a grin she decided to set him straight. "That seems to be the theme for this evening. Poor innocent woman needs a man to tell her what to do, how high to jump, and when to do it."

New flames lit his countenance, this time with the burst of indignation. "I don't push women around."

A huge pause loomed between them, eating up all the oxygen. She managed to speak a few moments later. "Then why do you care if I get eaten by the Jolly Green Giant, or fall in a hole and disappear from the face of the earth forever?" Sarcasm laced her voice, but she couldn't seem to stop it. "Why aren't you curled up in your bed at your hotel sleeping instead of trying to keep me from making a deadly mistake?"

His lips went tight. "You're a smart woman, Micky. I saw that during the nut case's rampage in the diner. You're resourceful and smart."

Micky stuffed her fingers through her short crop of hair. "Dumb luck."

"More than that. You were damned brave."

"Thanks, but I think it was what you called instinct earlier. A survival technique if you will."

"Call it any fancy name you want, but I've seen police officers freeze up in similar situations."

"Maybe I should change my career field to law enforcement."

"What do you do, by the way?"

Micky hesitated, afraid what other questions would be released by her truth. When she spoke again she worded the sentence with care. "Like I said before, you wouldn't believe me."

"Try me." His voice held a sensual nuance that turned two words into something sexual.

To her consternation her face flamed with heat again.

When she didn't elaborate, he continued. "You probably saved that waitress's life, and she didn't even thank you."

Her gaze fastened to his, captured without resistance as he looked deep into her eyes and plundered secrets without apparent remorse. Warmth traveled into her womb, generating a sizzle so hot, she couldn't believe either the force or quickness.

Her lips opened, words hanging by a thread of sound, wanting to speak.

Again his gaze dropped to her mouth.

She licked her lips.

"Damn," he said again and turned away, breaking the spell.

Micky wilted against the wall, released from the enchantment. Her knees felt so shaky she thought she'd sink to the floor.

When Jared turned back, he looked as ruthless as a moment ago, without the sexual heat crackling and snapping between them. "Trust me."

"Why should I? I hardly know you."

"Because I'm not here to hurt you. But there's a man out there who would. Women have died in this town lately and the month isn't even over yet. If I can prevent any other women from suffering the same fate, I'm going to do it."

"You're scaring me," she said truthfully.

His expression turned hard and fierce. "I'm glad to hear it."

"You get off on frightening women?"

His ragged laugh filled with sarcasm. "No, but if it makes you see sense, it's worth it."

See sense.

Micky had lost all concept of balance in the years since she'd lived with shadow people. Yet she couldn't tell him she'd been haunted her entire life, doomed to watch the night with dread in her heart. She tried to imagine this house without the pall of shadow people. She couldn't. The few moments where the house charmed her disappeared under dark feelings and even dimmer dreams.

God, I wanted it to be different here. Now it wasn't only the same. It was much worse.

"What's wrong?"

Micky had almost forgotten his presence, a difficult thing considering she'd felt a keen awareness of him the first moment she saw him back in the restaurant.

Jared approached again until he once again invaded her normally carefully guarded personal space.

She didn't know why she allowed him the small intimacy.

His gaze traced over her, the assessment of a self-assured man who knew what he wanted at all times. A niggling discomfort made her look away.

"You seemed far away, Micky."

"I was hoping this house would be the answer."

"To what?"

She sighed, suddenly beyond fatigued. "I came here to build a new life with my inheritance. My uncle was very generous leaving me this house."

"You want to run this place alone?"

She shook her head. "Probably not. I'll definitely need help."

"Why didn't your uncle keep staff here?"

She shrugged, her shoulder muscles tight. "I think he knew he was going to die, but he didn't tell anyone. He just closed the inn six months ago. He said he wanted to retire and not work so hard anymore."

"And you didn't think anything of it?"

"Not at the time." Guilt worked into her like a splinter. "I sometimes wonder if I hadn't been thinking about my own problems so much, I might have realized what was happening with him."

"Beating yourself up?"

"Sometimes."

"Is that why you want to open the place again? To make up for what you feel you didn't do?"

The question caught her at loose ends. Damn if he wasn't perceptive.

She crammed her fingers through her hair. "Maybe."

The cop's mouth, mobile and intriguing, caught her attention as he spoke. "You can't check out a creaking, half-haunted old mansion in the morning?"

Again, he was right. She'd been foolish to come out here at night. In the morning, once sunlight radiated through the dusty windows, she could see what needed to be accomplished much easier.

Then another idea came to her. "You think this place is haunted?"

Caution, reluctance and humor dashed through his expression one after the other. He rubbed one big hand over his jaw. "My aunt said the entire town is haunted. But then she believed in all that stuff."

"And you don't?"

"There's very little I believe in."

An ambiguous answer, yes, but now Micky knew she couldn't trust him with her concerns about shadow people or anything else that might inhabit this place.

When she allowed silence to grow, he asked, "Where are you staying in town?"

Suspicion rose inside her, even though she shouldn't be wary of a police officer. It's not like Jared Thornton stalked her, bent on destruction. "Jekyl's on Hyde Street."

He grinned, and for a split second she saw the boyishness beyond the hard-bitten male. "Pretty weird name."

She pushed away from the wall, finally feeling comfortable enough to move. "From what I remember as a kid, it wasn't a bad place."

"I'm already checked in there. The proprietor is kind of odd, though."

She nodded. "Mrs. Drummond gossips. It seems to be her favorite thing in life."

Jared nodded toward the front door. "Let's go then. I'm starving."

A strange creaking noise echoed out of the night.

She gasped. "What was that?"

He peered around the room. "Is someone supposed to be here besides you?"

"No."

He started toward the hallway that led back to a doorway into the basement. "It sounded like something in the basement."

"Wait." She caught up to him, gripped his forearm and brought him to a halt.

"Why?"

"Haven't you ever seen a slasher flick?" she asked with an attempt at levity in her voice.

He looked at her hand on his arm, and she released him immediately. "I've seen them. Stuff like that rarely happens."

Jared approached the basement door and unreasonable fear made her speak again. "Don't go down there."

She'd tried to inject humor into her voice, but he didn't smile. "If someone is down there, I should investigate."

"Please don't."

Suspicion narrowed his eyes. "Why?"

She didn't know, but the admittance caught in her throat. When she didn't answer he twisted the doorknob. It didn't budge.

"You have a key for this door?" he asked.

She dug into her jeans pocket where she'd stuffed the keys. Before she could protest he took them from her.

"Is this really necessary?" she asked.

"Yeah, it's really necessary."

"But if it's locked how could anyone be down there?"

"Let's find out."

Seconds later he unlocked the door and a draft of air wafted up from below. He flipped the switch and dazzling light flooded the area.

He threw her once glance before saying, "Stay here."

Without a second more hesitation, he moved down the steps at a steady pace. Micky felt every muscle tense as the wooden steps creaked and groaned. She stood at the door opening and watched him descend. She'd never been into the basement as a child, and she didn't want to go down there now.

When he reached the bottom of the steps he kept going. From here the basement didn't look large, but she remembered her uncle saying it contained nooks, crannies and various rooms used for food storage, and a wine cellar. He also mentioned once that tunnels led from the basement to the forest. He was never able to find out why the tunnels were there.

Micky almost held her breath as she heard Jared move about the area. Moments stretched into one minute, then two, then five. Tension drew tight as she waited. When she no longer heard Jared walking around, concern overran reluctance.

She took one step down. Then two. Three.

"Jared?" His name on her lips sounded foreign and strained. "Come on. This isn't funny. If you're trying to teach me a lesson, it's working, okay?"

She didn't care if he jumped from the shadows and screamed, "Neener-neener". She wanted out of there, fast.

An arctic cold breeze drifted over her body, and she shivered for what seemed the umpteenth time today. When she touched bottom, she surveyed the area. Huge stones paved the flooring and walls, assuring this place would last. A passageway led to the left, light touching rather than penetrating. Boxes were stacked up against the west and north walls, some looking as old as the house itself, others new as yesterday. Beyond the jumble of boxes, standing in the middle of the room, was a dress form. It stood naked and alone, singled out like a body ready for execution.

To the left and south a series of four passageways fanned out over the wall. Light didn't enter the hallways more than a few feet.

"How strange," she whispered into the silence.

When a shadow loomed up from the side of the stairs, she felt everything in her revolt. Fear jumped into her throat like a strangle hold and she couldn't breath. Before she could turn, the shadow expanded into an odd, hulking monster.

"Micky."

The deep voice made her jump, and she whirled.

"I told you to stay upstairs," Jared said as he approached her. He clicked off a small black flashlight and put it into a pocket in his parka. "Why are you down here?"

Defiance stomped on her trepidation and she bristled. "How dare you sneak up on me like that? I thought something had happened."

"Don't get your panties in a wad. If you thought something happened, you should have stayed upstairs."

"Right. I should have let you rot down here."

Again that irreverent grin brightened his face. "Who said I needed rescuing?"

"You were gone so long I figured Sasquatch had eaten you or something."

He smiled. "You're almost funny."

She sniffed. "Almost? Thank you very much. Now where were you?"

He nodded back toward the passageway to the farthest left on the south side of the basement. "I was in there. I think these tunnels might lead somewhere outside of the house, but I wasn't going to explore without a better flashlight."

"It could be dangerous in any of these tunnels. They might collapse."

"They look solid. The ceiling beams appear heavy and solid."

She turned to walk back up the stairs. "Great, let's get out of here."

"I'll help you investigate them tomorrow."

Abashed by his assumption, she turned back to him, placed her hands on her hips and pinned him with a no-nonsense glare. "Why would you want to do that?"

He walked closer to her, and once again superheated craving started deep in her stomach and vaulted straight downward to her loins. "Because you're irritating and challenging and I hate to admit it but..." He shrugged. "...I want to know what makes you tick, Micky Gunn."

"What if I don't want to be known?"

To her ultimate surprise, Jared slipped his fingers through the hair at the back of her neck, then leaned forward and whispered in her ear. "Oh, yes you do." He released Micky, then winked. "Come on. Let's get the hell out of here."

Chapter Three

ဢ

"Are you sure this is a good idea?" Andi Blossom asked her boyfriend Jeremy Nordice as they took the tunnel leading under the old inn. She tugged oh his hand and brought him to a stop. "I mean, when we were here last time I thought I heard something."

Her heart pounded, anticipation at making love with Jeremy mixing with her dread of the unknown. As the murders piled up in Pine Forest, she recognized a growing apprehension about living in this town. When Jeremy suggested they stop at the old inn on the way back from a friend's house, she almost told him he was crazy. After all, it was snowing like a son-of-a-bitch. On the other hand, they liked doing it in kinky places. They'd gotten caught the other day when a cleaning crew came by this place.

"I mean, women have been killed in this town. I don't know if this is safe, Jeremy."

"Don't worry about it." As he pinned her back against the hard tunnel wall she almost lost her flashlight. "Forget it. I can protect you."

Andi supposed she should feel safe, but she didn't. Jeremy possessed the body of a runner, lean and hard. But at five foot seven inches she stood the same height as him and he didn't inspire a sense of comfort inside her.

"Andi, nothing is going to happen," he said, a grin forming on his narrow face. He waggled his eyebrows.

She speared her hand through his hair and smiled into his green eyes. "Except..." she pressed a kiss to his lips, "...what we want to happen right now."

"Right now?" He sounded shocked, but the teasing in his eyes told her he didn't mean it. He dragged her closer against his body and kissed her with hunger.

Scorching need swept over her, staggering and almost frightening. They'd gotten it on in this tunnel more than once. At the same time, each adventure here brought her closer to a fear she didn't understand. Sex in this strange place, where darkness always seemed to linger even when light illuminated it, had given her a new sexual prowess. What twisted oddness made her feel hot and bothered each time she stepped into this forsaken place?

Jeremy leaned in and kissed her again, his tongue an aggressor she wanted deep in her mouth and deeper in her cunt.

She was ravenous.

She put her flashlight down on the floor and so did he.

Seconds later he unzipped her coat and pulled up her sweater. He reached for her bra. She batted his hands away and struggled with the front clasp while he wrestled with the buttons on her tight pants. He almost had them undone when her breasts, big and plump, sprang loose from her bra.

"Yes," he said with a low growl of satisfaction. "God, yes."

She smiled, happy he liked what he saw. His fingers clamped on her nipples immediately, plucking like crazy.

Andi gasped at the mix of pain and pleasure. "Jeremy." When he leaned forward and clamped his lips over one nipple, she moaned. "Jeremy."

He'd never been so aggressive, but then neither had she. Heat flushed through her body, and she ignored the cold brushing over her skin as an icy wind filled the tunnel.

She heard whisperings in the back of her mind, a soft utterance as cold as snakeskin gliding up her spine. She pulled back from Jeremy in time to see the night move behind him.

Andi knew, the way a man arriving at his execution knows, something hateful and evil waited in the shadows for them both. She didn't even have time to scream.

* * * * *

Settled in a cozy booth in a secluded corner of Jekyl's restaurant and bar with Jared, Micky turned her glass of cabernet sauvignon and stared into the liquid. She'd just received the wine, and yet she felt like she'd consumed two glasses. Perhaps once she ate she would stop feeling as if she floated in a weird dream.

Along with that sensation of unreality lingered an unexpected side effect. She felt safer than she did in a long time. Everything about this place said security, comfort and intimacy. While she welcomed the security and comfort, the intimacy bothered her a little. When Jared threw her one of those impenetrable, but accessing gazes, it disturbed her on several levels. It felt almost as if he could see right through her, to the most intimate recesses of her thoughts. Somehow, in the few hours she'd known him, he'd touched something inside her.

Of course, the atmosphere made it worse. Who would have guessed Jekyl's would have such a great restaurant nestled in the back?

Gentle, smooth jazz eased into the room from hidden speakers. Candlelight flickered in scones on the walls and in a holder in the middle of the table, the low lighting adding a romantic ambience. Delicious aromas teased her nose and her mouth watered as she realized how hungry she'd become.

Several patrons already occupied the establishment other than Micky and Jared. A few people threw curious looks their way then went back to their meals.

Jared took a taste of his chardonnay, his eyes locking on hers above the rim of the glass as he drank. Mesmerized for a full second, she couldn't look away.

"I could eat an entire cow," she said to break the awkwardness.

"I had my heart set on an artery-clogging hamburger and fries when that jackass back at the diner pulled his stunt." Rough and uncompromising, his voice rumbled the words.

"And yet you ordered salmon."

He shrugged and added a smile. "Women aren't the only one's who can change their minds." He put his glass down. "When I offered to take you to dinner after the creep almost shot you, why did you refuse?"

Because you make the RPMs on my libido hit red line? "I wasn't hungry at the time."

Doubt lingered in his eyes. "That's not it, but I'll leave it alone for now."

Tendrils of alarm ran up her spine. "For now?"

"I have ways of getting information out of people."

"That sounds ominous."

His gaze went smoky, his voice a husky compliment. "In your case, I think it will be a pleasure."

Her throat went dry. She grabbed her water and took a swallow while trying to think of a comeback that equaled his for cleverness. She couldn't think of a damned thing.

Finally she asked, "What types of torture do you employ?"

Again his gaze lingered over her mouth, then swept down to her breasts. Suddenly her breasts felt larger, swelling against her bra and sweater with a quick arousal that begged for more attention.

When his gaze traveled back to her face, Micky thought about being angry at his blatant show of appreciation for her as a female. Instead she liked it way too much. A dart of tingling pleasure pulsed through her lower belly when he watched her.

"Handcuffs," he said.

"What?"

"My form of torture."

"Oh."

Oh. Oh? Could you sound any less urbane? Less sophisticated?

She decided she would give herself a bit a slack. After all, how many times did a woman almost get shot and meet a knock-down, drag-out sexy man, all in one night?

One corner of his mouth tipped up again, and she snagged on the sight. She licked her lips. "Have you ever lost the key when…um…when you were applying the torture?"

"No. Now with you, I might make an exception."

Heat flamed in her face. She wanted to push his limits. Maybe she could forget the shadow people if she felt his regard, his embrace…perhaps even his kiss. "Do the handcuffs give you the results you want?"

"Always."

"Why?"

"Because I know just where to apply pressure."

"And how?"

"Absolutely. No pain, no irritation. Just confession."

"Oh." The word came out breathy and eager.

Jared took another sip of his wine, his gaze never leaving hers. "Want to know how I interrogate?"

"Yes."

He moved his glass to the side, then reached for her hands. As he looked down at her fingers, the heat from his skin made her shiver with pleasure. "There's always the stare-down method."

She grinned. "Sounds like kid's play."

"Ah, but when you do it well, it's an effective tool." He squeezed her hands gently. "Now look into my eyes."

It was crazy. Ridiculous. And it had nothing whatsoever to do with *anything*.

Micky looked into the cop's eyes.

Rolling heat rushed through her, a thrill dancing through her midsection, teasing until it swept between her legs. He wouldn't look away, and neither would she.

"I'll have you know I was a champion at this when I was ten," she said.

"You hadn't met me when you were ten."

She made a scoffing noise. "That's arrogant."

His fingers slipped over hers in a subtle caress, enough to make her inhale on a startled breath of pure excitement. "Yeah, isn't it?"

Another pass of his fingers over hers almost caused her to look down at his big hands. Yet she didn't, well aware he'd win the game that way. The last thing she needed was to lose anything to this man.

Including her sanity.

Inhibitions dissolved like fog in the morning sun. She suddenly didn't care if anyone watched them. She'd always disliked showing affection in public, trained at an early age by parents not to display mushy emotions in front of others. Their influence had worked into her brain like a disease, inoperable and indelible. Jared was the first man who made her want to show affection here and now. Hell, with him she might show lust.

How did Jared do it? How did he remove major reticence with one look, one touch? Acceptance and pure male anticipation shone in his eyes, and she wondered how she'd arrived at this place where she couldn't look away. How could she allow him to mesmerize her when she didn't care about anything but the next brush of his skin against hers?

"We'll have to stop when dinner arrives," he said softly.

Her fingers tightened on his. "Of course. Then we'll declare a tie."

"I don't think you'll be able to last that long."

A spike of exhilaration went straight up her spine. "How long do you usually last?"

Heat flared in his eyes. "As long as you want."

Micky's breathing quickened as forbidden craving quivered in her feminine depths and took root. Her skin heated, her palms warming against his, her body going soft with growing desire. "I was speaking hypothetically."

"I wasn't."

His hands slid over hers again, cupping, caressing. Quicksilver and molten, her desire increased two-fold. "Do you always try this with women you've just met?"

Jared's voice turned husky. "I've never done this with another woman."

Gratification made her smile the slightest bit. "Why should I believe you? I barely know you."

His eyebrows went up. "My point earlier. But now you know I'm not a serial killer and it's safe to hold hands with me."

"Safe? Not hardly."

"But you're in luck. I didn't bring my handcuffs with me," he said.

Before she could reply the food and common sense came out of nowhere. She jerked her gaze from his as the waitress brought their food.

Swaying across the room with the platter, the big woman walked with confidence and a smile. Her blonde hair, piled high, looked within moments of tumbling to her shoulders. Her generous hips performed a bump and grind wiggle as she took each step. The nametag over her right breast jiggled with each movement.

Long in the tooth, maybe, but this woman radiated a sweetness Micky could feel. Immediately Micky decided she liked her, regardless of the blatant stare the older woman planted on her booth-mate.

As she laid the food on the table, the older woman grinned again. "Now don't you two worry. This is the most delicious salmon in town. Enjoy."

"Thank you, ma'am." Jared winked at the fifty-something waitress as he released Micky's hands.

Although the woman's face boosted heavy lime green shadow, black eyeliner and crimson lipstick, her grin showed a friendly and sincere attitude. "Ma'am? Now if that don't beat all. You're a polite one. Well, like I said to you earlier, my name is Chessie. Short for Chestnut of all things. What was my Momma thinking? Anyway, it's Chestnut Buttercup Creed."

Micky's mouth popped open. "Wow."

Chessie laughed. "That's what everyone says." She flapped one liver-spotted hand. "Don't you worry none. I'm long over worrying if people like my name."

Embarrassed, Micky tried to make amends. "I'm sorry. I didn't mean to insult you."

"Honey, it isn't possible to insult me." A big grin parted Chessie's lips. "One's gotta accept reaction to a cotton-pickin' name like that. Now, where are you two from and what're your names?"

Jared put his hand out for the older woman to shake. "Jared Thornton from Denver."

Micky also shook the woman's hand. "Micky Gunn from Colorado Springs."

The lady's cat green eyes flashed with good humor as she looked at Micky. "What brings a young thing like you to this town, Sugar Plum?"

Unsure for a moment if the woman meant her or Jared, Micky didn't speak. When the woman stared, Micky broke from her silence. "My uncle, Carl Gunn, left the Gunn Inn to me."

"Oh, so you're *that* Micky Gunn. Welcome." She patted Micky on the shoulder. "Well, I'll let you two lovebirds get back to your cooing."

As the woman swung away to help more patrons, Micky found herself smiling big time. She glanced Jared's way. "Cooing? Is that what we were doing, Jared?"

Jared speared a piece of salmon and chewed before speaking. "I think it was more primal."

She wanted to agree, but it stuck in her throat like a piece of food.

"You lost," he said.

"I don't know what you're talking about."

"You looked away. There's a price to pay for losing."

She started eating, not daring to look up at him and see his expression. "Like what?"

"A kiss."

Micky gawked at him. "That's awfully presumptuous."

"Yeah. "

Simple. Undeniable. It was maddening.

She wanted to hate him for his arrogance and couldn't. "Do you always get what you want?"

"Sometimes." He looked up from his plate. "Mostly."

"And you think if you kissed me that would be it? I'd just let you do it?"

"Only when you're ready for it."

"When I'm ready for it? What if I don't want to kiss you?"

When his gaze snagged hers this time, it held more than building interest and desire, it owned certainty. "You will."

Heat bloomed in her face. Micky realized in one sweep she'd traveled a gambit of emotions with this man already and she'd only known him one day. How could he send her from desire to thankfulness, to attraction, to anger, and back to desire again?

Had this ever happen with Davy? No. Jared Thornton hurled into her universe with the force of a superhero, ready to protect and willing to command.

Challenged, she decided she would take what he expected and twist it around to her advantage when the time presented itself. She gave him a secretive smile and continued eating. Let him think for the moment he'd made a victory. They ate in relative silence.

A few minutes later he reached for his wine. He cradled the glass without lifting it for a drink, his expression thoughtful. "Tell me more, Micky. Why are you here other than to take care of your uncle's affairs?"

"I needed a vacation. I work for a psychologist as an executive assistant. It's been hell because my boss is an arrogant bastard. I'd stored up two weeks of vacation and managed to talk Jim-the-Jerk into giving me the time."

"A year without any vacation?"

"That's right. The man is a workaholic from the get-go. If he works, *you* work."

"Why haven't you changed jobs?"

"Comparable positions in Colorado Springs don't pay as well. I've been there six years already and built up my salary. I can't afford to go looking for a new position right now."

His frown held skepticism. "You'd rather be stretched to the breaking point?"

"I'm tough."

"No one is strong forever."

She pondered his statement before speaking again. "Few men would admit to not being hard-hitting one hundred percent of the time."

"That's because most of them are worried what women and other men will think of them if they admit any weakness."

"I think it's weaker for a man not to admit his faults."

Jared smiled and tipped his wine to her. "Then you're a rare bird."

She poked at her food, and although she loved garlic mashed potatoes, she already felt full. "You've had a lot of experience with women who put down men?"

"In my line of work, yes."

"Other cops?"

"Some. Mostly criminal types. "

When he didn't volunteer more information, she decided she'd leave it alone. At the same time, she wanted to know. She hated being attracted to a man she couldn't understand.

With casualness she didn't feel, she leaned back against the booth seat. "Who put you down, Jared?"

He quirked an eyebrow. "There was the time I bent over to retrieve a woman's purse and she tried to kick my teeth in."

"Oh, my God."

"I ended up with a bruised lip, but that's a story for another night."

Shortly after they'd finished the rest of their meal, Chessie came by and cleared off the plates and took their orders for coffee.

Finally he spoke again. "You're very quiet."

"I was thinking about the inn."

"It's a weird place."

"And old."

She looked through a window across the room and noted snow battering the hotel. Wind screamed around the building, adding to a deep sense of isolation.

"This whole town is weird," he said.

"Reminds me of a Poe quote." She cleared her throat. "'From that chamber, and from that mansion, I fled aghast.'"

"Which story is that?"

"The Fall of the House of Usher."

"Wasn't Poe crazier than a loon?"

"That's up for debate." She smiled. "And if you insult one of my favorite writers, I'll have to do you serious damage."

He waggled his eyebrows. "Oh, you can *do* me anytime you want."

Her mouth opened but no retort issued forth. Instead, she burned with embarrassment mixed with arousal.

Jared shoved his wine glass aside and leaned on the table. "Any other ghouls you have hiding in your background, Micky?"

She inhaled and let it out slowly. "God, I hope not."

He didn't look convinced. "Why don't I believe you?"

"Because maybe I'm not willing to explain my entire life to someone I just met."

"That's not it. It's worse. I see pain in your eyes."

Stunned by his evaluation, Micky played it cool. "I had a boyfriend once who was a cop. He was definitely a pain. Does that count?"

He grinned. "Yeah, he would count. Why was he a pain?"

"Because he—" She halted, too aware of old memories needling her like dozens of knives. "That's a long story for another time."

His eyes narrowed. "Was he abusive?"

So Jared didn't understand the meaning of the word no. She'd met enough police officers to realize they were often determined to get a straight answer one way or the other.

"Verbally and emotionally, he could be one cold bastard. So to answer your question, yes."

Jared's eyes turned icy. "Did he hit you?" Each of his words came clipped and sharp.

A little bewildered by his adamancy, she hesitated to speak again. "No. He could hurt me to the quick without laying a hand on me. His father perfected the talent of slice and dice humor and I guess that's where my boyfriend picked it up. You know, sarcasm disguising itself as humor."

Micky sensed a dislike for Davy broiling up inside Jared. His aversion felt palpable, as if she could reach out and touch Jared and come away with her hand singed.

"I've worked with men and women like that. It's a defense mechanism, but it doesn't make it right."

Amazing. Jared hadn't defended a fellow officer, whereas people in Davy's department looked the other way when he mouthed-off and put her down at station parties.

Before he could pepper her with another question, Chessie brought their coffee. She left with a smile and the check sitting on the table between them.

Micky and Jared went for the bill at the same time.

His hand landed over hers, and the hard heat encompassing her flesh felt solid and dependable.

"We're going Dutch," she said.

"All right."

He drew back, his fingers brushing over hers. When she saw how much she owed, she reached into her purse and drew out her wallet. She put money on the table.

He took his turn contributing to the payment, then pushed it to the side where Chessie could reach it. Even though they'd divvied up the check, she saw he didn't want to leave yet. No, his gaze kept chasing hers, trying to pin her into saying or feeling something she knew she didn't want.

They went silent for a long time and just absorbed the sounds of the jazz as it smoothed over the air.

Micky realized she'd been inconsiderate of Jared in too many ways. "I never properly thanked you for what you did today."

"What did I do?"

"You saved some lives, including mine. If you hadn't been there, I don't know what would have happened."

He looked uncomfortable, shifting in the booth seat and leaning back from the table. "Don't think about might-have-beens. They get you nowhere."

More stood behind the statement, but she didn't know where to start to ask him what he meant. "Well, thank you anyway."

"You're welcome."

"And thanks for being concerned about me. That really wasn't necessary."

His gaze trapped hers again. "My aunt died because of the killer roaming this town. I don't want to see another woman harmed if I can do anything about it."

"I'm sorry about your aunt. Were you close?"

He shook his head. "She was a recluse. I've met her exactly two times, both of them when I was a kid. I don't get to Pine Forest often, and she tended to stay in town. She was my mother's sister, and Mom's pretty broken up over it. I would have come here anyway to settle my aunt's property and affairs, but Mom also asked me to find the killer."

"Of course. Will the police here let you participate in the investigation?"

"I've already been to the station and I don't think they're interested in sharing information. It's not my jurisdiction."

"Still, I'd think they would understand why you wanted to help. I know some police forces get territorial about things but what could it hurt?"

"They must think it could hurt a lot."

She poured a bit more cream in her coffee, then took a sip. "What will you do if they won't let you in on the investigation?"

"I've got a game plan."

He let his statement hang. She had the notion if she didn't keep asking him questions, he would become the interrogator.

His sensual teasing earlier left her vulnerable, and she didn't like being exposed.

She backed up a step in the conversation. "You said might-have-beens will get you nowhere. Why do you think that?"

Jared shrugged. "Long time experience. I've learned a lot in the almost fifteen years I've been a police officer. Worrying about might-have-beens is natural, but at some point you have to work through the pain and go forward."

"You used to obsess with the past?"

His gaze returned to hers, all seriousness. "I almost beat myself to death with what-ifs about a year ago in the aftermath of a gun battle. I spent too much time covering up what I was really feeling. You know, doing the macho man act."

She understood all too well. Davy had shown her how closed-up and non-communicative a person could be. "Never talking about your work at home, always pretending the ugliness of crime can't touch you."

His gaze turned laser hot, but this time with curiosity and something else she couldn't define. "That's exactly right. You sound like you know from first-hand experience."

She nodded. "I dated a cop. Remember?"

When she didn't elaborate he continued. "It's tough being a police officer because everyone expects violence to just bounce off of you. People don't realize that if an officer doesn't get counseling for trauma soon after an incident, the chances for developing problems later on are likely."

"Bottled-up rage?"

"That's one possibility."

She wondered if Jared Thornton would ever show her rage. She hoped not. One sign of such behavior and she'd never see him again. Davy hadn't hit her, but his verbal slashing might as well have been fists.

Quiet settled between them and she allowed the jazz music to fill her with a mellow, sleepy sound. Jared finally spoke. "What about your uncle? He didn't have family other than you?"

She nodded. "My father. But he's unavailable to help right now."

Shame sliced through her that she couldn't admit her father's whereabouts. Not because any law prohibited her, but because she couldn't think about it herself. She decided now would be the time to retire. "I've got to go."

"To bed, I hope."

To bed.

The words hung there like a mantra or a plea. A simply said, but complicated scenario when a man this virile and disturbing spoke them.

She nodded and stood. She picked up her coat, then reached for her purse. "I'll see you around I suppose."

"I'll walk you to your door."

She didn't want him to accompany her. Heightened tension ebbed back and forth between them like waves against a shore.

He followed her up to the second floor, and when they reached her room at the end of the hall, she kept silent then, too. She dug in her purse for her keys.

Once again all seriousness, he said, "I'm not sure you should be alone at the Gunn Inn. It's too dangerous in this town right now for women to run around unaccompanied."

"Even in broad daylight?"

"Even in broad daylight."

Weary but unwilling to fight, she sighed. "What do you suggest I do, then?"

"When are you going over there again?"

"Tomorrow, of course."

"I'll take you over."

There it was, the insistence she expected earlier. "That won't be necessary."

"I don't like what I felt over there, Micky. You shouldn't be there alone."

Suspicion tickled her mind. "What you felt? What do you mean?"

"I'll explain tomorrow."

As he had at the inn, he took a step forward and backed her into the door. His hands came down on either side of her, blocking her in place. Micky tried to remember she didn't know this man well, that he trapped her between the door and the solid, powerful bulk of his body.

No, she didn't know Jared well, but she felt as if she'd been near him all her life. A strange comfort overwhelmed Micky as she dared to capture the sea depths in his eyes. She saw everything she wanted there—protection, an offer of comfort, incredible sexual possibilities. No man had given her so much in so short a time.

He brushed his fingers lightly over her cheek. Tenderness made her reach out. Her left hand touched his chest and heat shimmered through her at the feeling of his iron-hard muscles.

Wow. Every inch of Jared Thornton screamed unrelenting masculinity. She didn't want to feel this vulnerable but how could she avoid it?

Jared's intense regard drifted from her eyes to her nose, to her cheeks. When his gaze caressed her mouth, she felt the hot attention all the way to her womb. Her belly fluttered wildly in arousal, and she *knew* it. Acknowledged way down deep she could take the first step.

All her life she'd allowed inhibitions about life, love, and sex to isolate her from experimentation. She must take charge—from screaming at the shadow people to get out of her life, to grabbing Jared now and proposing he make love to her here and now.

With a noise of frustration, he slipped his fingers into her hair. "Tonight I just want this."

Before she could blink, Jared tilted toward her, his eyes burning with purpose. He kissed her forehead.

Surprised, she almost showed Jared she possessed some bombshells of her own. She almost grabbed his head and yanked him down for a full on lip lock.

He removed the choice from her.

Her handbag and coat dangled between them, preventing him from getting closer. Jared didn't seem to care, because he attacked another angle, his lips skimming from her right cheek to her mouth in a silken caress. As his mouth took hers, he tasted like his wine, rich and full of life.

Easing his other hand up over her shoulder, he traveled upward until he cupped her face in both hands. He held her immobile as he explored her lips with a continual tender assault. Nothing was voracious or demanding in his kiss, it made her heart speed up and her breathing come faster. His thumbs caressed her cheeks, and she shivered and responded. Slanting his mouth over hers, he tasted with kiss after kiss.

Wildfire streamed through her blood, hot and wicked and unrelenting. She felt like she'd known Jared forever, rather than a few hours. She responded, pressing and tasting, lingering and caressing.

His mouth gave homage to hers in a way no man did before. Micky moved nearer as her desire to explore him ran heavy inside her. His hands left her face and voyaged down to her neck. She shivered as he touched the delicate skin, pleasure doing another incredible flood through her body. He released her mouth and she gasped for air.

As he kissed her under the ear, Micky dropped her purse and coat on the floor at their feet. For a moment she wanted nothing between them but skin.

Frantic sexual desire demanded. She flushed from head to toe with pleasure, wondering if he would take the kiss to the next level. If she would.

Yes.

She flicked her tongue over his lips, and with a low male growl he stepped even closer. He imprinted his hard body against hers from chest to thighs. Rigid cock pressed into her, and she arched in shocked delight.

He gasped for breath. "God, Micky. God."

His mouth took hers again on a muffled moan. His tongue commanded and slipped between her lips. Instead of a slow exploration, he gave demanding strokes that offered no escape. He tasted wild and hungry, his approach a marauder asking for surrender. Again and again, his tongue filled her mouth, a relentless caress which set a fire between her legs. Although her mind drifted in a fog of sensual delight, Micky allowed her fingers to slip over the muscles in his shoulders, and she cupped the back of his neck to feel the warm skin there. She ached with increasing desperation to feel his naked skin against hers.

Deep yearning made her wonder how he would feel inside her. Broad and long? Would he press as deep as he could go, or drive her to a screaming edge with tender, slow pumps of his hips?

A door creaked open across the hall, and they jerked apart with a gasp.

An old woman with a thoroughly disapproving moue glared at them from the threshold of her room. "I thought I heard something out here." With a huff she threw them a disdainful look. "Get a room."

She slammed her door and engaged the lock.

To Micky's surprise, Jared chuckled. He released her and stepped back. His chest rose and fell with his rapid breathing, his face a little flushed. He reached down to retrieve her coat and purse and handed them to her.

"I have a few things to do tomorrow morning." His gaze searched hers, still fire hot. "Don't go to the inn without me, all right?"

"All right," she said before she could think of a reason to object.

He made a two-fingered salute. "Goodnight."

As he turned and walked away, she almost called after him.

There's a room right here, Jared. My room.

* * * * *

As Ronan Kieran strolled the almost empty streets of Pine Forest, the blizzard started to ease. Snow drifted in swirls about his booted feet, and icy wind blasted through his hair. He didn't feel the cold, his skin immune to everything including freezing. Still, he probably made a weird sight walking down the sidewalk in a long black leather coat and no hat and gloves.

Saints preserve us.

A dark mood drove him from his room at Jekyl's, and he'd decided a walk in the cemetery or the graveyard in back of St. Bartholomew's Catholic Church would do him some good. A nice reminder of his immortality, you could say. When he'd seen the man flirting with the delicate-looking blonde in the restaurant earlier, it reminded him of the mission ahead and the decree given to him by Yusuf and the seer. They'd insisted he must find a mortal female to fulfill the next part of the mission to destroy the ancient one. Only by combining the power of the mortal and immortal could he defeat an evil so dark.

He'd returned from Ireland that day, and although he should contact Lachlan and Erin to let them know information he'd gathered from the seer, he decided it was too late in the evening. He doubted the ancient one regained enough of his power to be a menace to them yet. A threatening disturbance ran through the air tonight, and while he felt no fear, he realized the sensation meant mayhem and perhaps disaster drew nearer.

The church loomed up, gothic elements stark and a little forbidding for a small house of worship, but beautiful all the same. At one time he'd been a Catholic, long before the life of a vampire took him. He felt no abhorrence for the Church, or anyone who prayed there. Vampires were not damned. At least not in the tradition of Christianity. They would suffer by their own evil, if such evil came. Like humans, they could reach the realms of heaven or nirvana or whatever their prior religion specified for their originating culture. Once they lost their immortality, depending on the life they'd led, they may discover paradise at their end. They recognized the three-fold law. Whatever vice they did or whatever good, it would come back on them three times.

As he knew too well, karma was a bitch.

He smiled and looked up at the large spire reaching high into the sky. Whirling snow fluttered in the darkness, more discernable to his night vision. Maybe in an odd way he found comfort in being linked with the living of the church and the dead of the graveyard. Whatever his motivations, he slipped through the broken open gate behind the stone church and cloaked himself in the night. Melting into the shadows assured him a night watchman would not see him. If a human felt his presence they'd think him a ghost, or a figment of overactive imagination. A mortal's penchant not to believe what they saw with their own eyes worked to Ronan's advantage.

Searching the area for signs of human movement, he saw nothing but the hump of gravestones small and large, flat and tall. Someone kept this yard of the dead in good shape. No weeds or grass overgrew the grounds. Flowers brought to headstones the day before now wilted under the force of the storm, most covered in snow.

A ripple went through his body. Someone roamed the area, though he couldn't see them yet. What matter of creature could it be?

Aye, and keep your eyes open for the ancient one.

Since he came to Pine Forest to assist his good friend Lachlan Tavish battle the ancient vampire, he realized something gnawed away at him late at night. He assumed the ancient one tainted the area, hiding, his everlasting evil a stain on the town.

He stuffed his hands in his coat pockets as snow and wind thrashed his face. Ronan decided he must work to vanquish the ache in his psyche as well as hunt and kill the ancient one.

A rustling in bushes behind Ronan warned him at the same time a wave of intense knowing hit him. A vampire hovered near. Whirling, he readied his stance for a fight. Knees bent, hands out, he waited. A dark shape walked out of the shadows, and a strange popping noise heralded the form's arrival, the sound of a vampire slipping from cloaked to visible.

"Aye now, look out," a familiar Irish voice said. "Don't be tryin' any fancy feckin' Ju Jitsu garbage on me, Ronan."

Ronan smiled as the small, skinny Irishman walked toward him. "Sorley, you bastard, would you give me some warning next time?"

"Why should I? Keeps you on your toes, as they say."

Ronan grunted. "When did you get into town?"

"Took me a hop, skip, and a long air flight to get here."

A mop of scraggly black hair tousled over the narrow-faced Irishman's head. Short and scrawny enough to thread through a needle, Sorley looked like a reject from a *Miami Vice* episode. Ronan couldn't help laughing. He gestured to the cream linen jacket and matching wide-legged pants Sorley wore. The coral-colored shirt made Ronan laugh again.

"Sorley, this isn't the tropics, man. Get into something more regional, unless you want to raise suspicions amongst the locals."

Sorley headed toward the gate leading out of the graveyard. He grunted. "Think these threads are square?"

"Adjust your language, too. You're speaking seventies."

Sorley stopped outside the gate. He put his hands on his hips, his eyes glowing slightly. Wind ruffled through his hair as snow alighted on his shoulders. "Now, surely you're not tellin' me how to dress and talk?"

"Damn right I am. I need your help, but if you don't blend in, people will get wary. Newcomers in town are being watched."

"Because of the murders?"

"Aye." Tired of his friend's idiosyncrasies, Ronan asked, "Where are you staying?"

"Not in a crypt, you can be certain. Too much time in Morocco on a cold stone bed, don't you know?"

"And?"

"I got the last room at Jekyl's'."

"Good. We can conference there, or at Lachlan and Erin's home."

Sorley cocked his head to the side like a curious animal, his smile broad. "So, he's moved in with her, has he?"

"Of course. He's bloody in love with her."

Sorley's eyes flared a second with a yellow glow like a cat. "You don't sound happy about the situation."

Happy didn't describe his feelings at all, but his sentiments didn't count with Lachlan, a mortal capable of many vampire powers.

Ronan stuffed his hands in his coat pockets again. "I never begrudge others to love."

Crossing his lean arms, the little Irishman peered at him. "Only yourself. I know. I've been your feckin' friend for how long now?"

"Since the American Revolution."

"Jesus." Sorley drawled the word, his accent turning the e sound to a long a. "Would you believe that?"

Wind blew flakes of snow across their faces and Ronan brushed dampness off his nose. Standing in almost total darkness, he could see the outlines of old gravestones with dates going back a hundred years. Yet he felt no awe at their age. When a vampire lived as long as he did, the word *old* became relative.

"Gettin' back to suspicious villagers, what is your cover story?" Sorley asked.

"A friend of Lachlan's. A tourist passing through."

Sorley's nose crinkled up. "That's not a bleedin' cover story, it's the truth."

Ronan started down the hill away from the church, and Sorley trotted to keep up with his long, steady pace. "I'm hiding in plain sight. No one would expect a vampire to run around in town where everyone can see him."

Sorley snorted. "If anyone catches me out of cloak, they will forget me as soon as they blink."

Ronan didn't plan to use invisibility cloaking or other vampire abilities to skulk around town unless it was absolutely necessary. Ronan trudged onward. "If people see me, I refuse to act like a ghost."

"Suit yourself, but I'd rather not be takin' chances. Besides, Mrs. Drummond is one nosy lady. She asked me about a million questions before she let me check in."

"Do you blame her? People are scared."

Sorley's sharp features screwed up in disbelief. "They ain't seen anything yet."

"There's another problem to contend with. A new mortal arrived in town today."

"How do you know?"

"I was in the right place at the right time, just outside a diner when the shit hit the fan." He explained about the young blonde woman and the cocky cop who'd encountered a mentally disturbed man with a gun. "I was walking by when I heard the man with the gun threaten the woman. Then I saw the whole thing happen. The cop was so fast I didn't have to interfere."

Sorley looked doubtful. "You would have jumped in to save the day, no doubt."

"I wouldn't have allowed the woman to be hurt. I would have figured out something."

Sorley shook his head. "Always the hero, you are."

Ronan decided to pay little attention to Sorley's sarcasm. He was used to the vampire's cynical attitude about mortals. "We still live in this world, Sorley, even if we don't like all the mortals in it."

The smaller man nodded. "Aye. And why are we talkin' about this blonde anyway?"

"Because she's fresh meat for the ancient one. Mark my words, we'll have to keep an eye out for her if the cop doesn't."

"We can't save all the women in this town from the ancient one."

Ronan didn't want to hear it, even though it made sense. "We can certainly try."

"What's so special about the new woman in town?"

"I'm not sure. Just a feeling I have. And you know my feelings."

Sorley shook his head and sighed. "That I do. Your feelin's have saved my arse on more than one occasion, they have." He picked up his pace, trying to match Ronan's longer strides. "On another subject all together, have you decided to take Yusuf's advice?"

Ronan reached the bottom of the hill and kept walking. "No."

"You told him you would."

"I can't do it."

"There's got to be at least one woman in this town that would be willing to screw you to help you generate enough power to kill the ancient one. How difficult can it be, eh?"

Ronan felt his temper cook, and walked even faster. Sorley would have to run, the little bastard. "I'm not going to fuck a woman just to get what I want. I'm not a user."

Sorley snorted. "Now that's a fine thing to be sayin'. You screwed Yusuf's daughter more than once to get you wanted."

"That's different."

"How?"

Ronan stopped, his ire reaching epic proportions. If Sorley weren't such a damned good friend, he'd probably have broken him into little pieces by now. "I shouldn't have to tell you. Yusuf's daughter was a newly made vampire. She had to have sex or die. You know how this shit works."

Sorley nodded. "All right, all right. I see the difference. But you couldn't feck a woman just once in this town just to get the ancient one in your clutches? A one-night stand with a hooker or something?"

Ronan's hands clenched into fists as he glared. "Damn it all to the tenth level of hell. Yusuf specified I had to make a woman fall in love with me. That takes a lot longer to accomplish than wall-banging a whore."

Sorley shrugged and looked at the ground. When he shifted from foot to foot nervously Ronan figured he'd made his friend think twice.

Ronan started walking again. "I'll think of another way to bring down the bastard, and that's the last word on the subject."

Chapter Four

ɛↄ

The ancient one waited in the dark, absorbing the stale air of the tunnels. As the ancient one took a cleansing breath, he sat up. The hard rock beneath his back gave him little rest any longer. He stood and tested his legs, uncertain about his strength after his long, long rest.

Restless, he wished the day would fade into night soon so he might prowl outside without draining his precious strength. Even in the pitch black tunnels he saw his surroundings with crystal clarity.

Eagerness mixed with a wish to seek revenge. He would take his time and lure those who'd hurt him into false comfort. Once again he'd destroy his enemies, as he'd shattered anyone who'd defied him in a thousand years time.

He stretched his arms straight into the air, grasping toward the low ceiling. He inhaled the pungent tang of questionable soil and wondered what iniquity he might tap in this shadowy place. As soon as he'd entered these tunnels the other day he'd felt it, and instantly drew the darkness into his undead heart. It powered him, regenerated him much faster than he would have normally. He could have expected to linger many more days in this abyss to mend. Instead he received this amnesty. For ancient history resided in this tunnel and all nearby land.

Since he'd stepped foot in the tunnels he felt strange shadows around him and saw them flittering here and there like pesky insects.

"Shadows, yes. Why do you come here?"

No answer.

No matter. Evil lurked close and he wanted to share the enmity with these creatures who came from nowhere. He realized the shadows had been here all along, deep in the soil and the walls and the ceilings of the tunnels and the house. He always recognized a fellow rotten soul...or lack of soul, as it were.

"Thank you shadows," he whispered, spreading his arms out and savoring the gloom. "Come into me and do your worst and we will work together. As one we will be even stronger!"

Like a hammer the sensation came down, driving the ancient one to his knees as pain spiked into his skull. He cried out, wondering for a second if he'd made the biggest mistake of his undead life.

Instead the feeling dissipated and he rose to his feet. Heat filled him, and unaccustomed to the sensation, he worried about it enduring. Instead it drained away and left him with his customary cold skin. He pushed his long hands through the tumble of hair around his shoulders and growled with the exhilaration.

Feeling stronger than he had before the silver bullet had entered his body, he proceeded along the tunnels in search of sustenance. Any rat might do in a pinch, but he saw nothing. Besides, his appetite had been fulfilled by the young couple he'd taken apart piece by piece last night. He'd left them in one of the offshoots of the tunnels, their eyes widened with dead terror. Humans tasted ever so much better when scared to within an inch of death. He would have liked to fuck the woman before taking her blood, but she'd screamed and collapsed at his feet when he'd torn out her boyfriend's throat with one bite. He thought she'd fainted. Instead he discovered the female had died. So much for the resilience of a youthful heart.

He started toward the end of one tunnel and observed all around him. Damp and mushy, the dirt floor stuck to his boots. The tunnel walls, shored up by wood and concrete, featured the stench of nightmares.

"Oh, what good evil I sense here. Good evil." He cackled, and the sound echoed in the tunnel. "Is that possible?"

As he stopped at the end of the tunnel and looked into the basement, he wondered when the young woman who now lived for the inn would visit him again. Oh, yes. He wanted her to stop by again.

Today he would wander, discovering in this blackness whether he could make a permanent home here. The graveyards wouldn't be safe any longer with Lachlan Tavish and Ronan Kieran patrolling by night.

In the meantime he would take sustenance from the strange beings surrounding the woman who traversed this inn by day. When she entered the house again, he would take opportunity. A succulent, most tasty diversion she would make. Tender, giving, full of sexual fire yet untapped. Perhaps, if she wandered into his path during his other nocturnal journey's she would discover a whole new meaning to awakening.

In the end he would give her more than ecstasy, the type of sex no mortal man could provide. Once she tasted him, she would never forget.

* * * * *

Micky decided reading the Pine Forest Sentinel in a noisy dining room at seven-thirty in the morning must be madness. She lifted her cup of coffee and after a healthy swallow, speared another forkful of scrambled eggs.

Mickey stared at the front article, a headliner about the strange incident in the diner yesterday.

Local authorities say Ben Wilkins of Central City just moved to Pine Forest a few weeks ago and did odd jobs. At this time it is uncertain why Mr. Wilkins attacked the people at the diner.

She skipped over more speculation, and her gaze snagged on her name and Jared's in connection with the incident.

Instant celebrity, of course. People in this little town hungered for news and gossip like any little city on earth.

Chessie stepped up and refilled her coffee cup. "Hi there, darlin'."

"Chessie, you're working again this morning?"

"Yep. One of the girls called in sick. They're willing to pay me extra for the double shift today, so I took it." Chessie gestured at the newspaper. "That article was something else, wasn't it?" Her eyebrows waggled. "That hunk policeman is a hero."

Micky nodded. "He did his job well."

Chessie put one hand on her hip. "From that there article it sounds like he's a decorated homicide detective back in Denver with a list of brave actions to his name."

Micky wanted to be impressed, then Davy popped into her mind, haunting her the way the shadow people did. Davy received several commendations for his good work, yet in the end it didn't save their relationship or his life.

The tall waitress batted her long eyelashes, heavy with blue mascara. "Matter of fact, he sounds like a real catch. And he seems to like you."

"I don't know about that."

Chessie made a *tsk-tsk* noise. "Open your eyes, girl. I saw the way he looked at you." She flapped her hand. "Well, don't mind me any. I tend to get a bit nosy, especially when I see a romance in the making. You eat up now. You look pale as a lamb, darlin'."

Despite the woman's prying, Micky liked Chessie's sincere friendliness. "Will do. Thanks for the refill."

When the waitress left to serve another table, Micky contemplated what Chessie said. Sure, Jared flirted, but that didn't mean a romance would come of it. She found him attractive in an elemental way, but lust often burned away after a short time, and she couldn't afford to be distracted by a relationship when she needed to put her life in order. How could she expect a man to understand the shadow people when she didn't understand them herself?

She turned to the next page and read another piece on the rash of murders. Since no new murders had happened lately, the paper postulated the serial killer may have drifted elsewhere. People could only hope the danger had passed.

Micky chewed over Jared's offer to escort her to the inn. A cautious person in general, she didn't know if she trusted him.

You trusted him enough to let him kiss you.

She rubbed her forehead. Kiss seemed too mild a word, too gentle to outline the extraordinary passion that erupted from them in the hallway last night.

Indeed, she'd almost invited him into her room. In a million years she'd never considered sleeping with a man she'd met a few hours before. Then again, she'd gone to a dark, abandoned inn last night. To a casual observer, she might not appear cautious at all.

I've got to pay attention to what I'm doing before I go down in the annals of too-stupid-to-live.

At the same time, she refused to rely on a man the way she'd relied on Davy.

The hell with it. I don't need Jared with me.

She closed the paper and after she finished her breakfast, paid her bill and headed out. Maybe once she'd gone through the entire house and assessed what she'd need to do to reopen the place, she'd feel refreshed and generate some energy. All night she'd tossed and turned, her sleep disturbed by strange dreams of Jared beckoning her, only to have him turn into a blood-sucking vampire.

Now there was an oxymoron. Didn't all vampires qualify as blood-sucking?

She crossed into the small lobby, her steps eager.

"Miss Gunn," Mrs. Drummond said from the front desk. "How are you this morning?"

For a moment Micky almost smiled, waved, and made a polite acknowledgment before continuing. Mrs. Drummond, though, moved from around the counter and came toward her. No escape this time. The gray-haired, fifty-something woman, tall and thin, always looked a little bitter. She also smelled like cigarettes.

Micky came to a stop and plastered on an agreeable smile as the woman caught up. "How are you, Mrs. Drummond?"

"I'm good." She held out an envelope, and Micky took it. "That police officer Lieutenant Thornton dropped this off for you."

Micky's full name was scrawled in blocky letters on Jekyl's utilitarian stationery.

"Thank you. I'll see you later."

"Wait."

Micky turned back, her body tensing. *She didn't expect her to open the letter right in front of her, did she?*

Mrs. Drummond pinched up her tanned, rough-hewn face. "I'm sorry the note didn't get to you earlier. He delivered it to the front desk about four o'clock this morning, but the desk clerk didn't think to tell me until a few moments ago."

More than curious about the note, Micky felt anxious to get to her car and read the missive. "No problem."

Her voice clipped and quick, Mrs. Drummond asked, "You aren't going out to that inn alone, I hope? I was telling some people the other day the place isn't fit for human habitation." The older woman crossed her arms, as if she needed to defend herself. "The last couple of months before your uncle died, he didn't exactly keep things up."

Again Micky put on a pleasant smile and kept her voice light, even when contemplating braining Mrs. Drummond with the nearest table lamp. "I imagine if he was ill it was difficult for him work around the place."

Mrs. Drummond's stony expression seemed to accuse her. *Why weren't you here to help him?* "You're probably right. But I didn't want you to be surprised when you went out there and saw it."

"I've already been there. Last night."

Incredulousness came over the woman's face. "After the incident at the diner? Weren't you afraid to go out there alone?"

She almost said it. Micky almost opened her mouth and said Jared arrived to save the day. No, not exactly. Not even mostly. She wouldn't and couldn't rely on him for another thing. "Of course not. Why should I be?"

Mrs. Drummond lowered her voice. "Because the place is haunted. Even old Carl mentioned it to me more than once. He talked about these weird shadows that followed him around the house."

Micky's entire body froze up. "What?"

"Shadows. He didn't call them ghosts. I always thought it was a weird way to describe ghosts." She shrugged. "But if that's what he wanted to call them, far be it for me to complain."

Mrs. Drummond's mention of shadows left Micky feeling apprehensive. She'd left Colorado Springs hoping to leave the paranormal behind. Maybe her uncle had been plagued by the same type of supernatural creatures.

At the same time, Micky didn't want to believe it. "You know how old houses are. I'm sure you've got some tales about Jekyl's. People couldn't help but think the place is haunted with a name like that."

With a smile holding surprising warmth, Mrs. Drummond said, "I called it Jekyl's just because of the place's reputation. It's one of the older buildings in town like the Gunn Inn. Lot of weird things happened over the years here. It stands to reason the place would be haunted, don't you think?"

Micky shifted her hobo-style denim handbag higher on her shoulder. "Of course. At least the town capitalizes on it for the tourists."

Oops. There you go, Micky. You've done it now.

Mrs. Drummond didn't seem offended. Instead she chuckled. "Some people think a legend of haunting is as good as a real haunting. Gullible people see things."

"Do you honestly believe you have ghosts here?"

"I've seen and heard some peculiar things around my establishment. My husband doesn't believe it, but I know what I've experienced. The whole town is haunted to the gills. I'm a sensible woman, Miss Gunn. I don't make things up. Well, anyway, you should be cautious around your uncle's home. With some nut-case running around murdering women, I warn all the female patrons coming through here." Mrs. Drummond's eyes held genuine sadness. "The town rolls up the streets early these days."

Deciding she'd had enough gossiping, Micky said, "Thanks, Mrs. Drummond."

Sun burst through clouds as Micky stepped into the freezing outdoors. She wanted to pretend the chill sailing up her spine had nothing to do with Mrs. Drummond's warnings and everything to do with the weather.

Snow had stopped sometime last night, but frigid temperature solidified the white stuff into a crunchy ice pack. About a foot of snow accumulated overnight, but someone had plowed the parking lot. After she climbed into her car, she cranked up the heater.

She looked at the envelope on the seat where she'd thrown it. Tantalized, she stared at the communication while letting the defroster go to work.

What the hell? She would have to get out in a second and scrape snow and ice anyway. With hurried fingers she ripped the envelope.

Micky,

I remembered late last night there are a few arrangements I still need to make to ship my aunt's remains back to Denver. It might take a good portion of the morning. I'd ask you again to wait for me, but on second thought, I doubt you would listen. If you do go to the inn, just be careful. And please don't explore the tunnels in the basement without me.

Jared

He listed his cell phone number below his name, as if she would have a reason to call him. Yes, he assumed much and somehow she'd have to break him of the habit. She wouldn't allow him to direct what she did or didn't do.

Shortly after she cleaned off the windshield, she cruised with relative ease through the snow.

Few people traveled the roads, Main Street almost deserted even though most shops looked open. Wishing now she'd thought about a take out cup of coffee to clear the cobwebs marring her thinking process, Micky decided the trip to inn would be a quick fact-finding mission. Despite Mrs. Drummond and Jared's warnings, she knew fear would be conquered by defiance and not giving in.

She thought again of Mrs. Drummond's assertions that Uncle Carl mentioned shadows and it almost made her stop in the middle of the road and turn back. Instead she gently pushed on the accelerator. Maybe it was a coincidence about the shadows. How else could she explain that as a child she hadn't seen the shadows in her uncle's house? Confused, she resolved to keep going.

The Gunn Inn loomed up before long, and to her good fortune, the driveway didn't have too much snow accumulation. She hesitated in the driveway, allowing the engine to purr while she thought about going inside. Doubts formed again, creeping up on her the way shadow people often did. She gritted her teeth against indecision, wracked by desire to enter her uncle's old place and by a warning at the back of her neck saying she should run and run fast.

Take a stand and make a decision. Micky took a deep breath. How much longer could she afford to be frightened by what-ifs? Since she couldn't escape the shadow people by coming here, what more harm could they do to her?

She turned off the ignition and listened to the howling wind. Sheer isolation crept into her bones, a tingling awareness of loneliness and the recognition no human save herself prowled these grounds. For one moment she almost caved into the trepidation as she stepped into the unknown once again.

Gathering her handbag and locking the car, she walked toward the inn.

As she entered the house her veins seemed to ice over. A shiver wracked her body. The inn seemed too quiet, as if it whispered earlier until she entered and broke the conversation.

"'There was much of the beautiful, much of the wanton, much of the bizarre, something of the terrible, and not a little of that which might have excited disgust,'" she said, quoting Edgar Allen Poe from *The Masque of the Red Death*.

An irrational thought sped by. Maybe if she spoke out loud the house would talk back.

Micky inhaled deeply. The place smelled stale and old, as if the centuries clung to the house like a live thing. She wondered why she hadn't noticed last night.

She slipped off her coat, hat and gloves and tossed them with her handbag onto a chair in the foyer. Light slipped through mullioned windows near the front door and threw diamond points of light onto the black and white checkerboard floor.

In the freshness of daylight she noticed more things. As she gazed around, she realized the house hadn't changed much since she'd last been here years ago. Although her uncle decorated in a Victorian style, he'd kept an eclectic style all his own that kept the place from being too rigidly defined. Dark wood merged with lighter oak, and fancier pieces of furniture nestled with more casual. It could have been a mishmash mess, instead it worked well.

She didn't know where to start. Taking a small pad and pen out of her handbag she made a room-by-room assessment of what should be repaired or updated. Many things, to her untrained eye, might look fine but need repair. As the number of items wracked up, a rising apprehension followed. Her uncle left money to her in the will along with the inn, but not enough to solve every problem she saw in front of her.

By the time she went through each room, truth kicked in. She might be better off selling the place. An ache started in her throat. She didn't want to give up so soon, but the task ahead seemed too daunting to contemplate. She forced the idea to the forefront. Maybe she would hire someone with expertise in restoration to check the place out and give her a professional opinion. Then she might know what to do.

Micky remembered she hadn't surveyed the attic, so she headed down to the end of the third floor hallway. As she walked the hall seemed to narrow, drawing down to a pinpoint where the door to the small attic staircase resided. Wood flooring creaked under her feet, a sudden snap and pop that made her flinch.

Seconds later a cold breeze drifted over Micky's shoulders and she shivered. The hair on the back of her neck prickled. Iciness slid over her body like a dip into a freezing pond.

A shadow passed to her right, and she started and gasped. She listened for any sign the shadow people would continue their assault, but nothing happened. She couldn't move, stopped in an instant by a wall of panic, the barrier of the unknown.

The day seemed to recede in this house.

Yawning, a chasm of indescribable dread took her breath. She couldn't move.

Shame flirted with resignation. She'd gotten used to running and hiding from the unknown. Muscling through the tightness holding her prisoner, she turned away and hurried down to the first floor.

Whispers taunted her. Sibilant and harsh, they verbalized all her weaknesses. She stopped at the top of the last set of stairs.

Another quote from *The Masque of The Red Death* came to her mind, whirling around in her memory as an explanation for what she heard. *And the rumor of this new presence having spread itself whisperingly around, there arose at length from the whole company a buzz, or murmur, expressive of disapprobation and surprise — then, finally, of terror, of horror, and of disgust.*

Weak light, filtered by encroaching clouds, seeped through the tall windows. A wave of renewed fear coursed through Micky. Half expecting shadow people to show themselves again, to own the voices, she waited.

Swiftly rising, the hateful voices told her a million secrets she didn't want to know. They demanded her attention, as sharp and ravenous as the bite of a serpent.

Hate is the answer.

She gripped the banister as a strange lethargy weakened her limbs. Her knees trembled.

Discord becomes you.

Her heart started to pound.

We are here. We are near.

Dizziness made her sink down onto the top step.

I am here.

The sonorous sound overwhelmed the others, and the weaker voices slipped into incoherent rambling. Shivering, she questioned what she'd heard and why.

She tried shrugging off apprehension, unwilling to collapse under the heavy atmosphere. She'd never heard voices with the appearance of shadow people before.

Never.

Another shiver rippled through her body. *My God. What's happening here?*

Swallowing hard, she tried to regain her equilibrium. She waited a few moments in case the voices started again, but she heard nothing but an eerie, almost suppressive silence.

Soldiering onward, she stood and headed the rest of the way downstairs. She almost dropped her pad and pen, her fingers clumsy as they trembled.

Take it easy. Get a hold on yourself.

Sure, Jared had asked her not to explore the tunnels, but she could check out the main room and list what she didn't want to keep. She headed for the basement door. Putting the paper and pen under her arm, she took out her keys and unlocked it. If she couldn't go certain places in this house by herself, what was the use of opening the inn? She must conquer this irrational fear once and for all. She waited, listening.

Nothing.

Half convinced she'd imagined the voices near the attic and the presence of an entity too evil to describe, Micky turned on the light. With a last gasp, her childhood hesitancy about the basement began to disappear. She put one foot on a step and then another, until she tromped all the way downstairs.

A musty, damp scent came to her nose. Dark, hollow, a place where light disappeared, the tunnels seemed ripe with danger. Fresh concern tickled at the back of her consciousness. Yet she stared into the abyss.

Seconds lengthened into minutes. A voice whispered in her head.

I am here.

Micky shuddered. Trapped in an icy cage, she held her breath and her body tightened. Each muscle felt stretched to breaking.

A movement deep in the blackness, at the farthest reaches of the tunnel, caught her attention. Shadows morphed, rolling in upon themselves like a writhing lizard.

Come to me.

"No," she whispered. "No."

While the shadows always terrorized her, a new malevolence lurked close. She could feel it in the way her skin prickled. A glacial draft brushed through her hair. She wanted to run, but she couldn't. Instead she took one step toward a tunnel. Then two.

Terror froze her heart as her feet continued to advance, dragging her along like a helpless doe into a predator's maw. When she reached the mouth of the tunnel, she tried to put her hands out to grab the sides and stop her progress.

"Mother of God, help me." What was she thinking? She couldn't reach the sides of tunnel. They were too wide.

Struggling with soul-staggering fear, she struggled for breath. Her throat felt like it might close up, her heart pounding in the most extreme terror she'd experienced. Her will was not her own, captured by something too strong to contemplate or understand.

Oh, please, please Jared, help me.

But Jared wasn't nearby, and she'd gone into this basement like a fool. A stupid, stupid fool.

The tunnel seemed to go on forever, and the waking nightmare continued as she tried regaining control of her body. Still she walked, one foot in front of the other, moving toward a goal she didn't understand.

As the darkness cloaked her, thick as a smothering blanket, she saw a tall figure in the near distance. She doubted her eyes a moment, unsure if she saw the mere outline of a person or not.

"Hello?"

A chuckle answered, deep and seductive. A wave of primitive heat wrapped around her midsection. It felt almost as if two hands held her by the waist and pulled her closer.

Before she could make a sound, she saw the face of her tormentor perched atop a cloaked body.

A gargoyle like face, as hoary and dismal as a stone statue on an edifice, grinned with sickening satisfaction. Red eyes, devoid of pupil or iris, burned into her mind and demanded compliance. The lips parted and whispered haunting words, brushing along her senses in a strange and devastatingly sexual rhythm.

"Come to me, sweet girl. Linger here and I will take you as you've never been taken before."

She tried to scream, to move in some way to escape this horrible dream. Nothing happened.

Then anger took over, refusing to allow defeat. Whoever or whatever this monster represented, she wouldn't go down without a fight. She closed her eyes and tried to wash her fear away with thoughts of being in Jared's arms.

"Stop thinking about him. He can't help you." The voice included a hard edge now, no longer seductive but severe. "You will submit to me."

"No," she said through the tight pain in her throat. "Never. Never. Go back to hell you sick spawn."

She coughed, her throat closing in a terrible moment. She couldn't breath. *Let me go, let me go, let me go!*

Then she heard new voices, much different from the gargoyle's rasp. Light and whispery, they taunted the gargoyle.

Lethergolethergolethergo.

Savehersavehersaveher.

"Leave me alone you sick bastard!" She shrieked into the darkness.

She could barely see, but she recognized in a heartbeat the gargoyle had disappeared. At least she could no longer see his hateful face or those hideous hell eyes.

Micky thought her heart would pound through her chest as she gasped for air. Confused, she struggled against the gargoyle's grip. With an effort she didn't know she possessed, she wrenched from the cold fingers pressing into her waist and stumbled backwards. As she fell, her body tumbled over a lump in her way. Pain radiated up her spine and into her head. She cried out.

Grateful for even the foul air of the tunnels, she drew in deep breaths. On her hands and knees she groped around and tried to find a tunnel wall. She thought she knew which direction she'd been taken.

She touched something soft. Soft and wet.

Flesh. A nose and perhaps the curve of a mouth.

A face.

She shuddered as she realized what she'd fallen over in the darkness.

"Oh, sweet God."

Reaching out, she patted around until she felt two bodies lay in the tunnel. A woman with long hair and a man. Trembling, on the verge of allowing terrifying madness to absorb her, she climbed over the bodies and stumbled down the tunnel. She felt her way, her fingers scraping over the rough wall surface.

Her breath rasped in her throat, her eyes streaming with tears.

Something had helped her escape the gargoyle and had given her strength, but she could only think of one person she wanted to see right now.

Jared, please help me.

Chapter Five

ಬಾ

Worry made Jared drive his old brown Bronco a little faster toward the Gunn Inn. Something nagged in the back of his brain, telling him to get his ass there pronto.

Arranging to have his aunt's body shipped to Denver hadn't taken as long as he expected. The medical examiner had released the body after the police decided they couldn't gather any more evidence from it. After that, his meeting with the chief of police went nowhere. Pine Forest didn't want a Denver detective horning in on their territory. He left their office and gave the impression, he hoped, that he wouldn't be back to interfere. Impression was the operative word.

He rubbed the back of his stiff neck. He hadn't slept worth a damn last night. *The* nightmare awoke him at two o'clock in the morning and he'd slept in fits and starts until three o'clock when he'd gotten out of bed. Then he'd obsessed about Micky as he'd eaten breakfast in his room. Thoughts of her worked in two ways for him, and he didn't know if he liked or hated it. If he thought of her he didn't spend much time milling over his aunt's death or allowing other intrusive and damaging negative crap into his head. At the same time, he knew thinking about Micky served little purpose other than to guarantee an instant hard-on.

Hell, last night at dinner he'd sported a hard-on almost the entire time. Staring at her rudely, pretending she didn't have power over him seemed to do little good. He shouldn't get involved with a woman now. Besides, didn't everyone tell him, including his shrink, that getting into a new relationship so soon after his divorce wasn't healthy? Kissing her had been a mistake.

Kissing her. Right, bucko. Sticking my tongue clear down her throat and almost fucking her in the hallway qualified as an A-number-one screw-up.

He hadn't felt a woman's sweet channel hugging his cock for at least six months, and the last time he'd lain with a woman, she'd told him he was a lousy fuck. Not exactly ego-inspiring.

At least he understood why he'd been a bad fuck.

His ex-wife Katherine. An image of her, petite and gorgeous with the most beautiful silver-blonde hair tumbling to her waist, popped into his head. Gorgeous, yes. Beautiful, definitely.

His heart no longer ached when he thought of her, but a year didn't dull the memories of how wonderful the sex between them had been for an entire twelve months. Correction. One year of making love without the benefits of marriage, then one year of making love within matrimony. Another year of staying celibate. Maybe when he bedded someone like Micky Gunn, he would fuck like a world champion.

Whoa, buddy. Where did that come from?

He couldn't forget what had happened the moment Micky's gaze first met his. He'd felt that electrical current sensation straight from his gut to his groin.

One hundred percent, unqualified excitement had made his blood run hot and his cock twitch. Oh, yeah. She'd felt the bolt of attraction jumping between them. Her pretty eyes had widened and her lips parted. Oval and delicate in appearance, her face had the fragile look of youth combined with the strength of experience.

Her tousled, waving short hair was a combination of blonde colors that gave her a fashionable yet natural appearance. Her indigo blue eyes, large and expressive, seemed incapable of hiding what she felt. No matter what she said, he'd been able to read the fear, anger, and confusion in those long-lashed windows to her soul. About five-foot-six inches, her frame held the willowy walk of grace and athleticism mixed into one body. Under her sweater and loose jeans she might have been curvy or thin. He couldn't say for certain.

But, man, he wanted to find out.

Jared gritted his teeth and felt his jaw protest. He debated the possibility of pursuing a relationship with her beyond the professional and swept the idea away in about two seconds. He'd come here to solve Aunt Eliza's murder, and that should be his focus beyond all else.

He arrived at the inn moments later and noted Micky's vehicle in the driveway. Urgency made him leave his truck quickly and he trudged through the snow to the front door. After leaning on the doorbell and not getting an answer for some time, worry pulsed through him. He tried the doorknob and found it unlocked.

"Shit," he muttered. Why the hell did she leave the door unlocked? Alert for danger, he went inside. The basement door was slightly ajar and the light was on.

"Damn it." He started toward the basement, his entire body tensing for action.

Footsteps rushed up the basement stairs. Seconds later Micky hurled through the doorway and straight into his arms.

She shrieked a sharp, startled exclamation of total fright. Wide-eyed and shaky, she stared at him before flinging her arms around his neck and burying her face against him.

"Jared." Her voice sounded tremulous and terrified beyond all reason. "They're down there." She sobbed a breath. "They're dead. Dead."

He'd never imagined the tough-as-nails woman he'd met yesterday quivering like a kitten and clinging to him. "What the hell happened? Are you all right?"

She drew back to look at him, her eyes glistening with tears. "No, I'm not."

His gaze searched for injury. "Are you hurt?"

Micky's lips parted and she drew a deep, shuddering breath as she clutched at his shoulders. "No."

When she continued to tremble, he held her close and smoothed his hands over her back to soothe her. "Come on sweetheart, tell me what happened."

"I don't...think...I...know."

Her hard breathing rasped, and he feared if she didn't calm down she'd hyperventilate. He cupped her head and held it against his shoulder. "Try to breathe deeply and slowly. I'm right here. You're safe."

She slipped out of his arms reached over to slam the basement door. "There's something horrible down there, Jared. Something evil."

When he took a step toward the door, she grabbed his sleeve. "No. Don't go down there. Not without enough firepower to bring down a bull elephant."

Micky saw the deep worry in his eyes, as well as the undeniable determination of a law-enforcement officer. When she'd launched into his arms she'd felt a relief so profound she could have wept with joy at the same time she wanted to scream in terror. Trying to get her control back didn't seem to be working. Her heart still jack hammered in her chest, and a cold sweat broke out over her skin. She felt dizzy and sick. She pressed her hand to her stomach.

"We've got to call the police," she said. "There are two dead people down there."

She reached for the phone on a small table near the staircase, but when her hand touched the receiver she couldn't seem to make her fingers close around it.

His big hand came down over hers. "Let me. You're saying there are two dead bodies in the basement."

"I tripped over them in one of the tunnels. A man and a woman. I could feel her long hair." She gulped, unable to continue.

As her heart seemed to stutter and shake in her chest, she wrapped her arms around her body. Her limbs shook, each jerking movement threatening to shake her teeth from her head. She couldn't get warm.

Jared called 9-1-1 and reported the situation to the operator. After he hung up, he urged her away from the basement door and toward the living room area. He cupped her face, the gesture warm and a little comforting.

"The police are on the way." He smiled for about a millisecond. "Never thought I'd hear myself say that." When she didn't respond to his humor, Jared clasped her shoulders. "You're shaking. Are you sure you're not hurt?"

The concern in his eyes softened the fright gripping her system. "I'll be fine."

Touching the side of her neck, he said, "You're shivering and your skin is cold and clammy. You're in parasympathetic backlash."

"What?"

"A fancy term for coming down from intense sympathetic nervous system arousal. It manifests itself in shock symptoms." He clasped her arms and brought her to him, bringing her into his arms again. "Take deep breaths. You'll be all right."

She did as told and eased her shaky, rapid breaths into longer, less frantic inhalations. "I'm sorry."

"There's nothing to be sorry about. You've just found two dead bodies. It's natural you feel this way."

"Natural?" Her voice went a little high. "Natural."

She gave a humorless laugh. Tears slipped from her eyes and she barely held back a sob.

"Easy. Easy. Come on, keep taking those deep breaths for me. That's it." His voice murmured against her hair as his fingers lingered on her neck, massaging the tight muscles. "You're safe. I won't let anyone harm you."

An image of the horrible gargoyle face flashed through her mind and she twitched in his arms. Could anyone, even a brawny cop with balls of steel, protect her from an abomination from the depths of someone's worst nightmare? In that frightening instant she wondered if she'd really seen the gargoyle.

Maybe the shadow people have finally driven me mad.

She couldn't tell him maybe the dead bodies were a part of an unspeakable mental breakdown. What if the police came and found no bodies?

No. She must believe she saw the gargoyle in the tunnel. She had to. Then she remembered the blood on her hands.

She burrowed into his arms like a child, enjoying respite from the gruesome world she'd encountered in the tunnel. Her hands clutched at his coat. The rough-soft feeling of fabric against her cheek reminded her she existed in the now rather than a horror movie.

Not long after the wail of sirens heralded the arrival of police.

* * * * *

Micky sat on the sheet-covered couch in the living room. She waited for Jared and the deputies to return from the depths of the basement. She didn't want to sit here alone, and thank God an officer hovered in the doorway.

She wrung her hands, then stopped. Almost thirty minutes transpired since Jared left her alone.

The officer outside the door shifted and his leather holster and belt creaked. His hand stayed propped on his holster at all times, as if the expected someone to jump out at him any time.

His shoulder radio squawked, and he spoke into it. A man's voice came through, obscured by static, and reported they'd located two bodies. She closed her eyes and leaned her head back. A weird relief filled her. At least she hadn't imagined the carnage. Then conflicting emotions rattled through her psyche. How could she be glad those poor people died? What a horrible, horrible way to think. She must be a cretin to wish death upon someone so she could prove she wasn't crazy.

But did I imagine the gargoyle? Did I dream up that disgusting face? And what strange force pulled me into the tunnel against my will?

She reached for the glass of water Jared had brought her earlier. She welcomed the cold liquid as she drank.

Down deep terror remained, hovering beyond her reach to banish it. It ate at her stomach, her mind, and dared her to try and remove its threatening presence. She couldn't banish the sight of the gargoyle, imagined or not, out of her mind. The scene she'd encountered in the tunnel threatened to run in inside her like an endless loop. She fought against the repeating tape, trying in vain to think of something calming. She turned her attention to the room and used it as a distracter.

Heavy blue velvet drapes hung on the large windows. Weak sunlight filtered through gathering clouds, and she wondered absently if more snow would come. She gazed around and took in the antique furniture, all of it her uncle's most precious positions. Each authentic piece gave the room opulence which screamed old-world money.

As Micky took another sip of water, her hand shook. She felt as if she'd dropped into a full color episode of *Dark Shadows*.

It took the police much longer to bring the bodies upstairs, and when she saw them, she turned her head away.

She'd already endured an interrogation by a detective. No doubt another grilling would follow. She understood the men were doing their jobs, but she feared they would think she'd killed those people. What would she do then?

Jared appeared with a tall, thin police officer by the name of Peter Barnstable. Danny Fortesque, another officer, brought up the rear.

Jared looked regretful, as if he had additional bad news.

"We need you to look at the bodies and see if you can identify them," Barnstable said.

She stood, alarm racing up her spine. "What?"

Fortesque gestured toward the hallway. "I know this isn't pleasant, but we need to know if you recognize them."

"Why would I recognize them?"

Jared reached for her arm and drew her toward the door, his intent clear, but his touch gentle. "A quick look, just to make sure."

She didn't want to see what her hands had felt. She shook her head even as she went into the foyer. Two gurneys sat in the foyer, black bags zipped over the bodies.

A man with a jumpsuit labeled *Coroner* drew the zipper downward over the face of one victim.

When she saw the young woman's face, marble white and tinged with a strange blue cast, her stomach lurched. The girl's throat sported two pinpoint, bloody holes on one side.

"My God," she said. "What did that to her?"

"Do you know her?" Barnstable asked.

"No. I've never seen her before."

"What about this guy?" Barnstable asked.

She moved a little closer to the gurney. The young man's pale skin looked almost translucent in quality. His throat also was ravaged, but with a long cut across the neck that must have caused instant death.

She gasped and backed up into Jared.

Jared's warm, big hands settled on her shoulders and pressed gently.

"Recognize this one?" Fortesque asked.

Like waxy mannequins, the victims looked unreal, a caricature of life. Or maybe horror washed over her sensibilities and made it impossible to believe.

"No. I don't know them."

After the bags were zipped over the unfortunates, Micky turned away and out of Jared's grip. She went back into the living room and slumped on the couch.

While Jared sat on the couch next to her, Fortesque and Barnstable asked her more questions about the incident. She stared at her folded hands.

"Strange situation, Miss Gunn," Fortesque said as he took notes on a pad. "You've been involved with two criminal incidents in two days."

Her head snapped up. "And?"

Jared put his hand on her shoulder and squeezed gently. "You have to admit it's strange as hell."

Barnstable pinpointed his sharp gaze on Jared. "And you've been involved as well."

Jared returned the man's intense stare. "If you're trying to make a statement, spit it out. Let's not pussy around with the meaning."

Fortesque's mouth tightened and Barnstable's face reddened.

"No need to get upset, Detective Thornton. You know this is procedure. Besides, I was making an observation, not an accusation," Fortesque said.

"Sorry, Fortesque. I guess I'm a little on edge." Jared stood slowly. His hands went to his hips and his feet braced apart enough to give him a Rock-of-Gibraltar appearance. "I'd like to take Miss Gunn back to the hotel to rest. She's had a shock to her system."

Fortesque nodded. "That will be all, then."

She scrubbed her hands over her face, weariness battling with anger over what happened in her uncle's house.

"Your plans were to open this inn?" Barnstable asked.

She stared at him as if his head had fallen off. He'd asked her that question three times. She drew on a well of patience. "Yes, that's correct."

Fortesque tapped his pencil on his own pad. "We found your pad and pencil lying on the ground in the tunnel near the bodies."

Being reminded of death, which seemed to hover near her, made her blood run cold.

"They've taken it as evidence," Jared said to her.

She shrugged. "I can always make another list at another time."

Barnstable and Fortesque exchanged deadpan looks.

The Pine Forest police officers headed back to the basement, and Jared said, "Let's get you out of here."

Micky grabbed her coat and purse and within minutes she'd bundled into her car and headed back toward town with Jared's truck following. She cherished the quiet, listening to the engine purr and watching snow clouds lower over the area. Somehow the impending weather made her feel isolated from what happened in the basement tunnels. At the same time she welcomed numbness from fear and uncertainty. Whenever the gargoyle face popped into her head, she shoved it away, determined to conquer the beast in her mind. She couldn't allow it to take over, whatever its origins.

As she turned onto Main Street, she noted the town bustled today, the streets thronged with people completing errands before a new snow blanketed the town. Maybe they also wanted to get home before dark.

Smiling faces crossed her vision, and she ignored them the way she disregarded the cruel grin of the gargoyle. She couldn't afford to feel anything right now.

She might come apart at the seams if she did.

When Micky reached Jekyl's, she left her car and didn't wait for Jared to catch up. As she walked into the lobby, she half expected the three people there to gawk at her.

No, that is silly. They couldn't know about the murders yet, could they?

No one seemed to notice her. She hurried to the stairs, tension blossoming in her body. She must get away. Must hide somewhere, anywhere she couldn't see the gargoyle and the murdered couple's faces.

Her hands felt boneless, and she dropped her keys on the floor.

A hand came down on her shoulder, and she jumped, startled. Jared stood there, his eyes deeply concerned and a frown tugging at his mouth. "You need something to eat. Come with me down to the restaurant."

She shook her head. "No, I couldn't. I just need to get away from it." She inhaled, her insides trembling with a force she didn't understand. "I just need to get away."

He picked up the keys and opened the door, then urged her inside. He closed and locked the door. When he tossed the keys on her dresser she flinched.

Jared looked like every cop she'd known, the band of brothers she met when she'd dated Davy. Though she shouldn't be afraid of him, the murders at the inn made her scared of everything right this minute.

"You can go downstairs without me," she said.

"I'm not leaving you."

"Why? Why do you care?"

He walked toward her and stopped near, his penchant for crowding Micky feeling more comforting to her than intimidating in this odd situation. "You're wounded. Not in body but in soul. You need to talk this out. Now."

"Why now?" She wanted to hit Jared for pressuring her. "Why?"

He held up one hand and began to tick off items. "Sudden trauma needs to be taken care of pretty quickly. You're going through fear you don't understand and condemning yourself for what happened."

His statement landed a punch. How did he know this? How could he possibly read her mind?

Micky moved to the dresser. She plopped the hobo bag onto it and then opened the top drawer. She yanked out a pair of utilitarian blue flannel pajamas and tossed them on the dark wood four-poster, queen-sized bed.

"If you don't mind, I want to crawl into that bad and sleep. I don't want to talk about any of this." She tossed her head in a dismissive gesture. "Besides, I've just been grilled over an open fire. I've got a headache about two miles wide and an attitude to match. It's beyond me why any man in his right mind would want to put up with the bitch I'm going to become in two minutes if you don't leave me alone."

A smile widened his mouth, a gentle and understanding grin that took her off the offensive. "I'm not going to ask you the same kinds of questions." He held up his hand again. "Point number two. You're going through several emotions right now and you need to talk about them at least a little. You need to let off some pressure." When she stared at him like he'd lost his mind, he crossed to the dresser and looked down at her with those incredible sea-blue and green eyes. "Because I guarantee if you don't talk about them now you're not going to sleep. Not now and maybe not for many nights to come. Other things will happen, too. Maybe you'll get belligerent with people you love and act out in ways you never would normally. Maybe you'll believe no one understands what happened to you."

Conviction tightened the skin around his mouth, and she saw a little muscle twitch near his left eye, as if he held back stronger emotions.

A lump grew in her throat. "What would you know about it?"

He drew off his coat and tossed it on a chair, and she knew he would stay for the long haul whether she wanted him to or not. With his red sweater and black jeans, he stood out against the drab beige walls. Power and confidence emanated from him, but so did kindness.

Jared stuffed his hands in his pockets and leaned back against the dresser. "You're trying to numb your emotions and that'll work for awhile. It worked for me the first twenty-four hours after the shoot-out last year. Sometimes it's too soon to talk about what happened, but often it's better to get it all out now."

"You mentioned the shoot-out at dinner the other night." Curiosity made her press for more information. "Tell me more."

He sighed, a resigned noise. "My best friend on the force was killed in a firefight with heavily armed bank robbers."

She sucked in a breath. "I'm sorry."

Pain flickered over his face. His eyes took on a haunted mien, an agony alive in his soul. Genuine hurt lingered within this man, deep and profound. Maybe what happened to her today drove him to help her. Perhaps he didn't do this out of special affection, but a necessity of one human being to another.

"Exactly one year ago last week," he said. "My partner Diego Jimenez and I had finished investigating a homicide. We responded to a call of officer down in a bank robbery."

"You weren't a detective yet?"

"I'd taken the test, but I was awaiting the results to see if I'd be promoted. One of the detectives from my division and his partner had gone into the bank before the robbery began..." He drifted off. His gaze latched onto the window where open curtains showed snowflakes drifting to the ground. "Diego always was a cocky son-of-a-bitch. He wanted to go into every situation with guns blazing. I was surprised he was a detective because many cops with attitude get fired or killed in short order. We got to the bank before anyone else. We'd exited the car and we didn't have time to blink before the perps burst out of there with automatic weapons spewing bullets."

"Oh, no." Her throat seemed to swell around the words, a sense of disaster coming with Jared's every word.

He moved to the window and stared out, and as she joined him there she watched the snow. Big flakes drifted downward, a peaceful balm on her naked soul.

"One bullet caught Diego in the neck. I crawled around to his side of the car. He was loosing blood fast and I tried to stop it. I'd already called for back-up and emergency medical services. No sooner than that, one of the bullets caught me in chest. Flipped me straight onto my back."

"Oh, my God," she whispered, imagining him seriously wounded.

The thought that he may have been taken from this world before she could even meet him sent a hard, painful surge of tears to her eyes. She inhaled and pushed the tears away.

Jared's profile looked frozen in ice and his jaw clenched and released. "The pain and the impact took the wind out of me. I managed to stay semi-conscious for all of a half minute before I passed out. When I woke up, two other police officers were dragging me around the side of the building. I could barely breathe and my chest hurt so bad I was sure the bullet made it through my vest. One of the other cops loosened my vest to see if I'd been hit. I kept visualizing Diego's blood all over my hands. I knew he was dead."

"Were you hurt badly?"

"The bullet didn't make it through the vest. I got away with a huge bruise and a cracked rib."

Tears filled her eyes again at the pain in his voice. When he turned toward her, Micky's breath caught as if she'd been the one punched in the chest with a bullet. "Why are you telling me all this?"

"Because I wanted to prove I understand. Trauma isn't something that happens only to people in shoot-outs. You've had two heavy-duty experiences piled on you in two days. One would have been bad enough."

She couldn't deny the truth, and gratefulness worked its way through her heart. "Thank you for being concerned."

He clasped her shoulders. "I don't want your thanks, I want to make sure you get some relief. It's not going to go away quickly. It takes time to get through things like this, but you can talk to me. Or you can talk to a counselor. I can get you in touch with my psychologist."

She put up one hand and it landed on his hard chest. "Whoa, there, cowboy. I never said I wanted a psychologist."

"He's a good guy. He's trained in Critical Incident Stress Management."

"What is that?"

His fingers caressed a soothing pattern over her shoulders. "A way to help people who've been traumatized by events. It starts with a defusing or debriefing of the trauma victim so they can decompress. To put it down to bare bones, you're expressing everything you feel, all your emotions now so you can hopefully prevent post-traumatic stress syndrome later."

It sounded clinical and scary. The suspicious side of her wouldn't grab onto the idea without more information. "And you're trained in this…this procedure?"

He smiled. "No. It's way more than a procedure. You're in a group setting usually and you explain what your participation was in the traumatic event. In your case, witnessing an assault and being assaulted in a diner at gunpoint. Then having the shit scared out of you when you find two dead bodies. That's enough traumas to last most people a lifetime, but you managed to stack them up in two days. You can't will the trauma away; you've got to work through it. Believe me, if you don't, you'll wish you had. "

"So you talked to this psychologist right away?"

Sadness entered his eyes, and she knew more hovered behind this story than one gunfight. "I didn't get help right away. I refused to talk when they put me in with a group of my peers spewing about how they felt. I thought none of them could understand those first horrible minutes when I saw my best buddy's blood spurting out everywhere. Hell, for the longest time I didn't even wear red."

"Blood. It reminded you of all the blood."

"Then I would flashback to the incident. It didn't matter what I was doing or where I was going. I'd be there at the bank with bullets flying and one of them coming for me."

He massaged her shoulders with persistent rhythm and some of the tension released. It felt so damn good to have his hands touching her.

Surprised he'd tell her about this experience, she peered at him with curiosity. She wasn't used to tough men letting their more insecure feelings show.

"Why are you telling me this?" she asked.

His gaze ordered her to understand. "Because I don't want you to do what I did. I don't want you to bottle it up until it explodes one day."

Caught up in his story, she asked, "Is that what happened to you?"

He nodded and released her shoulders. "Yeah. I had nightmares and these little attacks edging on terror whenever I thought about returning to work. I denied it and went to work against the suggestion of everyone two days after the shootout. Finally I was in the patrol car one day and my new partner and I were driving by the bank where Diego was killed. There was this car backfire. My throat closed up, I got pains in my chest. I thought I was having a heart attack."

Micky winced and she touched his chest again in a gesture of comfort. "Oh, Jared. What happened next?"

"EMS carted me off to the hospital. After a few tests they realized it wasn't my heart or anything else serious physically and that's when my new partner said he wouldn't ride with me unless I got help. I realized I could have crashed the patrol unit or otherwise hurt someone. It opened my eyes. I was a danger on the job."

Weary with upwelling emotion, she left his space and went to the bed. She sank down upon the comforter next to her cozy flannels. "So what do I do now?"

He sat on the bed next to her. "Talk to me. Tell me what you're feeling. What you fear and what you need. Tell me the worst parts of the two traumatic events for you."

Heaving a deep breath, she lay back on the bed and stared at the ceiling. "I'm not sure I understand what I'm feeling."

"Close your eyes. Think back. Remember it."

She visualized the day before when the quiet of the café disappeared under violence. "The man is ugly. Ugly with anger. He's pointing the gun right at me and my mind freezes. My life doesn't flash before my eyes. I just feel like the air has been sucked from me. Like my life isn't worth a plugged nickel."

"What did you feel when it was over?"

Restless, she sat up and then stood and paced, her hands going behind her back while she ran through the scenario in vivid color. "Stunned. Shocked. I almost couldn't breathe, it was so horrible."

"What about today?"

She went to the window again to watch the snow. "It was worse."

How could she tell him what she saw? He would never believe her. She could take a chance, but the one time she'd tried to tell her father and stepmother about the shadow people, they'd laughed and said her imagination worked overtime. This wouldn't be any different.

He rose from the bed and came so near she could feel the heat off his body. "How was it different?"

Micky hesitated. "I was terrified I wouldn't get out alive."

"Because you thought the killer might still be in the tunnel."

She nodded, afraid to give him the real scoop. No reasonable man of the law with logic on his side would ever believe her. *Sure, no problem detective. I saw a freaking gargoyle and I think he's the murderer.*

Stress pumped through her veins, and she put her hands over her eyes. He came up behind her, his hands touching her shoulders.

"It's all right. Rest for now."

Micky inhaled and emotions came tumbling out. Tears seeped from her eyes and ran down her face like rainwater. Her shoulders trembled with the effort to keep back the sobs.

"Hey, hey," he whispered in a deep, gentle voice.

Drawing her back against him, he wrapped his arms around her waist. Jared's body cradled her and gave the support she needed so much. Against all logic she leaned into his embrace, her head resting against him. He felt so powerful, so protective that some of her anxiety eased.

"Close your eyes and relax." He spoke close to her left ear, and his breath tingled over her.

She did as he suggested, dragging in one shuddering deep breath after another until tension filtered away.

"Why are you helping me?" she asked.

With a soft, lingering brush of his lips, he kissed her ear. "Because I think you probably keep a lot of things inside."

Wondering how he could know this much about her in a short time, she said, "That's not always a bad thing."

"It's always bad when it eats away at you until it makes you sick or you do something drastic."

She'd never heard a man talk like this before. Her father and Davy had never given into emotions other than anger. "I wish I could turn on the faucet and let it pour like you want. But I don't know if I can."

His chest heaved on a deep breath, and the movement made her more aware of him as a man and not only a human being willing to give comfort. "Don't do it for me. Do it for you, in your own good time. Just don't wait too long, or what happened the last two days could tear you apart for a lifetime."

No, she never would have imagined all this could happen in two days.

"You must think I'm like one of those too-stupid-to-live heroines who will go into the basement when she knows there's a monster in there. But I know there isn't a monster, and this isn't a movie. I can't let my demons..." She rubbed her forehead. "The basement is so strange. The darkness in there is like a siphon sucking the very life out of the earth."

"An interesting way to describe it."

"Didn't you feel it when you were down there?"

"Feel what?"

"The darkness. It was like a live thing."

"What do you mean?"

"Never mind."

"Tell me," he said. "Or I'll think of a way to get it out of you."

Micky shivered. Spoken in a deep, thrillingly heated rumble, his demand took on a double entendre. Heat shot into her belly.

Taking up the challenge, she smiled away her lack of confidence. She turned toward him, breaking his hold on her. "You mentioned handcuffs once. Is that what you plan to use?"

Heat notched up in his gaze. "I'll use whatever weapons I have."

His pupils dilated, his nostrils flared the tiniest increment.

A little nervous with the game, but wanting to play it out, she tried to appear nonchalant. "So you have an entire arsenal?"

"Oh, yeah," he said softly. "A very large one."

Warmth slipped through her body and replaced the cold terror she'd felt earlier. With Jared she felt safe, even though the expression in his eyes looked hungry and purposeful. A part of her felt totally out of control. She wanted him to leave but she craved this mad thrumming sexuality beating between them.

"Aren't you going to ask me where I keep my weapons?" he asked.

Oh, I know where you keep at least one weapon, Mr. Thornton.

"Turn around," he said.

She turned back around and his hands went to her waist.

Jared's touch brushed feather light, undemanding as he traced her waistline. Micky thought she could feel anything and everything in that second, a long sweep of tenderness and desire. When he'd kissed her in the hallway last night she hadn't imagined they'd be in her room now, edging toward intimacy. His body pressed against hers promised more than she could have dreamed. Every shift of his powerfully muscled frame against her held meaning, each touch profound.

Relaxing against him, she savored masculine hardness. His chest felt broad and supportive, hips nudging her ass so she could feel his growing erection. He tipped his hips more firmly into her, and his right hand splayed over her belly. Jared's palms seared the moment into her brain forever.

This was it. She could run now, or she could take him up on the offer implicit in the way he touched her.

As his breath tickled her ear, he placed an exquisite kiss to her lobe, then his tongue flicked and traced the shell with detailed attention.

"Tell me if you want me to leave. Tell me now," he whispered huskily. "Otherwise, I can promise I won't be able to keep my hands off you."

Chapter Six

ℬ

"Don't go," Micky said. Bold desires erupted inside her. "Tell me what you're going to do. I want to know."

He laughed softly. "You want me to tell you where I'm going to put my hands?"

"Yes."

"Micky, I don't know —"

"I never figured you for a shy man."

"You've had a rough two days. Maybe this isn't the time to go full throttle."

Frustration spilled into her arousal, but she wanted the distraction from the day's nightmares and the promise of his hands. "Then just tell me what you'd do. What will you do with your hands?"

She'd never asked a man something this intimate, this taboo. She had to know everything.

"I'll touch every inch on your body." His voice rumbled deep, vibrating into her skin. "Then I'll finger your nipples, stroke them over and over until you can't stand it. I'll slip my fingers deep inside you until you're so hot and wet you're aching."

His words fired deep arousal in her stomach, hot and heavy and ready for action. Excitement made her bold and she didn't stop to ask why she was doing this.

"That's all?" She grinned, knowing her question would infuriate his senses and he'd exact retribution. "That's all?"

"Hell, no." His voice went deeper, more desperate with desire. "I'll touch your clit and rub it until you're hot and creamy on my fingers."

His words, spoken in the most sultry, sexy male voice she'd ever heard, made her body tense with eagerness. "Then?"

"I'll stick my tongue inside you. Lick up the cream. Flick my tongue over your clit until you come."

Holy, holy God. A megawatt reaction started, like a nuclear reactor ready to go thermal. If he meant to drive her mad, he'd proven he recognized just how to do it.

"Then what?" she asked, not caring how pushy it sounded.

"I'll tongue and finger fuck you until you're begging for my cock."

Micky quivered in illicit anticipation. She moved in his arms, frantic to try out the heated suggestions. "Then?"

"You'll have to wait and see, sweet Micky. Wait and see."

Sweet pleasure slipped straight from her sensitive skin to her nipples. She inhaled sharply as the tingling in her breasts rose, sending incredible arousal through her torso down to her lower stomach. His hand slid to the area above her mons, not daring to quite touch, but coming dangerously near. Her breath caught.

She leaned back into his arms as his hands started sweet torture. Alighting on her ribs, his caresses smoothed her sweater over her body. As his kisses traveled down her neck, she tipped her head to the left, drowning in heady sexual appreciation. A mix of erotic textures and feelings exploded inside her.

His hot, manly scent. The size and pressure of his cock. The quickness of his breathing.

"Jared?" She moved in his arms as wildness built and blossomed.

"Mmm?" His sighing question came deep and husky as he burrowed his mouth in her neck and trailed lingering kisses along sensitive skin.

Like a small, hot brand, his nibbling touches heated her inner core. Arousal tickled and darted into her clit. She moan softly for something she'd never felt. Never realized until now she needed from one man.

"God, you're delicious," he murmured into her hair. "So damned delicious."

He turned her toward him and his eyes held the heavy-lidded expression of a man on fire, his desire evident in the way his pupils dilated and his lips parted.

Before she could speak, he drew her close and his mouth came down on hers. His fingers speared into her hair, holding her head in place as he treated her mouth to luxurious exploration. He didn't ease her into it. He slipped one arm around her waist and tugged her against his hard heat.

Jared treated her to drugging, deep, thoroughly impassioned kisses which made her mind reel and her loins clench. His tongue traced her lips before he slanted his mouth more securely over hers and his tongue plunged deep. With pumping, stroking motions mimicking sex, he seduced her. His hips moved against hers, showing her minute to minute how exquisitely they would join. All thoughts of resisting, of maintaining control, left by superhighway. Liquid and bold, her need for him made her wild, erupting with a force of passion she never expected.

Seconds drew into a minute, then two as his kiss drew out, until deep need throbbed in her body for more. Slowly his hands searched and palmed her back. He drew her deeper into the madness, his embrace a sensual world of textures, scent, and heady eagerness.

He drew back, cupping her head in his big palms. When he gazed down at her, Jared gave no quarter. He devoured with that look; he wanted, needed, must have.

Her fingers clutched at his sweater, then she allowed her arms to slide around his waist. With three short steps he urged her back against the wall. Again his mouth took hers. Hard, rampant cock grew against her, and she hungered for it, wondered what it would feel like with all that hot thickness buried as high inside her as it could go. Micky squirmed against him and Jared moaned deep in his throat.

When had she ever felt a soul-searing need like this one? Jared called to her, his demands forcing a red-hot spiral of desire to cut through inhibitions.

He cupped and stroked her ass, a touch intimate and reassuring at the same time. With a gasp for breath he released her mouth, then placed his hands on the wall either side of her.

"Turn around again." Hoarse with desire, his rough tone told her everything she needed to know about how much he wanted her.

She smiled, her head swimming with heady desire. She placed her hands against the wall in surrender. The surface felt scratchy against her palms, but she didn't care. "Are you going to frisk me, officer?"

He chuckled, and the low rumble sent a dart of fire between her legs. "Damn straight."

As his fingers traced a sweet path up her ass and over her waist, she gasped.

"Body cavity search," he said with a husky rumble. "Thorough."

Thorough body cavity search. Oh, yes.

Micky liked the sound of it more than she could have imagined.

"Where will you search?" she asked softly, her throat tight with excitement.

Jared leaned into her, his voice hot and enticing in her ear. He slowly cupped her breasts through the sweater. "Your sweet breasts." He pressed her mons through her jeans. "Your wet heat. Your throbbing clit."

She gasped. She writhed a little, dying for a way to assuage the heat pulsing and dancing in the wet channel between her legs. And she was wet. She felt slick and hot and engorged, wanting him deep inside and pounding into her until she screamed in ecstasy.

And oh, did she want.

She could feel herself moistening, opening and releasing in the rhythm of a woman ready to take a man inside her. She ached to experience Jared and forget everything she thought and felt in favor of his hardness sliding back and forth, high and deep to her center.

Then, with a slow movement he searched out her nipples. Through the thickness of her clothing he brushed over them, circling, rubbing, plucking with the lightest of touches.

Unable to stand it, she writhed against him, her hands landing over his to still his exploration and stop the insanity. Seconds stretched into torturous minutes. Finally, his hands rested on the waistband of her jeans. She held her breath.

He leaned down and helped her remove her boots and thick socks. He tossed them in the corner. Jared returned to her waistband and without hesitation unbuttoned and then unzipped her jeans.

Micky's senses went on red alert as he slid his hand down her pants to touch the hair at the top of her mons. He paused, as if waiting for permission. When she didn't protest, he worked his fingers lower. Lower.

With slow but certain movements he dragged her jeans and bikini panties down over her ass and legs until he dropped them. She stepped out of the garments and kicked them aside.

"Oh, man." His voice went hoarse as he cupped and rubbed her ass. "This is so pretty. I've never seen anything so damned delicious." His fingers challenged her, tracing slow patterns over her waist, then down her arms to her wrists. He took her hands again and plastered them against the wall. "Spread 'em."

She did as the cop asked, spreading her legs and keeping her hands on the wall. "What's the charge?"

"Resisting an officer. And for that there's a punishment."

His words made her breathless, aching for anything to assuage the throbbing craving in her center.

She almost moaned the next question. "How are you going to punish me?"

"Wait and see."

Pure excitement dipped into loins. She wanted to scream.

Seconds later he reached up under her sweater and unhooked the bra.

He cupped her left breast. Gently he tugged her back so that she once again leaned against him. He reached between her spread thighs and circled her labia with one finger. Micky gasped and parted her legs wider.

Heat drilled into her lower body again and again as he smoothed around and around her wet, tingling folds. Each pass over sensitive skin made her writhe and gasp with desire. Endless moments later, he tugged gently on her nipple and slipped two fingers slowly into her wet heat. She groaned as the sweet penetration demanded a finish.

Madness filled Micky with the wildest desire she could imagine. She couldn't stand it. Couldn't take the out-of-this-world longing anymore.

As if he read her mind, he drew one finger over her clit. Swollen and desperate for attention, her clit tingled and fired off one tiny, exquisite orgasm.

She gasped, her indrawn breath ending on an agonized groan. "Oh, Jared."

If she thought it stopped there, she was sadly mistaken. The orgasm popped and tingled through her as he strummed one nipple and rubbed her clit in a circular, then an up and down motion. Circle. Rub. Circle. Rub.

An ache burgeoned inside her, requiring more. Demanding his strength and hardness thrusting inside her to allay the carnal appetite he'd created.

Instead he continued tantalizing with strokes which searched and plied.

"Let it take you," he murmured. "Don't fight."

She allowed his words to wash over her like silk, a liquid urging with no beginning and no end. With each pluck of her nipple and stroke over her clit, she fought for control.

"Now." He whispered against her ear. "Take it all."

Urged by the passion in his voice, she permitted the horror of the last few hours to disappear with each feather brush of his fingers, each nudge of his cock against her backside. "Jared."

"Feel it." Ragged with passion, his voice fired instincts she didn't know she had, as primal as night and as dark as a jungle forest.

Her breathing quickened, her gasps for breath accelerating as his fingers played magic upon her body and soul, driving her emotions to heights of ecstasy equaled only by the torment of her flesh. Immeasurable pleasure surged back and forth like an ocean tide, daring her to go free.

She groaned in torment, unable to reach the plateau she longed for. "Please."

As she panted he increased the movements of his fingers on her nipples. He worked her clit faster.

Orgasm reached her, bursting up through her body until she shook. A loud moan burst from her throat as the burning pleasure shot deep into her womb, raced down into her cunt, and clit with ravaging force. She moaned again, a drawn out sound of exquisite torment.

Micky's entire body trembled as she writhed against his still moving fingers.

"There's more," he gasped into her ear. "More. Give me more."

With his right hand he palmed her ass, then stuffed his hand between her legs from behind and with excruciating slowness slid two fingers deep inside her. Both his hands worked her, the slow wet slide heating her from within once again.

Could there be more pleasure in the world than in this moment?

With sweeping strokes his middle finger played her clit. With deep, methodical plunges his other hand stroked, rubbing and rubbing.

With a shuddering wail she hit orgasm again, her muscles clenching over his fingers, then releasing on vibrating waves of mind-melting pleasure.

Micky sagged and Jared eased his fingers from her while aftershocks rippled like tiny earthquakes over her flesh. Every portion of Micky felt alive, humming with breath and blood and overwhelming pleasure.

She turned in his arms and looked into his eyes. A gentle smile tipped his mouth with a hint of male arrogance at his accomplishment. Hunger and desire to please made his gaze as stormy as a windswept ocean, as dark as a night that never ended.

With slow, gentle movements he pulled her underwear and pants up her legs, rearranging her as if they were finished.

"What are you doing?" she asked.

He hooked her bra and pulled her sweater down. "I'd better get going." He kissed her nose, then tucked her close for a hug. Then he released her and stepped back. "We've already gone a little crazy tonight. Maybe we shouldn't have done that."

Disappointment watered down the satisfaction lingering inside her. She darted a peek at his lower body. His cock pressed long and tantalizing against his jeans, and she knew he wanted her as much as she wanted him.

"Why?" she asked. "Why can't we finish it?"

A sad smile replaced his earlier grin. "That's just it. When we make love...if we make love all the way, I don't want it to be under these circumstances. I want it to be more than finishing it."

Frustration gave her tongue free rein. "You're going to walk out of this room now?"

He reached for his coat and slipped it on. Lucky for him, the length covered his hard-on. "Yeah." He leaned close to her, his tone still husky. "But we'll continue this on another night. When we can be sure we're doing it for the right reasons."

He kissed her nose, and in his eyes she saw regret mingling with enduring lust. Surprised and stunned into silence, she watched as he opened the door and hesitated.

"Why don't you sleep in tomorrow and call me when you get a chance?" he asked.

When the door closed, she stood for awhile in a type of shock. While she didn't want to take his rejection as a personal thing, she wondered if his honeyed words hid true rebuff.

How many men could refuse a ready, willing woman? A woman who was so aroused she became soaked with desire and had two orgasms?

She sat on the bed, then lay back, her emotions running from elation and relaxation, to fear and apprehension. As she inhaled deeply, sex lingered on the air. Acknowledging the musky scent gave a forbidden element to what they'd done.

While she'd denied it in her relationship with Davy, she was sick of pretending she didn't enjoy the taboo in sex. She had a wicked side and with Jared she might explore it.

She put her hand to her forehead and tried to analyze how she'd reacted to him. Wanton and in need of release, she'd taken everything he offered. Did she want all he could give so soon? Would time and temptation make another encounter sweeter?

I want it to be more than finishing it.

So they'd gone full circle, with her being the more aggressive sexual predator. When they first met she'd backed away from his attraction, fighting her own feelings. Now she wanted to get it on, and he didn't. The picture didn't add up, and yet she couldn't be upset with him. *Finishing it* really had been cold, a statement speaking of lust and little caring.

Weary and confused by the emotions bombarding her, she stared out at the black sky through the window and turned her thoughts back to the murders. Who or what could have killed those people in her basement?

She allowed her heavy eyelids to drift shut and her body to remember Jared's touch. As she eased into sleep, a smile touched her lips.

* * * * *

The ancient one cursed as he skirted one tunnel and plunged into another to avoid the police continuing to stalk the area. He could take them by surprise if he wished, and they would all die without a whimper. Yet where would the fun be in that? Wholesale mass murder wasn't his style. No, he preferred the methodical planning of a serial killer with keen intelligence, a sense of purpose. No helter-skelter, disorganized murder would do. Too messy, too gauche.

He'd known other vampires, some with limited brain power, who took the unsystematic approach. They often ended up staked in short order. Living a thousand years proved one thing if it proved anything. He knew how and where and when to kill.

Stalking, tormenting, and driving human fear to the highest level before devouring blood and flesh produced the best taste in mortal blood. Sweet and hot, the young couple he'd killed earlier had tasted astounding. Their hormones, full and hot with the need for sex, had drawn his hunger as much as the sound of their voices encroaching on his lair.

Darkness eased him from feeding lust as he plunged into the night and strode along the blackened streets where no one would see him. He cloaked so he would be a wavering of air, a shimmer. A figment of human imagination, a sensation of creeping, unusual horror and no more. Besides, materializing at the last minute added to human terror, and gave more pleasure to the kill.

Frosty air brushed his body as he searched the small town. While the tunnels provided evening shelter for feeding, the police who searched for clues to the young couple's death may come upon him when he slept in the day. That would not do at all.

Where to sleep?

Remembering the resting crypt he'd occupied before Dasoria, Lachlan and Ronan discovered him, he decided not to take sleep in a graveyard. He would hide where they least expected, somewhere even those who knew the truth about vampires never would think to look. He smiled as he thought about how myth helped his cause, how it led mortals toward folly of vast proportions.

He thought back to the woman who'd wandered too close after his kill tonight. While he could have taken her, given her the biggest ecstasy of her life before drinking her delicious blood, she fought his mind control with a will that astounded.

Perhaps only one other woman, his Dasoria, could resist him so well. Maybe he would toy with the other woman by night as he thought of a way to free Dasoria from the chain of her current lover, Lachlan.

Then there was the strange little voices whispering to each other to help the young woman he'd tried to take in the tunnels. His gut clenched in anger. Who were they? Despite his curiosity, he pushed thoughts of them aside.

So many things to do. He chuckled. All the time in the world to do them. A delicious shiver on anticipation ran through him.

He came to the bottom of the hill where the small, rough-hewn Gothic cathedral rose against the sky, its sanctuary bringing a smile to his lips. With his harsh laugh echoing in the air, he headed for St. Bartholomew's and his daily rest.

* * * * *

Lachlan Tavish put his feet up on the balcony railing as he sat on the back porch of Erin Greenway's home and absorbed early morning light. He tried to ease his mind, but the newspaper he held told all. No way could he pretend the ancient one hadn't killed again. Fury made him crush the front section of the newspaper. He lobbed it into open back yard with a curse.

Erin would be in danger for as long as the ancient one remained in Pine Forest. Perhaps as long as the cursed vampire trod Earth. Now a new innocent would be in the crossfire. This Micky Gunn couldn't have known what would happen to her when she came into town. First a gunfight and now a vampire attacking people in her basement. It all added up to one big mess.

While Lachlan went to work with Erin every day to guard her from an attack by the ancient one, he heard gossip. The Denver detective, Jared Thornton, might be an ally in this fight if he believed in the supernatural. Lachlan thought about approaching him and explaining that Thornton's aunt died because of the old vampire, but chances are the cop would think him insane.

Lachlan pondered ideas. If he didn't say anything to Micky Gunn or to Thornton, they'd be victimized by the world's oldest vampire. But what could he do to help them without telling them the real menace they faced? Frustration rose inside him.

He also must think of a new plan that called for more than guarding Erin day by day and night by night. What type of life would it be for her if she could never go anywhere without him?

He thought about asking her to immigrate to Scotland with him, since he hadn't established citizenship in the United States yet. Would she even like it there?

Tension coiled in his neck, and as he turned his head side to side to ease the pain, he decided to relax. He tried breathing deeply, taking in the crisp October air with appreciation. While flowers didn't bloom in winter here, tall ponderosa and spruce dropped needles and the occasional cone fell with a soft whisper to the frozen snow. A breeze wisped through the branches.

A strange sensation immediately overcame him, an awareness he acquired long ago after the ancient one had bitten him in Scotland. He knew when a vampire came near. He didn't know if this blood sucker was a friendly presence, or the kind that would as soon kill him as look at him. Pissed, he crumbled another piece of the paper and threw it over the porch railing.

He almost hit the vampire standing a few feet away.

Lachlan flinched, unprepared for the sudden appearance. Clothed in a head to toe cape, the figure also wore black gloves. Lachlan sometimes wished he had the ability to materialize out of thin air, or walk among mortals cloaked in invisibility. At the same time, he realized he would have to be a full-fledged vampire to accomplish this. Vampires, contrary to popular myth, could travel about in daylight. But each hour they spent in the sun meant their power would drain away until they could die. It limited their movements and therefore most of them went about their business in the wee hours of night. So either this vampire wanted to conceal himself for nefarious reasons, or he'd already spent too much time in daylight.

Lachlan smiled as Ronan Kieran tipped his cape hood back and showed an even, wicked smile.

"Get your ass up here and out of the sun before you fry, Irishman," Lachlan said as he stood.

Still grinning, the Irish vampire stepped onto the porch. "I never fry, my friend. I only bake."

Lachlan shook hands with his long time friend. Ronan embodied everything the ancient one wasn't. Good at heart, determined to hunt down evil vampires where they lay, and pledged to protect innocent humans. He might be cool, often unemotional and secretive, but a man couldn't ask for a better friend.

Lachlan led the way into the house. "Back from Ireland quickly I see. I hope you've got good news to report."

Ronan shrugged. "I wouldn't call it extraordinary news."

The dryness in Ronan's tone told Lachlan he shouldn't get his hopes up. "Sorley should be coming into town soon, right? I thought he'd be with you."

Ronan watched as Lachlan closed the shades in the kitchen. "Sorley is never with me. He's only where he wants to be, which can be just about anywhere. He's been looking for prostitutes."

"Why?"

"Because he claims the last time he had a good lay was over fifty years ago in Ireland. He didn't like the prostitutes in Morocco, apparently."

Lachlan laughed and reached in the pantry for coffee. "Decaf or regular?"

"You know me. Doesn't matter either way." Silence shrouded the room. Ronan pitched the cape onto a chair and removed his gloves. "Ah, that's better. It was getting hot under all that shit. Where is Erin?"

"Upstairs. She should be down in a few moments. I can tell she didn't sleep well last night."

"I can guess why." Ronan's smile told Lachlan exactly what he insinuated.

"Up yours."

"Well, remember I was the one who heard you and Erin feckin' away a few minutes after she met me."

Lachlan never blushed, but he paused in putting water in the coffee maker. "I know what's wrong with you. You haven't taken Yusuf's edict to heart. Why?"

Ronan's expression went from playful to stone cold, a sudden blast of white hot light igniting his eyes. Lachlan knew vampire anger when he saw it. His own eyes glowed the same way during strong emotion.

Ronan skirted the breakfast nook table and stalked to a kitchen window. He peeked around the shade for only a second, then turned back to Lachlan. "You know why. I've told you a dozen times, if I've told you a hundred."

Sensing he'd pushed the vampire too far, Lachlan decided to drop the subject. He switched on the coffee maker. "So what brings you here today other than to report in and say you're back from Ireland?"

"The killings yesterday. I'll be starting recon now that I'm back."

"I take it Sorley will do the same?"

"Aye. He will. I wanted you to know so you can stay with Erin. Be her guard as always."

"I would anyway. As much as I'd like to hunt with you, I can't afford to."

The coffee maker sputtered like a dying man, the choking sound spooky in the dim light. Lachlan didn't speak as his thoughts were a little chaotic.

"Sometimes, when I think of you and Erin, I get this bloody pang of envy."

As the coffee maker gasped one last time and finished brewing, Lachlan reached into the cupboard for mugs. "Why?"

"I don't believe in love for myself. But you…you have something special in Erin. She's a forever woman."

Sadness leaked around the sternness in the vampire's voice, and Lachlan wondered how Ronan withstood the loneliness.

Before he could ask, Ronan asked, "What about Micky Gunn? Do you think we should make contact with her? Let her know what's really happening?"

Lachlan was surprised Ronan would ask him. The vampire didn't often solicit human advice. "I was wondering that myself. The cop seems attached to her, but he's only human. He can't protect her alone."

"Shit." Ronan took the black coffee Lachlan offered him and swallowed a sip. "This will be an even bloodier cluster than I anticipated. I'll find the way into those tunnels under her home and see what I can find out."

Concern stopped Lachlan from drinking his coffee, the mug halfway to his lips. "What if you run into the ancient one?"

"Not to worry, I'll know if he's there, and I'll call for backup. I won't try and fight him without you and Sorley."

'That's a change."

"I've gotten smarter since our last encounter. Before I was being a tad too cocky. Call it bloody Irish arrogance."

Lachlan remembered their last encounter with the ancient one, not so long ago. While he wanted revenge in the worst possible way, he longed for the day it would all be over.

"Come on," Lachlan said. "Let's go into the living room and you can tell me what you found out in Ireland."

Ronan eased into a chair near the fireplace. Lachlan set his mug down on the coffee table and sat on the couch. He could tell by the pensive look on Ronan's face something bothered his friend.

"Okay, spill it," Lachlan said. "I take it you didn't find out anything earth shattering in Ireland, or you would have told me by now."

Ronan shifted on the chair, as if he'd found an uncomfortable spot to reside. "Yes and no."

When he didn't continue, Lachlan's patience came to a quick end. "We haven't got forever, Ronan. What did you find out?"

Ronan's fierce expression went harder, a stone-carved face filled with tumultuous emotion. "I went to Limerick, back to where I was born." A sarcastic smile lit his face. "Not much has changed. The seer is an old woman who's consorted with vampires all of her hundred years."

"Hundred years?"

"She's about on her last year I'd think. She gave me a book of formulas listing methods that have been tried on the ancient one by other vampires and humans before I was even born. None of them worked. When I told her what Yusuf prophesized while I was in Morocco, she agreed with him."

Lachlan leaned over to get his cup of coffee, his curiosity rising. "And?"

Apparently taking Lachlan's lead, the vampire reached for his coffee. After taking a long sip, Ronan seemed to relax. "She said I must find this woman almost immediately, or the entire town will eventually lose the battle."

Lachlan didn't like the sound of it and chose not to believe it outright. "She said the entire town's going to be killed by this fiend?"

Ronan nodded. "Unless they run away and never come back. You know how this place is haunted, man. The whole damned city is rife with the supernatural." Ronan laughed. "That sounds pretty feckin' strange coming from a vampire, eh?"

Ignoring his friend's attempt at humor, Lachlan said, "And you refuse to find a woman to fulfill your destiny because you don't want to use her."

Ronan's eyes turned faintly golden. "I explained that to Sorley just recently. I'm not going to subject any woman to my...to the desires of my flesh. I won't deceive a woman that way again."

"Again?"

Ronan's eyes glowed hotter with emotions. "Long story."

"You never used to be so philanthropic when it came to women, did you?"

"That was a very long time ago. A couple hundred years before you were even an itch in your da's pants."

Lachlan stood, his frustration building. "I don't give a rat's ass about your history right now, Ronan. We've got to deal with what's right in front of us. You went to Ireland to find a solution to this ancient one and came back knowing you have one choice. Why won't you use it?"

Fury sparked Ronan's eyes, and before Lachlan could blink the vampire popped to the other side of the room in a blink of an eye. Lachlan's heart jumped as Ronan stood behind the couch and slightly to the right of him.

"I don't fuck women just to be fucking them," Ronan said. "They have to know what I am and what I want. If they give it to me willingly that's one thing. Do you know any women around this place who are going to step up and say they want me to fuck them after I tell them I'm a vampire? That I'll have to take their blood and bang them repeatedly to keep up the energy I need to fight the ancient one?"

Curiosity made Lachlan's temporary wariness disappear. "Yusuf didn't tell you that, did he? He said you'd have to take a woman to defeat the ancient one. He didn't say *why* it was necessary."

"Right. But the seer did. She said the sexual power will be more incredible than anything between two mortals. Between me and the woman, we would generate a fierce opposition to the ancient one's preeminent powers."

Anger started inside Lachlan. "So you won't do what's necessary. Not even to save your friends."

Ronan's dire expression turned to an aching sadness. "You and Erin should leave Pine Forest. Run as far as you can. Sure, and I may not be able to save the rest of this town, but I can save both of you."

"You know the ancient one will follow us one day. He wants Erin."

"I didn't say I wasn't going to fight him. But if I fail and you've left town, at least I'll have given you a head start."

Lachlan stood, his heart starting a painful beat of recognition. "You're not saying what I think you're saying. You're not going to fight that son-of-a-bitch yourself."

"I am."

Lachlan stalked around the side of the couch until he stood close to the slightly taller vampire. "That's bullshit. We won't let you do this alone. You think we'd turn our back on a good friend?"

Ronan's eyes went into full boil, the golden glow turning almost russet red. "You may not have any choice." When Lachlan said nothing, Ronan continued, his hands out in supplication. "I will fight the ancient one with everything I have."

Lachlan figured Ronan's insistence covered something very traumatic in his past. At the same time, he didn't want the vampire's issues to cloud what had to be done. "You could mesmerize a woman. Make her willing to sleep with you. You know you can do it."

A throat clearing behind them made Lachlan jerk in surprise. Erin stood in the doorway in pajamas and a robe. Her black hair looked mussed, her grey eyes sharp with indignation. "I can't believe you just said that Lachlan Tavish."

"Erin, I—"

"No." Erin shook her head. "I won't be a party to it. And if you're willing to encourage him to do it, Lachlan, you can leave right now. I think the only way it would work is if Ronan finds a woman who truly wants him. Did you ever think that only real love or desire may be what it takes to make the sexual joining powerful enough to defeat the ancient one?"

Lachlan experienced the first spurt of anger he'd felt toward Erin in a long time. "Be reasonable. If it means sacrificing some moralistic high ground to save an entire town—" He cut himself off. Lachlan sighed and walked to her. He gathered her into his arms and hugged her to his chest. He kissed her forehead, and to his relief she snuggled closer. "I'm sorry. I'm desperate. I'll do anything to keep you safe."

"Then take her out of town," Ronan said. "Take her away."

Erin pulled out of Lachlan's arms and turned to Ronan. "No. We won't do that, either. We have friends in this town. We're not giving up on them yet. We'll have to think of something else."

* * * * *

A strange thumping noise woke Micky straight from stone dead sleep. She sat up, eyes wide as her heart pounded. Alarm made her stiffen in dread, last night resurrecting in her memory with fresh intensity.

When nothing dreadful happened and she didn't hear another noise, she lay back on the bed and took a deep breath. Sunshine leaked under the heavy curtains over the large window. When she glanced at the clock it read eight o'clock. She'd fallen asleep late last night, her nerves and body exhausted as much from two orgasms as the strange events earlier in the day.

Two orgasms.

Two incredible, creaming, toe-curling climaxes.

Pleasant sensations returned to her body, wiping out anxiety. Jared's gift last night still thrummed through her veins, as forceful as rain and lightning on a summer day. While she knew instinctively sleeping with Jared would have been incredible, she now welcomed the space he'd given her to heal a little before engaging in a life-affirming occurrence like full-on sex.

I've got to admire a man who places intimacy above raw animal pleasure.

She smiled and sat up again. "Well, there is a lot to be said for animal needs."

Micky didn't put down men's sexual needs or pretended they were somehow disgusting. She also didn't understand women who pretended as if sex itself was unnatural. Even less than satisfactory sexual experiences with Davy couldn't destroy the hope she harbored for a meaningful sex life with the right man.

Could Jared be that man?

As she walked to the window and parted the curtain, she imagined how he would feel inside her. She wondered if he'd be as hard and thick and long as she imagined.

Her stomach growling distracted her from sex for the moment and she could kill for caffeine. Coffee was a priority.

After ordering room service, she wrapped up in a long, cozy blue terrycloth robe. She opened the door and picked up her free copy of the paper on the floor. She closed the door and relocked it before looking at the headline.

Couple Murdered In Secret Tunnels Beneath Gunn Inn.

Of course it would be surprising if the story hadn't made first page headlines. At the same time, she feared publicity would create more problems. Her plans might be screwed seven ways to Sunday and this put new icing on the proverbial cake. She recalled the stories that made it to Colorado Springs recently since the murders began, and the ridiculous conjecture about a monster like El Chupacabra stalking Pine

Forest. Any sane person would realize a serial killer walked the town, and nothing more mysterious.

On the other hand, she shouldn't talk. She saw shadow people on a regular basis, and the gargoyle creature she encountered in the tunnels yesterday wouldn't qualify as sane perception.

She almost didn't read the article, then decided she'd rather be informed than ignorant.

Late yesterday afternoon, Gunn Inn's new owner Mick Gunn made a gruesome discovery in her basement. Twenty-two year old Jeremy Nordice and twenty-year old Andi Blossom were found murdered. The medical examiner's office would not give cause of death at this time, but an unnamed source reports loss of blood as likely.

These murders, according to the police, may or may not be linked with the other murders that have terrorized this town over the last few weeks. Police refuse to name a suspect. In light of these horrible murders, the community is once again jerked out of its complacency and reminded a killer is still on the loose.

How many murders, other than the two in her basement, had occurred since the terror spree began? She couldn't recall. Perhaps she didn't want to remember.

Alternatives came to mind. She could try and sell the Gunn Inn, which had always been an idea from the start. She could wait until the horrible memories of the murders left her, then she could move forward with reopening for business. Or she could wait for awhile and give herself the break she needed before making a decision one way or the other.

I've only got two weeks to decide. Then it's back to the salt mines.

A headache formed in her temples. Stress in action, she supposed.

She lay down on the bed again and relived, almost against her will, the ghastly situation she'd lived through last night.

The gargoyle's face intruded, cold stone, sharp angles, and vicious teeth.

"I can't do this to myself." She shook her head free of disturbing images once again.

First she would have breakfast, then head to the library to pick up a book to read. A good story could distract her from current events so they didn't invade her mind at unexpected moments.

No. I promised to call Jared first.

She reached for the telephone.

* * * * *

Jared stepped onto the icy curb outside the police department, glad for the ridged boots keeping him anchored. He breathed the icy air and welcomed the cleanliness into his lungs after the stale air inside.

Fusty more than described the air in the offices he'd left, it described the backwoods attitude of Danny Fortesque and many other police in this town. They'd called him out of a sound sleep at five in the morning and wanted him to come down for questioning. He almost contacted Micky, but decided against it. She needed sleep. And he required time to think about what they'd done last night.

He remembered how she'd looked when he'd first kissed her in the hallway, her eyes wide as he moved in for the kill. Then they'd danced on the edge of a knife last evening when he'd felt her pulsing in orgasm around his fingers. With her short hair tousled into a messy but somehow beautiful style, and her eyes asking him to take her, she'd looked like the answer to all his dreams. Her body, slim but lusciously curvy in all the right places, had driven him into meltdown.

But then so had Katherine.

Of course, the two women were nothing like in personality or looks, other than blonde hair. But while Katherine's blonde screamed brassy and bold, Micky possessed an innocence which stormed his defenses and demanded his protection. He wanted to keep her safe against everything.

He walked down the quiet main street and recalled how difficult it had been to back away from Micky. He almost took her up on the plea and freed his cock long enough to sink deep inside her. He would have fucked her long and hard. Probably for so long they would have both been sore this morning.

Shit, yes. It would have felt beyond heaven. When he'd touched her wetness, lingering over her slick juices, he'd almost...almost come in his pants. He couldn't remember any woman making him so desperate. He'd retreated to his room and jacked off in the shower.

He'd stood under the stream of water and imagined how her heat would envelope him, her passage pulling and sucking and caressing his cock like a mouth until he spewed inside her. While taking his cock in hand had emptied some of the pressure, he knew it would be damned difficult to keep his hands off her from now on.

Before he reached his vehicle, his cell phone rang. He grabbed it, anticipating his mother would call sometime and let him know his aunt's body arrived at the mortuary in Denver.

"Jared?" The warm, feminine voice belonged to Micky. A tingle started in his gut.

"Hey. I'm glad you called. Are you feeling a little better?"

"Yes. I thought I'd take it easy today and maybe go to the library. I need to be somewhere quiet."

Jared almost said he'd meet her there, but he knew instinctively she'd balk. "Good. You could use the rest. If I hear anything about what happened yesterday, I'll contact you."

Contact you. Thornton, that sounded fucking cold.

Silence came over the line, and he asked, "Are you there?"

"Yes. Well, I guess I'll talk to you later."

Come on, you asshole. Don't leave her like this.

"Wait. Have dinner with me tonight. We need to...talk."

He heard her inhale, a deep, almost resigned sound. "All right. When and where?"

A brisk wind whistled around his head and blew fresh snow across his boots. "I'm a little tired of Jekyl's. My aunt once said there was a great place outside of town called Ricardo's. We could try it out in her honor. What if I meet you at your room at five o'clock? I'll make reservations for six."

"Sounds good. See you then."

Without another word she hung up.

He stood in the freezing cold and stared at his cell phone, confusion reigning supreme in his mind.

Face it, man. You're sinking deep too quickly.

* * * * *

"Men. Who understands them?" Micky stepped through the big wooden double doors into the library. "Certainly not me."

An old lady with a welcoming smile tottered out the door as Micky held it open for her. The gentleness in the woman's expression banished Micky's grumpiness.

Negativity will find you if all you do is think of pessimistic things. An older friend, someone she'd lost touch with long ago, had once told Micky this. She knew her friend had been right, but remembering it didn't come easy.

When the wood door closed, Micky felt a strange disturbance in the air. She glanced around, and among some of the towering bookshelves, a shadow moved. She gasped. No one was there.

With a sense of inevitability, she realized what she'd seen. Shadow people.

Her gut ached. Okay, so at the hotel she'd escaped them. A small respite or perhaps Jared distracted her with his heady brand of mind-blowing sensuality and incredible pleasure. Top that off with seeing two dead bodies and it added up to sufficient distraction for anybody.

A few people moved about in the cavernous area, as well as sat at tables reading through books. Even if the place had shadow people and God knows what else, she wouldn't be alone.

Darkness lingered at the edge of the room, even though a chandelier twinkling above threw light across the long wood tables, the rows of books, and the polished floor.

She headed toward the main information and checkout desk, her boots making a wet squeaking noise. One older gentleman sitting at a table gave her a disapproving moue, as if she could control the sound.

A young woman with shiny black hair stood behind the counter, her smile welcoming. Petite and almost delicate in appearance, the woman's gray eyes sparkled with enthusiasm.

"May I help you?" The woman's soft voice asked.

Micky liked her right away. "I'm new in town and might not be staying permanently. Is there a way to check out books anyway?"

"We'll just need you to fill out a form. We'll give you a temporary card that's good for a month." As the woman reached for the form, Micky noticed her nametag.

Erin Greenway.

Instant kinship stirred inside Micky. She knew Erin had been attacked by the serial killer in this library. Micky didn't say anything. She took the form and filled it in right at the counter since no one else awaited Erin's attention.

When Erin saw her name on the form, she came to a standstill. Erin glanced up, a serious and perhaps sadness darkening her eyes. "You're Carl Gunn's niece?"

"Yes." Micky smiled weakly. "I imagine my name's all over town since the incident yesterday. Everyone in town will know me."

Erin's eyes shadowed, a glimmer of mental pain giving her a pinched look. "I know the feeling."

Unspoken understanding flowed between them. "I'll bet you do."

Erin began to make a temporary card. "This place has all the usual gossip and then some." She took a quick glance around the library. "Look, this is going to sound very strange, but if you need help, I've got friends who can assist."

Confused but curious, Micky leaned on the counter. "Why would I need help?"

The skin between Erin's brows creased as she frowned. "I don't know how to approach this. Did something else terrible happen down in those tunnels yesterday? I mean, other than the murders?"

Sincerity radiated from Erin, but the question shocked Micky down to her feet. Perhaps Erin could understand the strangeness surrounding her life since she'd come to this spooky town. How great to know someone here she could talk with and not feel as if she would be ridiculed.

Then again, she couldn't talk about the gargoyle to anyone, no matter who they were.

Micky took the card Erin handed her, the warmth from the laminating process heating her fingers.

"Micky?"

"I'm sorry. Nothing else happened in the tunnels. Just the murders."

"If you want someone to talk to, feel free. We could get together for lunch. I think we'd have some things in common."

Continued curiosity made Micky ask, "Why would your friends be able to help me?"

Erin nodded toward the middle of the room where a gorgeous, dark-haired man sat in a big cushy chair reading a book. "That's my fiancé, Lachlan Tavish. He's watching over me because of what happened here."

"Because you were almost murdered?" Micky's sympathy went out to her. "I'm glad he's looking after you, but what does that have to do with me?"

Erin sighed. "It's complicated. Lachlan could arrange for your protection as well." When Micky said nothing, Erin shook her head. "I'm sorry, I'm mucking this up. Can you wait about thirty minutes? I have a break coming, and I can explain in detail."

Although she believed she could trust Erin, the whole conversation went beyond odd. If she wanted to know more about the serial murders, she needed to investigate. Maybe Erin would have the answer.

Thirty minutes later, after Micky checked out a hardback suspense novel she'd lusted after forever, Erin showed her to a secluded seating area near the north end of the first floor.

Far above, sunlight from windows barely warmed the cushioned chairs. Glad she'd worn a heavy fleece top and flannel-lined jeans, Micky sank into an upholstered chair next to the librarian.

Erin clasped her hands in her lap, her small fingers worrying the sash belt hanging down from her blue broomstick skirt. "I'm not sure where to start." Erin's gaze went to the floor. "How much have you heard about what's happened in this town this month?"

Micky gave her a newspaper precise account of the serial killings. "Doesn't it make you nervous they haven't found the killer?"

"Lachlan watches over me. And like I said, he has other friends who are pursuing the culprit." Erin put her hands up in a helpless gesture. "I'm taking a big risk telling you the truth about what's happening in Pine Forest."

"How?" Micky's stomach tightened, suspense eating away at her patience.

Erin's voice dropped to a whisper. "Because most people, even the people in *this* town, wouldn't believe the truth."

"You'd be surprised what I believe."

Again Erin paused before continuing. "Pine Forest is a creepy place, but the events this month push it off the charts. You may be in danger, Micky."

Spirals of apprehension made her sit forward. "Why? From whom?"

Erin's eyes pinpointed to something above Micky's shoulders.

"From a vampire, Miss Gunn," a deep, slightly Scottish accented voice said behind her. "A vampire."

Chapter Seven

ಬಿ

Micky's fingers clenched the chair arms, and she twisted around to see who had crept up behind her.

Lachlan Tavish walked around to the chair grouping and settled on the couch close to Erin. When his arm slipped around Erin protectively, Micky experienced a pang of envy. Other than Jared, when had she known a moment of protection from a man? She thought back and couldn't recall. Lachlan gave Erin a warm, almost sensual glance, and Erin returned his affection with a love-filled smile.

Micky snapped back to reality. "A vampire?" She couldn't keep the total disbelief out of her voice. "You're kidding, right? Someone put you up to this?"

"I know it sounds insane," Erin said. "But you can trust us."

"Why should I?" Micky wanted to believe them. After all, didn't she have weird tales of her own? But vampires? *Come on.* "Are you saying there's someone who thinks they're a vampire and is committing these murders?"

The darkly mysterious man chuckled, and a soft golden glow touched his eyes. "I wish. It would make things so much easier."

The golden light increased in his eyes for a flash and gave him the dark, sleek danger of a stalking beast. Micky's breath caught. Had his eyes actually glowed? She shook her head, an internal denial. No wonder Erin found Lachlan attractive. The man packed enough sex appeal for two men.

Except for Jared.

Lachlan couldn't hold a candle to the cop's magnetic, powerful, masculine allure.

"I refuse to accept myth as an answer to these crimes," Micky said.

Erin's features softened, her gaze understanding. "It's difficult to believe. It took a lot to convince me."

Maybe Lachlan, with his smooth Scottish tones, controlled Erin more than the woman knew. Danger lurked around him, and Micky didn't trust him.

She glanced at her watch. *Damn it.* She was late for dinner with Jared. She stood up. "Thanks for the information, but I've got to go."

"Wait." Erin's expression held a plea. "There's more you need to know. Your survival may depend on it."

Unwilling to be made the cuckold, Micky said, "I'm sorry, but I can't accept the vampire theory."

"Have you seen him?" Erin asked quickly, rising to her feet. "Did you see anything or feel anything strange since you've been in town."

Micky paused. "No, why should I?"

"He may not have approached her yet, "Lachlan said.

"Who?" Micky asked.

"The ancient one," Lachlan said, his tone soft. "A thousand year old vampire with more power than any other vampire I know. Enough evil strength to take a woman against her will."

Micky's mouth popped open. "You've got to be kidding?"

Erin stood and her eyes held a beseeching expression. "We wish we were kidding and that it was only a Halloween joke. Have you noticed the fear in this community?"

Micky tightened her grip on her purse, almost as if she'd need to use it for protection. "Of course."

"People around here accept the supernatural, but before it was harmless," Erin said. "Now it's becoming a flaming nightmare, a horror flick on the late show."

The woman's intensity captivated Micky's attention, and she saw the honesty in Erin's eyes as she spoke. *But how could she be telling the truth?* "Prove it to me. Prove there's a vampire lurking around."

Lachlan smiled, lighting his serious expression until he appeared charming and not so grim. "We could always introduce you to Sorley and Ronan. They're vampires."

Micky smirked. "So you're saying now there's more than one vampire in town."

"Three that we know about," Lachlan said as he held up three fingers.

Okay, now that sounds way too weird to be believed.

"We know the ancient one is coming after me. He's already tried before." Erin inhaled deeply, and Lachlan slipped his arm around her. "But he's going to eat his way through a few more people before he tries."

"Why?" Micky asked.

"Sustenance," Lachlan said. "Blood. In our last encounter with him we shot him with a silver bullet. It drains his power and immobilizes him for a time. But it doesn't kill him."

Blood? Silver bullets? "No, this can't be true. I'm sorry I have to go."

She walked away.

On the way out to her car, Micky tried calling Jared on her cell phone but the battery went dead. She'd charged the phone just last night. Frustrated, she tossed it onto the passenger seat.

Murphy's Law applies big time.

As she pulled out of the parking lot she made a right.

Wait.

Damn it, the hotel is the other way.

Wondering where her common sense had departed, she decided at the next intersection she'd make a loop.

Come to me, lovely one.

The voice came out of nowhere, a masculine, compelling voice with a drugging quality. Husky and intimate, it droned in her head. *Come to me. You know me as I know you. You have seen my face.*

Fear ran over her body with freezing tentacles. "Who is it?"

The master of all you need. I can do for you what the weakling cop could never accomplish.

Dizziness made her slow the car, her senses drifting as the voice intoned. She shook her head and realized she'd passed through the last intersection and hadn't made the loop back to Jekyl's. At the corners of her vision shadows drifted like wispy smoke. She looked one way then the other, but as usual, the shadows alluded a full on glance.

"Leave me alone." She muttered her wishes. "Please, please. Go away. Get away from me."

Come to me. Come. Come. Come.

"No!" Micky struggled to regain her sense of control, but she couldn't move her hands from the steering wheel or pull over. Her body didn't follow orders anymore, at least not from her. "Stop it! Stop it!"

She didn't know who she shouted at, but maybe if she yelled it would break the bizarre trance gripping her.

Fog drifted down until the street and buildings seemed far away. Murkiness closed over her mind, an obliterating darkness sending contrary messages to her physical being. Again the voice demanded.

Only I can give you what you need. Your body needs satisfaction. You will come to me.

Trembling, she used all her will to resist the voices pull. When she saw a police cruiser driving toward her, a plan formed. She could swerve toward it and maybe break the voices hypnotic quality.

No. No she couldn't. What if the officer was hurt or killed? She couldn't take the risk.

Her head pounded, her heart picked up speed. Sweat broke out all over her body. Nauseated, she struggled with the voice's haunting, evil nature. "Jared, help me."

Foolish woman. He can't help you. He's a mere mortal and they are highly ineffective creatures on the whole. He doesn't know anything is wrong. He won't know until it's too late. There is no need to resist, lovely one. With me there is much pleasure to be had.

Another chorus of whispers invaded her hearing.

Resisthimresisthimresisthim.

Savehersavehersaveher.

The voices were the same as the one's she'd heard in the tunnels.

Puzzled, she resisted the drugging quality of the sultry voice.

With a curse parting her lips, she stomped on the breaks and wrenched the wheel to the right. The car skidded, then came to a stop on the shoulder. Shuddering with adrenaline and fear of the unknown, she waited until a semblance of control returned.

Worry encroached. She'd never seen shadow people in her car before. What did it mean? Did the seductive voice belong to one of the shadow people? Thinking about it made her head pound. Micky leaned her head back and took deep breaths, hoping the relentless ache would recede. After about five minutes she felt more normal and turned the car back toward town.

All the way back to Jekyl's she replayed what the entity had said to her and it made no sense. What did it mean by saying she knew it and had seen its face? By the time she made it to the hotel her equilibrium returned and her nausea and headache completely disappeared. She could almost imagine the entire thing had been her imagination or a bad dream.

As she walked through the lobby, Mrs. Drummond stood with another woman behind the front desk. They didn't appear to notice Micky as she passed by, and she caught part of their conversation.

"You'll be perfectly safe," Mrs. Drummond said to the middle-edged, frowzy looking woman. "No one will try anything in a public place like this."

The woman sniffed. "I don't know. Are you sure your husband can't take this shift? I mean, other than that kid the other night, a man's never been attacked by whatever this thing is."

Mrs. Drummond laughed. "Are you kidding? After a full day's work over the butcher shop, he isn't putting in another shift of any kind."

Micky hurried upstairs, not wanting more reminders of the murders.

When she reached her room, she found the light on her phone flickering like crazy with two messages.

Jared's deep, sensual voice provided the first message. "Micky, it's five ten. I'm in my room. Give me a call." The second message played. "It's five thirty. If I don't hear from you in ten minutes I'm going out looking for you. Call me on my cell phone number."

"Tried that," she muttered.

Great. He sounds more annoyed than concerned. How long had the extra little trip out of town taken? She looked at the digital alarm clock on the bed stand. Five fifty. She'd lost almost twenty extra minutes or more trying to get back to town.

She groaned and put her fingers to her temples as her head started to ache again. Two aspirin might be in order.

She started to reach for the phone to dial Jared's room number when knocking on her door made her stop. Jared's deep tone came through the door. "Micky?"

What will I tell him?

She couldn't tell him what happened to her on the road. He would turn away from her in a heartbeat and suggest she needed counseling.

Micky hurried to the door, and when she opened it, Jared stood there with a bristling power that reminded her of the first time she'd seen him. His hair stuck up on his head, as if he'd run his fingers through it. Dim hallway lighting made his eyes dark emerald.

When she stepped back to let him inside, he entered and closed the door with a solid click. "Where were you?"

Rigid disapproval, like ice chips over exposed skin, tinged his voice.

She bristled. "I lost track of time."

Ire drained from his expression by slow degrees. "I was worried."

"I appreciate that, but it wasn't my intention to be late or make you worry."

When she rubbed her temples to ease the tension, he moved closer. His gaze caressed her, sweeping over her features with a lingering, hot appraisal that wiped away her own anger. She couldn't seem to stay mad at this man when his eyes devoured like he wanted to kiss her, but wouldn't because of misguided chivalry. As always, her body responded to Jared's heated, longing expression.

"Micky, I'm sorry. I shouldn't have barked. When you were late I imagined all kinds of disaster. With the murders in this town, it made me nuts when I didn't know where you were."

She smiled, gratified. "A woman could start to wonder why you're so protective. You are protective, aren't you?"

"Sometimes I imagine bad things happening to people I care about."

Jared's big hands cupped her shoulders. Fire danced over her body when his gaze traveled over her hair and then captured her eyes for a moment before settling on her lips. His face held promises, cherishing, affectionate and admiring.

"I overreact sometimes," he said huskily. "And yeah, I'm protective."

Wanting to reassure him, she placed her hands on his chest. Masculine power emitted from his torso and she absorbed with the greedy adoration of a woman who can't deny a man's sexuality.

Oh, yes. Jared Thornton was walking sex and she couldn't resist him.

He'd worn a teal sweater that molded his sculpted chest and arms to perfection. Tucked into a pair of black jeans, the sweater showcased his flat stomach and the entire ensemble made him look good enough to eat. Silky material glided against her fingers, her appreciation for his hard-muscled body firing her excitement to new heights.

Their gazes clashed and a smoldering fire ignited in his eyes. Before she could think of a coherent reply, he slipped his hand into her hair and anchored her close. With tender contrition his mouth settled over hers, hot and strong and mint-flavored.

Staggering heat bloomed deep in her stomach and she wanted him with lightning quick passion. Sweet longing grew and she clutched at his shoulders, needing the anchor of his strength. Jared's cock grew rock solid, thick and long against her belly. She gasped into his mouth. The sensation of rampant maleness ready exclusively for her made Micky want to slide her pants off and get down to business. Feeling wet and swollen, she arched against his cock.

She tore her mouth from his. "God, Jared, you're so hard."

He groaned against her lips. "We gotta stop or we'll be late for our reservation."

She could barely draw a breath to respond. "We can eat in. Cancel our reservation."

He took her mouth again, a lingering, loving taste. "We've got things to talk about."

"Such as?"

Jared's lips touched her chin, then lingered over her cheekbone. "What I learned today from the police and how it relates to the murders at your uncle's inn."

She moaned in exasperation. She did want to know what he found out, but the riot he created in her body threatened to topple ideas of leaving the room. "Then you're going to have to stop driving me crazy."

"Crazy how?" He kissed her forehead, then traveled down to her other ear. He nuzzled the sensitive area alongside her neck. "By kissing you, or by acting like a madman and threatening to hunt you down if you didn't call me."

"Both. Are you a possessive man?"

His lips catalogued a slow, agonizingly sensual path to her neckline. "I've never been before. Must be something about you."

"Is it entirely my fault, then?"

"Definitely. Whenever I see you, all I want to do is get close."

His breathing increased and the slightly gruff nuance in his voice acted like an aphrodisiac. Sexual craving roared into her system, a river overflowing its banks. One of his hands took up residence on her ass, the other slipped along her ribcage and toured toward her breast. He stopped just short.

"I want to touch you," he said. "Everywhere."

Molten metal couldn't have been any hotter. If he kept his up, she'd melt into her shoes. Shivering, Micky felt moist and hot with need. She squirmed a little and his grip tightened on her ass, then loosened.

"I can't believe we're doing this, Jared."

"Why?"

"We hardly know each other."

He pressed a tender kiss on her cheek. "I don't understand it either. Earlier today I tried to tell myself I wasn't being a gentleman, and that I was taking advantage of a woman who'd just suffered major traumas. I want to hole up in this room and do nothing but stay inside you for hours."

Hours? My God, what would that be like? Heady excitement washed over her. "That long?"

He whispered in her ear as his touch traveled up her back, then back to her ass. He pressed her against his groin, all subtly shot. "God, yes."

"I can't believe you'd want that with me." She cleared her throat. "A man's never said —"

When she cut herself off, he asked, "What?"

Still she stayed silent. He captured her gaze with his and his eyes narrowed, but the heat never left them.

Embarrassed around the edges, she decided honesty would be best. "I've had two lovers, Jared. I get all tense and I can't…"

"It's all right," he said softly in a coaxing tone. He brushed his fingers through her hair, the gesture making her stomach tumble with desire. "Tell me."

"I'm always so tense that making love sometimes hurts."

His eyes widened. "Didn't they stop? Didn't you tell them?"

"I just endured the pain for a few seconds and finally told them to stop. They didn't mean to hurt me."

His brow furrowed, then he put his forehead to hers and closed his eyes. He held her gently. "Damn it, Micky, I wouldn't have pushed you like this if I'd known."

"How could you know?" She laughed a little sarcastically, then pulled back so she could see his expression. "It's not something you do when you first meet a person, you know. 'Excuse me, but I may not be able to have sex because it hurts.'"

He shook his head. "Wait a minute. Was one of the guys you're talking about that cop?"

Part of her didn't want to talk about Davy again, but she didn't have much choice if she planned on being honest with Jared. "Yes. Davy Benjamin. He didn't understand and said it was my problem. "

"Shit." He caressed her hair. "What an asshole. I think you didn't feel anything with him because unconsciously you knew he was an idiot. Your body tightened up because it didn't' want to let him in."

She'd run the idea around in her head more than once to test it out. But what if it happened again? She didn't think she could stand it.

He released her with reluctance and sadness made her heart ache. She may have destroyed any chances with him. An awkward silence ensued, and she turned away in disappointment. Maybe it was good she'd told him before it went any farther. After all, if he found her admission disturbing or it turned him off, she didn't want to go to bed with him anyway.

Right. So why am I burning up inside with the need to make love with him?

She reached for her coat on the bed. "We have enough time to make it to the restaurant if we hurry."

He helped her on with the coat, then turned her around. He tilted her chin up with his index finger. "Let's have a nice dinner, and then we'll come back upstairs. I'll show you sex doesn't have to be like what you experienced with those two men."

Her disappointment eased a little. She gave him a mischievous smile. "That's awfully smug of you, Detective Thornton."

"Damn right." He plunged his hands into her hair. "I'm so hot for you I can barely stand to leave this room. But I promise before we even get back here you'll want me so much all you're going to feel is pleasure."

Her face flushed and when he took her mouth again, this time he held nothing back. His tongue plunged inside, and she gasped at the heated invasion. Her belly swirled, the sensation hot and welcome. His tongue stroked hers and mimicked the deepest sex imaginable. She didn't know if a person could come only from kissing, but with this man she just might.

God, I want him inside me, pumping out his lust. Hard and fast, slow and deep. Anyway I can get him will be the right way.

Jared drew back too fast for her liking, but if they remained longer they never would make it to Ricardo's. Before they left the hotel room she swiftly changed into a black skirt made of a shimmering fabric and a multi-colored sweater that reminded her of a black night strewn with a jeweled sky.

As they left, anticipation made a delicious shiver through her body. She had a feeling tonight would be special in ways she never anticipated.

* * * * *

"Did you find a prostitute?" Ronan asked Sorley as they walked up the hill toward St. Bartholomew's.

Ronan felt the beginnings of a headache in his temples, an indicator the weather changed again. Soon the snow crunching under their feet and the brisk wind whistling in their ears would turn into another blizzard.

Sorley grinned. "No. Had to resort to strangling my own chicken. There isn't a prostitute to be found anywhere in Pine Forest."

"Imagine that," Ronan said dryly.

Ronan tried not to think about Sorley jerking off because it reminded him too much of his own long-ignored appetites. Despite the thorough screwing he'd given Yusuf's daughter not so long ago, a vampire's lust went beyond mortal requirements. Still, he knew the longer his desire built without satisfaction, the higher his frustration would become. When he finally did get his mitts on a woman, he'd be hard pressed to reign in his desire to shag for hours. The woman would have to be ready and willing to spend hours engaging in sex. Hell, she'd have to accept that his lust dictated sex on a frequent basis. A very frequent basis.

He brushed away errant thoughts of finding a woman for a good lay and instead took a deep inhalation of icy air. Tonight new cloud cover darkened the land, and it suited Ronan fine. The darker the better for prowling.

"So you think this priest will talk to us if we ask him about suspicious vampires hiding around this place?" Sorley asked.

Ronan grunted. "Hell, no we aren't asking him about vampires. He'd think we were of the devil, or some other such rubbish. Besides, there isn't usually anyone around here this time of night, not even the priest."

Sorley nodded. "Pity. I was looking forward to seeing the man's expression."

"You are sick, Sorley. Very sick. Scaring a poor, innocent priest."

Sorley's delighted laugh trickled over the wind and echoed in the tall trees. "All right, all right. So what are we looking for again?"

"It's possible the ancient one is using several places to hide out. I've scanned over many of them since I've been here, but with your help we can get through more hiding places."

"I thought you explored this area before?"

"Yes, but that's before the murders at the Gunn Inn. The church isn't far from the inn. It would make a convenient hiding place for him now the police are poking about and investigating the tunnels. Sure, and the ancient one wouldn't want to be anywhere mortals could stumble upon him easily."

When they walked around the side of the church to a side door, Sorley came to a stop and nodded toward the doorway. "You go first."

Ronan grinned, his friend's tendency to wimp out at the last minute was legendary. "You can stay out here."

Sorley snorted and planted his hands on his hips. "I'm going in with you."

"Then what the hell are you afraid of? You're a vampire for God's sake."

Sorley's face twisted, his boney features giving him a scary mask that would frighten mortals with ease. "Sometimes I forget that crosses can't hurt us and that holy water doesn't even give us a burn. It's hard to remember when mortals keep spreading that shit around."

Ronan glared down at him. "Get some balls. We don't have time for this."

Ronan turned the doorknob and to his surprise it swung open. No need to walk through walls, which they could do if they needed to.

As they stepped into the church, Ronan blinked and adjusted his eyes. At the best of times he found bright light annoying, and even the somewhat subdued glow almost made his eyes ache.

Ronan closed the door behind them. "You take one side of the church and look for anywhere the ancient one could rest easily."

One of Sorley's eyebrows twitched upwards. "And what if I find him?"

"Run."

Sorley's high-pitched cackle rang through the nave and bounced like a ping pong ball.

Ronan grimaced. "Good. If the priest didn't know someone was here before, he does now."

Sorley hurried away, quickened by his old friend's severe expression.

Shaking his head in dismissal, Ronan started a search of the old structure. He admired the architecture, even if he didn't plan to make a steady diet of coming here. Stained glass windows soared high, their designs obscured by the night. He looked through each area with a meticulousness he reserved for graveyards and cemeteries. Although he didn't feel the essence of the ancient one nearby, he sensed the vampire crossed through here at some point tonight. Something dark and unclean had passed this way.

He stopped in front of a pew and scrutinized the worn surface. Centuries ago, when mortal blood ran through his veins, he'd found ease in the quiet of a holy place. Now it left him somewhat cold and indifferent.

You're too jaded, old man.

Ronan felt Sorley's surprise and disgust a few seconds before he heard the vampire's swift steps through the nave.

He heard his friend's customary litany. "Jesus, Jesus, Jesus."

Holy sinners. Sorley's thoughts flew into Ronan's head like gunshots. *Holy Mother.*

Before Ronan could formulate a mental reply, Sorley rounded a corner and appeared nearby, popping out of his cloaking ability with an audible snap.

Ronan walked toward him. "What the hell is going on? What are you shrieking about?"

For the first time in his life, Sorley looked scared. He pointed back in the direction he'd come. "I found him."

Ronan's muscles went on alert, his body taut and ready to fight. "The ancient one?"

Sorley shook his head, the motion jerky. "The priest. What's left of him, anyway."

* * * * *

Jared watched Micky order her dinner as they sat at the booth table in a secluded part of Ricardo's. Their table suited what he planned to do to Micky very well. He could sit close to her with the tablecloth draped over their legs.

He enjoyed perusing Micky, the way her mouth moved, and the way her eyes danced with amusement when the waiter made a subtle joke. Hell of it was, he'd enjoyed everything about her tonight. She looked beautiful and unearthly. Everything about her glowed with vibrancy. Her skin held a rosy glow, her eyes a delicate sparkle. Her hair possessed the silver sheen of an angel.

God, he loved pushing his fingers through the soft, golden and platinum lengths of Micky's short, cute hair.

When he'd first seen her standing in the doorway of her hotel room, he thought she looked pale and troubled, but the idea disappeared in a heartbeat. Sex simmered beneath the surface of everything they said and did. He might have rejected having sex with her last night, but now he couldn't think of anything else.

She is just so incredibly fucking cute.

They might be in a stylish, out-of-the-way restaurant, but she fit right into the glitter here. Something about her felt old-fashioned in the best sense of the word, as if she could enter the past and blend seamlessly. He vowed he'd know more about her tonight and fill in some of the gaps he needed to discover.

Before he left their table, the waiter explained the old Queen Anne house had been converted into a restaurant some time ago, and it extruded opulence. Red velvet brocade dominated the room, and while it seemed a bit much to him, he figured women probably liked it. Two huge chandeliers sparkled with low, romantic light. China, gold utensils and expensive green table linens added to the ambience. Subdued classical music played in the background and a huge gas fireplace at one end of the large dining room danced with flames.

The place screamed romance.

Yeah, a good place to bring a woman you can't wait to fuck. And he did want to fuck her. Never mind trying to be slow or sweet about it, he wanted her so much he got hard whenever she spoke a little breathy or her gaze pinpointed part of his body. He'd caught her attention lingering on his lips, his chest, and even his cock on more than one occasion. It made him crazy to realize she liked his body. If she wanted to treat him like a sex symbol, let her.

Face it. Her admiration is the biggest turn-on you've ever had.

When she'd caressed his chest through the sweater he'd about moaned in ecstasy and decided to stay at the hotel.

Then he remembered the promise he'd made her. She would discover only pleasure when they came together. Determined, he knew he couldn't let her down.

Then he recalled the last time he'd gone to bed with a woman, and his ego wondered if he would disappoint Micky.

Shit, man, have I lost my mind?

Yes, he'd lost it when he came to Pine Forest to hunt his aunt's killer and instead spent almost twenty-four hours a day wanting to protect and be with this woman.

He felt possessive in a fiery, get down and dirty way he'd never sensed before, not even with Katherine. Whenever Micky came near him his heart banged in his chest, he felt a little breathless, and he wondered if he spoke like a fool or a damn fool.

While he suspected she hadn't told him everything about what happened down in the hell-hole tunnel, he couldn't keep away from her. She fascinated him in dozens of ways he couldn't define at this point.

Damn it, he knew this feeling. He'd experienced it with Katherine once. Could he be making the same dumb ass mistake?

Maybe. He'd have to keep his heart on a leash. Sure, he could keep lust from turning into something deeper if he concentrated on the physical. Maybe they could both enjoy sleeping together without getting twined in some messy relationship thing that would implode in the end.

When their chardonnay arrived, he took a taste and then focused his full attention on her. "Great place."

She glanced around, her eyes sparkling with enthusiasm and enjoyment. "I'm feeling a little underdressed."

When he cataloged the people around them, he could see most people wearing finer clothing. He shrugged. "You look great. Pretty, in fact."

Her smile widened and a flush touched her cheeks. She opened her mouth as if to deny his compliment, then she swallowed hard. "Thank you."

He could flatter her all night, loosen up her inhibitions before they did the wild thing back at the hotel, but several things needed their attention beforehand.

"You went to the library?" Jared asked.

"I checked out a thriller I've wanted to read. Erin Greenway gave me a temporary card in case I decide I don't want to stay in Pine Forest."

Two things caught his attention, but he concentrated on one. "Erin Greenway. That name sounds familiar."

She took a sip of wine before she answered. "She's one of the women who was attacked by the serial killer and survived."

"Right, I remember now."

Micky brushed at her bangs, pushing them away from her eyes. "Something weird happened while I was at the library.

It's crazy, I suppose, but then in this town it figures. Erin and her fiancé, this Scottish guy, said a vampire is the killer."

Stunned silent, he waited for more explanation. When she didn't give it, he tried a police officer's line of questioning. "You want to start from the beginning and tell me everything she said?"

"You're not going to say she's nuts and I should forget about it?"

"Well, they both sound nuts, but tell me what they said."

After another sip of her wine, she leaned back in her chair. Lines of strain around her eyes showed she hadn't slept well last night. Maybe tonight, after a good, long bed session with him, she would get the sleep she needed.

Easy. Maybe what she needs is a slow work up to this. Tease her until she begs you. She'll be so excited she won't tighten up when you get inside her.

He wanted her aching to hold his cock inside her, her hot body opening wide to take his thrusts.

Aggravation made him curse mentally when he realized she'd been talking and he'd been too busy thinking about seducing her.

"I couldn't believe what I heard. Vampires? It's too crazy." She worried a strand of her hair, flicking it back with an impatient movement. "Maybe the attack on Erin rattled her sanity."

"People would use about any excuse around here to explain a horrible event when they don't know the real facts. It might be a defense mechanism for her and the boyfriend."

Her brows tipped down again as if she pondered the questions of the universe. "They seem so normal, Erin and Lachlan."

"Appearances can deceive."

"I know."

Time to cut to the chase about what he'd learned. "I found out a few things at the police station that might shed some light on this case. I talked to Danny Fortesque. He knows Erin Greenway well. He thinks Lachlan has something to do with the killings, but he can't put a finger on what yet."

Micky looked troubled. "Do you believe Fortesque?"

"I'm not sure. I don't think I can trust him with information, but it's hard to tell. According to Fortesque, all the people attacked were ensanguined."

Micky's face paled. Shadows seemed to form in her eyes, haunting her like ghosts. "Drained of blood. That lends a little credence to this vampire theory, I suppose."

"These murders have a logical basis. It's a human killer with sophisticated methods, an organized murderer. He's damned good at it, too."

She shivered.

"Cold?" he asked, knowing her quiver might be from fear. She nodded, and he shifted nearer. "I'll share my body heat with you."

Her grin told him she didn't believe him. "Share more information about what Fortesque said."

Resigned, he spilled the rest. "There doesn't seem to be unifying factors with any of the victims, or at least none the police have been able to detect. Age isn't a factor. My aunt was the oldest person attacked and this Andi girl the other night was the youngest. They all had different occupations and didn't know each other that well if at all."

"Wait a minute, what about Erin and that woman she works with? They're friends."

"Probably it has as much to do with them being in the library at the same time than anything."

"What do you think made the killer stop draining their blood?"

"The only factor is Lachlan Tavish. He showed up in time to save Erin. Erin walked upstairs and heard some strange sounds. The other woman, Gilda, may have struggled more with the culprit and it made her a problem for the perp. By Erin arriving, she probably saved Gilda's life. Lachlan shows up and negates the second attack on Erin."

Micky rubbed her forehead, a habit he noted she possessed when she was concerned or thinking hard about a situation. "Did the medical examiner's office explain how the victims were drained of all their blood?"

"I wondered about that, too, but Fortesque said the ME couldn't come up with a definitive explanation."

Before he could elaborate, their dinner arrived and they settled into eating. His ahi tuna tasted great, and she said she loved the prime rib. They ate for some time in quiet, their companionable silence putting him at ease. Maybe neither one of them wanted to talk vampire legends and murder over a plate of delicious food.

When the waiter cleared away their dinners, they decided to linger over their wine and talk more about what he'd discovered. She sighed and contemplated her wine glass, fingering the stem again in a way that made him wish those small fingers glided across his cock right now. He gritted his teeth, but it didn't do any good. His cock jerked and surged, pressing against his fly with insistence.

Shit. Shit. Shit.

Think of fruit. Vegetables. Man, anything to get this permanent hard-on under control.

He caught her hand and held it still. "Don't babe." Because he sat so close to her, he could lean in and look like he was having a simple lover's conversation. "You're turning my cock into a railroad spike."

Her mouth popped open and she inhaled a surprised little breath. Her fingers tensed under his, and he fixated on her ripe, pink mouth. Would her nipples be as pink? Would they be brown and large or tiny and red? Every woman came packaged differently, and the idea made him want her with a grinding need he couldn't contain. When she swallowed hard, he watched her throat work, and he imagined his lips buried there as his hips thrust, pumping his cock between her slick walls until her mouth opened on a high scream of climax. He couldn't wait to see her naked, to lick and suck and drive his tongue inside her so she knew the true meaning of pleasure.

Vulnerability entered her eyes, a sadness drawing her perfect lips downward. Did she know what her sexy pout did to him? No, Micky didn't seem to have a conniving or deceitful bone in her body. He hated her lack of sexual self-confidence because he knew a tigress lurked deep inside her. She needed the last push to bring her over. He knew she wasn't a little innocent, but he also realized she probably hadn't done many wild or kinky things in her life. He'd bet his cock on it.

He licked his lips. That was it. He must know. "Have you ever had an orgasm?"

Micky thought her throat would close up. Just having Jared this near made her heart hammer and her body prickle with forbidden sensations. She clenched her thighs together. His audacious question startled her and made her body moisten with superheated anticipation.

Her eyes widened. "What?"

Jared slipped one arm onto the table so that it crossed in front of her. He covered her fingers with his big hand so they rested on the tabletop together. His thigh touched hers, and the leashed power made her want to touch him. What would he do if she reached over and put her hand over his cock? Just did it now? No one could see. The tablecloth would conceal anything they wanted to do.

Again she pressed her thighs together, her arousal notching upward moment by moment. Though she thought about looking away, his hypnotic eyes held her.

All right, Jared. You win. You have the most gorgeous, compelling eyes I've ever seen.

"Have you ever had an orgasm?" he asked again.

She wanted to be embarrassed, expected to be mortified. Instead more heat pooled low in her belly and she shifted on the plush blue seating. "Um...yes."

His smile grew warm with seduction and hot with promises. "How?"

"I'm not sure I understand. You know how people have orgasms."

Jared released her hand and slid his big, hot palm onto her right leg just above the knee. With a hushed tone, he plunged right into the next question. "Have you given yourself an orgasm?"

For several seconds she considered telling him to mind his own business. Then a little devil on one shoulder told her to go for it. Tell him the truth and see how it affects him to hear it. *Okay, he wants honesty; he's going to get it.*

"I have, yes."

His hot smile said he liked the answer.

Jared smoothed his hand higher, roaming with gentle brushes of his fingers. With a gliding motion he reached down again, and then she felt his hand burrow under her skirt and sweep over her stocking-clad right leg. She'd always found thigh-high stockings more comfortable than pantyhose, but maybe the extra barrier would have been safer. *Then again...*

Heat rose in her face, and her breathing quickened. Jared's fingers felt so strong, yet forever gentle. A tiny thrill, mixed with alarm, rocketed through her.

They were in a restaurant with people all around them. They spoke in hushed tones, yet his hand crept up her leg with determination. She knew without a doubt what he wanted, how he needed her to spread her legs for him. Jared wanted her so hot she couldn't see straight and would beg him to take her.

What do I want?

"When?" His touch slipped down to her knee. "When was the last time you gave yourself an orgasm?"

"Actually, it was three months ago. Then my vibrator broke."

He chuckled, his laugh soft and husky. "But you could use your fingers, right?"

"I could. But I didn't. I was busy with work and every night when I came home I was exhausted. No time to feel sexy."

"When was the last time you felt sexy? Was it when we kissed in the hotel?"

"Yes."

"Hmm. We'll have to make you feel that way again."

"We?"

"You and I. Together. You've heard sex is really all in your mind, haven't you?"

"Yes."

Micky's earlier worry about being in this public place and maybe getting caught seemed to drift away the more he caressed her. Warmth spread new ringers of fire over her belly and down between her legs. Gliding, gliding, his hand went to the top of her stocking, tracing the lace edge with gentle strokes. Somewhat ticklish, yet turned on by his teasing touches, she squirmed. Her thighs parted almost against her volition.

God, if he keeps this up, I'll combust.

Jared's eyes burned into her as he leaned closer. He slipped his other arm around her shoulder and tucked her close. She enjoyed the comfort of his embrace and at the same time, she feared the crazy way he made her feel.

In a low, intimate tone he asked, "What kind of vibrator?"

"One of those small ones about the size of a Lifesaver package."

"And you didn't buy another one?"

"No."

"Why not?"

"The other one was a gag gift from a bunch of friends. I never ordered one for myself."

He perused her wordlessly. With a lingering, tender touch his fingers brushed over the top of her mons, then down over her clit in a quick flick that made her inhale sharply.

"Pity," he said. "I'll bet you would have enjoyed it."

Micky felt a momentary panic, something she couldn't seem to control. She blurted out, "How many lovers have you had?"

"Six."

"I don't believe you."

He quirked one eyebrow in amusement. "I don't know whether to be insulted or not."

Her cheeks turned pink. "I meant that you've probably had more lovers. I know for a man that can be an ego boost."

"Sorry to disappoint you, but I'm afraid not."

Micky's eyes widened. "Wow." She blinked. "I'm sorry. That was a really rude question. You should have told me to mind my own business."

He grinned, then eased back in his chair. "I'm flattered. Do you like the fact I've only slept with six women?"

She nodded. "In a way, yes." She made a helpless gesture with one hand. "I sort of had this image of you as a wild, hot, consuming sex machine."

He laughed. "One of them was my ex-wife. Then there was another woman a few months back. We were on a blind date and she sort of jumped me."

"I can understand that. You're..." She swallowed hard, as if the next words would mean life or death. "A very attractive man."

"She told me I was a lousy lover. She's the last woman I slept with." He waggled his eyebrows. "So all these ideas you have about me being a sex machine is unfounded. But thanks for the compliment."

With slow persuasion he slid his hand into the cradle of her thighs, and she parted them. The wildness of what he did, the utter boldness made her heartbeat pick up the pace. Slow and deliberate, he nudged aside the crotch of her panties until his middle finger could brush her labia. Excitement made her shiver, her gasp a testament to her enjoyment. Each unbearably slow movement made the heat notch up.

She grew wet and the lips of her labia parted and swelled with arousal. He brushed around and around, spreading the growing moisture around her opening. Micky didn't think she could remain coherent much longer if he kept this up. Her clit throbbed, engorged with desire to be touched, licked and sucked.

Oh, God. Yes.

"Tell me more about your meeting with Erin and Tavish," he said nonchalantly, as if his fingers hadn't become the center of her world.

"There isn't much more to say."

His fingers circled her clit, the pressure now steady, rhythmic, and designed to drive her into major meltdown.

She swallowed hard. "Lachlan has that dark and dangerous thing going on." Micky managed a flirtatious smile. "But then so do you."

He gave her a devilish grin. "Dark and dangerous? You're kidding."

"No." She dared to keep her gaze locked with his, enjoying the heady pleasure of seeing his own arousal increase. "You've got something I noticed from the first time I met you."

His pupils dilated and his lips parted as his finger manipulated her clit a little more. "Yeah?"

With slow deliberation he inserted two fingers deep into the melting hot slit.

She bit back a groan and answered him. "Yes. You have an intensity that could be scary. I wouldn't want to meet up with you in a dark alley if I was a criminal."

"Thanks. I pride myself on being able to scare criminals since it's my job." He kept his fingers imbedded, and she tightened her muscles over the delicious sensation.

"Wait. You're not afraid of me, right?"

He started to move his fingers, caressing her deep inside, then drawing back into retreat. With deliberation he made sure the movements stayed subtle; no one could see his muscles in action.

God, help me, I'm going to scream. No I can't. I'm in a public place. My God! I'm in a public restaurant with people all around me eating and drinking and Jared has his fingers buried up inside me.

"You asked me that before. The answer is no," she said.

With excruciating slowness, he worked his fingers back and forth and she fought to keep her wild arousal a secret from anyone who might look their way. A heated flush spread over her skin, her heart did triple time and her body trembled.

"You're sexy as hell, sweetheart, and I know you've got it in you to let go."

She inhaled, trying to reign in her crazy thoughts and needs. "Let go?"

He kept his voice down, his eyes slumberous with arousal as his fingers massaged her inner core. Then his hand came out to touch her aching clit, and she moved her hips a little, trying to get relief. Again his fingers slipped inside her, and the excitement throbbed and burned deep. He spread his fingers slightly, using the motion to caress her inner walls and open her to invasion.

"I think given time, attention, and the right man, you'll have a healthy and exciting sex life. You've got a lot of passion to give a man."

"Are you sure you aren't a therapist instead of a cop?"

"Hell, no."

"How did you get to be an expert on sex?"

"I didn't say I was an expert. I'm going with my instincts." His eyes, flaming high with arousal, kept her prisoner. "What I feel right here. You know what it does to me to be able to touch you like this and not have my cock where my fingers are? I want to be inside you so much."

His heavy artillery words set her off, her libido ramming into an overdrive. She knew she wouldn't stop him now, and a forbidden scenario rolled through her sex-steamed mind. Jared pulling his fingers out and laying her on the table in front of everyone, ripping his pants open and plunging right into her for all to see.

Holy shit.

She knew he wouldn't do it, but the idea of it thrilled her.

He gently worked to capture her clit in his fingers. With a deliberate, but not rough action, he plucked at her clit. She gasped.

Beyond the crazy tumult in her mind and body, she wanted to discover the mysteries lurking inside Jared. She stalled her orgasm, wanting more anticipation before her passions roared to full burn. Despite the fact her cunt contracted and released, aching and dying for him to fill her, she couldn't believe what they did together. The boldness, the utter cheek made her arousal spiral higher.

He whispered in her ear. "Are you going to come? Nod and tell me."

She nodded. "Yes."

Again he said softly into her ear. "Imagine it's my cock. Do you think my cock moving back and forth inside you would feel good?"

"Yes."

"Think of it stroking deep, reaching high up in there until I touch your womb. I'm hard and thick and so deep you won't be able to deny what you feel." He licked her ear. "Thick. Deep. Hot. Hard."

She closed her eyes for moment and allowed herself to imagine. *Oh, yes. Oh, yes. I'm going to come. Oh God, oh God, it's wonderful.*

She reached a stage where she must anchor or be carried away. She clutched his thigh with her hands, her fingers digging in.

If anyone had told her she'd be in Pine Forest sitting in a ritzy restaurant with a man's fingers buried inside her, she would have laughed.

Again and again his fingers lingered and caressed. He smoothed the essence of her excitement over her plump labia and desire rose to heights sweet and more real than anything she remembered feeling. Sensations grew and grew until she couldn't think about anything but the hot, pulsing rise to the top.

She shuddered, reached a pinnacle and allowed the building shivers to slam into her gut and burst between her legs. She held back a moan, closing her eyes for a second as his fingers brushed continuously over the throbbing, exploding bud.

When she opened her eyes she glanced around to see if all eyes were on her, accusatory and repulsed. No one looked in their direction. Music continued, mellow and sweet, utensils clattering and the murmur of soft voices. Only Jared's attention remained trained on her. When he drew his napkin down to her lap and wiped his hand, she realized how much she wanted to touch him, to show Jared what she could do with her hands and mouth to please him.

In his regard she saw tenderness and passion. "Was that good?"

She licked her dry lips. "Good is an understatement."

"Let's get out of here, and I'll show you how much better it can be."

They refused dessert when the waiter came back to their table, and they left moments after paying the check. Jared insisted on paying this time.

In the car, Micky felt the tension sliding through her, demanding a finish to the high-grade sexual inferno he'd started inside her. While she'd felt the sweetest orgasm she could remember having, she realized what she would experience with Jared back at the hotel would be earth-shaking, profound, and a new direction for her life.

All the way back to Jekyl's, her mind tried to wrap around the incredible possibility she'd found a man who understood her a little. A man who could maybe, just maybe, take her to bed and make her orgasm with his cock deep inside her. Not come with the touch of fingers to clit or tongue to nipple, but the bold thrust of cock into warm wetness between her legs. Heady excitement left her breathless.

"I can almost hear your thoughts from here," he said.

She glanced over at his strong profile as darkness cloaked his true expression.

"Oh? What am I thinking?"

"You're amazed that I finger fucked you in a public place."

His blunt words only served to make her clench her thighs together in a low-grade sexual misery. "Good guess. How did you know?"

"I'm psychic."

"Really?"

"No."

She laughed.

"You're not too embarrassed about what we did?" he asked.

"No. It was...exciting. And no one knew. It was so dark in there anyway and I think most of the couples there were...you know."

"Good."

"Better than good. It was wonderful." Silence returned until she said, "You said you aren't psychic. Do you believe in the supernatural?"

"No. I can't say that I do."

Disappointment wedged into her. *That's it then.* No matter how intimate they became, she couldn't reveal the shadow people to him.

"You've never seen anything...strange?"

She felt his gaze land on her for a moment. "Such as?"

Maybe this hadn't been a good idea, leading him in this nonsexual direction. She wondered if she did this to avoid the sex. "Ghosts?"

"No. Have you?"

"I'm not sure."

She wasn't lying, really. How could she define the dark shapes that chased her as ghosts? And the creature that killed in the tunnel couldn't be a ghost.

Again they fell quiet, a constant hum between them laced with sexual energy. A momentary segue into the supernatural didn't seem to break the mood.

Once they reached the hotel, she felt her nerves mix with excitement laced with doubts. Fear of the unknown tightened all her muscles until she felt taut as a longbow. So she started talking again, breaking the quiet as they walked down the hallway.

"Your room or mine?" she asked.

Chapter Eight

๛

Jared's arm slipped around Micky, and before she could blink he backed her against the wall. One hand landed on the wall next to her head, the other stayed around her waist. His growing erection pressed against her.

His hot breath sizzled over the delicate skin of her right ear. An excited shiver ran through her. One step away from the rest of her life, she wondered how long this ecstasy could survive.

"My room," he whispered into her ear. "I've got everything we need."

He pressed a kiss to her nose and released her long enough to unlock his door and draw her inside.

When he locked the door behind them, he gently crowded her against the door. Intimacy closed around them as the low light from a bedside lamp barely illuminated the room. She smelled his aftershave lingering on the air, the intoxicating exotic musk teasing her with promises. She cupped his face and realized he'd shaved late in the day. She closed her eyes and fantasized about his skin brushing over hers, naked to naked contact.

With him she could find a few hours of respite from the strangeness surrounding her. No shadow people and no gargoyle faces, no bodies drained of blood. In his embrace a peace resided among the turmoil boiling at the surface. A tumult born of sexual desire so strong there could be no answer but completion.

Animal power radiated from Jared in the way his hands anchored her waist and brought her tight against him. A man about to lose control, his fire called to her with primitive rhythms established since man first touched woman. She felt claimed, captured, and wanted.

Against her stomach, his cock told her all she needed to know.

He couldn't wait any longer and she didn't want him to hesitate.

She opened her eyes and his attention caressed her, going from her eyes to her lips, her body came alive from semi-arousal. The one orgasm she'd experienced wasn't enough. Hungry to experience the depths and heights of ecstasy with him, she gave up all inhibitions.

Without another word, his mouth covered hers. She fell into the kiss, thrilled by his male aggression. A muffled growl ushered from his throat as he moved into a devouring kiss, his tongue plunging deep.

He thrust his tongue against hers with a determination mimicking fast, hard sex.

The time for subtlety was over.

As one melting kiss blended into another, he slipped the jacket from her shoulders. It fell to the floor. He pulled off his own coat and let it drop away. He clasped her waist as he tasted her ear, his touch measuring as they drifted up her ribcage and teased the sides of her breasts. His kiss drifted to her throat, incredible affection belying the urgency. Tender brushes along her collarbone burst like tingling fire, a tribute to her skin that seared and soothed in one unbelievable emotional and physical need.

Between soul-deep kisses he inched her sweater upward until he could cup her bra-clad breasts.

He looked down at her round flesh, measuring them in his hands. "God, these are gorgeous."

His voice held roughness, a gravelly quality on the edge of combustion. With one quick movement he opened the front hook bra and her breasts spilled free.

"So damn beautiful," he said.

She allowed her ego to enjoy the way his eyes hungrily devoured the sight of her. Neither too small or too large, her breasts fit in his hands as if meant for Jared. Her nipples flushed red with arousal, hard and ready for his taste. Again he encompassed her in his hands, his hot gaze driving her to within an inch of begging him to take her. Quickies never worked for her because she couldn't get aroused fast enough.

Until now.

Oh, Jared. Now, now, now.

He nibbled, then drew his tongue over her with a lathing, long lap that made her gasp. His fingers clasped the other rosy red bud and held it, while his tongue played a wet path around the other pebble-hard nipple. He pinched and stroked the captive, playing with it until a new ribbon of fire danced straight to her womb.

She writhed against his hold, tortured and insane for more. "Jared."

"Mmm," he mumbled against her nipple before he captured it between his lips and sucked deep. "Like strawberries."

She groaned as his tongue darted and licked.

He released her long enough to pull the sweater over her head and it landed on her coat at her feet. Her bra followed, pooling at the top. Seconds later her skirt joined the pile.

She sighed with pleasure as Jared picked her up in his arms. Burying her face against his shoulder, she surrendered all. Textures blended, became a mix of soft and hard, rough and smooth. His sweater felt warm, but the muscles under her cheek felt hard as rock. The power in his body thrilled her, tantalizing Micky with a searing desire to see all that naked strength.

He placed her on the bed and reached for her boots, slipping them off in record time. Tossing them aside, he looked down on her with a growing appreciation she could feel straight to her soul. New feelings blossomed, a tender understanding of his needs and his wants. She catalogued everything about his face, wanting to remember him and this moment until she reached forever. With loving attention she noted how his eyes sparked, allowing the conflagration to grow.

He drew her to her feet and said, "I want to see what's under all this. Take it off slowly." He lay back on the bed and propped himself up with his elbows.

"A strip tease?" She smiled.

"Only if you want to. Otherwise you can just take off everything right now."

Instead of intimidating her, his suggestion sounded down right inflaming. She stood almost naked, her panties and stockings the only thing covering her. For a millisecond self-consciousness threatened to intrude. What did she need to erase the last, lingering anxiety?

It came to her easier than she expected. She decided he needed a little defiance. Hell, she needed spice. "No."

One of his eyebrows twitched up. "No?"

She slid the utilitarian white panties down her legs, wishing she'd had sexy lingerie to show him. His gaze centered and fixated on the pale hair covering her mound, and she allowed her hand to touch the fine hairs. She stood in thigh high stockings and nothing else and suddenly, by his spellbound expression, she knew he found her beautiful. In his eyes she felt pretty, no doubts to linger or destroy her elation. His attention, the tender, loving light mixed with animal need made all her worries slide away. New moisture dampened her aching channel.

"I'm leaving the stockings on," she said, the words hoarse.

He grinned, self-assured. He knelt on the floor in front of her and touched her taupe nylon-clad thighs. Jared's breath wisped through the pale curls covering her secrets as his hands reached behind her and grasped her naked ass. With a light squeeze and a gentle caress he tested her buttocks. She shivered.

He grinned, the wide, sexy smile turning her knees to mush. He pressed his lips to her wet, warm cunt like the brush of a butterfly. "So pale and pretty."

Compliments didn't often excite her during sex, because she'd never believed them before. Now, with his eyes smoldering as he examined her, she believed each word.

"Are you still wet?" he asked quietly.

He brushed a finger over her clit and she gasped again, writhing in his hold. "Yes, yes."

"Damn, yes." His affirmation came husky. "Part your legs."

At his demand she opened to him and waited. Her eyes closed. Her hands reached for his shoulders and she gripped him.

"Jared, I don't think I can take this. I want you now."

He brushed kisses along one of her thighs. "A little longer, baby. I want to make you feel good."

She shivered. "I can't stand it. I need you...I need you inside me now."

"Shhh...just a little longer. Then I'll be so far inside you, so deep."

Husky with emotion, his voice made her open her eyes and look down at him. What she saw there made tears of joy and excitement blossom inside Micky.

"Oh, yes," she said.

"I'll fuck you any way you want to be fucked."

Micky trembled, his blunt words making her hotter than a forest fire. "Tell me."

"Deep. Hard. Slow. Anything that gets you off."

Getting off. It sounded forbidden and beyond wild. She loved the way he said it, his eyes flaming with need.

Dipping between her thighs, he swiped his tongue over her swollen folds. She whimpered at the hot, wet, silky wonder. Gasps came from her throat as he did with his tongue what he'd done with his fingers in the restaurant. Circling her labia with warm, slow strokes, he built her fire to a fever she couldn't contain. She clutched at his head, trying not to dig into his scalp as he slipped his tongue into her and tasted. Rapture burned deep in her womb, and as she moaned he thrust his tongue inside her again and again and again. Without a pause he used his thumbs to part the folds over her clit, then his tongue fluttered against the delicate, aroused tissue.

She cried out as orgasm took her immediately. Her entire body shook as he settled his mouth around her flaming clit and sucked. She stifled a full-blown scream as she quaked again and again with the craziest ecstasy she'd ever experienced. Her fingers clutched in his hair as she held on for dear life.

"Yes." He whispered against her thigh, pressing tiny kisses against her hot skin.

Micky's heart pounded so hard she thought she might pass out.

When he looked up at her she saw the answer in his eyes. They wouldn't stop, they wouldn't pause, the time for foreplay long passed.

Jared sat back on the bed and removed his boots. When he stood again he drew his sweater over his head and then flipped the garment aside. He worked at the waistband of his jeans, then shoved them down his hips and off. With another swift movement he slid his black briefs down and off his legs.

She'd imaged him naked on more than one occasion, but reality staggered her. Jared Thornton defined raging, hot, primitive sexuality. Her mouth literally watered as she devoured the sight of the most gorgeous male body she'd ever seen. If she could have imagined perfection, Jared would be it.

173

Strength and determination seemed drawn in every line, every solid muscle.

With appreciation she took in his wide shoulders, defined by curved muscles. Long, powerful arms and forearms were sprinkled with dark hair and ended in big, capable hands. She imaged those hands on her again, treating her body to a sensual feast of sensations. A neat tracing of dark hair covered his developed pecs and trailed down to his six-pack stomach. Her gaze ate up his body with healthy appreciation, his striking muscular structure turning her on more than she could have imagined. Her gaze snapped up to his eyes, almost afraid to take a full measure of his cock.

Eager, overwhelming need burned in his gaze and convinced Micky he wanted her admiration and enjoyed the way she consumed him with hungry desire. Again she measured his entire body limb by limb until she reached the dark hair that thickened around his erect cock.

And oh, what a cock.

She could just reach out and touch it if she wished, but instead she waited. Grew into the anticipation as her heart picked up the pace and warm, wetness thickened between her thighs and started a new ache. Her first boyfriend's cock had been impressive, maybe even a little large. She'd always thought maybe that's why it hurt when he put it inside her. Davy had been an average man and it was still uncomfortable.

Normally she would never judge a man by the size of his erection, knowing it was what he did with it that counted. She couldn't help but be impressed by Jared's cock. His thickness and length would reach her depths in new and exciting ways.

Again she looked up at him. Jared's hands clenched and unclenched, his lips parted and he licked them. "Micky, if you keep looking at me like that I'll…"

"What?"

He didn't answer, his eyes blazing down at her in sexual frustration. She liked the power, the realization this man needed her so much he couldn't take it any longer.

"You'll what?" she asked.

"Touch me. Please touch me."

The plea in his voice, rough with sexual intensity, made her ache and swell with the need to have him inside her.

All the events of the last two days came into the picture, and she knew his pleasure would be her own. She dropped to her knees and clasped him in her right hand. Burgeoning with heat, his cock felt hard and incredibly strong. Would they make love all night as he'd once mentioned?

His head fell back. "Holy shit." As she slipped her hand up and down his cock, he groaned. He opened his eyes and then clasped her hand to stop the motion. "No. I won't last. I want you too much."

She freed him, but then Jared lifted her from her kneeling position and captured her lips in a ravenous kiss. His tongue took control, stabbing deep as they tumbled onto the bed in a heap of legs and arms. Micky writhed with need. Seconds later he released her and fumbled in one drawer of his bedside table. Sheathed by protection, he wedged his hips between her legs. With one hand he clasped her ass, cupping her butt possessively. She felt the head of his erection teasing at her entrance. Again she wiggled, tormented by the sensation, by the mere promise of his ownership. She wanted to be his with everything inside her, with a deep ache.

"Now," he said, "tell me. Do you want to fuck me?"

His blunt question made her desire spiral higher. She whispered, "Yes."

He kneaded her ass cheeks. "Feel it. Feel it as it goes in. It's going to be so hot."

This time his erotic words pushed her to the limit. She couldn't take it any more. Her arms came up and wrapped around his neck.

"Close your eyes and feel every inch," he said.

She did as commanded, the sensation beginning as the head of his cock probed inside her, dipping one inch, then retreating.

"Oh." Her gasp made him stop.

"Does it hurt?"

"No."

"More?"

"Yes."

Another dip, this time a little farther, then a retreat. Sensation bombarded her, the ecstasy of solid, broad cock probing inside her beyond imagination. She couldn't think anymore, only writhe upon the little bit of cock he inserted. Micky circled her hips instinctively, trying to reach for what he denied her. He was right. It was hot.

"Tell me when you want more," he said.

She clasped at his shoulders, looking for any anchor in the storm. "More."

Another inch slid inside, rubbing with tiny back and forth motions that inflamed her more than she thought possible. Again she twisted on the impalement, dying for, begging for more. She'd never experienced anything more exquisite.

"Jared, please. All of it."

She whimpered as his hips pushed gently, then retreated, giving her only a couple of inches of Jared's searing hot cock.

"Please." She arched her back, her lower body aching with need for release.

When he dipped yet another inch deeper, then retreated, Micky thought she would die. This was it.

Panting, gasping for air, she moved her hips, undulating and trying to force more of him inside her. With a growl signaling his final release on control, he thrust home the rest of the way.

Moaning and trembling, she felt the blaze rise, a fire whipped to superheated status. Forced to the hilt inside her, his cock stretched and spread her. Her walls shivered around the heavy hardness and it felt so wonderful her entire body sang with pleasure.

He drew back and plunged.

She came.

Agonized groans of rapture parted her lips as she shook in his arms. And as the orgasm went on and on he pulled back and rammed forward. She cried out at the hard stab and reached a new escalation.

His hips plunged, each movement building speed until he grunted with each hard, determined hammer of his hips. He groaned and picked up the pace.

He urged her with erotic, forbidden suggestions. "Take it all. That's it, sweetheart."

She couldn't remain silent. Her cries spiraled upward, caught in the throes of sex so mind-bending she became nothing but physical body. Her muscles burned, her breathing hard and rapid, her panting loud in the room. Friction inside her heightened as he pounded deep into her channel, sliding through hot cream and building more inside her.

The headboard started to *thunk* against the wall, a rapid bang, bang cadence that added to her continued excitement.

And as the ecstasy took a final jump, she exploded against him. Literally sobbing with bliss she accepted his ramming thrusts. As each stab hit inside her, another orgasm blasted inside her until sensation melded into one climax after another.

Her cries muffled as Jared covered her mouth with his and gave one last plunge straight to the heart of her. She felt him grow even larger inside her, then he burst.

He tore his mouth from hers and buried his face in her neck. As his entire body shook, he roared like a beast. She felt his muscles go tight as he shuddered against her continually, his climax setting off pulsations deep in her cunt. He collapsed against her, his body heavy. Wrapping her arms around him, Micky held on to his hot body, tracing her fingers over his muscled back, feeling evidence of their exertion in rapid breaths and trembling muscles.

Stunned by the incredible force of what happened between them, she couldn't say a word. Jared's lungs worked like bellows as he regained his breath, and the realization she'd done this to him made the experience even more profound. She'd driven a man to this level of madness.

Beyond that, he'd given her the best sexual experience of her life.

Now she knew, at last, the true meaning of being fucked out of your mind.

Raw, tender emotions welled up, overruling the physical until tears came to her eyes.

With another groan he rolled off her and drew her into his arms. His fingers plunged into her hair as he kneaded her scalp with a gentle motion. Peppering her forehead with tiny kisses, he sighed.

Overwhelmed by his tenderness, by the enormity of what she'd experienced in his arms, she started to cry again. At first he didn't seem to notice.

Suddenly he stiffened in her arms and drew back so he could tilt her face up. His gaze, lambent from expired passion, turned worried.

He rolled her onto her back and cupped her face with one hand. "What is it? What's wrong? Did I hurt you?"

"No."

"Oh, shit. I did. I was too rough." His voice went hoarse with self-recrimination.

She sniffed again, then smiled. "*No*, you didn't. I'm crying because I'm so happy."

He brushed his fingers down her arm. "You're sure?"

Micky reached up and traced his face with a tender caress. "I've never felt anything like that before, Jared. I've never imagined anything so good."

Concern ebbed from his eyes, replaced in degrees by one shit-eating, gratified male smile. "All I could think about was fucking you so hard you'd come for a century."

She laughed and pulled his head down for a soft kiss. "I would have been happy with one climax."

With another grin signifying how much he liked what she said, he sighed and buried his face against her throat. "There's more where that came from."

Exhausted but happy, she accepted his arms as they cradled her protectively. Content, she drifted into a sleep safe from unknown danger.

* * * * *

Ronan wanted to scream out his frustration about the priest's death. Instead he pounded on Erin's front door and waited.

"Jesus, I can't believe it," Sorley said for what seemed like the hundredth time. "The priest is dead. Don't you know the bloody ancient one is gettin' feckin' bold."

"Shut up will you?"

Ronan considered strangling his friend, then thought the better of it. He felt shaken by the priest's death, too. Moreover, the fact the ancient one had committed murder in a church somehow made the whole thing even more distasteful.

When the door popped open, Lachlan stood there bare-chested and wearing a pair of jeans. "What's going on? What are you doing here this late?"

Ronan took a deep breath. "There's a problem. We need to talk to you."

"Lachlan, who is it?" Erin's voice asked with caution, a hint of fear residing in her sweet voice.

Lachlan stepped back and let them enter. "The usual suspects."

Erin wore a green terrycloth robe belted around her and her eyes were a little bleary from interrupted sleep. Ronan supposed he should feel guilty for breaking in on them so late, but he didn't.

"This may be a matter of life and death for the mortals in this little drama," Ronan said. "A priest is lying dead up at St. Bartholomew's."

Erin gasped. "What?"

Ronan gave them the quick version of how they'd found the priest drained of blood with the telltale two holes in his neck. "For all we know, he'll come back as the only vampire priest in town."

"Oh, God," Erin said.

"Just looking for the ancient one's new hiding place, we were," Sorley said as he slumped on the couch. "Then I see blood smeared along the pews at one end of the church. Next thing I find is the priest with his neck twisted, drained of blood and part of his—plain sick it was—part of his sexual organs ripped off."

Erin put one hand to her mouth and went pale.

Ronan grimaced at his friend's shortness of tact. "Do me a favor, Sorley. Let me tell this story from now on."

Lachlan went to Erin and clasped her in his arms. He glared at Sorley. "Could you try being a wee bit more careful about what you say?"

Erin lifted her head from Lachlan's shoulder. "It's all right. I'm not usually so squeamish. Are you sure the ancient one did this?"

Ronan started to pace, his mind speeding along with ideas on what to do next. "I'm sure of it. I've heard of him killing other priests this way hundreds of years ago. He did it during the Spanish Inquisition."

"Why?" Lachlan asked.

"I guess he didn't like the hypocrisy and took retribution into his own hands," Ronan said.

Lachlan's disgusted expression said what he thought of the idea. "You're condoning what he did then?"

Ire built in Ronan. "Of course not. I just don't believe in revisionist history. I'm telling you what he did, nothing more."

Lachlan released Erin. "I'm sorry. This whole thing has us on edge. It's getting a little old."

His friend looked remorseful, and Ronan let his anger dissipate. "No, I'm sorry. I shouldn't have snapped at you. None of this is your fault."

Erin walked across the room, her gaze pinning Ronan to the spot. "But it is our fault. We didn't stop him the last time."

Ronan shook his head. "We can't beat ourselves over the head. There's no time for it."

"I take it you didn't stay for the police?" Lachlan asked.

"Are you feckin' crazy?" Sorley's eyes widened with disbelief. "Of course not. We left the priest there. I pity the sod that finds him next."

"Never mind that," Ronan said, his patience wearing thin. "We've got to approach Jared Thornton and Micky Gunn once again. Otherwise their lives will be forfeit. You know it and I know it. We need Erin with us to help convince Micky."

"She seemed to trust Erin at least a little," Lachlan said.

Erin's wry smile made her look less troubled. "Of course. With two gorgeous, stunning men—" She glanced at Sorley and gave another smile. "—three gorgeous men approaching her, she probably wouldn't know what to think. Let's get on it."

"The lady has spoken." Lachlan drew her into his arms for a hug. "Let's do it."

* * * * *

Micky woke some time later, the security of a powerful arm banded about her waist. She wiggled her ass against Jared. Jared's already erect cock slipped between her thighs. She clamped her thighs on his flesh, determined she'd feel his granite hard shaft thrusting inside her soon. Broad, masculine hands traced a tender path over her body. He traced a tingling path over her hips and down her thighs.

"Oh, yeah," he whispered hotly. "If you don't stop teasing me you're going to get fucked again."

She giggled as he pressed tickling kisses to the back of her neck. "Promises, promises."

He licked her left earlobe, then took it in his teeth, holding it prisoner for his tongue. When she gasped and writhed in pleasure, he chuckled. Rumbling deep in his chest, the laugh sounded so sexy that hot arousal poured into her stomach.

Gently he tested her, spreading the hot cream of her pleasure around and around.

When he rolled away from her, she murmured a protest. "Where are you going?"

"Don't go away."

As if I'd consider it. It would take an atom bomb to blast me from this bed.

Within moments he settled behind her again. He drew her leg up over his. With a slow, even slide, he thrust his sheathed cock inside her.

A gasp parted her lips.

He clasped one nipple between thumb and finger and began to play. Whimpering, she accepted the agonizingly slow pump of his cock deep into her heat, the gentle thrust and drag immediately carrying her to the top.

Micky couldn't stand it.

It was as if once he showed her how hot sex could be, her body wanted it over and over until the earth shattered and the sky exploded into fragments and never came back together.

He slid from her body and rolled her over onto her stomach. He urged her to tilt her hips up until he could put a pillow under them.

With urgency in his deep voice, he said, "Hang on."

She clutched at another pillow, her fingers digging into the soft surface like the last rope needed to keep her from falling off a cliff.

Jared wavered on a threshold, his mind asking him to control his animal passions so he couldn't hurt her. When they'd made love earlier he'd lost all sense, his instincts sending him into frenzy as he took her hard.

Now if he didn't get into her soon, he'd simply spew on the sheets. He palmed her ass, enjoying the staggering sight and amazing feeling of warm, soft, white butt cheeks.

He spread her thighs far apart with his hands. Seconds later his took his cock in his own hand and brought the tip to her labia lips. Unable to wait a moment longer, he thrust.

With a gasp of pure delight, she called his name.

It was the sweetest sound he'd ever heard and almost as delicious as the sensation of pushing between her tight, creamy wet folds and feeling her part for him in welcome.

Thrusting with assurance and steady power he worked her back and forth. Her breathing became rapid, little sobs of sound punctuated with begging.

When she asked for a finishing stroke he denied it, pumping steady and sure. He measured her, taking all he had to give and spiking it inside her.

Pure, primeval male emotions cascaded inside him.

My woman. Mine. Mine.

He increased the pace, each motion promising ecstasy but never quite giving it. He paused long enough to spread her legs even wider, and his next deep thrust made her squeal.

Oh, yeah.

She bucked against him, slamming back onto his cock until every slide of her tightness over his engorged flesh threatened to be the last one before he burst and filled the condom.

With a growl he lunged into the motion, gathering strength until he fucked her mercilessly.

Micky stiffened and with a little scream, she came.

With a last grunt of powerful male animal he spurted with jet after jet of hot cum.

When they collapsed in a heap on the bed, Jared felt a melting deep in his heart, a signal for something he thought he'd never feel again. Hell, maybe he'd *never* felt this way before. He drew her close, pulling her half on top of him so he could cup her butt to brace her against him. One of her thighs slipped between both of his, and her head rested on his shoulder. He liked her close to him. The grinding possessiveness inside him disturbed Jared on one level.

Afraid to think much about what the feeling meant, he savored instead her soft, female musk and the unmistakable scent of sex.

Sex.

It sounded almost crass now. But it was definitely sex in the more raw sense of the act. The way they'd gone at each other described nothing else on the planet but animal need.

With a soft moan he shifted against her, and realized from her calm breathing she'd fallen asleep. Slipping out from under her body, he headed for the bathroom. When he came into the room again he stood by the bed and watched her for a moment, fascinated and frightened by new emotions boiling inside him. He turned away and went back into the bathroom to stare in the mirror.

For he'd changed in a definite way the moment he'd entered her body.

He hung his head and closed his eyes, trying in vain to sort feelings. He wanted to do more then keep this woman out of trouble, to give her the advice of a police officer on what happened at her uncle's old house. Jared wanted her warm, womanly body against his at all times, to shield her from any conceivable harm.

No matter how improbable, he'd done the one thing he never would have expected in a thousand years.

He didn't want it. Couldn't have it. Tenderness grew inside him until his heart ached.

Whether he liked it or not, he was falling in love with her.

"No, damn it." Jared looked into the mirror again and scrubbed a hand over his stubble-roughened chin. "Shit."

* * * * *

The ancient one discovered where Micky resided, following her scent. Once he touched someone, they could not hide from him.

He could find them anytime, anywhere he wished.

As he stood outside Jekyl's, cold wind blowing in his face, he almost laughed at the peculiar humor displayed by mortals. A strange, most sinister name for a hotel, but he liked it. Perhaps mortals thought if they played with the macabre they could avoid real monsters. They pretended at Halloween that they could evade evil by dressing up. Little did they know, poor dim-witted creatures. This Halloween there would be no shelter for them. When the veil between the worlds became thinnest, he would bring havoc to their lives in the worst imaginable way. He would stalk and destroy until he'd taken his fill.

I am the monster, and the darkness.

He took a deep breath and scented other vampires nearby. Whether they were in the building or somewhere around it, he couldn't say. Of course, Ronan would be here, and if he enlisted any of his hangers-on cronies, they would be here, too.

He rather liked the idea of fighting a whole contingent of other vampires. He'd done it before and could do it again. He always won and that's the way it would remain.

If he didn't hurry, there would be no time to get into the hotel without Ronan detecting him. That is, if he hadn't already.

Another breath brought the ancient one brought the scent of sweet woman, this one the unmistakable bouquet of Erin Greenway. Ecstasy churned in his loins at the thought of her. Good. He would find Micky and then take Erin as well.

He laughed, aware others might hear the disembodied sound and wonder where it originated. As he surveyed the dark streets he saw no one. Humans continued to fear the night, and it suited him well. Those venturing out would be too thick to realize what risks they took. Deep satisfaction and anticipation led him to venture out more as his strength increased. Those who hunted him would soon regret what they'd done. He would assure their deaths and would turn Erin back to the sweet Dasoria he loved.

He waited outside the main doorway to the hotel. He peered inside the darkened glass and saw beyond the muted lightning to the clerk behind the front desk. She looked tired, disgruntled, and ripe for his picking.

Her negativity washed toward him and he drew on it, delighting in the empowerment. If she'd known how her pessimism made him stronger, how all human suffering made him potent, would she have chosen a positive life? Would she have stopped bitching, complaining, and demanding?

He wondered maybe an instant, then closed his eyes and drew a deep breath. With his building strength he cloaked himself and then pushed open the door a little bit. It thumped back into place, and the woman looked up. She squinted, a suspicious look forming on her already dour expression. The woman walked around the desk, then headed toward the front door. He needed her outside or she must invite him inside.

Since he doubted she would invite him in if she saw him, he would have to trick the stupid woman into it.

Open the door.

The woman stopped dead in the middle of the floor, her eyes widening.

Good. Her thin, weak mental barriers would be no defense against him. She'd heard him, but now he must exert the mental pressure to force her obedience. He couldn't afford for her to run away screaming.

Open the door. Open your mind to the ecstasy.

He heard the questions running through her mind, the fear stiffening her muscles and sending her into a shock not unlike a deer caught in the crossfire.

Stupid wenches were always easier to seduce, their screams of excitement mixed with a frantic fear. He savored it, could almost taste it as he pressed at her meager opposition.

Open to me. Accept what I can give you.

He pushed at the woman's mind, swallowing her fears in a bath of contentment. The woman struggled with her strange thoughts, fighting for her sanity and the repugnance caused by her hidden desires. She was repressed, afraid of sexuality.

What a waste. She would have found exhilaration in a good humping as a youth, but she buried her true nature in ridiculous pious beliefs. He would give her a taste of what she'd missed and she would do what he willed.

Moments later, her mouth slack and expression filled with staggering terror and awash in forbidden sensuality, she stood at the door. She reached out and touched the doorknob, hesitating.

She took a deep breath and opened the door. As she stepped back, he sent wind through with a firm brush. Helplessly she gestured him forward. As he walked through the woman looked toward him, obviously wondering if the wind blew hard enough to open the heavy wood. She stared right through him and he stalked into her proximity with intent. He would make this fast and quiet.

* * * * *

Micky woke to silence. Cold, she burrowed under the covers and drew them up to her chin. For a few seconds she didn't know where she was, her mind a fog of half formed images. A man's gentle touch, his murmured words of farewell.

Goodbye?

Blinking, she tried to clear her vision. A light burned on the bedside table, and as she glanced at the bed beside her, she saw the dented pillow and the rumpled sheets.

Then it came back to her with a blast.

A companionable dinner with Jared turned into a burning hot encounter.

His mouth on hers as he muffled her orgasmic screams.

Then Jared making love to her twice more with enough power to make her forget everything in her life but him.

She sat up and looked around the room. "Jared?"

Where had he gone? A smidgen of worry screwed with her confidence. Maybe he'd left because he didn't want to wake up with her. Davy had done that on more than one occasion, too much a coward to depart while she lay awake.

"Forget about Davy," she said into the room. "Just forget about him."

For the first time in her life she'd experienced sexual ecstasy with a man, the incredible rightness of being cherished and loved.

Loved?

Maybe not quite yet, if ever. What man and woman in their right mind fell in love in such a short amount of time?

She smiled, remembering how he'd given her bone-melting pleasure and challenged her beliefs about her sexuality. She could learn a lot more from him given time.

Lying naked and satiated, she glanced over at the night stand and noted the late hour. Midnight. Was that all? Where had he gone at this time of night? A slip of paper, propped up by the lamp, awaited her attention. She reached for it, apprehension making her cautious.

Blocky male handwriting scrawled across the paper.

Micky,

Be back in a few minutes. Don't go away.

Your personal sex machine, Jared.

She laughed with relief. "As if I have any other sex machines in my possession?"

Micky glanced around the room, curious. She hadn't paid much attention earlier when she'd been bowled over by a sexual stupor. She stretched, yawned, then sighed dreamily.

She left the bed and located one of Jared's blue T-shirts hanging over a chair. After she slipped the big shirt over her head, she looked in the large mirror above the chest of drawers. She looked, to be blunt...thoroughly fucked. Her hair was snarled and a small whisker burn along one side of her neck gave evidence.

Micky grinned. *Excellent. I've always wanted to look fucked.*

With a chuckle she turned away from the mirror.

A delightfully childlike curiosity ran through her. His suitcase beckoned, sitting on the suitcase stand wide open. With guilty pleasure she walked to the closet and opened it. Numerous sweaters and shirts hung wrinkle free. She fingered a couple of soft Italian designed silk-blend sweaters, one brilliant blue and the other flaming red. Both jeans and dress slacks hung in the closet. She closed the door, her guilt calling on her conscience to stop snooping.

Instead she went to the bathroom and noticed his shaving kit wide open. Nope, she wouldn't look in there.

Humming with remembered bliss, Micky decided to lie in bed and wait for him. She smiled, hoping they'd *work out* again when he got back. As she sprawled stomach down on the bed, the sensitive, well-used area between her legs gave a twinge.

She winced. Maybe she was too tender and needed a break, even though she wanted him again as soon as possible.

She sighed, more contented than she could remember being in all her life.

Then the voice came.

Come to me.

The words leaked into her brain like insidious, obsessive thoughts.

Come to me and slake my craving and yours.

Her skin prickled. "Who are you?" Her throat tightened, muscles tensing. "What do you want?"

A knock on the door startled her and she yelped.

Jared? Why would he knock?

She started for the door, then realized she could hear murmuring outside the door.

She heard a deep male voice say, "Hurry, he's coming."

Dread made Micky waver for a few seconds before she looked through the keyhole. Erin Greenway, Lachlan Tavish, a short, skinny man, and a striking, ruggedly handsome man stood outside the door. Astonished, she scurried to retrieve her clothes. She couldn't stand around in nothing but the T-shirt. After she took off the T-shirt, she quickly slipped into her underwear, sweater and skirt. Pantyhose and shoes would have to wait.

The knocking on the door came again.

Micky unlocked the door, suspicion keeping her alert. She kept her voice calm and modulated. "What are you doing here?"

Erin looked spooked, her eyes round. "Micky we have to speak with you. It's urgent. May we come in?"

She shook her head. Her glance snagged on the thin face of the short man who was dressed in a sweater and jeans too big for him. The tall, powerful man standing next to Lachlan gazed at her with a hard look that made his gorgeous face intense enough to frighten.

"No." She straightened her backbone, putting grit into her words. "It's late and I don't let strangers into my hotel room."

"Micky, please," Erin said, her eyes sincere. "There's a creature coming and he's very dangerous. He's right downstairs."

"Who?"

"Trust us," Lachlan said. "You need our protection."

She searched Erin's expression for deception and found none, but the men scared her.

Erin gestured toward the men. "Micky, these are our good friends Sorley Dubh and Ronan Kieran."

Ronan's melting dark eyes held hers, their power latching onto her like a grip of iron. She sucked in a deep breath.

"She is frightened," Ronan's velvet voice said. "We shall have to remedy that."

Husky and tinted with an Irish accent, his voice held incredible enticement. It shook her down to the core.

Let us in. His voice filled her head, seducing her into compliance. Unlike the other voice she'd heard in her head lately, his imparted comfort and not evil. She heard sex, sin, and something ancient in his tone. She imagined every woman would succumb to the suggestive, silky seduction in his voice.

Over six feet tall, Ronan Kieran was one devastating hunk. Micky might be falling for Jared, but no woman could deny Ronan's intriguing good looks. His almost black eyes compelled and demanded. Ronan's long black leather jacket hung below his knees, but under it he wore a black sweater, jeans and boots. Shadows defined him, the true meaning of dark and dangerous.

Cursing her lack of judgment, she stepped back and they entered the room. If she was wrong about them, she may not live to regret it.

Ronan closed the door and leaned against it. Her heart jumped and the fear returned. The tall Irishman moved away from the door, his expression turning to a small smile. "I'm not trying to scare you, Miss Gunn."

Does the man read minds?

Lachlan took up a position next to Ronan, near the door but not exactly guarding it.

"What is it you want?" Micky asked the group, feeling self-conscious. "Were you looking for Jared?"

"No." Erin sat on the edge of the rumpled bed. "We wanted to talk to you first about your strange experiences."

New skepticism rose inside her. "What are you talking about?"

Sorley planted his thin hands on his hips and grinned. "It's a right confusin' thing. But listen to us and we'll explain."

"So talk," Micky said, leaning against the dresser for support.

Erin put her hands out in entreaty. "We know you've had a tough time lately. Your uncle dies and leaves you property to take care off, then you suffer from that incident in the diner and the murders at the inn. It's all stressful."

Micky nodded. "Okay, so you understand what's happened. Why would you want to talk with me about a series of unfortunate incidents?"

"Do you believe in vampires, Miss Gunn?" Ronan asked.

She quavered, her fear rising. "Of course not. I've already had this ridiculous discussion with Erin and Lachlan at the library. And I don't understand why you've come here in the middle of the night to talk about some half-baked —"

"Wait." Ronan held his hand up. "We get the picture. But you'd better start believing in vampires or your time on this earth is numbered."

"Ronan, back off." Lachlan sat on the bed next to his fiancée and put his arm around her. "What Erin and Ronan are trying to say is that your life is in danger. Anyone who gets in this fiend's way is in trouble. The murdered people in this town weren't killed by an ordinary serial killer. As far as we know, most of them are killed outright and are not brought over to be vampires. We haven't tried staking any of them to be sure—"

"Staking them?" Micky asked. "Are you insane? You're going around staking corpses through the heart?"

Sorley grinned. "It takes a silver stake, to be exact. None of this horse hockey about wooden stakes."

Ronan stepped forward, impatience clear in his face. "As we said, we could have staked them, but we haven't. If they return as vampires, so be it."

Micky wrinkled her nose in sheer disbelief. "Why would some of them come back as vampires and not others? Sounds like you can't get your story straight."

Ronan crossed his arms. "If they become a vampire or not will depends on several factors. We don't have time to explain right now."

"So who is this so-called murderer running around?" she asked.

"He's called the ancient one," Ronan said.

Lachlan, Sorley, and Ronan all pitched in to explain.

"He's a thousand years old," Sorley said.

Lachlan added more information. "More evil than any human on earth could be."

Ronan elaborated. "There is much more to know about him. He killed Lachlan's family, bit him and gave Lachlan some vampire powers. And the ancient one killed my…"

As Ronan trailed off, his eyes going bleaker, Micky realized the tall man struggled with whatever he wanted to say. She knew emotions powerful and destructive raged inside him. His intensity crackled and snapped, the danger around him palpable.

Ronan swallowed hard and took a few steps toward Micky. She pressed back against the dresser. When she looked into his eyes a glow lit them, making his eyes more golden than black. She gasped and he looked away.

"The ancient one has harmed people we knew and loved." Lachlan's hand shifted through Erin's hair, his touch tender and possessive. "Although we stopped him from taking Erin and harming her, he is intent on getting her for his own. He believes she is the reincarnation of his long lost love Dasoria. He is demented and evil."

Ronan's glowing eyes diminished back to brown. "He will work his way through as many people as he can to rebuild his strength. He needs blood to live because he continues the old way of feasting on human blood. Sorley and I no longer consume human blood on a regular basis."

Micky sneered. "You're saying you're vampires as well? You're all vampires?"

"Only Sorley and Ronan," Lachlan said. "As we told you a while ago, I was bitten but not killed. With that experience comes extraordinary powers. I'm not as strong as a vampire, but I can do things other humans cannot."

As Micky listened to the absurd story, her heart started to pound and her throat went dry. She wondered if Erin had been brainwashed by these men. Another more awful, frightening thought came to mind. What if they were the killers?

She tried to think fast, to devise a plan for how to get them out of the room. "Even it all this was true, I don't understand why you're telling me."

"Because you're in danger." Erin twisted her hands together, her eyes filled with pleading. "I've been through this, and I've fought the ancient one alongside Lachlan and Ronan. I know what this creature can do. A mortal is defenseless against his power."

Ronan shook his head. "I think there is something we don't know about Micky. Something she doesn't know about herself."

She glared at Ronan. "What makes you think this...this ancient one could care less about me?"

"Sure, and there's the rub," Sorley said, his eyes now glowing with that strange golden light. "Did you see somethin' besides dead bodies while you were in the tunnel?"

"And if you did, how did you escape the ancient one unharmed?" Ronan asked.

Stunned, she delayed answering. How could he know about her experiences in the tunnels? Renewed dread rolled through her body in a nauseous wave. "Yes, I saw something, but—"

"What did you see?" Ronan snapped his question, stepping toward her and grasping her arms. "How did you escape?"

His grip was firm but not hurtful, but Micky struggled a little against it. "Let me go."

"What did you see?" Ronan asked again.

Lachlan stood and clasped Ronan's shoulder. "Let her go, you're frightening her."

Ronan's eyes grew brighter, flaming up with antagonism and desperation. "She may be a key to stopping him. We have to know."

"Not this way." Lachlan kept his tone calm and low. "We need to take this slow and easy. She's already frightened."

Ronan's eyes slowly lost the yellow fire, sliding back to heated brown.

Micky started to believe something was very, very odd indeed about Sorley and Ronan, if not the others.

Straightening her spine and putting as much courage into her voice as she could, Micky pointed toward the door. "I want you all out of here or I am calling the police."

A rattling at the doorknob caught everyone's attention, and Micky's heart surged with joy. Jared must be back.

Feeling a little safer, she started toward the door.

"Micky, wait," Erin said, her voice worried. "It might not be who you think it is."

Angered, Micky tossed the other woman a sarcastic smile. "I'm done with this."

Before she could reach for the door, it swung open and Jared stepped through. Eyes sharp and mouth tight with determination, Jared appeared ready for a fight.

He leveled his hard gaze on the men. "Who are you and what the fuck are you doing in my room?"

Chapter Nine

ஐ

Relief and fear jumped inside Micky as Jared took another step into the room.

Lachlan edged in front of Erin, his gaze also now golden, hard and wary. Ronan and Sorley stood stiffly, as if they expected action. As the weird glow returned to their eyes, they reminded Micky of cats watching prey.

"I'm only going to ask one more time. Who are you and what the hell do you want?" Jared asked.

"We're trying to help Micky," Erin said over Lachlan's shoulder.

"Just the way you helped the clerk downstairs?" Jared asked.

"What clerk?" Lachlan asked.

"Listen, old buddy," Sorley said with a smile, "we aren't here to do harm to your woman. The ancient one is near. We could feel that he was here already when we arrived. When we came in the lobby there wasn't a soul at the front desk."

Jared's lips twitched in sarcasm. "Right. First you knock off the night clerk and now you're looking for other victims. Well, I don't fucking think so, *sport*."

Erin's eyes widened. "Knocked-off, as in killed?"

Jared nodded, his gaze cold and determined. "You got it. There's one very dead clerk behind the front desk."

Micky saw the genuine horror in Erin's face over the news. If they'd killed the night clerk she didn't think Erin would be able to fake such surprise. "Jared, I don't think they've hurt anyone."

Jared's gaze caught Micky's for a second. "You all right?"

"Yes," she said.

Before Micky could take a move toward Jared, a silhouette, much denser and more menacing than any of the shadow people she'd seen before, appeared behind Jared. The figure towered, a black cloak swirling about the entity's body.

And within that cloak was the gargoyle's head.

Razor-sharp fear clutched at Micky's throat, along with soul-staggering surprise.

Somehow she managed to speak. "Jared, look out!"

Jared was blown off his feet by a tremendous force. He sailed across the bed and into the desk with a thundering crash. He crumpled onto the floor in a heap. Micky cried out and started toward him.

She took one step before she suddenly couldn't move at all. All her muscles went rigid, her breath strangled in her throat. She tried to breathe and couldn't. Terror gripped her as a buzzing filled her ears.

"No!" Erin's voice cried out.

Lachlan kept Erin behind him. Ronan and Sorley went into a vigilant crouch, their gaze fixed on the figure behind Micky.

She is mine for the taking. The harsh voice rang in Micky's head. She recognized the evil rasp as the voice she'd heard on the road earlier in the evening and in the tunnels. She managed to gulp a little oxygen. With the oxygen came strength, and she moved her arms and tried to thrash. The paralyzing force field returned and this time with a tighter grip. Consciousness started to waver, a languorous sensation taking over.

"Drop her!" Ronan challenged the entity. "You don't need her. She's an innocent."

A laugh, ominous and overflowing with a sulfurous stench that made Micky ill, filled the air. "She is but a taste on the way to heaven. I will have her, then I will take Erin. And then I will send you all back to the hells where you came from."

"Let her go you sick bastard!" Erin started to move forward, but Lachlan blocked her.

Weakness swamped Micky's limbs and the world around her went fuzzy. She felt her feet leaving the ground. Determination to live rallied her strength and she struggled against the immobilizing pressure.

We can release her. Ronan's voice?

"Now!" Sorley's voice rang clear.

Ronan held his hands up to the heavens at the same time Sorley and Lachlan did and the strangling feeling started to retreat.

All three men muttered in a language she didn't understand but thought she'd heard somewhere in the mists of time. The same ten words chanted once. Twice. Three times.

I'm not going to die this way. She inhaled and savored the tiny bit of air. Strangely, she thought of the shadow people, and wondered in a small corner of her consciousness if they could help her. *Please, shadows, if any of you can hear me, please help.*

She blinked and tried to clear her vision. The lamp on the bed dimmed, a sudden gust of wind swirled around the room. Shadows, how many she couldn't be sure, spilled into the area like ghosts in a horror movie. She heard sibilant, unintelligible whispers. Garbled voices struggled for space in her head. Pandemonium threatened to split her skull with pain as contrary voices yelled louder within her mind.

Savehersavehersave her.

She whimpered as pain almost caused her to pass out.

Seconds later an angry, horrible cry vibrated her body and her ears hurt. The pressure on her body released and she fell. When she hit the floor she landed on her back and lay gasping.

A sulfurous wind swirled through room and whirled out the door. The door slammed shut.

"He's gone." Sorley's voice sounded shaky. "What the feck were those things helpin' us?"

Soft hands touched Micky. "They looked like shadows," Erin said, her voice trembling with fear.

"Help the cop," Lachlan said.

Weak and unable to open her eyes, Micky lay helpless as hands lifted and placed her on the bed.

Micky heard sirens and this time she could open her eyes. Sorley and Ronan stood near the bed, their gazes worried and yet glowing with the unearthly light.

"Somethin' mighty odd is goin' on here," Sorley said.

Ronan snorted. "Sure, and you're just now figuring that one out, then?"

"Jared?" Micky bolted upright and swung her feet off the bed. "Jared?"

Jared groaned and started to sit upright, his eyes glazed and a trickle of blood on his temple. Erin dabbed at his head wound with a tissue. He struggled to his feet, but when Lachlan tried to help him, he shrugged him off and staggered toward Micky.

Micky sprang off the bed and rushed to him. She wrapped her arms around his waist the same moment his arms came around her shoulders and held her tight. Micky sank into his embrace, feeling his strength. His lips touched her forehead in a tender kiss.

"Did they hurt you?" Jared asked huskily.

She looked up at him and saw the pure worry in his eyes. "No. They were trying to help. What about you? Are you all right?"

"I'm going to ache like hell, but nothing's broken except maybe a little pride." Jared kept her close in his embrace and scanned the strangers with suspicion. "Now that's all over, someone tell me what the hell is going on?"

Sirens came closer.

Erin sank onto the bed. "Perhaps we should start from the beginning again."

* * * * *

Five o'clock in the morning came and went at Jekyl's.

Jared wished he was in a new hotel making love to Micky and none of this other shit had happened. Instead he sat on a loveseat in a far corner of the lobby, Micky tucked under his arm, and his gaze directed away from the bloody stain on the floor near the front desk.

Flickering blue, white, and red police cruiser lights flashed across the windows. A gaggle of nosy people bustled around outside, and he thought he could hear their muttering through closed doors.

Dismal thoughts intruded, threatening as they had in the past. Post-traumatic stress reared its ugly head and sawed at his defenses. He realized fresh trauma resurrected old feelings. He'd get through this, not only for himself, but for Micky.

He closed his eyes and a vision of the bank robbery flashed into his head. His partner lying on the ground, blood spurting from his wound. Feeling the punch to his chest, the lack of air, the pain, and then blackness. Waking up to gasping breaths as paramedics ripped his vest apart to assess injury.

Then he saw the hotel desk clerk as she'd been before her body was taken away. Her throat punctured by two holes, life's blood gone and eyes staring at the ceiling with glassy vacancy. A small, half-surprised, rapture-filled grin had been affixed to the clerk's mouth. He remembered the stark horror filling Mr. and Mrs. Drummond's faces as they'd come into their hotel and seen the commotion and the dead body.

Jared shook his head and opened his eyes. *Screw this.* He wouldn't think about crap in the past and relate it to the present.

Hell, anyone's brain would be scrambled from the recent insanity. Especially when they listened to bull crap about how vampires roamed the earth. Top all this off with a throbbing skull from hitting the desk in his room, and it came up to a major pain in the ass.

He tightened his arm around Micky's shoulder, his hand rubbing up and down her arm. When she put her head on his shoulder and sighed, he kissed the top of her head. Tenderness swept through him, and he decided he'd better get used to feeling gentle emotions about this woman.

His walk outside earlier that evening had cleared his head a little, but not much. Confusion ran deep, but for the moment he could push aside chaos and concentrate on her. He could also focus his ire on the people who'd entered his room upstairs and brought death and destruction with them.

He also understood for the first time how it felt to be interrogated by other police. Sure, he'd fielded some questions when police investigated the murders at the Gunn Inn. This time, the cross-examination instilled a strange guilt in him he didn't appreciate. He couldn't blame the cops. If he'd been the investigating officer, he would have questioned people the same way.

Maybe if he hadn't gone outside for a walk to clear his head, the clerk wouldn't have been murdered.

Right. Where was the logic in that?

"Jared?" Micky's soft voice broke into his thoughts. "It looks like I'm next."

A weird spurt of fear went through him. Could she also be the next to be harmed by the serial killer? Staggering alarm ran though his psyche as he thought about the possibility. Determination reared up and shoved away his apprehension.

Over his dead body. He wouldn't allow anything to happen to her.

He stood up with her as Fortesque gestured for her to come over. Jared followed, passing by the watchful gazes of Lachlan and Erin.

"We need to talk to her alone, Detective Thornton," a Detective Menton said when they reached the questioning area. "I'm sure you understand."

Gritting his teeth against a retort, Jared nodded. He brushed the back of his fingers across her right cheek in what he hoped would be reassuring gesture. He retreated to the loveseat across the room, and Erin and Lachlan came up to him.

"So where are your weird friends?" Jared asked them.

Lachlan and Erin glanced at each other warily. Lachlan crossed his arms. "We told you. They're vampires. They can disappear at will."

"And you've been bitten by a vampire and have some of their powers. Yeah, I heard you the first time." Jared snorted. "Maybe I should tell the local cops about your bizarre friends and they can put an all points bulletin out on them."

Lachlan's face hardened. "Why haven't you? Since you seem to think Erin and I don't have anythin' better to do than to lie." The man's Scottish accent became thicker the higher his irritation rose. "Why dinna you tell your cop friends we're hidin' their whereabouts while you're at it?"

Lachlan's chest rose and fell with indignant breaths. Instinct told Jared the big Scot didn't lie, but his logical side overruled. *Why didn't I mention the skinny Irishman and the guy with the long black leather coat to the police?*

Jared kept his voice cool. "If you had anything to do with my aunt's murder or the other deaths, you're going to pay."

Lachlan pointed at Jared. "And you're being a fool. You were tossed clear across a room by a powerful force and you're pretending it didn't happen. As a cop, I'd think you'd be interested in the truth when it's right in front of you."

Grinding anger built inside Jared. He rose to his feet with slow deliberation so the Scot wouldn't think he planned attack. He had a feeling Tavish could kick major ass if tested. "I can't explain right now *who* tossed me across the room, but you can be damned sure it wasn't a vampire."

A sarcastic grin widened Lachlan's mouth. "Okay, go ahead and be deliberately stupid. But you're putting Erin and Micky in greater danger. Remember that."

Erin, pale and looking stressed, reached up to touch Lachlan's arm. "Come on. Let's go." She gave Jared a somewhat aloof expression, a cross between pity and understanding. "I just hope you can protect Micky from now on. Why don't you ask her again what she saw? She wouldn't answer you before. Maybe that tells you something." They started to depart, then Erin turned back. "If you ever change your mind about us, call my house. You're welcome to stay with us if the trouble gets too extreme."

Seething, Jared watched them leave.

For Micky's part, she couldn't wait until the interrogation ended, and when it did, she hoped she'd done a good job being untruthful to the police. She almost felt like running from the lobby in shame because she'd lied.

Detective Menton's guarded look made her nervous. "You're free to go, Miss Gunn. But stay in town. It appears each time something freaky happens around here you're the center of it."

"You, Tavish, and Erin," Fortesque said under his breath. His mouth went tight, his eyes sharp and suspicious.

Micky sensed a personal agenda in Fortesque's words, but she couldn't say what.

She turned away and Jared approached carrying their suitcases. When she reached him, his stern expression dissolved to a tenderness that melted her heart. He put down the cases and squeezed her shoulders.

Then he cupped her face in his big palms. "Hey, you okay?"

"I'm fine. Just tired, I think."

He released her and picked up the suitcases. "I've checked us out."

Micky retreated across the lobby with Jared. "I'm glad that's over. My head feels like it's going to pop off."

He paused in the foyer, his gaze probing and concerned. "We'll get you some food and sleep."

She scrubbed one hand through her hair. "Where are we going?"

"We can get some groceries and stock the pantry and refrigerator at the inn."

"The police are done investigating there?"

"That's what they told me when I asked earlier."

Micky hesitated, the horror of what happened in the tunnels almost making her refuse. "I don't suppose it's any worse than staying here."

"I checked with the other hotels and they're full of reporters from out of town. Otherwise I would have checked us into one of them."

A sinking feeling entered her stomach. She knew she'd have to talk with him about what happened up in his room. The visit from the gargoyle-faced, so-called vampire would be foremost in the conversation. Going back to the inn didn't rank up there with her preferences, but they didn't have much choice if they couldn't leave town.

She nodded. "All right. Let's go."

* * * * *

Micky drove her SUV behind Jared's truck. As they headed down Main Street, loaded with provisions for staying at the inn, Micky tried to ease her fears.

She didn't know whether to smile because she'd discovered mind-blowing sex or shiver because she'd entered a *Twilight Zone* episode.

Brilliant morning sun spilled over the treetops and mountains, heralding a new day free from strange people who claimed to be vampires.

Nothing else explained her seeing the gargoyle face again, or Jared being pitched across the room. Nothing else explained Lachlan, Ronan and Sorley's glowing eyes.

As she turned the heater up a notch higher to drive away the thirty degree temperature, she savored time to think, to bring perspective to the odd events over the last few hours. Number one, they'd experienced otherworldly beings, whether Jared wished to admit it or not. She knew, despite earlier skepticism, that horrible things lurked in the night. Had the shadow people saved her from the gargoyle's grip, or had the combined efforts of Lachlan, Ronan and Sorley? She didn't know.

After they arrived at the inn, they brought in their suitcases and plunked them inside the kitchen door.

It took some time to unload groceries and when she put the last bag on the kitchen counter, she sighed. "Looks like the kitchen needs cleaning before we can cook a good breakfast. Unless you'd rather nap right now. We didn't get much sleep."

He started taking off his gloves and then his coat. "I need to wind down before I sleep and my stomach is empty. I'll take the suitcases upstairs and see which bedroom we'll want. I'll strip the sheets and bring them down to the washer."

Bedroom.

She noted he assumed they'd share a bedroom, and it gratified her. Obviously he wanted to continue their intimate relationship.

Before she could say yea or nay, he headed upstairs, leaving her in the quiet kitchen. Large and hinting at old-fashioned, the kitchen still had all the modern accoutrements a person could want. Micky allowed domestic chores to dominate her mind, making it easier to forget recent events.

Determined, she toiled faster, wiping down the sink and counters and the stovetop. Sunlight streamed through the lemon yellow curtains over the sink, brightening the room and eliminating ghoulish thoughts. She could almost forget how her life turned into a horror flick.

A dark shadow flickered in her peripheral vision near the sink. She started and gasped. Turning, she took inventory of the kitchen. Nothing. Her heart beat quickly, testament to her uncertainty.

So what if I see shadow people here? They helped me, didn't they?

Edgy and perturbed at her own vulnerability, she turned to the small closet in the utility room and retrieved a dust pan and broom. As she worked, she wondered if Jared felt the same sense of inevitability as she did. Did he reflect on everything that happened with the same intensity, the same qualms? She doubted it. A man like him feared little, no matter how much he should.

Jared came back a few minutes later, an armful of sheets and pillowcases. Without speaking he went to the utility room off the kitchen and started the washer. He returned to the kitchen and stared at her with disconcerting intensity.

She stopped sweeping the floor and brushed by him to put away the broom and dustpan. When she came out of the utility room he snagged her arm and tugged her toward him.

"Come here," he said softly, a husky nuance growling in his voice.

His lips captured hers as his arms went around her. Micky absorbed the tender, almost pleading caress of his lips. He drew her deep into sensuality with a mere brush of lips against lips, his eagerness never overshadowing his sincerity. Without aggression he molded and shaped her lips, not intruding with a thrust of his tongue. But it burned down through to her stomach and straight to her womb. She moved against him, her hips arching and wanting to feel evidence of his arousal. When she deepened the kiss, his right hand slid down over her butt and clutched one ass cheek.

She smoothed her tongue over his lips. With a growl of breaking restraint, he slanted his mouth over hers and opened wider for her invasion. Tentative at first, she plunged her tongue inside, gaining confidence as he accepted her. Stroking along his mint-flavored tongue, she dueled with him for a tender moment. When Jared pulled back a few seconds later, his breathing came faster.

"I'm sorry," he said. "I shouldn't have left you alone at the hotel. Not even for one minute."

She drew back slightly. "You went outside to clear your head. You couldn't have known what would happen."

His gaze held mysteries, deep and questioning her as much as she queried him. "Why did you let those people into my room?"

She smoothed her fingers over his strong shoulders, then up to his face where she cupped his head and kept her eyes linked with his. "Because I trusted Erin. When I talked to her at the library I never got the impression she was dangerous or malicious. I can tell that she's not lying, Jared. Whatever she says, she believes."

His grim smile mocked. "Just because she believes what she sees doesn't make it real."

With a gentle push against his chest, she disengaged from his arms and went back to the sink. She slipped on plastic gloves again and tried to remain nonchalant under his continuing scrutiny. She washed utensils that couldn't go into the dishwasher, rinsing them and putting the shiny instruments into the drainer.

"Are you angry?" he asked.

When she glanced over at Jared, still standing where she'd left him, she heaved a sigh. She shook her head. "No. I'm tired and starving."

He volunteered to cook, and moments later he assembled ingredients for scrambled eggs, sausage, and wheat toast. They worked in silence until he plugged in a small, dusty radio sitting in one corner under some cabinets. He fumbled with the dial until he found a rock and roll station that played older hits.

She smiled. "My kind of music."

His returning smile sparkled with music. "Yeah? I never figured you for a rock kind of woman. More classical maybe."

She shrugged. "Oh, I like classical well enough, but I'd rather listen to smooth jazz or big band or rock."

He narrowed his gaze, seemingly intent on learning everything about her. "You're a study in contrasts, you know that?"

Did she want to hear this? "How?"

He took the large spoon and stirred the eggs. "I feel like I know everything about you and yet nothing."

If he only knew. "A little mystery can be a good thing."

When she glanced at his solid expression, at the shape of his profile, she wondered if the feelings stirring inside her for him could be the beginnings of love, or the leftovers of sex. A glow like this, burning down in her soul, didn't mean she wanted happily-ever-after with him. She needed to remember the facts and not the fantasy.

"Maybe it's the cop in me. I don't like too much ambiguity. I have this driving need to understand you," he said.

"Why?"

"I don't know. Maybe because you're the most intelligent, sexy woman I've known in a hell of a long time."

Micky couldn't help laughing gently as gratification moved inside her. "Thanks. Anything you want to know, I'm an open book. No arrests, not even a traffic ticket. I did come close once with a speeding ticket but the cop let me off because I didn't give him any lip. Said I was so cooperative he felt guilty for giving me the ticket."

Jared's irreverent grin said he appreciated the humor. "I had fun playing cop with you."

A warm tingle darted into her belly. "Oh, you mean the threats to cuff me and the cavity searches?"

"Yep."

Heat filled her face as she remembered. All of a sudden she felt innocent, a woman who had much to learn about sex. "Last night was…it was fantastic. No matter what happens, I wanted you to know."

As he turned a curious gaze on her, she felt the heat in her face notch up a degree. "No matter what happens?"

She nodded and didn't elaborate, and he let it go.

"I could say you're a mystery, too," she said. "Although I could have guessed you liked rock and roll. It seems like you."

He waggled his eyebrows. "Oh, yeah. I'm a real wild man." After a pause he continued on another vein. "Tell me what you think happened in the hotel room."

His request threw her off. She slipped off the plastic gloves as she finished with the last dishes. "You mean what you and I did together?"

A gentle smile curved his lips. "I know what we did. I mean when Erin and the others came into the room. What do you think happened?"

"Official version or the truth?"

He lowered the flame on the gas stove and the sausage sent up a tantalizing aroma. He moved with subtle assurance, a man who knew what he wanted, yet understood it might take him some time to achieve the goal.

He put the bread in the toaster but didn't toast it yet. "The truth."

"Everything they told you is what happened. It may sound incredible, but that's what happened."

His eyes hardened. "You really believe the crazy story about vampires doing the killings and this Ronan Kieran and Sorley are *good* vampires?"

"It would explain many things, including why the victims were drained of blood. The police certainly can't explain it any other way."

"Just because they can't explain it doesn't mean vampires are doing the damage."

"Of course not."

He wandered away from the stove, his hands on his hips as he paced a little. His boots made a *thunking* noise over the linoleum. His navy sweater and well-fitted jeans hugged his body with an affection that never failed to distract her. They might be talking about vampires and disagreeing, but watching him walk still sent warm arousal spiraling deep into her womb.

He caught her watching him and smiled. Inviting and sensual, his grin made her forget momentary strife. Jared stalked toward her, his intent this time clearly not conversation about vampires. Flustered, she couldn't take her eyes off him.

"You'd better stop looking at me like that, or the eggs will burn," he said.

Her mouth popped open a second. "Looking at you what way?"

"Like you'd rather fuck me than eat breakfast."

With another gentle smile, he leaned down and kissed her softly before returning to the meal.

Oh, yes. She would rather go to bed with him than eat any day. Her stomach growled and overruled the idea. "I had a wonderful time last night, Jared. Up until the vampires, of course."

"I'm glad."

His voice sounded almost sad, and instinct said she should pay attention to the implication.

Maybe she should stick with talking about the incident at the hotel. "What do you think threw you across the room? That certainly wasn't your imagination."

He crammed one hand through his short hair, tousling the strands. "Good question. I haven't figured it out yet."

Micky heard the determination in his voice and decided she wouldn't push him to accept her reasoning. "You didn't see what happened to me when you hit the desk. Like I said before, I was caught in some sort of vice and I couldn't move or breathe well. I suppose you'll tell me that was a panic attack."

"It could have been."

She decided maybe she'd sacrifice explanations for the moment. Maybe after they had some sleep they could discuss the situation again. In silence she set their table and poured orange juice. He scrambled mushrooms, tomatoes, and onions into the eggs.

A short time later they filled their plates with food and settled at the small table. She stared at the utensils on the table and memories flooded back. Her uncle used good china for the guests at the inn, while utilitarian white plates had served his own needs.

"Something wrong?" Jared asked, his dark brows pinched in concern.

She unfolded her paper napkin and placed it in her lap. "I was thinking back to when I sat at this same table when I was a kid. When it came to updating furnishings and keeping the inn beautiful for guests, Uncle Carl went the distance. He kept his own accommodations frugal."

"He sounds like an interesting guy."

"Oh, he was interesting all right. He was quirky in a pleasant way."

After a few silent moments eating, Jared took a sip of his orange juice. "You said you spent a lot of time here when you were a kid? With your parents?"

Okay, so he wanted to keep probing. She supposed she could tell him more. "Before I was born Dad and Mom brought my brother here off and on."

His eyebrows rose. "You've got siblings?"

She stopped with a forkful of eggs halfway to her mouth. "One. Rich is the oldest. He's a software engineer in Chicago, married, and has three kids."

"Where do your parents live now?"

She swallowed, her last bit of egg settling in her stomach like a hard lump. "Mom died when she was twenty-five." She inhaled deeply. "Having me."

Jared put his fork down and sat back, his eyes sad. "God, I'm sorry. What about your father?"

Pain, dull but still there, touched her heart. She chewed her next bite of food thoroughly before responding. "Well, he's an interesting story all in himself. I'm not sure you'd want to hear it."

He returned to eating. "Sure I do."

Micky remembered back to the first time Davy heard about her father, and the impact had made her wary from that point forward about telling anyone. Jared would dig until he discovered the truth, so she might as well spill it now.

With slow deliberation she said each word, afraid it would come out in one big gush.

"Dad remarried much later when I was eighteen. I liked his second wife Candita. She was this beautiful woman who'd emigrated from Spain a year before that. She was very strong, very independent." She smiled. "Not that we always got along, but I respected her. I thought it was a bit strange dad

213

would marry her. He didn't care for women who were too modern."

When she paused for a long time, he said, "And?"

Here it comes. You can't avoid telling him when you've gone this far.

"About two months after they married, Dad strangled her in a fit of rage."

There. It was out and Jared looked more stunned than anything else. She waited for him to speak, half afraid rejection would come.

Jared sat back in his chair, his thoughts spinning as she dumped the startling information on him. Her gaze held his without flinching, little hint of emotion in what she'd told him. He guessed she was an expert at keeping feelings at bay when she wanted to hide. What a shitty thing to happen in her life. He understood her a little better with this new revelation, and his eagerness to comfort her arrived full force. He shoved aside his empty plate. Simple words often remained the best when comforting someone.

"Micky, I'm sorry. You weren't around when it happened, were you?"

He expected her to clam up after the revelation, but she continued, her eyes turning hard with something that looked like anger. "No. I was in college in Texas at the time getting my Bachelors in Humanities. I had no idea they were having problems. My father was often demanding and cold. I sometimes wondered how my mother stood him. And I didn't really understand what Candita saw in him other than his looks. He should have been a model, he was so good-looking. He had this beach boy appearance with his blond hair and blue eyes. But I knew something wasn't quite right about him."

"Was he mentally ill?"

"When his trial came up his defense attorney tried to use the insanity plea because a psychiatrist diagnosed him as having manic depression. But I knew that wasn't the final factor in what he did. I came to the conclusion Dad was just plain evil."

A little surprised by the mention of something as esoteric as evil, he didn't comment at first. Instead he drank a big gulp of his juice and finished in one swallow.

"I guess that depends on what you mean by evil, doesn't it?" he asked.

Her gaze snapped to his, a hint of caution and maybe a little mistrust lurking. "There were things he did when I was a child. He talked pretty bluntly about my mother." A shiver went through her frame. "He said she was freaky. That she saw and heard things that weren't there."

She took a deep breath and paused. Jared leaned on the table. The tension inside him rose, anticipation making him hang by the edge. "Such as?"

"Things."

"What sorts of things?"

Micky shook her head. "I'm surprised you want to hear this, considering you don't believe in the supernatural."

He smiled, but it felt brittle. "Just because I don't believe in the supernatural doesn't mean I don't want to hear about it."

Jared saw new pain enter her eyes, and part of him wanted to pull her into his arms to comfort her. Instead he waited, not wanting to do anything to compound her discomfort. "Is your father in prison?"

She took a bite of toast and nodded. After she'd chewed, she said, "He was given life in prison. At first he tried to say it was a crime of passion, that they weren't getting along and he just snapped. But there was evidence it was premeditated."

Jared's head started to ache with fatigue and he rubbed the back of his neck. "Do you believe that?"

"I believe he knew what he as doing and planned Candita's murder." She rose from her chair and took her nearly empty plate to the sink. She stood there, her expression thoughtful until she scraped a couple of scraps into the garbage disposal. "I try not to think much about it. I thought for awhile I might have prevented it. You know the old arguments. If I'd just warned Candita that Dad had strange moods. I did tell her my brother and I asked him to get psychological assistance. Not that it mattered since she didn't listen to us. I keep telling myself she lived with him every day and must have known. Maybe she was in denial."

"When is the last time you saw him?" he asked.

She closed her eyes and hung her head before she spoke again. "I haven't seen him since he went into prison."

When she looked at him with expectant light in her eyes, he wondered what she believed he would say. He suspected the cop who'd messed with her head was a gage she used to measure every man, and maybe her father instilled suspicion in her as well.

His heart ached for the hurt she'd experienced. "How long has he been in prison?"

"About ten years...a little more. I don't keep track of it if I can help it."

"You don't still think you could have helped him, do you?"

"No. No, I don't."

His appetite ebbed and he was almost finished, so he stopped eating and helped her clean up the cooking mess. His mind went back to her mother and the shadows Micky mentioned earlier.

"Tell me about these things your mother saw."

A tiny smile graced her full lips for a moment, reminding him how delicious she'd tasted earlier. "Okay, then. But don't say I didn't warn you. Mom saw shadows in the house. They could be dense and have a human shape, or they would be blobs in the corner of her peripheral vision. She apparently saw them all her life. They're called shadow people."

Jared frowned. "There's a name for this hallucination?"

As soon as he said hallucination he saw Micky twitch, as if he'd hit a live wire inside her and she barely held back a response. "If you believe it's a hallucination. Not everyone does."

"I've never heard of them."

Resolve flowed over her features and she seemed ready for battle. "Most people haven't."

She seemed content to drop the subject, but now she had him interested. "Tell me more about these shadow people."

Micky's incredulous expression, her eyes widened and her mouth open, made him want to smile. He liked surprising her.

"You're sure you want to hear it?" she asked.

"I wouldn't have asked."

"Let's go somewhere more comfortable then to talk. I'm exhausted."

"Why don't we take the clean sheets upstairs, make the bed, and you can tell me then."

They left the kitchen and went upstairs with clean linens in hand. He directed her to the bedroom he'd picked out for them.

As they made the bed, she explained about the mysterious shadow people. "No one knows who or what they are. There are dozens of theories."

"Ghosts are one of them, I'm guessing."

She smoothed a sheet with her palm. "Yes. Some people say they are time travelers from the past or the future. Or maybe they are inter-dimensional beings only some people can see. Some say they are other people experiencing an OBE, out-of-body experience."

He slipped a pillowcase over the end of one pillow. "What do you think they are?"

"I don't know."

"But you don't believe your mother was mentally ill?"

"No."

He wanted to press the issue that she couldn't know for certain. Yet what good would it do? He shouldn't mock her mother's so-called beliefs.

"And you have a penchant for Edgar Allen Poe. Why?"

She shrugged. "He's atmospheric. By today's standards he's flowery and difficult for many people to read, but I love the pictures he creates in my mind." She gestured with one hand, making a flowing motion. "His way with words brings the cold darkness alive." She smiled and shivered. "Not something I think I'm going to read while I'm here in Pine Forest. I thought about it, but the last thing I need to do is read something that might scare the hell out of me."

He smiled. "I can understand that."

As they pulled comforter over the king-sized bed, he wanted to sink down on this bed with Micky in his arms. Instead he yawned. "Look, I'm going to have to get some sleep."

She nodded. "I need to take a shower."

He watched her walk into the bathroom with a pair of flannel pajamas and a makeup bag in hand. The flannels made him smile. She was a contrast, this woman. All fiery in bed, then cool with her flannel.

Maybe, after he'd slept a while, he'd slip her out of the flannel and into his arms. With a smile of anticipation, he sank onto the bed and closed his eyes.

Chapter Ten

∞

Micky woke around two in the afternoon, her head clear of the fog she'd floated in while having breakfast. Jared wasn't in the bed beside her.

Her mind whirled with a half dozen questions. So many things happened over the last few days, she wondered if she'd gone crazy and dreamed it all. She rolled onto her right side. *Of course you didn't imagine it.* Yet how could she believe in vampires and people like Lachlan who'd been bitten by vampires? Could a person become a half-vampire creature? Had the shadow people saved her from the being with the hideous gargoyle head? It didn't seem possible on any level considering the shadows always frightened her.

She pressed her left hand to her temple and rubbed at the slight headache forming there. *Caffeine withdrawal. That's what's wrong with me.*

After she crawled out of bed with reluctance, she unpacked her suitcase and put away her clothes. After dressing in a blue cotton cable sweater, black leggings, and boots, she decided to head downstairs and make coffee. She'd engage in serious thinking about her uncle's property and if she wanted to stay here and run the place.

As she went downstairs, the wood creaked and popped as old wood often did. Maybe she should take a vacation that didn't include Pine Forest with its weirdness. Ghosts, murders, vampires — she didn't want or need any of it.

Right. So your responsibilities are going to disappear because you want them to? Not hardly.

In the kitchen she started a full pot of coffee. She puttered around the kitchen trying to decide what to do next. Her mind jumbled ideas, forcing unpleasant tasks to the forefront.

A flash of the gargoyle's face popped into her head without warning and she flinched. Then she imagined the priest's horror and the clerk's violent death. She almost knocked a coffee mug off the counter when a vision of Ronan, Sorley, and Lachlan's glowing eyes came to mind. Sweat popped out on her forehead and her throat tightened. As her breathing quickened, she put her hands over her face and sank onto a kitchenette chair. She took one wavering breath and then another.

No, don't think about any of it.

Instead she thought of Jared and the pleasure she'd discovered in his touch. As she reviewed their lovemaking, she smiled. The tightness in her muscles eased and her breathing slowed.

Excellent. She'd discovered a cure for obsessive bad thoughts. Sex. Or at least fantasies about sex with Jared.

While the coffee pot gurgled, she went into the utility room and grabbed her coat, hat, and mittens. She decided a quick trip around the property in the cold air would clear her head more than caffeine. Besides, she'd be back shortly and ready for coffee.

"Where are you going?" a deep voice asked.

She whirled around, her heart in her throat. Jared stood in the utility room doorway, a frown punctuating his face.

"You scared me. I was going for a walk."

He put his hands on his hips. "No, you're not." She opened her mouth to protest, but he moved in quickly and planted a swift peck on her mouth. "Not without me. And sure as hell not before I get some of that coffee in me."

If he hadn't looked so mouth-watering she might have considered getting mad at him for being so bossy and scaring her. What right did one man have to be so adorable? He wore an old long-sleeved white T-shirt and his jeans rode low on his hips. He wore white athletic shoes. With sleep-mussed hair, stubble-rough chin, and a sleepy expression, he defined delicious.

She sighed. "I wasn't thinking. It isn't safe for me outside."

"That's right."

Unexpected frustration welled in her gut. "I can't do this for the rest of my life, you know."

His brow furrowed. "Do what?"

"Rely on you to protect me. Pretend that what is happening isn't happening. That I didn't almost get shot in a diner, stumbled over dead bodies under this house, and got attacked by something you tell me isn't a vampire. I can't pretend I like having you tell me where and when I can go someplace, even if it is common sense."

She shook her head and peeled off her mittens, then her hat, then her coat. She tossed the coat on a small chair rather than hang it up, a mini show of defiance against something unnamed.

Jared looked at her with a scarcely masked condescension she wanted to smack off his face. "You're still stuck on that vampire idea?"

"I think I have a right to my opinion on what happened."

"Of course you do, but you don't have any evidence to support it."

She stalked toward Jared until she almost bumped into him nose to nose. "What more evidence do I need than men with glowing eyes and paranormal strength? What more evidence do I need than a force I can't see strangling me?" Annoyance made her muscles tighten with stress. She stayed in place, unwilling to move an inch until she had it out with him. "Do I need photographs? Hair samples? DNA?"

"Yeah, that's about the size of it. Don't expect me to operate off anything but evidence, Micky. It's my job."

"Just like a man." Her words startled even her. She didn't normally generalize male behavior. This time she couldn't seem to stop. "Men think they can come into any situation and advise a woman to death. Give her counsel but don't listen to her feelings."

As her ire escalated, his expression toughened into *cop face*. All staidness and skepticism, he generated exasperation within a blink of an eye.

He stuffed his hands in his jean pockets. "Let's get some coffee and have a reasonable discussion."

She didn't feel sensible. In fact, she felt downright strange, as if a fire lit inside her she couldn't and didn't want to contain. "I don't think I'm in the mood. Besides, you wouldn't want me around you right now. I might be too emotional."

His frown became a glare. "You're letting your feelings completely overrule what you need to think about. There's a dangerous man out there willing to hack and slash his way through this community for some gruesome purpose no one understands."

Micky poked him in the chest with her index finger. "We do know who he is, what he is, and is purpose. He wants Erin Greenway because he believes she's the reincarnation of his old lover. He may be a demented vampire, but he's real."

"According to a weak-minded woman and her cohorts, yeah."

"She is not weak-minded. She's intelligent. And as for her cohorts, I think if it hadn't been for them we would both be dead. The vampire or whatever it was would have killed me and then probably you when you came into the room." She waved a hand in dismissal. "Oh, forget it."

She started to brush passed him, but he clasped her arm and twirled her back toward him. Before she could gasp in outrage, he pulled her into his arms and settled his mouth over hers. With deep, drugging sensuality, he tasted her. She wanted to struggle, even considered it. But her body betrayed her, wanting him more than anything to blot out the fear that haunted her no matter how hard she fought it.

When he released her a second later, he nuzzled his nose into her hair. "God, you smell great. Instead of coffee, maybe I should sip you."

She smiled and leaned into his touch. Before she could think about the consequences, she pressed her hips into his and felt his growing arousal.

"God, honey, if you don't want me to do you right here," he whispered hoarsely against her neck, his hands reaching up to brush the sides of her breasts, "walk away."

She swallowed hard, her voice going soft and strained. Tears touched her eyes. "I don't think I can walk away. I don't think I want to."

He drew back enough to look into her eyes, and what she saw there frightened her on a level having nothing to do with fearing him as a person. No, she feared how much she felt for him.

"I'm sorry," he said. "Forget what I said about the vampires for now. We can agree to disagree, right?"

"Yes."

With her permission, he dived into a new kiss. Fraught with desperation and yet a kind of tenderness she'd never expected resided in a man, his kiss took her to new heights. With sweeping tastes he lingered over her mouth, each brush of lip against lips bringing ecstasy to her mind and body. Every time he brushed his hands over her with worshipful feeling, she knew this man would bring her great joy and perhaps sorrow.

He broke off the kiss and swept her into his arms. "Bedroom."

"Hurry."

She grinned as he left the kitchen, his stride strong and sure despite her weight in his arms. Rippling and bunching, his powerful arms acted like an aphrodisiac to her heated blood. She wanted him now with a breathtaking quickness. Lightning arousal pooled low in her stomach.

Oh, yes. I want him now and damn the consequences.

She couldn't deny the fervent demand in her mind for a fulfilling sexual relationship. Few men had come into her life that made her feel burning desire, and none of them had quickened her like Jared could. None made her feel protected, cherished, and maybe even a little bit loved like Jared.

As he crossed the foyer and headed up the stairs, she knew with a sense of fate this time with him would be special, a treasured moment tasting as rich as fine wine. When they reached bedroom he edged open the door with his foot. He sat her on her feet and allowed her body to slide down his with lingering, sensual intention. She purred at the feeling, digging her nails into his shoulders for a second like a playful cat.

One corner of his mouth turned up, a teasing grin playing with his lips. "Ever been a love slave?"

Micky shook her head. "No, but I think I'm about to try it."

Clothes went flying as she yanked off her sweater and tossed her bra in a corner. She moved away from him long enough to remove her boots and socks. Seconds later her leggings and her black silky panties ended up on top of the bra.

The devouring looked in his eyes gave her an ego trip she couldn't resist. Having a man in her power felt gratifying in a way she'd never expected. She glanced at the bulge straining against his jeans. He took the hint. With almost jerky movements, he pulled his T-shirt over his head and then reached for the button on his jeans.

"Wait," she said. "If I'm your slave, shouldn't I do that?"

A wide grin parted his lips and he waggled his eyebrows. "Get over here love slave and take off my pants."

Micky hurried to his side and unbuttoned his waistband, then peeled the zipper down with a quick *snick*. He groaned as her fingers brushed over his brutal erection straining the fabric.

He grabbed her fingers and held her hand over his cock for an electrifying moment. As he gazed at her his eyes darkened. She felt she knew what he wanted and needed. Despite her gnawing arousal, she'd give him the one thing all men seemed to want.

She went down on her knees and after peeling the jeans down over his hips, she also slid his white briefs down to his knees. She admired his entire body, chorded with superb musculature and defined power.

"You're the most gorgeous man I've every seen. And even when I don't agree with you, you make me hotter than any man ever could."

A moan, deep with masculine appreciation, rumbled passed his lips. "Micky, you don't know how crazy it makes me to hear you say that."

She clasped his cock at the base, holding on firmly but not too tight. She started a movement, up then down. Up, then down.

He groaned and breath hissed between his lips. "Oh God, yes."

His head dropped back as he closed his eyes, and his excitement spilled from his lips as she stroked. She cupped his balls, caressing them with careful, gentle movements that made his hips twitch and his entire body tremble. She loved the sensation of silky heat and hardness inside her grip, adored how much he wanted her.

Micky added her tongue to the torture, and when she licked up the underside of his cock, he groaned deeply. "Hell, yes." With a moan of tortured pleasure, he whispered, "Lick it, baby. Suck it deep."

As his slave, she complied, liking what she did to him as it added excitement. Her mouth encompassed him, sliding as far down as she could. She sucked and kept her hand clutched around the base. With swift motions she started to suck him; her mouth and hand worked in unison to bring him the biggest climax he'd ever experienced. At least that was her goal.

She wanted him moaning.

She wanted him incoherent with pleasure.

She wanted him to beg for more.

Jared started a motion with his hips until he fucked her mouth with deep, persistent strokes. His breathing quickened and she heated inside, his excitement becoming her desire. Everything inside Micky centered on pleasing him, to bring him the biggest cock-spurting event he'd experienced. Her mind raced with wicked thoughts, a million ideas forming about what she could do with and to him. Animal longing rose inside until she pumped him quicker, her hand and mouth around his cock a persistent rhythm demanding fulfillment.

Yes, she would give to him what she'd never given to a man before.

Her essence. Maybe even her love.

He growled low in his throat and she kept her mouth wrapped around him as he gasped, "Honey, pull back now or I'm coming in your mouth."

Yes. I want that. She didn't verbalize it, she kept up the motion. Seconds later another hard, male animal groan broke from him and he burst. Warmth spilled into her mouth as his cock jerked once, then twice with long, full explosions. Jared's body shook with each pulsation, his fingers clutching in her hair as he held on for dear life. She pumped his cock, sucking and sliding her hand back and forth over him to drain the last drop.

"God, woman." He panted the words as he tried to catch his breath. "You're wonderful."

226

As she swallowed and enjoyed his taste, she managed to say, "There's more where that came from."

He laughed, his magnificent chest rising and falling with deep inhalation and exhalation. "I hope so. I could get used to this."

As she licked her lips with female satisfaction, he pulled her to feet. Again he picked her up in his arms. Jared's look said things she didn't dare assume, but wanted with all her heart and soul. Melting with gentleness and a heat that said he couldn't wait to take her, his eyes held mysteries ages deep and eons strong. She felt they tapped into ancient rituals, the most profound act a woman and man could experience.

He placed her on the bed and headed for the bathroom, and she knew he went for condoms. She didn't want foreplay, didn't need it. All she required was Jared's long, thick, hard erection pumping her to completion.

Her breasts felt full and tender, her nipples ripe with arousal. Clenching and releasing, her cunt heated and her labia lips engorged. One touch from him and Micky believed she would explode on the spot. Dazzled with the possibilities, amazed at how fast he aroused her, she lay back with her arms and legs spread wide.

When Jared came back into the room he'd stripped and his new hard-on was sheathed with protection. He climbed onto the bed with Micky. Almost as if he read her mind, he slipped between her thighs and pushed his cock slowly but inexorably through her folds and deep into her hot, tight channel. She moaned as the feeling of his cock parting and spreading her depths made her wild. She wrapped her arms around him and planted her feet flat on the bed. Tilting her hips upward, she assisted him as he thrust deep, deeper, deepest. He touched bottom, coming up tight and hot against her center. This time the sex felt singular and new in ways she couldn't understand but wanted to explore.

"Oh, Jared," she whispered, unable to keep back a shiver of delight.

He kissed her, his mouth ravenous as he explored with his tongue hard and deep in her mouth. He started a rhythm, his tongue thrusting and retreating.

Her hips twitched, and she moaned into his mouth. She wanted him to fuck her hard, but he seemed content to rest inside her. Relaxing into his non-hurried approach, she decided to enjoy him second by second, minute by minute.

Breathing long and deep, she enjoyed the way her sensitive cunt stretched around his hot thickness invading her core. If she hadn't been so hot and excited, the demanding length might have hurt. Instead Micky wanted his hardness in her forever. As she tightened her arms around him, he shifted his hips the tiniest bit and the movement inside her sent sparks of electricity along her veins.

As his tongue plunged and retreated inside her mouth, Micky groaned and counterattacked by clenching her vaginal muscles around his cock.

His breath caught and he moaned into her mouth. Pleased with the effect, she started a rhythm of tighten and release. He tore his mouth from hers and buried his face in her neck, his breathing harsh with restraint, as if he wanted to take her hard and fast but wouldn't. His hips moved the tiniest bit, stirring his cock inside her.

"Oh, Jared." She whispered out the words, afraid to take another breath, the pleasure felt so intense.

As he licked her ear, she shivered and rotated her hips again. He took up the challenge. Jared moved, grinding his cock inside her and moving back and forth the tiniest fraction. It was a thrust but not a thrust, a tentative request designed to drive her insane with craving.

And she felt desire like never before.

For eternity they maintained the subtle plunge and withdraw. The motion became the beat, like a sensual song created by their bodies. Muscles burned with effort, running toward a finish line tempting on the horizon.

Thrust and retreat.

Thrust and retreat.

Inhale and exhale.

Momentum gaining, breaths rasping hard and deep.

When Jared leaned down and sucked one nipple, she gasped out an excited cry. He added this bliss to the others, a continual suck and lick, suck and lick as she writhed in his arms.

Their bodies moistened with exertion, heat building as stimulation rose. Micky clutched at his shoulders, her single anchor in the extraordinary storm. She became wholly physical, her mind receding in favor of her body's requirements. Nothing entered her thoughts but sensations, and she locked onto the singularly corporeal dimension. As his hips pumped with the subtlest of thrusts, her cunt tingled and pulsed, verging on a wild orgasm a fraction out of reach. Her blood sang and boiled, the sexual crescendo building without remorse. She gasped, oxygen second to the screaming climax rising on the tide.

Her arms twined around his neck and she kissed him, determined he would know her taste when he came. She gently pushed her tongue into his mouth and he accepted her conquering with a vigorous, unexpected thrust of his hips.

Micky squirmed against Jared at the mind-blasting sensation of his steel-hard, hot cock skewering her cunt. She lifted her hips to accept everything he had. Again, a jabbing thrust.

Oh. Oh yes. Oh yes!

Lights seemed to explode behind her eyes as orgasm rippled up and tore through her body. She shivered and moaned as her muscles shivered around his cock.

He growled and started pounding into her, each spearing thrust punctuated by a sound of pure, male animal. He slowed down just long enough to loop her legs over his arms and press her knees back toward her shoulders so her hips tilted high for penetration. At the next plunge she gasped, then moaned as he pierced deep with ramming thrusts into her center.

Another climax rushed forward, startling her with such exploding pleasure she jerked in his grip and her entire body quivered as she screamed. His roar followed hers as he centered deep in her cunt, his cock spewing forth long streams of cum before he sagged onto her with a sigh. His body quivered, his breathing still quick from exertion.

Content and lightheaded with delight, she rested in his arms. Micky held him tight, absorbing the aftershocks rushing through them. Her gaze snagged his, and with a smile he rolled off of her. He disappeared into the bathroom for a few seconds, then returned to pull her into his arms. Snuggled close against him, she savored the quiet and the comfort of this incredible man for a long time. He'd given her the world and something more in the way he made love to her. While she might not express it, might not know how to tell him, she would cherish this satisfaction and safety in her heart forever.

As silence grew longer, Micky knew he held something back, just as she did. But what? Words of affection? Words of love?

No. There was no guarantee he'd ever love her, and mind-spiraling sex was no pledge a man would change his plans. She realized then she didn't know much about him, and he knew twice as much about her. Avoiding the mushier emotions, even if they stirred inside her, might be a good thing.

He tilted her chin up and kissed her on the nose. "Damn, girl, you know how to make up after a fight."

"Was that what we were doing? Fighting?"

"Close enough for me."

"You don't believe couples should discuss problems?"

She heard the word *couples* in her sentence and froze. The intimacy of the word surprised her. Yes, they were a couple whether they liked it or not. But it was always possible Jared wouldn't like the idea and would think she read too much into their relationship.

"Yeah, I believe they can fight, as long as they don't do it to hurt one another. Couples who never disagree at any point are fooling themselves."

"My Bachelor's degree was in Humanities with a Human Communication minor. The more I discovered about human communication, the more I realized most of us aren't very good at it."

"Depressing but true."

Maybe she *could* tell him about the being with the gargoyle head, the creature some claimed was a vampire. "You value honest communication no matter what?"

His arms tightened a fraction. "Absolutely."

They settled into quiet again, and his hands smoothed over her back in a gesture both arousing and comforting. God, being in his arms felt so wonderful. She wished reality meant she could stay here day and night until whomever or whatever stalked Pine Forest gave up and went away.

"What was your childhood like?" she asked.

He drew back slightly, his eyes wide with curiosity and a smile parting his lips. "What?"

"Your childhood. I told you about mine. Turnabout is fair play." He swatted her butt gently and she squeaked. "Hey!"

"Who says anything about being fair?"

She squirmed out of his arms. She sat Indian style, knowing good and well he'd have a full view of her charms. "I know about the horrible experiences you had a year ago, but not much else."

His grin turned unrepentant. "You know my body. Very well, as a matter of fact."

"But not your mind."

He stretched his arms above his head and his rippling muscles bunched and reminded her of how powerful this sexy man could be. As if she needed reminding. His stomach muscles moved and so did the long, well-carved brute force in his long legs. Micky's gaze snagged on the semi-erect status of his cock and wondered when he'd want to love her again.

"All right." He sat up, pilling pillows behind him and leaning back against the headboard. "I was born in Denver and as you know I still live there. I've made sure to travel whenever I get a chance. I refuse to be someone who knows everything about the world from books, movies and the History Channel."

"That's good. Some people have lived nowhere and know everything."

A smile burst over his face. "Very astute observation. Is that a way of telling me I don't know diddly about ghosts and other strange phenomena?"

"No, that wasn't what I meant, but now that I think of it—"

"All right. You think about it all you want, but right now there are no ghosts or vampires in my immediate future, okay?"

She nodded, unwilling to break the light mood by telling Jared he had it all wrong.

He continued. "I have a Bachelor of Arts in Humanities and a Masters in Criminal Justice with a psychology emphasis."

Impressed, she leaned forward and brushed her index finger over his chin in a teasing fashion. "So we have that in common. I never would have figured you for Humanities. The criminal justice certainly fits, though."

His gaze centered on her cunt, and she knew he could see she was still wet, still swollen with leftover arousal. Gratified, she watched as his eyes caressed her intimate places and his mind seemed to lose complete track of the conversation. She cleared her throat and he jerked his gaze back to her face.

"Anyway, I've got a nice condo in Lakewood, but I want a house someday. Right now I'm at work long hours and don't need the space." He paused, apparently reflecting. "I have two older sisters. Aimee is divorced with no children. She is a beautician in Englewood and has her own shop. Danielle is engaged to a sergeant I know on the force. She has a nineteen year old boy, Mack, by her first marriage."

She waited for him to continue, but when he didn't' say anything she asked, "Have you ever been married?"

She saw the hesitation start, and she wondered why he'd balk. Seconds later his expression cleared. "Yeah. I was for a year."

This information didn't surprise her really. Tentatively she decided to push for more information. "What happened?"

"My wife Katherine and I dated a year before we married and we seemed perfect for each other. We were married about six months when our relationship started to erode and by the time our first anniversary came she wanted a divorce."

"Oh God. I'm so sorry."

He nodded, but kept going. "I agreed to the divorce because I knew we couldn't work it out. I moved out of the house and into an apartment a few days before the bank robbery I told you about. She visited me I the hospital and for a few moments I thought maybe she wanted me back."

Micky imagined the mental and physical pain Jared must have experienced. "What happened then?"

"She figured out after a day that she really didn't love me anymore. Her concern was more like one friend for another and not so much a wife for her husband. Not the kind of love two people should have for marriage."

"What do you think went wrong?"

Jared shrugged. "I'm not one hundred percent certain, but she had a lot of anxiety about me being a cop. She complained about my hours and seemed very insecure. I think I was so damned blinded by lust when I was with her I didn't realize she wasn't a very independent person. She needed me with her all the time, wanted me to shirk my duty to the force. I couldn't do that."

She nodded, understanding. "Why did she marry you if she worried about you all the time?"

Jared's gaze pierced something deep inside her. "Would you worry?"

She didn't hesitate. "Of course. But I would also understand it's a part of the job. I'd have to take the good with the bad."

A brilliant smile touched his mouth. "You're so different from her. You've got strength and you know what you want."

She'd never heard herself described that way before, and his admiration and assurance made a new warmth glow deep in her soul.

He locked his hands behind his head, and once again her attention went to his physique. She wanted to reach up and touch his finely-sculpted arms.

"My father and mother have given up on the idea of grandchildren coming from me," he said. "Besides, I've seen how my dad's career in the police force eroded his marriage."

Surprised, she leaned forward again. "Your parents are divorced?"

"No, but they probably should be. Dad is a tough old bastard in a way. Mom met him in college and they married before Vietnam. He was drafted early on and made it through one tour and didn't have to go back. He entered the police force and rose all the way to police chief before he decided to retire. Mom put up with a lot of crap from him over the years. They seemed to have settled into a mutual understanding now. I don't know what you'd call it. Tolerance, maybe?"

"They don't love each other?" The thought made her heart ache, because she'd certainly seen what lack of love could do.

"I think they do in their own way. It may not be a comfortable relationship, but they're content with it."

Surprised at the ease in which he revealed his past, she plowed forward, eager to know more. The words came before she could slow herself down. "I could never marry a man for anything but love."

She half expected Jared to bolt as many men did when confronted by a woman spouting words about love.

Instead his gaze intensified, like she was a suspect he wanted to interrogate. "You shouldn't have to. Don't settle, Micky, whatever you do."

With another blinding smile that set her heart pattering, he left the bed. "Come on. The coffee is probably stronger than hell by now, but I need to wake up."

After dressing and heading down to the kitchen, she decided she couldn't keep him in the dark any longer about what she'd seen in the tunnels. If she wanted a relationship with Jared she'd have to be honest.

When they'd settled at the table, she decided to edge into the conversation slowly. "Until the killer is caught, I can't do a thing with this inn. Tourists aren't going to come here."

He stirred cream into his coffee. "You're right." When he looked up, his eyes held a sadness that disturbed her. "Maybe you need to head out of here until this is all over."

Giving him a wry smile she said, "Trying to get rid of me?"

"I want you safe." The gruffness in his tone assured her Jared meant it. "I don't want you to go, but you should."

Silence descended as she thought about his suggestion. Staring into her coffee as if the dark depths might offer answers, she wished she'd met Jared under different circumstances. Then again, if they'd met in Pine Forest under any other circumstances, would they have hit it off? She couldn't know.

She tucked her hair behind her ears and took a deep breath. Time for the truth.

"There's something I need to tell you," she said.

One of his eyebrows twitched upward. "That sounds ominous."

"I'm afraid to tell you."

"Why?"

"Because what I'm going to say will sound very strange."

Jared settled back in his chair, his eyes assessing her much the same way they did the first time he saw her. "Strange seems to be the order of the day." A smile touched his mouth, his eyes filled with curiosity. "You've got me intrigued."

She took a deep breath. "When I was here by myself the day the murders happened, I didn't plan on going into the tunnels. It was the last thing I wanted to do. But I felt something drawing me toward them."

Micky saw the turn in his gaze, the natural skepticism making his eyes somehow colder. "Like a force?"

"I know it sounds bizarre, but that's what it felt like. I couldn't resist it. I saw the creature that killed those people."

It took him a minute to answer, his face deadpan. "What?"

"I saw the murderer."

Anger entered his expression. "You saw the killer and you didn't tell the local police?"

Bracing for disapproval, she revealed the truth regardless. "You wouldn't have told them either if you saw what I saw. I went in the basement thinking I'd make a list of what to get rid of. While I took notes I made the mistake of glancing at the tunnel where the bodies were. I couldn't see anything, but there was this...I know this is going to sound weird...this energy that drew me toward it. I couldn't resist going into the tunnel. When I got there I stepped into the blackness and the gravity held me. It felt like hard, cruel hands drawing me forward."

She waited to see disbelief and condemnation in his eyes. Instead he wore the impenetrable mask of a cop interrogating a witness.

Swallowing hard, she continued. "I saw a face. The face of evil."

"What did it look like?"

"You won't believe me."

"Try me."

She put her hands over her face and mumbled the answer. "A gargoyle with red eyes."

The image flashed into her mind and she quivered with revulsion. She managed to drop her guard and look at Jared. His brows pinched together, a definite frown turning his mouth into a sharp line. Nope, he didn't believe her.

"I don't blame you for thinking I'm two jokers short of a deck," she said. "But it's what I saw."

He nodded. "You're right, I don't know what to think."

As conversation came to a halt, she received the impression the house waited for an explanation as well. Subtle and dark, the expectant air in the structure bothered her on a profound level. As if a sinister core, more evil than the shadows residing here and threatened their peace. When wood creaked and groaned in the bowels of the house, she started. Chills sent goosebumps down her arms. Maybe the old inn disapproved of her telling its secrets.

Right. Maybe Jared's skepticism isn't off the mark if you're starting to think of this place as a living entity.

On edge, she clutched her hands together in her lap. She shivered a little as a cold breeze passed over her neck. She glanced around, half expecting to see a window open. All of the windows remained closed, just as she thought.

"What's wrong?" he asked as he leaned on the table, his expression concerned.

"It's as if...as if this place is alive. Did you ever see the movie, *The Haunting*, based on the Shirley Jackson novel? The old version made in the early sixties?"

He shook his head. "I'm not much into horror films."

She took a deep sip of her cooling coffee, hoping the caffeine would enliven her sagging energy. "The first time I saw the movie I was a little kid. There was this one scene I never forgot. Two women huddle together in a room because they've been awakened by strange sounds. At one point it's like the house starts to breathe. The doors start to suck inward, then outward, then inward. The wood was flexible like a pair of lungs. It was the most chilling thing I've ever seen." She rushed forward with her explanation. "I'm not saying this inn has done anything similar, but it does feel alive. Like someone watches us from the corners." She took a calming breath. "Whatever force is behind the gargoyle, something made him release me while I was in the tunnels, and the time I was in the hotel."

Jared tilted his head to the side a little, his gaze hard. "What do you think that something was?"

"I'd like to say it was my own will. But I don't know anymore. When the creature attacked me in the hotel room, I thought I saw..."

No, she couldn't tell him that like her mother, she also saw shadow people when he didn't seem to believe her about the gargoyle.

After a short silence Jared stood up and went to the coffee pot. He brought the carafe back to the table and poured them more coffee.

As he applied fresh cream to his brew, he drew in a deep breath. "Everything you've told me sounds like classic haunted house stuff."

She made a scoffing noise. "You call being sucked into a tunnel by an unstoppable force standard haunted house fare?"

He shrugged and wrapped his big hands around his mug. "In the movies."

She caught his sardonic lilt, and decided then and there she'd made a big mistake telling him her true thoughts about the gargoyle. "You're saying you don't believe me."

His critical expression assessed her like a criminal with a mile long record. "How can I, Micky? None of what you've told me is logical."

Antagonism roared to life inside her. "So if something defies logic is must not be true."

"For the most part, yeah."

Deciding she wouldn't change his mind about what happened, she said, "Just forget I said anything. This was a stupid idea."

"Maybe the strain of the diner incident and seeing the murders caused some low-grade hallucination. You've been under pressure. You remember what I told you about critical stress management? Hallucinations are not as unusual as one would think after a significant trauma."

Doubt made her waver. "You've encountered some people with full blown hallucinations like that before?"

He shook his head. "Not personally, but I've read about it. It's not unheard of even in mentally healthy people."

Micky gave him a cynical smile. "Good to know you don't consider me a nut case."

Jared slanted an irked look her way. "You're someone who's experienced several bad things in a short amount of time. That's going to cause problems. "

She turned sideways in her chair so she could cross her legs. She propped her forearm on the back of the chair and let her fingers dangle. Could he be right and she had experienced delusions?

But I saw the gargoyle as plain as day, as if he were sitting right across from me now.

"I saw the gargoyle in the hotel room before you were pitched across the room into the desk. I wished you could have seen it too, then you'd understand."

He sipped his coffee, his expression thoughtful. "Think about what you're saying here. Not only are you saying you believe in vampires but living gargoyles as well?"

What did I expect? Full belief?

No, she'd gotten what she expected.

When it came down to it, he didn't believe her.

Micky stood and went to the kitchen sink to dump her coffee, her body weary and her mind fatigued from dealing with events the last few days. Maybe she should relax for a few hours. She'd experienced enough gargoyle heads, shadows and murder for a lifetime.

She started to turn away, half expecting him to speak. When he didn't, she kept on walking and said, "I'll be in the library."

Jared didn't stop her, and her heart went heavy with worry. She may have ruined any chance she had with him, and at what cost? Then again, if he didn't want to be with her because of what she'd seen, did she want to be with him?

Once Micky stepped into the library and turned on the lights, she found the dark-paneled room soothing. White sheets still covered the furniture, but she might spend a little time in here looking for a book and then return to her room. She walked from one end of the enormous bookshelves to the other. She could crawl up on the tall ladder and look at the books on the highest shelf, but she decided to stick with the rows at the bottom.

After spending at least thirty minutes perusing old mysteries such as *The Moonstone* by Wilkie Collins, she settled on an old Edgar Allen Poe volume of stories. She paused, a smile marking her lips. It didn't matter what happened in her life, she could always count on ole Edgar to entertain with a depth of mind-bending chill and intrigue.

"Do I really want to read spooky tales in a house like this?" She shrugged. "What the hell?"

Besides, if Jared was right and nothing supernatural was happening at the inn or in Pine Forest, then why should she be frightened by fiction?

She left the library and went into the foyer, intent on heading for her room. Right before she reached the staircase, she realized the door to the basement stood wide open, the light on. The air seized in her throat as an icy breeze whooshed from the basement like a breath from a glacier.

No. I won't go over there. I won't close the door. It can stay open for all I care.

Her practical side immediately seized on the implications. Why did the door stand open in the first place? She hadn't been in there since the murders. Jared? Maybe the fearless cop in him decided to investigate.

All the hair on her body seemed to stand up at one time.

Maybe the murderer returned to strike again.

Her heart began to hammer, her breath quickening. She turned and went to the kitchen in search of Jared, but when she arrived the room was empty. She hurried back to the staircase and rushed to their bedroom.

When she reached the closed bedroom door, she knocked. "Jared? Jared, are you in there?"

After three knocks she simply opened the door and double checked the room. Frustrated, she tossed her book on the bed and hurried back downstairs.

Seconds later she heard it. A voice, deep and familiar, penetrated the depths of the basement.

"Micky! Micky help me!"

Jared.

Micky froze at the sound of his voice pleading for help.

"Oh, no," she whispered, her throat tightening in terrible anticipation. "Jared!"

Instinct thawed her. She ran toward the door, her heart pounding an erratic beat as she stopped at the doorway and looked down the steps.

"Jared, are you all right?"

"Micky! Micky help me!"

"I'll be right there!" She sprinted for the kitchen to retrieve a flashlight.

After digging frantically through a couple of drawers and finding nothing, she cursed and looked in yet another drawer. "Shit, shit, shit!" She came across the large, baton style flashlight she'd brought with her. "Yes!"

She ran back to the basement door and heaved a deep breath, determined to conquer her panic. Damn him for not believing her when she talked about the vampires and the gargoyle. Damn him.

Micky headed downstairs. Chilly dread raced up and down her body with a slithering caress. As the steps squeaked, she quickened her pace.

"Jared?"

Reaching the bottom, she looked around for any sign of him. Instead she felt the cold air that seemed forever locked in this subterranean lair. The dirty floors sent up puffs of dust as she walked. As she breathed, the air felt gelatinous with something creeping and foul.

Moments later she heard Jared's distinctive voice luring her forward. "I'm in here."

This time the voice sounded deeper, less frantic than before. She couldn't be sure where it came from. Indeed, it sounded as if he was all around her.

She stepped deeper into the room, then heard a strange sound right behind her. Cold hands descended on her shoulders and gripped with ruthless pressure that sent pain sinking through bone and muscle. She gasped.

"Hello, my darling," the voice said.

Chapter Eleven

ॐ

Micky woke to something hard and painful pressing into her back. Her head felt as light as a cloud; thoughts wouldn't string together one after the other. While she lay on her back on a stone-hard surface, she couldn't remember anything about how she'd gotten here.

Disjointed and aching from cold, she felt tears burn her eyes. She writhed a little, but she couldn't move her arms or legs. She tried wriggling her fingers and couldn't. Her arms were pressed down along her sides.

What on earth?

She listened, trying to get her bearings. Water gurgled, the distant whistle of wind repeated in her head. As she caught a whiff of a musty, damp scent, she recoiled in distaste. It smelled like...

A newly turned hole for a grave.

Dread trickled along her spine and fear mocked her to remain composed.

Am I in a grave? Oh God. Oh God.

She launched into self-talk. "No. It'll be all right. I must remain calm."

She tried opening her eyes and succeeded. Intense blackness, penetrated by the barest of light, enveloped her in a coffin of darkness.

Coffin.

Perhaps she lay in her grave, forever separated from everything and everyone she knew. Death seemed to hover near, a symbol of fear deep in her soul. Insidious, the terror rose like a smothering blanket.

"No," she rasped again, her throat dry and aching.

Tears pressed at her eyes, demanding attention. Stubborn, she refused them, unwilling to give into screaming horror even as it clawed at her with razor sharp talons.

She heard whisperings, the voices familiar in an awful way she'd rather not recall.

Was it the same shadow people who flickered at her side day and night and haunted her no matter where she went? Or were they something different?

Voices grew louder, their half-formed words prodding her mind and pushing for her notice. The voices mixed, all angry and wanting a different outcome.

"Are you here to help me?" she asked.

For a second their tones wavered, the voices rising like an ocean tide to overtake her senses and press her into submission.

Another set of voices battled back, urging her not to give in.

Fightitfightitfightit.

Micky whispered back. "Who are you?"

Then, before anything could answer, her memory slammed her back into full awareness.

She remembered the staggering pain along her shoulders and the ice-thickened voice, more evil than anything she'd heard. The voice had sounded familiar. Yes, it was the same voice she heard at the hotel room and here in the tunnels when she'd seen the gargoyle face.

Fear slammed her like a punch to the gut, tearing away her ability to breath. A vice seemed to clamp on her chest, refusing to allow her air.

Micky gained one sucking breath to scream. "No, no, no!"

She cried out as terror wrapped her throat, an uncontrollable knowledge she lay in subterranean night bound by unseen hands. Something bit into her wrists, and a thousand fingers held her ankles and feet to an unforgiving surface.

"Help!" The word parted her lips without thought, a desperation born of heart-wrenching dread. "Someone help me!"

She guessed she must be in the tunnels, and when she turned her head to the right, she saw a pinpoint of light in the distance. An opening? A way out of this hellish nightmare?

Jared. Where was Jared?

Worry rocketed through her. What if something had happened to him because of her? Because she couldn't reach him in time?

"Micky." The voice whispered out of the darkness, as wicked and deep as the darkest pits of an unknown hell. "Your concern for your man is admirable."

Anger overran her fear. "What have you done with him?"

A low chuckle reverberated around the vast area.

As fingers touched her torso, she realized with horror that her coldness and vulnerable feeling came from more than fear. She was naked.

Bare-assed exposed.

She shivered as cold fingers traced her belly button. Startled, she gasped and tried to twitch away. She sensed the invasion was in her mind, and not the touch of a real person. Micky trembled with the knowledge that whatever the fiend did, she couldn't stop him.

Stophimstophimstophim.

"Discover what I can give you," the male voice said, tone seductive. "I can do things for you a human lover cannot. My delights are of the ages, my experience accumulated over a thousand years. I have wonderful pleasures for your breasts, your precious pussy, your tiny clit. I can make you wet, I can even make you want a cock up your ass."

As the voice spoke it licked over her ears and suddenly fingers floated over her skin with enough pressure to warm. Gentle and yet persistent, the fingers first encompassed her hips, then her thighs, down to her calves. Seconds later they encircled her ribs. They landed on her breasts, fingers immediately clasping her nipples in a teasing grip. Rolling, plucking, flicking, the fingers drew her nipples into instant arousal. Astonished by the intensity of her response, she screamed in rage.

She licked her parched lips and swallowed hard before she could speak. "Whoever or whatever you are, I don't want to do this. I don't."

"You will."

A laugh, deep and rumbling, played with her ears and wrapped around her body like a blanket. Unmistakable, it reminded her of a nightmare from one's deepest childhood fears. Disembodied and yet near, it spoke of deeds she didn't want to know.

"I will draw the blood from you as I give you the greatest pleasure you've ever experienced. And you shall be my slave until I find Dasoria."

"You don't want me," she whispered in desperation.

More fingers added to the torture, and she realized it wasn't one pair of hands or even two touching her, but dozens. Warm tingling played with her body and teased like a thousand tongues and fingers. She shivered, not with revulsion, but overwhelming lust.

Need for sexual satisfaction ripped through her like the worst flood, the hottest firestorm. She wanted and she wanted *now*.

As fingers manipulated her nipples, another slipped between her legs and brushed over her clit. With mortification Micky felt her vaginal lips plumping as they slicked with moisture.

A mouth descended on hers and a hot tongue thrust inside. She arched against the hands, writhing under inescapable torture. Fingers stroked her clit with barely there touches, plucked her nipples, and a tongue fucked her mouth with insistent strokes.

Micky's fear vanished under the onslaught. Swirling demands overtook her, sensations both panic ridden and urgent with lust. Excitement darted through her and yet a tiny part of her mind screamed for her to escape, to not allow the bloodthirsty creature to win her body. A furious assault of sensations overtook her, and thoughts of escape slipped through her in mind-numbing despair.

Again and again the tongue plunged into her mouth, the fingers on her nipples tugged non stop, the rubbing over her clit driving her higher and higher.

Something hot and broad touched the lips of her cunt and she gasped. She didn't have time to register a protest, and couldn't have if she'd wanted to as the mouth continued to kiss her. With one spearing thrust the hard object breached her cunt. The mouth released hers and she gasped and screamed as the thick heat speared straight to her center and lodged deep. The object, hard, thick and unrelenting, pushed even harder and she moaned at the exquisite feeling of being stretched tight.

Seconds later something smaller, but no less heated, parted her ass cheeks.

What?

Tentative and probing the warm object played with her puckered entrance, teasing and playing. The fresh erogenous zone made her shiver with forbidden craving.

Seconds later the teasing turned serious as the cautious tickling turned to pressure and invaded. She quivered as her back entrance widened to accommodate the probing. Stunned amazement hit her as penetration continued and dipped into her with slow, easy plunges. Filled fore and aft, she shook as sexual feelings flooded her with remarkable strength.

She whimpered, caught between shame and wanting the never-ending pleasure of being physically overtaken by a thousand hands. With an inevitable sense she couldn't escape, she knew she would have to endure whatever happened.

The creature paused, as if to give her a moment to acknowledge she couldn't resist. One glimmer of loud resistance started at her center, but then it melted as a wavering confusion fogged her senses into submission.

The tiny voice, trapped down deep inside Micky, commanded her attention.

Resistresistresist.

The tongue thrust in her mouth, fingers rubbed her nipples, a hot tongue manipulated her clit, a huge cock fucked her wet channel, another object moved inside her anus with continual strokes. She couldn't take it.

Jared. Oh, Jared.

All she could do is hold on to a fantasy, grip an idea that Jared took her and not this demon of the night. She had no choice. She started to imagine Jared's hands possessed her, tasted her, loved her.

Then a hot pain lanced her neck and she screamed. Whimpering, she tolerated the hurt, writhing what little she could, until the pain faded. A strange languor overtook her, and then pleasure rocketed with pulsating waves. Surging like an ocean against the shore, orgasm ripped through her like a bomb, shredding her defenses as ecstasy tore her to pieces. She couldn't say how long her pleasure lasted. An eternity perhaps, or maybe a few minutes. As she sobbed with rapture and mortification, the torturing tongues, fingers and cocks disappeared, leaving her cold and alone. Her only salvation came in realizing nothing physical had touched her. Her violation had occurred only in her mind.

Everything faded to darkness.

* * * * *

"There must be something else we can do to help Micky and Jared," Erin said as Lachlan stood behind her and massaged her tight muscles. "If we don't something horrible is going to happen. I just know it."

Standing near the roaring fireplace in her living room, her gaze turned to Ronan and Sorley, permanent fixtures in the house. Ronan sat in one easy chair with his legs sprawled apart, his mouth holding an impudent curve she couldn't remember seeing on his fallen angel face before.

Lachlan manipulated her shoulders a few more seconds before he let her go. She groaned with guilty pleasure. It felt so good to have him close to her, and she felt safe with him near. She loved him for protecting her, and for everything within this sexy, wonderful man.

Ronan stood and started to pace. "This is—what would you call it?"

"Soddin' lame?" Sorley asked with a sneer.

"Thank you from the peanut gallery," Erin said.

"Huh?" Sorley's face twisted in confusion.

Erin sighed. "Never mind."

The room dropped into silence again. She felt frustration pouring off Lachlan and the two vampires.

"We can't force Micky to listen to us, lass," Lachlan said. "As much as you want to help her, she has to help herself, too."

She heaved another sigh. "I know, but I feel so useless, and I hate that. I have to take some sort of action. Maybe we should talk to Micky and Jared one more time."

Lachlan turned her to face him. He pressed a warm kiss to her forehead. "And say what? The same stuff we've said before?"

Ronan shrugged, his gaze indolent and almost disgusted. "Bloody mortals, you never can make up your minds. First we say aye, then we say nay. Which is it going to be, then?"

"Cool your jets," Lachlan said with recrimination in his tone. "Erin wants to help. I won't have you talking to her like that."

Ronan's expression changed to contrite, and he walked toward her. His clear gaze, golden with feeling, held sincere apology. "Erin, you know I didn't mean any harm by what I said. Sometimes I forget what it's like to be mortal. It's been so long for me."

Erin understood. "It's all right, really. Maybe you and Sorley are feeling a bit as if you failed? Am I right?"

Sorley nodded and walked away from the fireplace mantle to stand alongside Ronan like a true friend. "We are at that. Every time we've gone to the tunnels the ancient one is off somewhere else. We're timin' this all wrong."

Lachlan made a soft, doubtful snort. "We found him before, we can do it again."

Erin knew her next idea wouldn't be popular. "Perhaps I need to put myself out there as bait. With all three of you around me most of the time, it does make it more difficult to get to me."

A chorus of three voices went up. "No!"

Exasperated, she stuffed her fingers in her hair and held her head as if it might fall off. "This situation is getting worse. More people are being killed almost every day and the police aren't going to be able to stop him because they think they're dealing with a human."

Lachlan slid his hand over her back in a soothing motion. "She's right. We need a better idea. Everything we've come up with lately has fallen flat."

She stopped mussing her hair and turned to him to look him straight in the eye. "What if Micky and Gilda and I present ourselves as bait? A triple treat for the bastard? You could all watch out for—"

The three voices roared again. "No!"

Realizing she wouldn't get what she wanted that way, she spoke from sheer vexation. "Well, do you have a better idea?"

Quieted settled in the room.

Finally, Lachlan said, "You know Tom won't let Gilda participate in this."

Saddened, she realized she hadn't talked with Gilda in a couple of days. "She doesn't even know what's going on. I mean with us. She has to have heard about the other murders. No one can escape that. The reporters running around, the newspaper talking about it. There's just no way anyone could avoid it."

"Why don't you give her a call and assure her everything is all right here. She's probably working at the library right now," Lachlan said.

She reached for the phone and punched in the numbers to the library.

Lachlan turned to Ronan and Sorley. "Let's make it impossible for Thornton to disbelieve."

* * * * *

Jared awakened with a pounding head and wondered what the hell made him groggy and bewildered. He opened his eyes to a room dimmed by approaching night and realized he'd fallen asleep in the attic.

His body ached in each bone, and sudden nausea made him wonder if he was coming down with some shit. He sat up, weaker than he'd ever felt before.

Correction. Maybe he'd felt worse after first regaining consciousness after he'd been shot. But not by much.

Vague memories whirled through is mind and he closed his eyes to quiet his mind. He couldn't remember anything about falling asleep. A slight panic slipped into him, and he fought it back. He couldn't afford to fall down on the job.

No, Micky isn't a job. She's my woman and I want her safe.

My woman.

It might be a primitive way of thinking, but from this day forward he didn't want another man to touch her in a sexual way. She would be his forever.

Forever.

Jared opened his eyes and glanced around the dim room.

He remembered coming into the attic earlier in the day after Micky had stomped out of the kitchen. He knew she needed some time alone, so he'd traipsed up here with the idea of exploring the attic for a few minutes. He'd found a plethora of junk, some valuable antiques, most useless items no one would want. He'd brought a flashlight with him because of the low light in the room. Wintry, dying light cut through the small window, but it didn't illuminate much.

Confusion still held him in thrall. "What the hell is going on here?"

Jared couldn't remember a damned thing after walking into the attic. Frustration added to his jumbled state of mind. He reached for the flashlight and turned it on. He tried standing and found his legs wobbly but strong enough to support him.

Where the hell is Micky?

He shrugged, realizing that if she hadn't gone looking for him, he couldn't blame her. He'd been a bit overzealous in his skepticism. After all anyone, cop or not, would be hard pressed to explain the bizarre things happening in this town. He hurried to the attic door and turned the knob. It wouldn't budge.

A strange, creeping apprehension darted through him. "What the hell?"

He struggled with the doorknob a little longer, then paused. Unless he busted down the door, he wouldn't go anywhere.

So be it.

With the confidence of a man who'd done it before, he kicked at the door with all the force behind his body, allowing a battle cry to usher forth. One kick. Two.

The wood gave and the door swung open. Triumphant, he stalked out of the room and down the stairs. As he reached the second floor, he saw the whole damned house was almost dark. Rather than flick on the lights at each landing, he used the flashlight.

Confusion battled with aggravation as he tromped down the next set of stairs. The amnesia bothered him. *How the fuck did I fall asleep in there?*

His heart pounded a little at the implication something was physically wrong. He knew he was in the best health of his life, but that didn't guarantee anything. He pumped iron and ran almost every day, although he'd been off the regime since coming to Pine Forest.

When he reached the darkening foyer, he saw a light on in the library. He flicked on the light and the chandelier above went bright with illumination. Maybe Micky had fallen asleep in the library.

A crawling sensation rolled over his skin. Then again...

She wasn't in the library. Trepidation sent curls of worry through him. He returned to the foyer and looked out the front windows. In the fading light he saw the shadows of their vehicles.

He rushed to their bedroom and retrieved his weapon, then searched the house room by room. As his concern increased, so did his annoyance. Would she leave the house by foot despite the danger?

Micky, where are you?

With a gut-wrenching epiphany he admitted one thing. If anything happened to her, he would never forgive himself.

When someone pounded on the front door, he ran downstairs and looked through the peephole, every muscle tense. He saw Erin's worried expression, and nearby he could barely see Lachlan.

Speak of the fuckin' devil.

He opened the door quickly, keeping his weapon in hand.

Before Erin and Lachlan could speak, Jared gestured for them to come in. "I'm glad you're here. You've got some explaining to do. Where is Micky?"

They entered, Lachlan's cautious expression pinpointing on Jared's weapon. "First things first. Could you put away the weapon?"

Jared closed and locked the door. "Not until you've answered my question to my satisfaction."

Erin held one hand out. "We're not here to cause trouble. I know we're probably the last people you want to see, but this is very important."

"Wait a minute," Lachlan said. "You asked where Micky is."

Jared nodded, holding his weapon against his thigh. "Yeah." He gave a quick version of what he'd experienced in the attic, and even admitted the disagreement that sent Micky and himself to different parts of the house. "I've been searching the house and I can't find her anywhere."

Jared shifted his stance and Erin gasped. "Jared, your neck."

He flinched, her words catching him off guard. "What?"

"Damn," Lachlan said. "Look in the mirror."

Suspicious, Jared walked to the gilt-edged mirror near the front door in the foyer. There, right near his collar line, were two fine puncture holes. He stared in amazement and disbelief. Speechless, he turned back to them. Jared didn't know what to believe, a sense of otherworldliness making him dizzy. He felt ill again and his stomach lurched. With a groan he touched his stomach as a wave of weakness washed over him.

"He's been bitten by the ancient one." Lachlan's voice sounded hollow, ringing with a nuance of the inevitable. "That must be what happened to you in the attic. You don't remember the attack?"

"No, I—" Jared stopped, irritation increasing by the moment. "No, damn it. I don't remember any vampire attack. That is all crap. I don't know what you did to convince Micky. Now she believes in this vampire stuff as well."

"So you said a bit earlier." Erin's eyes held sadness. "But we didn't have to convince her. She saw what happened in the tunnels and in the hotel room. She saw the face the ancient one presents to humans. The gargoyle face."

"Then why isn't your face like a gargoyle?" Jared asked Lachlan.

"Because Lachlan isn't evil and he isn't a vampire," Erin said.

"Malevolence twisted the ancient one's features into one of the most horrifying faces imaginable," Lachlan said.

A rustling came from behind Jared and he heard two strange popping noises. He turned swiftly, weapon at the ready. "What the—"

Before Jared's disbelieving eyes, two figures materialized out of thin air in less than a blink. Both bodies, one tall and one short, were covered in brown cloaks from head to foot. Jared's heart rammed into overdrive and added to the sickness in his stomach and the increased pain in his skull.

The figures tipped back their hoods. Ronan and Sorley appeared in full glory. Sorley gave Jared a sarcastic grin, as if he liked scaring the shit out of people.

Sorley said, "Do you think you believe us *now*?"

Jared didn't know what to think, and as his heartbeat sped up even more, he cursed his inability to control his physical response. Sweat popped out on his forehead and his palms felt sticky.

"Lower the weapon," Ronan said. "You could pump Sorley and me with a dozen holes, and it wouldn't make a difference. Of course, you're welcome to try if you like."

"Aye," Sorley said with another grin. "If it would make you feel any better."

"Shit, shit, shit, shit." Jared swallowed hard. He felt his skepticism start to dissolve. "All right. Maybe there is something to all this. How long were you guys back there?"

"Oh, just long enough to hear your story, old boy," Sorley said as he let the cloak fall to the floor.

"And what's the deal with the cloaks? Some sort of ridiculous Halloween costume?" Jared laughed, a weak, disgusted sound. "As if a real vampire would need a costume."

Sorley winked. "Oh, you'd be surprised at the outfits I've worn—"

"Can it, Sorley," Ronan said. "The cloaks are to block the sun. Unlike vampires in books and movies, real vampires can spend time in daylight, but it weakens our systems and depletes our powers. That's why we still prefer to operate at night. As for the cloaks, it reduces the effects of the sun. And our ability to go invisible allows us to transport from place to place more quickly and easily."

"No bats, eh?" Jared asked.

Sorley grunted. "Bats, my ass. You mortals really do come up with the most ridiculous fantasies."

"Very few vampires are capable of shifting into animals, but some have developed the talent," Ronan said.

Jared looked from one vampire to the other. "Do either of you shape shift?"

Sorley shook his head.

Ronan grinned. "I don't give that information out to anyone."

Jared snorted. If he wasn't so damned worried about Micky and feeling like he might collapse, he'd see the humor in the conversation.

Renewed weakness assaulted Jared's knees. He felt as defenseless as a newborn and it drove him nuts. "So...which one of you bastards bit me on the neck?"

Sorley chuckled. "Wasn't me."

"Nor I," said Ronan. "I prefer to taste beautiful young women. Men's blood always did leave a bad taste in my mouth. And even at that, I haven't consumed mortal blood in a very long, long time."

"Friendly vampires?" Jared still didn't want to believe, but what choice did he have at this point? "Who bit me then? This ancient one you've all been talking about?"

Lachlan nodded, his expression serious. "That's the one."

A sickening wave of heat passed over Jared and he didn't know how much longer he could hold out against the nausea and vertigo. If he passed out now, he couldn't help Micky. Fresh terror made him stiffen his knees and stand more erect.

Jared swallowed hard around the tightness in his throat. "What if Micky's been taken by this ancient one?"

Ronan's fierce expression eased a little, as if he understood Jared's distress. "We're here now to help, if you'll allow us."

"Allow you? Like I could stop you."

Erin frowned. "Jared, once and for all, you've got to trust us. Micky's life may depend on it. Now you understand you can't fight this creature alone. He attacked you and you can't even remember how it happened. He probably grabbed you first, then snatched Micky. You're lucky he didn't kill you."

Jared's knees threatened to dissolve like melted butter and he struggled to stay upright. He staggered toward Lachlan, not caring if the vampires took him down for a feast. He'd bargain for Micky's life if he must. "All right. What's the first move? I'll do anything to get her back."

"You're in love with her," Erin said, her voice soft with understanding.

"Fuck yes," Jared growled. "I love her."

Jared groaned as another punch of sickness rolled through his body. At the same time, admitting once and for all he loved Micky seemed to give him temporary strength.

"You're sick from loss of blood, man," Ronan said. "Why don't you take rest and we'll—"

"No. I'm going to find her now." Jared looked toward the basement door. "God, I should have looked there first. How could I be so stupid?"

"Take it easy," Lachlan said. "You're injured and weak. It's amazing you're even standing. When I was bitten by the ancient one I was unconscious for a considerable time longer than you were. You're doing damned well as it is."

Jared didn't care. "Help me find her."

Suddenly, Ronan stiffened as if someone had popped him between the eyes.

Lachlan gazed around warily. "What is it?"

Sorley frowned. "Oh, aye. I hear it now, too."

"Hear what?" Jared asked.

"A whimper." Ronan started toward the basement. "And I think I know where it's coming from."

* * * * *

As they crossed the basement, Jared realized he could sense things he never noticed when he'd been here before. The drip, drip of water somewhere. A deeper musty scent. Evil and dark, this placed vibrated with a thousand imps, elementals, spirits willing to torture and maim. Jared shook as he recognized them. Did he feel these things now because he'd been bitten by a vampire?

His mind couldn't seem to take on the concept, even though deep inside it rang true.

A deep male voice, recognizable as Ronan, spilled into his mind. *It is true. Accept it or your reluctance will get you killed. Ignore the evil. It cannot harm you if your soul is pure.*

Jared started, half sure the vampire spoke out loud. *You can read minds? Can I?*

I can read minds any time I want. Lachlan can project and sometimes read some minds. You are much the same as him now.

Does that mean the ancient one can read our minds?

If he is so inclined. Most of the time he doesn't care. He feels too invincible.

Sweating, Jared wiped his forehead, determined to forget this unholy illness and the fear crawling through him. He knew he could learn to live with the changes. He had to.

I can do this. Micky needs me. I've faced worse things in my career.

No, damn it. He had not. He'd never feared for his loved one's life.

As they turned to the left and went down the same tunnel where Micky discovered the young couple, Jared saw more puzzle pieces come together. He realized, too, that if he shut off the flashlight he could see somewhat without it.

"Fuck me," he murmured.

"What's up?" Lachlan asked.

Jared smirked. "I can almost see without the flashlight. Is this because I've been bitten by the vampire?"

"You got it," Lachlan said. "You'll be able to see, hear, and smell much better than you have before."

Jared glanced at Ronan. "So Ronan tells me."

"Reading minds again, eh?" Lachlan said to Ronan with a nonchalant inflection.

Ronan didn't answer, his concentration apparently on surveying the area.

"They're here," Sorley said as he tramped ahead.

Erin beamed her flashlight ahead. "Who?"

"The shadows. The strange creatures that helped us protect Micky in the hotel room."

"Micky mentioned these shadow people." He explained what Micky had told him about her mother seeing shadow people. "Are they guardian angels?"

Ronan moved to the front of their pack. "Perhaps. We're not certain."

"Should I be able to see them?" Jared asked.

Ronan pressed ahead, quickening his pace. "You may be on overload right now. Lachlan, can you see them?"

"I sense something, but I think it's all mixed up with the intensity of everything else that's in these tunnels. Everything that's happened. I can't sort it all out."

Anxiety flared inside Jared. "Will you know if the ancient one is nearby?"

Ronan nodded. "Most definitely. But he isn't here now. We'd know."

This time Jared thought he heard a tiny whimper, so faint as to be almost null. "What was that?"

"*Shhh.*" Ronan put his finger to his mouth as they all came to a stop. "There. At the junction between this tunnel and the next. I think she's there."

Before Jared could blink Sorley and Ronan disappeared.

Jared couldn't help gasp a little, taken by surprise. He looked at Lachlan. "Can you go invisible at will?"

Lachlan smiled grimly. "Not exactly."

Erin clarified. "He can disappear for a much shorter time. Just enough to scare the crud out of me." She took Lachlan's hand and squeezed it. "He moves so swiftly the eye can barely see it. Not quite the same as disappearing entirely like Ronan and Sorley. They can not only disappear, but materialize wherever they like."

Jared shook his head and started to run toward where the vampires had disappeared. His heart pounded a relentless, painful beat at the same time his mind chanted. *Please, Micky. Please be all right. I love you.* Anguish made his gut tighten with a pain more profound than the sickening commotion rushing through his stomach and the throbbing behind his eyes. Nothing mattered but finding Micky and holding her in his arms. He'd battle this weakness no matter how long it took to find her.

A jolt of pain in his stomach made Jared gasp, and he stumbled to a halt. Erin and Lachlan grabbed his arms.

"Whoa," Lachlan said.

Jared wrestled from their grip and kept going. Nothing would stop him from getting to Micky. He rounded the bend and found a surreal scene.

Ronan and Sorley knelt next to a woman's naked body sprawled on the floor.

Not any woman's body. Micky's.

Chapter Twelve

ᔎ

"Micky!" Jared ran toward her and almost knocked Sorley out of the way. "Micky!"

He fell to his knees beside her and checked for a pulse at the side of her neck. When he found a strong pulse, he closed his eyes in relief. Erin and Lachlan crouched next to him. When Jared opened his eyes, he saw bruises around her small wrists and ankles. Her upper thighs also possessed a few small bruises.

Jared lost it. "God, the bastard hurt her!"

Ronan's voice, normally gruff, hushed to a gentler tone. "She'll be all right. Her vitals are strong." Ronan's dark eyes held bleakness. "We need to get her out of here now."

Jared took a shuddering breath and tried to control his temper. He started to reach for her, to pick her up in his arms.

"No," Ronan said. "You can't carry her in your condition. We'll take her upstairs to the living room."

Ronan lifted her in his arms, and in a flash disappeared. Sorley also popped out of sight.

"No!" Jared started back down the tunnel toward the basement.

Erin placed a hand on his arm as caught up to him. "He isn't going to harm her."

Jared's heart rebelled against the vampire touching Micky. He kept walking in spite of fatigue threatening to bring him down.

When they reached upstairs, Jared heard Lachlan secure the basement door. Ronan appeared at the top of the stairs leading to the second floor. "Up here."

Jared didn't give Ronan a glance as he passed him and rushed up the stairs to the connecting rooms. Micky lay in the bed covered by sheets and comforter. Sorley stood over her like a sentinel.

Jared sat on the bed beside her and brushed his fingers over her cold cheek. Dark circles marred her closed eyes, her skin milky white. He grasped her wrist gently and looked at the bruises. "Son-of-a-bitch. I'm going to kill him." He looked up at the others, renewed horror in his heart. "The bruises on her thighs. Tell me the truth. Do you think he raped her?"

They didn't answer, all their gazes solemn.

"Tell me the truth." Jared glared at the vampires. "Tell me now."

He wanted an answer before he allowed this gnawing sensation in his stomach to overtake him.

Ronan kept a straight face. "We'll talk about it later. You need rest. You can't help her now."

Jared wanted to rage at the injustice, the disgust he felt at the probability she'd been raped. His stomach boiled with newfound hatred. "I can't rest. She needs protection."

Ronan clapped one hand on Jared's shoulder. "It'll take more time for you to recover completely from the attack. If you don't want to leave her, sit in a chair and close your eyes. We'll be right outside."

"Are you crazy?" Jared asked as he stood and then looked down at her face. "We've got to get her as far out of town as we can."

"Do you really think this vampire couldn't get to her anywhere on this planet if he really wanted to?" Lachlan asked from the doorway. "We can stay with her and protect her." Lachlan looked at Erin, standing beside him. Jared saw love and concern in the man's eyes for Erin. "We've protected Erin by staying near her at all times."

Erin stepped farther into the room, her gaze straying to Micky. "Let's get more blankets for her and try to make her more comfortable. And I think Lachlan's right. By staying near her we'll keep her safe. And you'll be right by her side when she awakens and needs you."

Jared shivered as a round of shakes made him sag into the chair nearby the couch.

As his consciousness faded he heard them leave the room and close the door.

* * * * *

Micky awoke. This time, though, a soft and comfortable surface cradled her and blankets kept her warm. In the gentle yellow light of the bedside lamp, Jared sat in the big chair to the far right of the bed on the other side of the bedside table. His head tilted back, his eyes closed, his hands griping the chair arms. Alarm and relief raced through her in one sickening jolt. Jared was alive, but he looked so ill with dark circles under his eyes and a strained touch to his lips.

Then she remembered where she'd been and what happened. Her throat closed up with horror as she recalled the methodical, frosty seduction of the ancient one. She shivered, her heart breaking with shame.

Jared would never speak to her again when he learned what she allowed the vampire to do to her.

He would never love her.

The knowledge pierced to the core, blinding her with a flood of tears so abrupt she sobbed.

Although she lay in her bed rather than on a cold floor in the tunnel, quivering raced through her limbs. Sickness swamped her, and for a moment she thought she might vomit. Instead she put her hand over her mouth, and a muffled sound of distress and despair left her lips.

The door creaked as it swung wide and she gasped. Jared's eyes popped open and he jolted from sleep, his body tensing as she sprang from his chair.

"Whoa," Sorley said as he looked into the room. He entered, the rest of the crew ambling behind. "Just checkin' up on you, we are. There's nothin' to fear."

"I can see you're doing well," Ronan said to Jared. "Very well."

Jared's dire frown said he didn't care what Ronan thought. Jared glanced over at Micky and she started in renewed alarm.

She saw his eyes glowing golden before she glimpsed the puncture wounds on his neck. "No. Oh God, not you."

Jared's harsh expression, his hands clutched into fists, made him appear like a hardened, determined vampire. His chest heaved up and down with his breaths, his gaze locked on hers with hypnotic effect. Then his fierceness cleared so quickly she thought she could have imagined his expression.

"Micky." He reached out for her and she flinched. He drew his hand back, a hurt expression narrowing his eyes and drawing his mouth into a deep frown. "What is it? Why are you looking at me like that?"

"You're eyes." Lachlan walked deeper into the room, his gaze watchful with understanding. "I'd tell you to check the mirror but it's too late."

Jared looked in the mirror over the dresser anyway. "What are you talking about?"

Erin sat on the opposite of Micky's bed. "When you feel any deep, intense emotion from now on, there's a good chance you're eyes will turn golden. It's a legacy from a vampire bite."

Micky shivered and nestled deeper under the covers. Her gaze darted from one person to another. "How did I...how did I get here?" Her voice felt raspy, as if she hadn't spoken in years. "The ancient one had me in the tunnels. I couldn't get away. I couldn't...I couldn't..."

"*Shhh.* There's nothing to fear right now."

Erin's soothing tone moved over Micky, but she couldn't stop the fear as it continued to rise. Confusion added to her trepidation. She felt the dull pain in her neck and touched it. "Did the ancient one bite me, too?"

Erin's pained expression and everyone's silence answered her question.

She closed her eyes. "I'm a vampire, then."

Erin reached for one of her hands and held it. "No. You're not a vampire."

Micky tried to feel relieved, but she couldn't. She opened her eyes to look at Jared. "Do my eyes glow?"

Jared sat on the bed next to her, his movements slow. "They did a moment ago when you woke up."

Ronan stepped further into the room. His swagger held an indelible arrogance, something Micky imagined he couldn't remove even if he wanted. At the same time, Micky saw rare compassion and understanding in the vampire's eyes. For a moment she detected something she'd never noticed before in both Ronan and Sorley. They may be egotistical, they may be vampires, but they owned a civilization some mortals didn't possess. She no longer feared them in any way.

You can hear us in your mind. Ronan's deep voice penetrated her psyche.

She gasped and looked at him. A smile parted his lips for a second.

"I heard you in my mind," she said.

A pause existed as reality filtered into her ravaged system. Trauma wracked Micky, and yet part of her refused to be cowed by what happened to her in the tunnel. "I wouldn't have gone down there." She looked at Jared and tears threatened. "But I heard your voice calling me for help."

"He tricked her, he did," Sorley said. "The ancient one can project his voice to sound like any of us."

Jared cursed under his breath, his voice guttural with hate. "Damn that vampire to hell. May he fucking rot."

Micky trembled as she saw the rage build inside Jared, a wildfire anger crossing his face. She feared the level of his temper and yet the fact he cared this much for her—it seared her soul deep. She didn't know what to think, her mind fogged with exhaustion and worry. Erin squeezed her hand, then released it. When she looked at the other woman she saw compassion and a willingness to assist.

Ronan's voice came again. "Perhaps with our combined powers we can send his miserable ass into purgatory."

"Bullshit," Jared said with venom. Jared's voice grated harshly on Micky's oversensitive hearing. "You can't do anything. You didn't stop that bastard from using my voice to lure her into the basement, or from biting my neck and turning me into some sort of fucking freak."

His anger burned Micky like a live thing, hot and bleeding and writhing. "Please Jared, it's not their fault." Again tears came and this time she let them flow down her face. "Please, stop it."

Jared's expression filled with heart-breaking remorse and tender regret. "I'm sorry."

He scooped her from under the covers and into his arms. She stiffened in his tight embrace, wanting his touch so much, though she feared him as well. She'd thought at one point in the tunnels she would never see him again and although Micky nestled into his powerful, protective embrace, the memory of what happened tore at her insides. Too shaken to be embarrassed by her nakedness, she clung to the man she loved.

Loved.

Yes, she'd fallen for him. Hard.

As tears rained down her cheeks, she buried her face in Jared's shoulder. He crooned to her in a tender voice, so unlike the fierce cop or the pseudo vampire face she'd seen moments ago. "Easy, sweetheart. No one can harm you now."

"You'll both be all right," Lachlan said. "It took me longer than it's taking both of you to recover from the bite."

She felt Jared's chin move against the top of her head as he spoke. "How can we be all right? We're not completely human anymore."

When Lachlan spoke, his voice was steady. "You *are* human, as I am. You just have extraordinary abilities. Give yourself time, but not too much time to accept it. Then use your skills to help you survive."

Micky noted the wisdom in his advice and pocketed it away for when she could think clearly.

"Leave them be." Ronan gestured to the door. "We'll be back later to tell you what we'll do from this point forward."

Micky didn't watch them leave as she burrowed deeper into Jared's embrace. He swept his hands over her back with tender regard and affection. He ran his fingers through her hair and over her shoulders.

"You're going to be all right." His voice, thick with emotion, made her tears flow harder. "We both are. If it's like Lachlan said."

He kissed her forehead and then explained how he'd awakened in the attic unable to remember the attack. He then recapped how the others had arrived to help, refusing to back down.

"I suppose I should be grateful to them," he said huskily.

She brushed the tears away from her face and took a deep breath. "Yes, we should be."

He swallowed hard. "Micky, I'm sorry I couldn't protect you. Maybe if I'd believed what you told me about vampires —"

She put her finger over his mouth. "No. Please don't blame yourself. Anyone would be skeptical."

"You weren't."

"At first I was." She told him about the mesmerizing voice that drew her out of town. "That's why I was late that day getting back to the hotel to have dinner with you. But I decided not to tell you."

Remorse entered edged his eyes with regret and his mouth into a frown. "Shit."

"There's more."

She explained about her experiences since childhood with shadow people, and before she finished the story, she knew he believed her. "I didn't want to tell you any of it because of your disbelief."

"Damn it, if I'd only been—"

"No. Please don't. Stop blaming yourself for what's happened. Do you understand?"

A smile reached his eyes and mouth. "Yes, ma'am, I'll try. I'm not sure I can forgive myself one hundred percent. At least, not right now."

She savored his heat and drew the regenerating strength into her body. "You're the bravest man I know, Jared. But you weren't fighting mortal forces in all this. You were up against something evil and powerful. None of us is as powerful as the ancient one. That's obvious." She shook her head. "God, Jared, there's so much to tell you. So much, but I don't think we have time. Lachlan is right. We've got to accept what's happened quickly. I don't think the ancient vampire is going to wait for us to think this through."

Jared's face, so dear to her, filled with understanding and warmth. Although she saw new lines of stress around his eyes, she also witnessed strength growing inside him. He may have been taken down, but he wasn't out for the count.

She cupped his face and kissed his chin. "Are you all right?"

"Now that I have you back in my arms."

Before she could tell him more, a wave of sleepiness came over her. She yawned.

So tired.

He stood up with her in his arms, her naked body plain for him to see. A flare of heat entered his eyes. *There's nothing more I'd like to do than to make love to you right now, but you need rest.*

Jared, we're talking to each other in our minds.

He grinned. *Cool.*

She laughed as he put her on the bed again and helped her slide under the covers. *Wait, can you get my pajamas out of that drawer?* She gestured to the chest of drawers and he retrieved her flannel pajamas.

Her soul filled with renewed spirit of well-being. Despite pain and suffering she'd experienced, she felt lighter of heart, ready to fight for her life and for the man she loved.

He helped her to stand while she slipped the pajamas on. He groaned.

"God, baby, if we weren't both so damned tired, I'd fuck you right now," he said, his voice hoarse with restrained desire.

His rough words, hot and arousing, made her body tighten with arousal. She might have been assaulted by the ancient one, but her desires seemed heightened rather than suppressed. Maybe she needed the cleanness of Jared's touch, the pleasure his body could give her.

His fingers reached to help her button her top and his knuckles brushed over her sensitive breasts. Fiery pleasure prickled through her nipples. When she looked into his eyes the golden glow returned, and the heat in his gaze no longer frightened her.

"I feel different," she said as his gaze traveled over her with longing. "Do you?"

He nodded and licked his lips, hunger etched into his face. "Yeah." But instead of leaning down to kiss her, he stepped back and let her pull the flannel pants up over her legs. "Yeah. I don't think either one of us will be the same. Lie down and get some rest. We'll talk more about it later."

Weariness edged out the building arousal. She yawned again. "Later."

"I'll be right here if you need me."

No sooner than she closed her eyes then she heard a knock on the door. When Jared replied for them to come in, the door creak opened and Ronan's deep voice spoke. "Jared, I need to talk to you a moment."

Jared squeezed her upper arm gently. "I'll be back."

Too tired to worry, she sank into a deep sleep.

* * * * *

"Sit down." Ronan's command set Jared's teeth on edge as Ronan led him into the next room, a large suite with a fireplace and a sitting area. "We have a few other things to talk about."

Although Jared didn't like the vampire's cool tone, he didn't give a shit about arguing. The ache running through his body commanded rest. Earlier he'd felt awake and alert after the nap. Fatigue crept in around the edges of his psyche, his mental processes slowing down to the consistency of porridge. Without a word he sank into a chair.

Ronan stood in front of the fireplace, his gaze strong and uncompromising. The man never had a hair out of place. Without the long black coat that gave him the appearance of a sinister bat, Ronan still looked invincible. A blue sweater, utilitarian and a little worn, covered the man's torso. His jeans and black boots made him appear almost ordinary. Yet nothing about this vampire could conceivably be commonplace.

Despite Jared's new trust in Ronan, his impatience arose. "Okay, let's get on with it."

Ronan crossed his arms and leaned back on the mantle. "There are several things you need to know now that you possess enhanced abilities. You also need to understand something Micky experienced while she was down in that tunnel."

A flicker of fear made Jared sit up straighter. Before he could question the man, Ronan continued. "All of the people murdered in this town this month were taken by the vampire. He came to this town when he tracked Erin here. He believes she's the reincarnation of Dasoria, his lover. She's not his reincarnated lover, but he is insane enough to believe it because she may have a superficial resemblance."

"So he's a criminally insane vampire."

"Exactly."

Ronan lowered his voice and looked over at the connecting door to Micky's room. "Erin was traumatized by her experience with the ancient one when she was attacked by him in the library. But Lachlan was able to get to her before she was bitten. Her friend Gilda wasn't so lucky. Gilda was bitten and seduced." Ronan strode across the room to the window overlooking the back yard.

"And Gilda now has some of the same extraordinary senses?"

Ronan kept his attention pinned to the window. "Aye, but she suppresses them. Eventually she's going to have deep problems if she doesn't acknowledge and accept what happened to her. She's a fine woman, but she's allowing what occurred to isolate her. Erin is very worried about her."

Jared rubbed the back of his neck. "So the long and the short of it is you're warning me about the same thing happening to Micky and me."

"Unless you take control of yourselves as quickly as possible." Ronan turned away from the window and impaled Jared with the weight of his stare. "There's more."

"Of course there's fucking more."

Ronan ignored Jared's harsh words. "You asked if she'd been raped. I didn't answer you for a reason."

Jared's neck muscles tensed again, and his hands clenched into his fists. "Why?"

"With a vampire like the ancient one it's a thin line between seduction and rape. It's more likely he seduced her."

"What?" Jared's heart sped up, his stomach dropping into the cellar. "How can it be a thin line?"

"It's complicated and the details aren't important right now." Ronan shifted, his stance straighter and less relaxed. "No mortal woman can resist the seduction of a vampire, especially not one as strong as the ancient one. A woman's will is not always her own when under the influence of a vampire."

Jared's mind whirled with what he'd just heard. "So she was taken just like Gilda. You're telling me that fucking asshole vampire raped her?"

Ronan put up one hand, as if to ward off the anger bouncing off Jared like powerful waves. "Not in a physical sense, but a mental sense. Because vampires can control other people's minds in many ways, he kept her in place with sheer domination of his mind. You'll have to ask her exactly what he did, but my guess is he gave her a mental sexual experience so mind-blowing she is ruined for mere mortal copulation."

Jared's laugh choked from his throat as he gave into sarcasm. "Copulation is a damned cold word, but that must be what it was. She wouldn't give herself willingly to him."

"No, she wouldn't. The ancient one feeds off unwillingness and takes a victim's fear and anger and it empowers him as much as their blood strengthens him. All of his humanity is gone, and he gets more pleasure from mesmerizing, controlling, and making her so wild she can't stand it."

"You're saying he's given her the best mind fuck she's ever had." Jared heard the bitter sound in his own words.

Ronan nodded.

Jared stood and paced the room, rolling abhorrence for the ancient one coming full surface. "That bastard is going to pay. He's going to pay."

"Micky will need your understanding right now." Ronan's expression didn't change when he said, "She'll have sexual appetites that would seem ravenous to most mortals. At first she might have trouble controlling her needs. She may want an extraordinary amount of sex. If you want to indulge her—"

"Shut up, vampire." Jared stalked toward him. Ronan put up one hand, and Jared felt a clear, but solid wall come between them. He couldn't move past it. "Another parlor trick, vampire?"

Ronan moved toward Jared this time, keeping his hand up and the wall in place. "Call me Ronan. Vampire isn't a word I like used to describe me. I don't hurt innocents and I don't drink mortal blood anymore. I told you that."

Continuing to brim with chained frustration, Jared decided to return the conversation to Micky. "What do you mean an extraordinary amount of sex?"

Ronan let his hand drop and the wall fell with it. "She may want to do things you never imagined she'd want. If she was inhibited before she'll become a bloody wanton in your arms."

Jared couldn't believe what he heard. "She'll want sex frequently?"

Ronan chuckled. "What have I bloody well been saying? I've been trying to be subtle about it, man, but you give me no choice. She'll want to fuck and she'll want to fuck often. If you were highly-sexed before, now you'll be even more so. You should be able to keep up with her appetites."

Jared groaned, but a smile lit his face. "Hell."

One of Ronan's eyebrows tweaked up as he crossed his arms and stared at Jared. "Not exactly what I'd call hell, but then as a vampire my needs are even more incredible. A human woman can rarely satisfy my need to fuck. I imagine Micky would be able to take me—"

"Don't even think about it," Jared said harshly. "If you touch her, I'll—"

"What? Kick my bloody Irish ass? I don't think so."

Jared knew he couldn't hurt the vampire either, but when it came to Micky, he'd do anything to protect her.

Ronan smiled. "Ease up. I don't steal other men's women. Even though I could if I wanted to."

The arrogance in his voice didn't surprise Jared. "Her sex life is none of your business."

"No, but it is *your* business, isn't it?"

Shaking his head, Jared groaned and gave a laugh. "And here I told Micky all about how to deal with trauma after the incident in the diner and the murders in the tunnel. No damned stress management program is going to help us with vampires."

Ronan smiled, and his sudden change startled Jared a little. The vampire possessed mercurial moods out the ying-yang. "You'll get through it."

Jared felt his cynicism rising out of old habit. "Easy for you to say, you can't die."

The vampire winced, almost as if he could feel mortal pain and sadness pass through him. "I died a long time ago." He shrugged. "Go to her, man. She'll need you when she wakes." Ronan headed for the door leading into the hallway. "I'll take the first night watch. Sorley will follow after. That way the rest of you will be able to sleep as normal."

"Normal. Do you think anything will be ordinary again?"

Ronan nodded. "We have to believe that. What else is there?"

With the knowledge that Micky may have been mentally seduced by the ancient one, Jared vowed he would keep her safe if he had to die for her. And he would die for her without a second thought. Above all, he wondered how he could erase the ancient one's sexual talents from Micky's mind. He vowed he would find a way.

* * * * *

In a half doze, Micky almost didn't hear the door open from the hallway. She jolted in fear, her senses hyper with awareness.

Erin stood at the threshold. "I'm so sorry. I just wanted to see if you were all right."

"Come in."

As she sat on the edge of the bed, Erin smiled. She patted Micky's arm and pulled the comforter up a little farther.

"Where's Jared?" Micky asked, a low grade concern starting inside her.

"Lachlan's getting him something to eat. Jared needs sleep, but he also needs sustenance to build up his strength. Just like you do."

"I'm not hungry."

"You will be later. Ravenous, as a matter of fact. Everyone who is bitten by a vampire and survives reacts differently."

Micky pressed her fingers to her temples. "I'll be glad when this headache goes away." She attempted a smile, but it vanished almost before it started. "I'm sorry. I'm whining like a two year old."

"Understandably."

Silence dropped over them until Micky spoke out of curiosity. "What made you come here to help Jared and me?"

Erin sighed, the sound heartfelt. Sadness turned her eyes dull. "I knew I couldn't live with myself if anything happened to either of you. Of course, something did anyway. But I wanted to help."

Micky tried to imagine what Erin or any of them could do. "What's your plan to defeat this vampire?"

Erin stood and walked to the window. She remained silent a long time. "You haven't heard all the details about what happened when Lachlan and I encountered the ancient vampire." Erin turned back to Micky. "It seems like a long time ago, but it really started about two weeks ago. So much has happened since then."

Micky listened as Erin explained Lachlan's encounter with the ancient one, from the burning of his ancestral castle to his parent's death. When Erin reached the part about Lachlan being bitten, tears formed in Erin's eyes.

"Whenever I think he could have been killed and I never would have met him, it makes my blood run cold." Erin rubbed her sweater-clad arms. "Lachlan had heard the ancient one might be here trying to find his long lost love. He also understood the ancient one was working his way toward me and he worried about me."

"He was falling in love with you?"

A gentle, satisfied smile parted Erin's lips. "We had a powerful attraction right from the beginning. When I finally discovered why he could mesmerize me so easily, I thought maybe it was just his powers and not a genuine attraction. But he's proved differently to me."

Erin continued the story, backing up in time to explain how she'd met Lachlan and how he'd devoted his life to hunting the vampire. Erin explained about Lachlan's extraordinary powers and what abilities Jared would have.

Hovering between curiosity and amazement, Micky sat up in bed and asked, "What about Ronan? How does he fit into this? As a vampire I'd think he'd want to help the ancient one, not slaughter him."

Erin returned to the bed, settling onto the edge. "When I first met him I was terrified of his power. But if Lachlan trusted him, I realized I could, too. Ronan is a very, very complex vampire. He won't tell anyone why he hunts the ancient one most exclusively."

"A vampire bounty hunter."

Erin's wry smile said it all. "Of a sorts."

Micky pondered everything Erin told her and one question lingered in her mind. "Do you think we can beat the ancient one?"

Erin's eyes filled with determination. "Lachlan and I are going to Gilda and Tom's house early in the morning to ask them if they'll help us, too."

"You've got another plan?"

Erin nodded. "Lachlan isn't certain it will work, and neither are Sorley and Ronan. But we have to try every avenue. We don't have any other choice."

"How can Gilda and Tom help you?"

"When Gilda was bitten by the vampire she probably absorbed powers just as you and Jared have. One more powerful person against the vampire can't hurt."

Micky frowned. "You don't sound too positive about this."

Erin twisted her fingers together. "Gilda's changed since she was bitten by the ancient one. She doesn't want to deal with the fact she has special powers. She's bottling it up. Instead of making her anger productive she's going along as if life never changed."

Micky remembered her discussions about critical stress management with Jared and Gilda's reaction made sense. "She's trying to avoid the hurt of admitting what happened to her."

"That's right. We talked but I sensed it wasn't enough. She's closed off and I know she's…"

"Yes?"

Erin shook her head. "No, that's confidential. I know her feelings about the ancient one are powerful. She hates him and wants him out of this world."

Micky pulled the covers higher up. "I can't say I blame her."

"Then maybe, just maybe, she can help us get rid of him forever."

Chapter Thirteen

ഇ

Micky awoke before dawn, her senses alert and a surge of incredible energy tingled over her skin like a fuel ignition. She could see well enough despite lingering darkness. Normally night came to the forest so deeply it would be difficult for human eyes to see through the gloom.

Then she remembered. At first she didn't want this extraordinary ability any more than she wanted the others, not for the price she'd had to pay. But as everyone said earlier, she must accept the inevitable to survive.

Taking a deep breath, she felt a hot, hard warm body lying to her left in bed. At first a panic darted through her and she gasped. Then she acknowledged Jared's warm male musk and relief replaced her unease. His hard, dependable presence so near eased dark fears, her jumpiness removed and replaced with pleasure.

I love him so much.

She rolled to her right side. Maybe she could lie here and pretend nothing changed between them.

She hadn't told him everything about the vampires attack, but she must sooner or later. Anything less wouldn't be fair to him. Her conscience wouldn't allow it. If he turned from her in disgust, she would have to live with it.

Jared turned over, his arm sliding over her waist to tug her close. She sighed and nuzzled back against him with satisfaction and contentment.

"Do you want me?" he asked, his voice sounding husky.

The hoarse, tender tone in his voice about broke her apart. "Yes. More than words can say."

"Then show me."

His arm tightened and brought her closer. Enjoyment sighed from his lips and straight into her like a hot fire through tinder. Nothing felt more comforting right now than his touch, his obvious enjoyment of her body, and the deepness of love.

With Jared perhaps she could escape the ancient one's taint forever.

He kissed her shoulder. A fluttering started in her belly and turned to sharp desire. Primitive, her natural call to mate charged forth like a lioness, ready to give in to every hunger she anticipated. Heat blossomed over her skin, a fever from outside and from within.

She wiggled her ass against him.

"Oh, baby, yeah," he whispered low and throaty.

Melting anticipation made her breath catch and she did as he asked. His cock jumped against her backside, growing longer and thicker by the moment. His arousal made her desire run hot and thick. She creamed, and the sensation increased her wanting a thousand fold.

"Yes, yes, yes, yes." She mouthed the words without thought, an affirmation and call for more.

As his lips explored the side of her neck with increasing fervor, tingles raced along her body. He cupped her breast, gently squeezing. His touch felt possessive, claiming and capturing without remorse.

Warm, wet tongue touched her earlobe. "Tell me what you need. I'll give it all to you."

"Oh, Jared, I feel so strange."

"What is it?"

"My desires. They're so hot. So high I feel like I'm in a fever."

Though he said nothing out loud, his mind spoke to hers. *Move against me. Give me your heat. I want it spread over my fingers, over my cock, my lips.*

She shivered as his mind whispered the forbidden. *I'm here to give you everything you want, Micky. Any desire, any position, and any way on earth you want, I'll make it happen.*

His cock rubbed her ass cheeks, a test speaking of forthcoming explorations.

A moan slipped from her lips. *That feels so good.*

How about this?

He palmed her belly. Deep in her most private world, his mind called to her, asking questions. *I know you need me.*

Yes. I want it now.

His breath rasped in her ear as he plucked her nipples, touched her pubic mound. She shivered in profound ecstasy. His middle finger smoothed over her clit, then retreated, then darted over it, then retreated. As the teasing made her flow with cream, she allowed all her senses to center on what he did and how he made her feel.

Nothing in the world mattered but this.

His breath rasped against her ear, his skin rubbed hers. Micky cherished the hair-rough skin against the back of her as his long, muscular limbs twined with hers. Over and over he rubbed her nipples, tweaking and pinching with a consistent rhythm she could no longer withstand. As her gasps and moans accelerated, she breathed deeply of his hot, male scent, taking in his essence. She could never forget him or the moment, no matter what happened from this day forward. Desire built, demanding aggressive fulfillment. They may not have tomorrow, but they had this second without question.

Please, Jared.

Patience.

I want you now.

A wild, feral, unimaginable scenario roared through her head. With a flash she saw what she wanted. Must have. Would have from him.

She wanted his cock in her ass.

His voice, spoken to the air this time, came harsh with excitement. "Oh, God, yeah. Whatever you want."

She didn't care about being embarrassed, worried, or inhibited. None of it mattered now with their lives still threatened and a raging sexual craving eating her up from the inside out.

"Jared." Her voice sounded frantic.

"We need you ready. Very ready. I don't want to hurt you. We're going to do it all. All of it."

Wildness ripped through Micky as her entire body quivered. She couldn't remember feeling this out-of-control before. Something extra crept into their lovemaking, a crazy need to stamp ownership on each other's souls.

His voice came into her mind again. *I'd never hurt you.*

"No," she whispered.

Heat sluiced through her stomach as he stroked her silky pubic hair, then back up with agonizing significance.

As she moved her ass against his erection, he wedged his long length into the crease again. Her gasp of excitement spurred him into more stimulating exploration. With a barely there movement, he moved his hips. He lifted her leg over his thigh so he could reach between her legs. Jared's touch caressed hot, wet flesh.

As he spread her juices with slow touches, a deep ache started in her stomach and pounded between her legs. Her cunt tightened, wanting something desperately to hold onto and caress. She reached down and slipped her middle finger over her clit. Fire burst and she moaned. She threw her head back and his mouth zeroed in on her neck, licking and caressing.

"Yes, touch yourself there," he said.

She didn't hesitate, flicking over the tight, oh-so-sensitive clit.

"Slow and easy," he said in response.

When he turned her over onto her back, golden heat flared in his eyes. He wanted everything she needed right now. Love shimmered in those familiar but different eyes, changed by their recent experiences.

His mind whispered to her. *I do love you. God, I love you.*

Before she could respond in kind, her heart bursting with happiness so profound she could barely draw breath, Jared's special brand of torment returned.

His mouth took hers, his tongue ravenous as he plunged deep inside. As he explored, he kissed like he might never see her again. The erotic slide of tongue against tongue started a hotter reply deep in her slick cunt.

His mental voice came again. *I know what you need.*

His fingers left her breast and with deliberate but careful execution, he dipped two fingers slowly into her dripping channel. *Now play with yourself.*

She did, enjoying the freedom. As she strummed her clit, his fingers sank deep into her, then out again. Deep then out. Deep then out. His mouth clamped down on one nipple and sucked hard, then moved to the other with merciless attention.

Micky cried out. Ruthlessly he sucked her while his fingers did a deep massage treatment, pushing in and out to the beat of her touch over her clit.

All her world centered down to sensations. The brush of finger against clit, fingers stuffed in her cunt, his mouth latched onto her nipple.

She burst into hot, pulsating orgasm, the eruption coming from nowhere as it roared up and swallowed her.

It didn't stop, the throb continuing in her aching cunt, requesting a finish. "Please, please." She couldn't stand it. "Now!"

Jared watched Micky, enjoying the way she begged as it heightened his arousal to a screaming frenzy.

She was beautiful.

Her cheeks went pink as he stared down at her. Lips pouting and red, her eyes glazed with the aftermath of orgasm, she looked like a wanton, thoroughly satiated. Yet he knew she needed more, demanded more. All their sexual encounters before felt weak in comparison to this union, this blending of mind and spirit.

Cloud soft and mussed around her face, silver and gold strands of hair teased at her cheeks and at her mouth. A deep ache started inside him, this time not from a desire to take her, but a desire to love. He knew this feeling would never happen with another woman, a deep need to cherish and protect. He thought he'd loved Katherine, but now he understood what he'd felt for his wife long ago was lust and caring. Not the deep, abiding love of a man mated for life. Jared wanted Micky in his arms forever. Wild, uninhibited feelings raced through him, hammering hard at more tender feelings. Ravenous and ready, he knew he'd do anything and everything to make sure his woman came until she couldn't take any more.

Again her hips arched up, bumping her wetness against his cock. He hissed in a breath. "Easy sweetheart."

She whimpered, her eyes fluttering closed as she rose up against him, her hands searching his back and shoulders with frantic want.

His cock felt tight and so hard he could barely see straight. His balls ached, his body primed for a union that would bring them together once and for all.

He retrieved protection, and seconds later he moved between her legs. Propped on his forearms, he looked down at her once again. A tender smile warmed her parted lips. Then she did something that broke him. Her pink tongue came out to swipe her lower lip.

Thoughts, hot and feral, raced through his mind.

God, God, God. I'm going to fuck her so hard.

Her feathery plea launched into his mind. *Please, Jared. Yes.*

She was going to get the fucking of her life.

Right now.

With a groan he complied and sank deep inside her with one swift plunge. Sliding through furnace-hot folds, sinking as high as he could go brought him paradise. She seemed tighter and hotter than she'd been before, and he groaned as her cunt twitched around his cock. He drew back and slowly thrust. She whimpered in stunned enjoyment.

With a gasp she shimmied against him and he felt her walls ripple around him.

A startled shriek left her throat.

Male satisfaction ripped through him as she spasmed around him in orgasm, her entire body shaking.

"Fuck, yes," he said, his voice guttural.

The delight in her mind penetrated his thoughts. *So hot. So hard!*

He moaned. *There's more.*

Jared started a driving fuck, his enormously hard cock grinding inside her with short thrusts. He pushed up on his hands and arched into her, pressing deeper, deeper yet. Opening his eyes, he watched her eyelids flutter and her mouth open as she gasped for air.

On and on he continued the reaming thrusts. Her pleas turned desperate, begging for achievement. By damn, he would give it to her if it took him all night. In a flash he knew what would get her off. He looped her legs over his arms and pressed her thighs back against her body so her hips came up off the bed completely. As he stabbed deep into her she moaned and bucked in his arms. Jared circled his hips, the motion brushing and tantalizing her clit as he thrust and pressed, thrust and pressed.

Micky thought she would die.

Bliss didn't come any better than this.

She gave herself over to sensation, dizziness encroaching as she breathed in short pants.

Never once in her life did she remember feeling a man's cock like this. Each time he rubbed and stroked high up inside her, touching places she didn't know existed, she thought she would splinter apart. Each movement of his hips as he gyrated drove her to within an inch of screaming finale. His paced quickened as her breath rasped through her lips.

"Oh, shit," he groaned. "Oh, yeah."

Like a wildcat she clutched at his shoulders, feeling her fingernails dig in. As he gasped at the pain he fucked harder, the drag and thrust of his cock sending Micky to insanity and back. His breath came fast and hard, his male grunts adding to her excitement, his occasional murmur of lusty appreciation acting like an aphrodisiac.

With a growl parting his lips he held hard and deep inside her. She shimmied around his hardness, a plea escaping her lips.

"Don't stop. Don't stop."

Before she could draw another breath he drew back and plunged hard.

She gasped.

As if he'd opened a door to a long-buried treasure, her climax burst like a detonation.

She stifled a scream, her fulfillment coming forth as whimpering. Her entire body shot through with pleasure, pulsing out from her clit, throbbing through her belly. Her vaginal walls expanded, then contracted in hard, rippling excitement around all that hard, uncompromising male buried inside her.

For a minute she thought it was over.

Jared drew back and thrust. Again and again and again and again he fucked, pumping until her cunt began to vibrate with yet another climax. She screamed as it hit her, and he came down on top of her and covered her mouth with his. As he thrust his tongue into her mouth, he shoved his hands under her ass to anchor her against his hips. He pumped through each of her contractions until she felt nothing but a long drawn out orgasm taking her up, down, up, down. Tortured by the continual throbbing, she screamed out in her mind.

Finish me!

He thrust one last time. He stiffened, fingers clamping on her ass as he shuddered and quaked and a guttural groan left his lips. Finally he rested quiet against her, his weight pressing her down.

Micky thought it might be finished, but her body felt other wise.

His mind spoke to hers. *More.*

Yes.

Although her limbs trembled, she felt stronger than ever. She knew what she wanted and needed, what she had to have.

What he wanted, too.

He rolled off of her and retreated to the bathroom.

Although astonished by the bestial way they rutted with each other, she didn't want anything else. She also understood the way they made love came from the desire to live, to take each moment like their last. Her love for him ran strong in her veins, a reminder of all they'd experienced and would experience.

Sweat tickled her skin, and although the room was cold, she felt hotter than the fire coals of hell.

She reached down and touched her clit and it throbbed. Amazed and pleased, she caressed her labia and drew moisture from it, then brought up the proof of her arousal and rubbed it over her clit.

With what seemed like only seconds later, he returned.

As she lay on the bed, her thighs spread wide and her hand between her legs, Jared's expression grew blistering with anticipation. His gaze latched onto her hand as she fondled her clit. Hard, male delight flickered in his eyes as he watched her. His chest expanded as he took a deep breath and let it out slowly. He climbed onto the bed and shifted between her parted thighs. Uncertain what he would do, she kept the rhythm on her clit steady.

As he watched her, he reached down and grasped his cock. His sex thickened immediately as he stroked from root to tip.

Root to tip.

Root to tip.

His eyes grew fierce, and his exhilaration created more thrills deep in her stomach and an unrelenting desire for another climax.

Love swamped her, tender and fierce. "I love you."

His smile grew wider, reaching his eyes and spreading in a tender glow. "And I love you." He released his cock. "Turn over, up on your knees."

She did as he said, anticipation warring with the slightest hesitation. She felt like a virgin initiated into ritual, uncertain and yet thrilled by possibilities.

Micky never imagined in a million years she'd be having sex like this. Especially not what they were going to do now.

Startled by the fierceness of her desire, she stopped touching her clit and gave herself over to whatever would happen next.

"Wait." She smiled and left the bed. "I'll be right back."

When she returned from the bathroom moments later, she carried a small bottle of personal lubricant. She climbed back on the bed.

With a sense of anticipation, she said, "To make things even more exciting."

He grinned in appreciation and took the bottle as she handed it to him. She turned her back to him and got down on her hands and knees. His hands rubbed over her hips as he kissed her ass cheeks, then gave them a playful swat.

She squeaked in surprise.

She heard him open the bottle of lube, then the startling sensation as he gently spread a generous amount around her puckered anus. She jerked, startled by the sensation. Part of her was surprised by how much she liked it. Jared massaged her, and it felt decadent and wicked and accustomed her to the sensation of being touched in so personal a place.

"Relax," he said softly.

She felt one finger penetrate her, widening it enough to slip in up to the second knuckle. She gasped.

"All right?"

"Yes."

She shuddered as he removed his finger, then gently pushed inside. His lubed finger felt good, moving with tender strokes designed to arouse.

The sensation felt so different and good she tilted her hips up and leaned down on her forearms to give him better access. For a long time he thrust his finger into her, keeping the tempo gentle.

Thrilled by his tenderness, she closed her eyes and enjoyed.

In.

Out.

In.

Out.

He pushed in a little farther, and suddenly she realized he'd gone farther. Up to the last knuckle, she thought.

In.

Out.

In.

She couldn't stand it. The heat was rising again. She whimpered with the force of it, and she rubbed her clit.

As if sensing her urgency, Jared rolled away from her long enough to sheath himself with another condom.

Although she wanted to climax with a madness that drove her to the edge, she wanted the ultimate experience to come with him inside her. Everywhere inside her.

Oh God. I want him in my ass!

Though she'd told him with her mind what she'd wanted, and he'd started to prepare her, the wickedness, the illicit aspect at once excited and terrified.

Her desires, so much more than before, frightened her.

She slipped from his touch and got off the bed. "What's happening to me?"

Before she knew it, she stood at the other end of the room near the bathroom.

All she could think about was escaping her sinful desires.

"Micky." Jared's low voice, a little surprised, came low into her ears like the purr of a big cat. She caught the flash of his golden eyes as he growled a little in this throat, her name on his lips like a curse. "Micky."

She blinked and he was there.

With gentle hands he pinned her face first against the wall, his big body pressing but not forcing. He slipped his hands around and caught her breasts, immediately trapping her nipples between thumb and finger.

He whispered in her ear, and his hot breath caused shivers to race up and down her body. "If you don't want this, just tell me to stop."

"I do want. God, I want it more than anything." He twisted her nipples and she gasped. "I was just..."

He licked her earlobe, then stuck his tongue in her ear. Again he played her, drawing her nipples into longer and harder points.

"You're afraid of what's happening to us. That we *want* so damn much."

"Yes."

He kissed her neck. "I love you, and I want whatever you want. If this is too much, too soon, we'll stop."

Stop. No, not in a million years.

"I've never done this before, Micky."

A little surprised but gratified, she leaned back in his arms. "You've never taken a woman...that way?"

"Never. You're the only woman I've ever wanted this way."

She hummed with mental and physical pleasure at his confession, her body an instrument of primitive needs.

"I'll tell you right now, though," he said huskily, his voice thick with desire, "All I can think about is getting my cock up your ass."

Micky's libido exploded into overdrive at his explicit description.

The last of her inhibitions slipped over the ravine and crashed at the bottom. "I want you..."

"Yes?" He caressed and cupped one of her butt cheeks. "Tell me."

"In me. I want you in my ass."

"I won't hurt you."

She swallowed hard. Shivering and quaking with passion. "I know."

They returned to the bed, and Jared urged her to place her hands on the bed and lean over. He applied lube to his condom-covered cock.

He encouraged her. *Slow. Slow. We need to take it soft and slow and not too much.*

Micky sucked in a breath as he parted her ass cheeks. She felt his cock probing, then the very tip of him slipping inside her anus the tiniest increment.

Fire ripped into her, a desire so incredible she moaned.

He pulled out. "Did I hurt you?"

"No," she gasped. "Again."

First he reached for her left breast and feathered the nipple, then captured it for rhythmic tugging. As she wriggled against him, Jared tucked about a half inch of cock into her anus. In a little. Out. In a little. Out. The endless cadence made her groan with each thrust and each withdrawal. He punctuated gentle movement into her with a tug on her nipple. Then as he increased the pressure and her excitement escalated, he nudged a little bit more cock into her.

Soon she couldn't think of anything but the drum inside her head, pulsing out the count as he thrust inside her with increasing speed. Micky felt different, her eyes opened to new sensations. Seconds stretched as she opened to his slow, slow touch.

The carnal nature of what they did, the tautness of her around his body, brought her exquisite new pleasure. As he probed deeper she inhaled, amazed, enthralled at his tenderness, and her willingness.

All this combined to set her off. Her body clenched, shivering around his cock as a sweet, incredible orgasm burned deep inside her. Jared let her quick pleasure spread through him. As she tightened over his cock, he gritted his teeth and closed his eyes. Her excitement multiplied his desires. His erection felt so heavy and ready to burst; he wanted her to come until she screamed.

Her nipple stabbed against his fingers as he rubbed it. She shivered and he moved again, sliding into her sweet tightness with the utmost care.

He pushed a little higher until she gasped at the extreme excitement.

Micky thought it couldn't get any better, but it did.

With a growl he tugged her nipple.

She flicked her clit.

Jared stuffed about four inches of his cock into her, but no more. And she knew he was concerned about hurting her.

Her mind whispered. *Just enough.*

With a groan he picked up the pace until his cock slid back and forth in her with steady movements, gentle but enough to increase her delight.

Her finger moved faster over her clit.

Jared's breathing accelerated.

A mind-detonating climax blasted through her, rippling and shaking her body as he pushed in one last time and roared.

She felt his cock grow harder and thicker inside her. Her asshole rippled as her cunt tightened over and over with orgasm. When Micky finally stopped coming, he withdrew from her and wrapped his arms around her waist. His chest worked like bellows.

Quivering with profound satisfaction, she allowed love to swamp her. Wordless, she enjoyed his skin plastered against hers, his hot, hard body a part of the pleasure.

When he left her side, she collapsed onto the bed and snuggled under the covers. Despite the sexual energy once heating the room, it now grew cooler.

Jared returned moments later, and she turned toward him. She swallowed hard as she allowed her gaze to travel over his incredible body. *Jared is raw, ripped, gorgeous masculinity and I love him so much.*

A gentle smile touched his lips as he slipped under the covers with her and brought her close. As her cheek pressed against that solid chest, his powerful arms protected her. What could be better than this?

Nothing is better than this. Jared said to her in her mind.

She smiled. "So you know that I think that you're the most disgustingly handsome man I've ever seen?"

Humor filled his voice. "That's what you were thinking."

"Hmm...I don't know if I'll get used to the fact you can read my mind."

"Only some of the time."

A pause came, but it didn't last long. "Do you think we can learn to control some of these things we can do and feel now?"

He shrugged and his arms moved her in his grasp. "Probably."

Silence gathered around them, and Micky could almost forget they still must be vigilant against the ancient one. What happened to her in the tunnels haunted her, and not even the explosive sex she'd experienced with Jared removed the memories.

"Tell me about it," he asked softly.

She stiffened, fear returning. She squirmed in his arms and he released her. When she sat up, she looked down on his puzzled expression.

"Yes," he said. "I read it in your mind. I felt your fear." He drew in a deep breath. "I know what happened to you, remember? At least, I know part of it." Jared sat up, shifting back on the pillows. "I didn't expect you to be able to make love with me. At least not right away. I figured what happened to you might be too..."

When he didn't finish, she guessed what he meant. "Traumatic?"

"Yes."

She nodded, then shoved her fingers through her tangled hair. She winced when her fingers caught in the mess. "Maybe the trauma pushed me to this edge. You know. Experience sex as raw and primitive as you can to reaffirm life."

He didn't touch her, his gaze cautious. "That isn't a bad thing."

"No."

"But you're thinking maybe what we just experienced won't last."

Damn him for being so perceptive. She didn't want to admit it, so she said nothing.

He crossed his arms. "Micky, what I feel for you isn't going to go away. It isn't an illusion, and it didn't form because we've been bitten by a vampire." He chuckled. "God, I never thought I'd be saying that. I mean, that I've been bitten by a vampire."

He stood up and went to the mirror above the chest of drawers. He turned his head slightly to the side. "The scars are fading a little. Almost as if they're healing. Come look at yours."

She did, standing in front of him to peer into the mirror and peruse her wound. Now the punctures looked like mere raw, small dots. "Amazing."

He put his arms around her and they stared at each other in the mirror.

Jared kissed her head. "You can tell me what happened in the tunnel."

She shivered and his arms tightened. "I don't know."

"Too soon?"

She smiled weakly. "Is this more of that critical incident stress management stuff?"

Returning her smile, he said, "Yeah. Think of it that way."

Again she lapsed into silence, until the quiet grew intense. "I couldn't get away from the ancient one." She caught his gaze in the mirror and held it. "And I couldn't stop being aroused."

Micky's face went pink with embarrassment, and she wished she hadn't said anything.

"It's all right." His hands palmed over her stomach in a motion more soothing than sexual. "You can tell me."

When she shivered he urged her back to bed. Once again warm under the covers, she told him each excruciating detail of the ancient one's mental violation. When she spoke of the anal invasion, his arms tightened around her.

Fear sluiced through Micky. "Maybe that's why it was so easy for me with you. He—"

Her voice broke as tears clogged her throat.

"No, no." He brought her closer, his touch warm and forgiving. "You opened to me. You allowed me to love you. Together we'll erase what happened to you. Together. The ancient one was in your mind, Micky. He made you believe certain things were happening to you when they weren't."

Reassured, she snuggled into his embrace and allowed cleansing tears to flow.

"I'm sorry you couldn't tell me about the shadow people earlier, or the other times you had contact with the ancient one." Jared's voice held true remorse.

She pulled from his embrace and propped up on one elbow. "You needed evidence first. I understand that."

He caressed her shoulder, then touched her face with the backs of his fingers. "Thank you, Micky. God, I wish I'd met you long ago. Long before I met Katherine."

Her breath caught at the implication behind his words. Speechless, she saw the turbulence in his eyes. She searched with her mind.

What are you saying, her mind asked him.

He grinned. "I would have fallen for you then."

He drew her back into his arms and kissed her. Deeply, hotly, with a power that needed no translation, his kiss devoured resistance.

His mind said, *I would have married you then.*

Startled bliss made her break his possessive kiss. "Married me?"

Jared's eyes glowed, green-gray sparkling with shimmering, molten gold, hot with desire and the need for her to understand. "When this hunt for the ancient one is over, will you marry me?"

Micky's heart leap, staggering pleasure bursting over her. Her eyes filled with joyful tears. "Yes. Yes."

* * * * *

As Lachlan and Erin drove down the semi-deserted streets of Pine Forest that morning, Erin realized one thing. "Halloween isn't going to be the same anymore after this year."

Lachlan grinned. "That's for sure."

They passed store-fronts still decorated for the season, and some even presented posters reminding people of the upcoming community party.

"October will come around every year and each time we'll think about what happened this year," Erin said.

"But we'll have to forget it some day. At least the pain will have to ease."

"Or we'll never be able to stay here."

Lachlan glanced at her, then immediately went back to the road. "Exactly, lass. Old wounds will heal if we let them. But maybe, after this is all over, you and I can leave for awhile."

She smiled. "I wondered when you'd bring that up."

His returning smile, filled with love and a moment's laughter, made Erin feel light and without care for at least one moment. "What about Scotland?"

"You know I've always wanted to go there."

"Then it's a deal."

At least they'd have something to look forward to, and Erin cherished the thought deep in her heart.

As they passed some news station vans from Denver and Colorado Springs sitting on Main Street, Erin said, "All this publicity."

Lachlan grunted. "You'd think the reporters would be afraid for their lives coming here."

They arrived at Tom and Gilda's house and pulled into the driveway. Although they'd called ahead to let them know they were on the way, Erin half expected her old friends not to be there. Tom's voice on the phone had been distant and nothing like the man she'd known before the attack on Gilda.

She stopped halfway up the sidewalk. "How can I ask Gilda and Tom to put themselves in danger for us?"

Lachlan slipped his arm around her. "You wouldn't ask if we could think of any other plan."

They proceeded to the doorway and knocked, then waited for Gilda or Tom to open the door to their home. A few moments later Tom stood there, his gaze more cautious than welcoming.

"Come in," he said with a slight smile.

Once they stepped inside and Tom took their coats, Gilda came into the foyer and spotted them. Her long red hair was piled in a bun, and her pale face looked pinched with worry. Dressed in a thick white cable sweater and jeans, she appeared uneasy. Nevertheless, she came forward and greeted them with hugs and a kiss on the cheek.

Lachlan spoke as they headed into the living room. "We're sorry we gave short notice."

"It's all right." Gilda gestured for them to take a seat on the couch. "You wouldn't be here if it wasn't important."

Tom came back into the room and offered them drinks. Erin decided maybe wine would settle her rattled nerves, while Lachlan asked for water.

When Tom left the room, Gilda talked about non-consequential things, as if she didn't want to launch into a serious discussion until he returned. Once he arrived with the drinks, she accepted her whiskey and took a sip. Tom settled on the love seat some distance from Gilda, his attitude striking Erin as remote. Something just wasn't right; Tom normally sat next to Gilda and showed undeniable interest in being near her.

They'd both changed, and it seemed not for the better. A lump grew in Erin's throat as she recognized how much the ancient one's attack tainted Gilda and Tom's relationship. She thought back to Micky and Jared and hoped the same thing didn't happen to them.

Lachlan told Gilda and Tom the proposal. When he finished, Tom eyes flashed with barely suppressed anger. "You're suggesting she join up with the rest of you to use her so-called powers to fight this monster. Do you realize how dangerous this is?"

"Of course," Lachlan said. "But right now Pine Forest is in the ancient one's grip. We've got to do something. If there's one universal truth I've figured out in my life, it's if you do nothing, nothing happens. Right now we're maintaining, but we'll never be free of this vampire if we don't act."

Erin jumped into the conversation, eager to make her friends see Lachlan's point. "Gilda, you've noticed that there are things you can do now that you couldn't do before the vampire bit you. You can use those abilities to benefit Pine Forest instead of hiding from your new skills."

"You think I can make a positive thing out of what happened?" Gilda asked.

Erin felt the answer with all her heart. "Yes."

"She isn't going to do this," Tom said, his voice firm.

Gilda tossed a glance at Tom, her lips going tight as she took a deep breath. "I'd like to speak for myself, please."

Tom's eyes went from flame to twin chips of ice. The freezer burn came through loud and clear. "Gilda's not strong enough for this."

"I understand how you must feel, Tom," Lachlan said. "I know when I've thought Erin would be in danger I've tried everything I could to protect her."

"So why are you asking me to let Gilda do this, then?" Tom asked.

Lachlan took a deep breath and let it out slowly. "Because this is her life, and she's got to reclaim it. Sitting here in this house isn't going to do that."

"Things are still dangerous, I'll admit," Erin said. "The newspaper said they're going to have the community party no matter what. Even the people of Pine Forest are trying to living their lives despite everything that's happening." Erin's throat felt like it would close up. "The paper said there's going to be a community meeting today to discuss the murders. The natives are getting restless, I guess. They've lost confidence in the police to catch the murderer. But you and I know they can meet all they want. If they don't understand who the enemy is, all their planning comes to nothing."

"Why does it have to be Gilda to help you out?" Tom's gaze pinpointed them with laser-sharp disappointment. "She's already been through enough hell to last a lifetime."

Eager to assure him, Erin said, "Micky Gunn and Jared Thornton are now in the same boat." She explained about the attack on them and their transformation into people with extraordinary powers. She also told them about the shadow people who may have helped Micky and kept her from being murdered by the ancient one.

Gilda's gaze cleared of tears as she took a deep breath. "I understand what I need to do. I've been...I've been hiding away. I go to the library and then come home and I don't go anywhere else ever." She glanced at her husband, then down at the whiskey glass in her hand. "I've been sticking my head in the sand pretending this menace doesn't exist and that if I only do that, it can't harm me."

"But that sick bastard vampire *did* hurt you," Tom said, his voice rising. He glared at Erin with unusual menace. "And why hasn't this ancient one come after you again? I thought he believed you were some reincarnation of his old lover."

Erin shook her head. "I'm not sure, but I think it's because he's been preoccupied with regaining his strength and he toyed with Jared and Micky because they were convenient. It's not as easy to get to me because Lachlan, Ronan, and Sorley have been around me most the time."

Gilda put her glass down on the coffee table and turned toward him, her eyes pleading for understanding. "I can't hide here in the house for the rest of my life. That's no kind of life at all."

Tom stood slowly as he looked at Erin and Lachlan. "I'm not sure we can do what you want."

As Gilda shot an annoyed look at her husband, Erin felt emotional pain grinding in her heart. She never wanted her friends to alienate from each other, but it seemed it was too late.

Gilda said nothing as Tom headed down the hall toward the bedrooms.

We may be at a dead end here. Lachlan's voice rang in Erin's head and she looked at him.

Why don't you talk to Tom alone and I'll stay here and talk with Gilda?

Lachlan nodded and stood. "I'll be right back."

After Lachlan left, Gilda gave Erin a weak smile. "I take it you were communicating telepathically? I can't do that with anyone, not even with Tom."

Erin hesitated to speak her mind on the subject, but she did anyway. "My guess is that if your connection is weakened you might not be able to communicate telepathically. Apparently these powers are random. Lachlan can read minds, move quicker than the blink of an eye, and he can sometimes mesmerize. He's also stronger than the average man. Ronan says it's different for everyone." When Gilda nodded but said nothing, Erin continued. "Listen, I know it's none of my business—"

Gilda laughed softly. "But you're going to ask anyway." Her smile this time warmed her eyes. "Go ahead. Ask away."

A little more relaxed, Erin reached for her wineglass and took a sip. "I noticed the tension between you and Tom. You've gone from being one of the most secure couples I've known to cool distance. Is it my imagination?"

Gilda shook her head, and she looked down at the floor. "No. I was honest with Tom about what happened between me and the ancient one."

An ache started in Erin's gut. "When did you tell him?"

"Yesterday morning. I was reacting differently to him and he kept asking me what was wrong." Gilda shrugged. "So I told him. I broke it to him gently and explained I didn't want it to change our relationship. But you can see it has."

Erin felt Gilda's hurt down to the bone. "He knows you couldn't help what happened, right?"

Gilda looked up slowly. "He says he does, but that's not the way he's acting. We'll just have to work through it."

Conflicted, Erin hesitated to press forward with any demands. "Maybe Tom is right. Perhaps you shouldn't join our little coalition against the ancient one."

"Is there ever going to be a right time?" Gilda stood and went to a window. Sunlight streamed in as the day gathered strength. As rays fell over her face, Gilda tipped her head back and took a deep breath. "Maybe he thinks I'll be seduced by the ancient one again."

Erin wanted Gilda's help, but how could she continue to ask now? "We shouldn't have asked you."

Gilda's eyes filled with regret. "No, I'm glad you did." She leaned back against the window sill. "I love Tom with all my heart, but I have to follow the path I think is right."

Renewed hope surged in Erin's heart. "What is the right path?"

Without hesitation, Gilda said, "I'll help you."

Chapter Fourteen

ॐ

Early afternoon sunlight speared into the formal dining room at the inn, the dazzling brilliance of hard-crusted snow hurting Micky's eyes. Before she turned away from the wintry portrait and back to the group, she pulled the shades over the windows in deference to the vampires present. Although they would only be in the light a little while eating lunch, she wanted to accommodate them. Erin flipped on the overhead chandelier light.

Because the house became chilly overnight even with the central heating on, Micky wore her heaviest sweater. The clink and clatter of utensils and dishes dominated the room for several moments.

Things still seemed a bit loud to Micky, noises reverberating in her ears, her eyes seeing details they never could have seen before. Being transformed into a half state of vampirism had its disadvantages.

"We've come up with a new plan now that Gilda has agreed to help us," Ronan said as he glanced at Micky. "We'll need Micky's approval."

"Why my approval?" Micky asked.

Lachlan put down his coffee cup, his eyes solemn. "Because this is your property. Your life."

"Her life?" Jared asked. "What the hell are you talking about?"

Jared's typical bluntness didn't surprise Micky. She felt a war coming on, not between the men, but between forces of both good and evil dancing within the house and this town.

"Tell us about it," Micky said.

Sorley launched into explanation first, his lilting voice grating against her ears a bit. "Good forces seem to surround you and so do bad."

"The shadow people?" Jared asked.

Sorley nodded. "I've caught some looks at them while I've been here and so has Ronan. Yet they seem to communicate most clearly to Micky."

Micky reached for her coffee. "I've always seen them in flashes, nothing else. No full images." She pondered for a moment. "Although when I first came to the inn this time, I heard them."

"Heard them?" Erin asked, her eyes curious.

"I forgot to mention that earlier. They whisper to me. I've heard them in the main house and the tunnels. I can't understand what they're talking about most of the time. Mrs. Drummond told me Uncle Carl used to talk about seeing shadows, too. My mother saw shadow people apparently. It must run in our family to be able to see them."

Ronan cleared his throat as he took a small bite of toast, then grimaced and put it down.

"Something wrong with the human food?" Lachlan asked with a grin.

Ronan's returning smile said he didn't begrudge his friend the teasing comment. "Frankly, I need another shipment of blood."

"Please, let's not talk about blood at the table," Erin said as she glared at Ronan.

He laughed. "Sorry."

Micky liked the levity, her stomach up to the task of talking about blood. She didn't even mind segueing in to a different direction. "What's your theory about shadow people, Ronan?"

He leaned back in his chair, his relaxed posed arrogant and powerful. "The shadow people, as you call them, are still a mystery to those of us who've been around hundreds of years."

"Glad to know there's something you don't already know," Jared said with a dry tone.

Instead of rising to the bait, Ronan continued. "Vampires have known about shadow people as long as there have been vampires."

"Which is how long?" Jared asked.

Ronan narrowed his glittering gaze on the other man. "For as long as there have been mortal humans."

Jared put one hand up. "Someday I'm going to need a better explanation about how vampires came to be."

Sorley laughed. "Now that's a long, long story."

"One we don't have time for right now," Ronan said. "Shadow people are of both varieties, good and bad. I think you've had the good variety, the protective kind hovering around you all your life, Micky. They frightened you only because you didn't know who or what they were." Ronan shifted his chair back and propped one booted foot over his knee. "Then there are the shadow people who've arisen from the depths of evil."

"From hell?" Jared asked.

Sorley snorted a laugh. "Vampires don't believe in hell." Before anyone could ask for an explanation as to why, Sorley said, "Shadows come from the highest and lowest forms of life. They are as all things are, good and bad. Sure, and without one there can't be the other."

Ronan took over where his friend left off. "As with humans, elements of the spirit world must make decisions on which way they'll go."

"Such as?" Micky asked.

Ronan paused, and the room moved into eerie silence.

Ronan blinked. "Shadows decide whether they will turn to the darkness or to the light."

"I thought all vampires were damned," Jared said.

Sorley's disgusted expression said it all, but he spoke anyway. "That's rot. Stuff of movies and books. Vampires are a natural state of this earth."

Jared's eyes took on a sharp element scorching with golden light. "Like shit."

Ronan's eyes flashed with fire, then Sorley's gaze echoed it.

A little alarmed at the heat rising in the conversation, Micky reached out and touched Jared's shoulder. "Down boys. We haven't got time for testosterone overload right now."

Lachlan chuckled, and even though Sorley looked offended by Jared's remark, Ronan's antagonism disappeared like a lightning bolt.

Things started to fall into place for Micky. She chewed a last bite of toast. She took a deep breath and looked from face to face. Everyone's expressions showed confusion and interest.

"What do these shadow people have to do with the ancient one?" Jared asked.

"With our combined powers, we'll hunt the ancient one," Ronan said.

Jared's mouth popped open, his eyes burning yellow with heightened emotion. His mouth thinned into a frown. "That's crazy. We're going to confront him head on?"

Lachlan put his coffee cup down on the saucer and it clattered. "That's what we did last time we brought him down."

Micky knew what they'd done in the graveyard with Erin shooting the ancient one with a silver bullet. "You've got more silver?"

Lachlan nodded. "But that will only be a standby. We may not need it this time."

"Pretty ineffectual on the whole, I'll admit," Erin said as she shook her head. "It may not prevent the ancient one's return any more than the last battle did. All we can do is experiment until we get it right."

Ronan's gaze once again took on the heated glow of a vampire. If Micky hadn't known he possessed goodness, she would have been frightened by the mere sight of his bristling force. "We must train today for what is ahead."

"How?" Jared asked.

"Much as we did when he attempted the attack on Micky at your hotel room," Lachlan said.

Jared's voice stayed cool and cynical. "Well, I was having my ass thrown across the room at the time. I don't remember much about that. Explain again."

Ronan took his knife and held it in his hand like a dagger, the grip facing down and the pointy end at the table. "Our main objective is to drain the ancient one of power."

Jared looked skeptical, and Micky could tell that although he wanted to accept the supernatural, he sometimes slipped back into incredulity.

Sorley also moved his plates aside, and he placed his hands on the table. Lachlan and Ronan did the same. All three men closed their eyes and took a deep, coordinated breath.

Before she could blink, she heard Jared gasp. His eyelids fluttered and he started to slide down in his chair. Alarm raced through her as she reached for his arm. "Jared."

"It's all right," Erin said. "They're demonstrating how they can sap someone's power."

"Stop!" Micky said as Jared's head went back and his eyes closed.

Lachlan and the vampires opened their eyes and removed their hands from the table. Jared's eyes flickered open and Micky noted the hazy, somewhat dazed expression in his eyes.

"What did you do to him?" Micky asked in irritation.

Sorley put up one hand in defense. "Getting your panties in a wad, you are."

"You're damned right I am." Micky's voice rose as she took Jared's hand and rubbed it. "Jared, are you all right?"

His eyes cleared immediately, but to her amazement he didn't look angry. He kept her hand in his and his grip tightened. "I'm all right. I understand what they're trying to do."

Sorley's long suffering sigh would have been funny if it hadn't goaded Micky. "Thornton here seems to need constant demonstration."

She started to protest, but then Jared squeezed her hand gently. "They're right. You know what they say about old habits. I do need proof despite everything I've seen."

Micky started to understand more herself. "The ancient one doesn't need to maintain contact with someone physically to drain them. That's an advantage he has."

Ronan crossed his arms. "He can do pretty much whatever the hell he wants."

Jared's frown deepened as his grip on her hand increased. "What you're telling me is that we'll have to all touch as we confront the ancient one. And one of us will have to touch the ancient one."

Sorley and Ronan nodded in unison.

Silence covered the room before one word came from Jared's lips that described the whole situation. "Shit."

"Even then there's no guarantee we can beat him," Sorley said.

Micky felt a lump growing in her stomach like her food didn't want to digest. She stared at the sparkling crystal goblets on the table in front of her. "How do we get him to take the bait? Micky gazed around at her friends. "I'll do whatever it takes. I'll dance naked in the snow if I have to."

Sorley chuckled. "Bugger. That would do it for me."

"Fuck you," Jared said with a growl.

Sorley bristled, his half-smile turning to a sneer. "Sorry, buddy, you're not my type."

Micky glared. "Damn it boys, cut it out."

Jared turned toward her and clasped both her hands, forcing her to face him. "You're not going to be bait for that asshole. Naked or not."

Micky stared at him for a long moment. "I've got to. We must end this now and it's my decision."

Ronan broke through the heightened tension. "You'll be there to protect her, man. We all will."

Ronan explained how they would train for an hour projecting their auras around their body as shields and how they would use white light as a projection to attempt a draining or destruction of the ancient one.

"What if we're trapped with him in the tunnel?" Erin asked. "What will we do then?"

Ronan and Sorley looked at each other. Ronan finally spoke. "I'll have the gun with the silver bullet and I won't join the circle."

"At the very least," Lachlan said, "the bullet will slam him down like it did the last time."

"You mean you just can't stake the bastard?" Jared asked.

Sorley laughed. "More bullshit tales made up by mortals. Only if you have a stake made of silver, and only if you can somehow drain his power enough to keep him prone."

"So how do you fight vampires on your own?" Micky asked Ronan.

He sighed and made a dismissing gesture. "It's always a one-on-one fight with other vampires. Only a fool would fight the ancient one alone."

Micky realized she'd committed to a path that could end with her death. In all their deaths. She didn't know whether to run in stark terror or face her demons.

Ronan speared her with a glance. "You can do this. We all can."

Jared's eyes held fear and continuing objection. "We need to talk, Micky. Alone."

She pushed back her chair and stood. "We won't be long."

Without further hesitation, she followed Jared out of the room.

Jared led the way upstairs, and she went silently. She felt the tension crackling off him like a live, exposed wire. When they arrived at their room he drew her inside and closed and locked the door.

When he turned to her Jared's eyes burned. "Don't let them pressure you into anything you don't want to do."

She went to him, eager to erase his worry. She cupped his face in both hands, brushing over his skin with a tender caress. "I'm doing this because if I don't, the killing will go on."

He brought her into his embrace and buried his face in her hair. His voice held despair. "I won't let you."

"You can't stop me." She twined her arms around his neck.

"Fuckin' A, I can't," he growled. "I love you. Do hear me? I love you."

Tears filled her eyes. "And I love you."

With one hand he stuffed his fingers into her hair and wrapped his other arm about her waist. Before she could protest his mouth came down on hers.

Lightning seemed to flow through her, the crackle of emotion filled with heat. A heat more brilliant than fire, more lasting then the sun, just like her love for him.

With a sob against his searching lips, she clutched him closer and surrendered to a burst of lust. She would take him now and brand him on her soul forever. No matter what happened today she would have one last taste.

His tongue searched her mouth like a starving man.

She tore her lips from his. "Make love to me now."

He stared down into her eyes, his passionate gaze more potent than anything she'd seen from him before. Within those depths she saw love, hunger, and strength. With that knowledge she reached for the waistband of his jeans.

He helped her, and when Micky freed his erection for her touch, he groaned in enjoyment. Almost frantically he lifted her sweater and opened the front clasp of her bra. Without preliminaries he clamped his lips over her nipple, sucked hard and drew his tongue over her flesh as he tasted.

She writhed in beautiful torment, her breath sluicing in and out as heat filled her breast and swirled all along her body.

Wanting to give him equal pleasure, she pumped his cock once. Twice. The silky texture, the raging heat under her fingers made sweet, hot liquid form in her center.

He stilled her caress, his cock growing full and hard within seconds. "No more."

As their breathing increased, love and lust running hard, Jared helped her remove her shoes, then worked on her jeans and yanked them down her legs. Within a few moments he'd stripped her naked. He paused long enough to devour her with his ravenous gaze.

Micky wanted to scratch and beg and bite. She'd never experienced a more primitive desire, a more needful sensation clawing at her insides. She didn't take the time to wonder if what she sensed had anything to do with her new state of being, or if she would have felt this with him before her transformation. Now she wanted Jared inside her with a driving passion eating at her insides and glowing in her mind like star fire.

Shucking his clothes quickly, he grabbed a condom. She took it from him, eager to roll it over his cock. After tearing the package, she took her time sliding it down, down over his thickness. He groaned as he watched her cover him. When she reached the base, he put his hand over hers to stop any more tantalizing touches. Instead he drew her into his arms and took her down on the bed with him. He covered her body and nudged his erection between the hot, needy folds between her legs. She gasped and surged up against him. Now was the time. Now.

"Look at me." His voice filled with hunger. His eyes flamed into golden sunset, and she knew her gaze must look the same.

Vulnerability almost made her refuse. Nakedness came from more than lack of clothing, but from bearing one's soul.

"Please." His voice, this time equally defenseless, asked for her compliance.

She kept her gaze linked with his as she gripped his broad shoulders. Steady and true he pushed, sliding hard and high into her body. As he touched as deep as he could go, she shimmied around the sensation.

A gasp of bliss left her lips. "Feels so good."

An eager heat begged her to ask for completion, to demand a hard fucking to reach the pinnacle sooner. Instead she kept her gaze locked with his as he withdrew, then plunged slow. He pressed hard each time he bottomed out inside her.

While they'd rushed to make love, now he kept the motion measured, a sweet thrust and recoil. Again he pulled back, again he parted her hot, sensitive folds. She wondered if she could stand it, enthralled by the way he made love to her with gentle regard. They may have gone after each other like animals, but something had changed.

She needed to remember this time, if indeed it was the last time. What they did here and now became a union of love and lust, a proper tribute to their need for each other.

Jared's withdrawal and thrust seemed to last a lifetime. She could no longer keep her eyes on his as the ecstasy rose, threatening to throw her over orgasm with the next soul-spearing thrust. She closed her eyes and surrendered to sensation.

As she dug her fingers into his arms to anchor to the world, Jared buried his face in her neck.

He thrust and she moaned softly. "Yes."

With a growl he drew back and slammed inside her. She writhed as every inch of steel-hard cock penetrated, then retreated. Again and again he moved, his pace mounting. Push and pull back, the driving motion gaining strength as her cries escalated. She felt the inevitable rise to the top, the call to her senses to submit.

Micky knew in that moment the man she loved now would be the man she loved forever. She grasped onto the knowledge fiercely, like a tigress defending her own. Jared was hers and she'd be damned if any vampire would take him from her.

Bathed in elation, she followed the cadence of their bodies as her breathing quickened and her heart pounded. As he drew her to the top with a last stabbing thrust, she whimpered in the greatest pleasure she'd ever known.

Jared's voice echoed in her head. *Give in to it. Feel the freedom.*

She did.

Allowing climax to fling her to the skies, she moaned as furious pleasure rocked her and took her to heaven on earth.

* * * * *

Sun broke through shimmering high clouds as Micky stepped outside into the crusted snow. The burden of her decision to step into harms' way reminded Micky this wasn't a game. Jared slipped an arm around her as the stood in the back yard. The amazing love she'd found with Jared sustained and gave courage. Yet she worried about him and the others.

Gilda and Tom stood nearby, while Ronan and Sorley were nowhere to be seen. Erin and Lachlan slipped into the yard, their pace steady as they walked toward the grouping.

Micky's attention turned to the man and woman she'd met only today. Gilda's stocking hat covered her long deep red hair, her features pale. Gilda had nervously looked about when Lachlan explained earlier that Ronan and Sorley would remain cloaked until they deemed it the right time to appear. If what Lachlan and Erin said about Gilda's reluctance was true, Gilda felt more than awkward about her growing powers.

"Sure you want to do this?" Tom asked as he looked at his wife. Worry drew his mouth into a deep brown.

Gilda nodded and drew her hat farther down over ears. Her gloved hands shook a little. "I'm ready as I'll ever be."

Micky's compassion mixed with a raging desire to start tracking the ancient one. Since the vampire had mentally violated her and changed her so that she would never be the same, Micky realized she was a more assertive person. Maybe, in some ways, the added capabilities she owned would be productive in other ways.

Slipping away from Jared's side, she went to Gilda. Gilda's eyes flashed with emotions, fear and jumpiness foremost among them.

"I understand how you feel, Gilda," Micky said. "I'm sorry we don't have time to get to know each other better right now. We're asking you to do something very dangerous. I can't tell you how grateful I am that you've come to help us."

Gilda's gaze cleared to calm as she took a deep breath. She twisted her gloved hands together, her breath puffing in the cold air. "I thought about the innocent people that thing killed just in the days since he attacked me. It's the least I can do."

Jared came to their side, his footsteps crunching as he walked. He looked at Tom. "You know I understand how you feel. You're worried you can't protect Gilda. But I think if we all work together, we can't be stopped."

Tom smiled, but his eyes held desolation and apprehension. "Thanks. I'll do everything I can."

Lachlan moved toward them. "We'd better get going." He looked around the area. "I feel something —"

Two strange popping noises came out of nowhere. With a *whoosh*, two brown monk-like cloaked figures appeared near them. Gilda gasped and drew back.

"Easy." Lachlan put up one hand in caution. "It's just Sorley and Ronan."

The vampires pulled back their cloak hoods enough to reveal their faces, keeping their heads covered against the sun. Ronan's fierce, domineering expression made Micky recoil from him a bit. No one in their right mind would want to meet this vampire in a dark, lonely place. Sorley's sardonic expression always held enough humor it would be difficult to fear him. Micky supposed it worked well for deceiving victims; they could be lured into peril before they knew what bit them.

"What about your eyes?" Gilda asked, taking one step toward the vampires she feared. "Don't you need something like sunglasses to keep them from hurting in this sunlight?"

Ronan smiled, easing his sardonic expression into something calmer. "You'd think so, aye. But that's not the way of it. We can do without the sunglasses."

"Are we ready, then?" Sorley asked. "Let's kick some ancient vampire ass."

Erin looked at Lachlan, then at Micky and Jared. "How about you? Ready?"

Micky nodded. "As ready as I can be."

Jared took Micky's gloved hand and squeezed gently. "Ready as I'll ever be."

Micky's confidence surged. While she didn't want to be too cocky about what she could do, she also felt that whatever happened would happen. She loved Jared with all her heart, and yet she couldn't control the entire outcome today.

She turned a smile on Jared. *I love you.*

Jared's gaze sparkled with affection. *I love you, too.*

Ronan grinned, his broad smile raw masculinity. God, if he ever did decide to seduce a woman, the man wouldn't have any trouble. One look from those sin-and-sex eyes and about any female within a hundred yards would succumb.

"Okay, lovebirds, let's get this show on the road, eh?" Ronan asked.

"Aye," Sorley said as he headed away.

As they'd discussed earlier, Jared walked ahead of Micky, and Erin followed Micky. Lachlan came behind Erin. Gilda walked behind Lachlan, then Tom. Ronan took up the rear.

As they walked Micky's mind churned with possibilities. For a second the walls she'd built around her trepidation dissolved and new apprehension rushed inside. What if they couldn't do this? What if?

We can and we will. Ronan's voice filled her head. *You can and you will.*

At peace again, she let security brush away her fears.

They tracked into the woods about a hundred yards before Sorley stopped at the wooden doors tucked into a small mounded hillside. The doors looked like those to a storm cellar.

"Does anyone know what these tunnels were for?" Gilda asked. "I mean, they all lead to this one point, don't they?"

As the group gathered around the doors, Ronan answered. "Yes. Micky? Did your uncle explain how these tunnels came to be?"

She shook her head. "He never explained it to me. When I was a kid I didn't go in the basement, and he always told me these doors were for a storm cellar. That was as far as he explained."

"How old is the house?" Jared asked.

Micky thought back. "Late 1890's."

"Maybe the tunnels were here before the house was," Tom said. "As long as I've lived around here, though, I never heard about these tunnels. Carl Gunn kept it a secret."

"No more time for speculation. Let's go," Ronan said.

Without waiting for Micky to unlock them, Ronan wrenched open the doors, breaking the lock.

Micky gave him a disconcerted look. "Thanks, Ronan."

His eyes glowed with unearthly light. "My pleasure."

When they reached the bottom of the ladder they turned on flashlights. Although they could all see in the dark rather well now, especially Ronan and Sorley, Tom couldn't.

Tom asked, "How do we know he's here?"

"Trust me," Ronan said.

"We can feel him." Sorley wrinkled his thin nose. "It's a creepy sensation."

"It's like a dark, hard punch to the diaphragm," Micky said as she acknowledged she could also feel him.

Jared nodded when she glanced at him. "You've got that right."

"So we've all got a feckin' radar for him. Let's get it on," Sorley said as they walked into the mouth of hell.

* * * * *

As the day wore on, the ancient one grew tired of games.

He popped in and out of buildings, his power undiminished by the light as he wore his cloak and remained invisible. He walked among the mortals in Pine Forest with the omnipotence of long acquired iniquity. He enjoyed watching them grow more fearful, their petty conversations forgotten as they whispered to each other with terror in their eyes. Like people caught in a war zone, they now understood they weren't safe.

As he stalked the library, he remembered how he'd tasted Gilda here and how he'd almost had Erin for his own. His full power restored to him, he could now do what he couldn't a short time ago.

He could have Erin once and for all.

If the motley grouping thought they could stop him this time, they would experience a rude awakening. He could have cloaked in their presence at the Gun Inn, but the other vampires would have felt him. Perhaps the one's he had taken and bitten would also sense him. A nasty byproduct of his bite, unfortunately. Too bad he'd left them alive; perhaps if they hadn't fought to live he would be rid of them all and Erin would be Dasoria. Be his own.

He enjoyed toying and terrorizing them with uncertainty. All mortals could be manipulated into animal actions, into going by the base in their natures. What a glorious feeling to torment mortals. They were so easy to guide in the direction he wanted.

No, skullduggery wouldn't do. Direct, deadly intervention was required to achieve his ultimate goal.

Tired of reminiscing about his attack on Erin and Gilda, he knew a little sleep would bring him even more power. Remaining invisible, he traveled like a bat, floating on air as all vampires could, traveling with a preternatural speed. Once at the tunnel entrance he saw the lock broken on the doors and knew someone walked within. Inhaling deeply he closed his eyes and sought the identity of the intruder.

Ah, Erin was with her invading gang of friends. The ancient one felt the disturbance as he materialized into the tunnels beneath the Gunn Inn. Bloodlust pushed him toward greater needs, toward the continuing malevolence he loved so much.

Omnipotent, he grew stronger by the minute. With a smile of evil intent, the vampire popped into the farthest reaches of the tunnels, where he'd first encountered Micky not so long ago.

He smiled as his old skin crinkled. He would await them here and when they found him, they would wish they'd never been born.

* * * * *

As they walked into the dark tunnels, going deeper into a maelstrom, Micky thought of a passage from another Edgar Allen Poe story. She quoted softly, "'There are moments when, even to the sober eye of reason, the world of our sad Humanity may assume the semblance of a Hell—but the imagination of man is no Carathis, to explore with impunity it's every cavern.'"

"What?" Sorley asked.

Jared chuckled, his laughter guarded. "It's another of Micky's excursions into Edgar Allen Poe."

"*The Premature Burial*," Ronan said as if he talked about the weather. "A rather wise but narcissistic gentleman, old Edgar."

Surprise ran through Micky. "You knew him?"

"I did," Ronan said.

"And a weird experience it was, I'll bet," Sorley said.

Ronan sighed. "I liked him, idiosyncrasies and all. He was an insightful man and not always appreciated."

"Being a vampire, I wouldn't think there would be many people you'd think were weird," Jared said.

Ronan kept walking, on the face of it unaffected by Jared's snide remark. "I don't know, Thornton. I think you could even give old Edgar a run for his money."

To head off another testosterone laden confrontation, Micky said, "Maybe it's not appropriate to be spouting quotes, but—"

Tom halted. "*Shhh*. What was that?"

Everyone eased to a stop and Micky thought she heard wings rustling. An image of bats flying about in the darkness took hold of her imagination. She shivered.

"More misunderstood animals," Ronan said, apparently reading her mind. "Bats are fine creatures."

"Do you turn in to a bat?" Gilda asked.

Sorley chuckled. "Vampires are more sophisticated than that. Most of us can't turn into animals."

"Most of you," Gilda said, her voice becoming wary.

Sorley shrugged. His golden eyes, shining in the darkness, flicked to Ronan. "Aye, most."

Words spilled from Micky's mouth before she could. "Then why does the ancient one have the face of a gargoyle?" When no one answered she asked, "Well?"

"Some vampires adopt such a countenance because of their malevolence," Ronan said. "A gargoyle is only one representation of evil."

Sorley made a grunt of agreement. "Sure, and in the case of the creature we're hunting, a true image."

"I thought gargoyles were put on medieval buildings to ward off evil," Erin said, her voice almost too soft to be heard.

"That's true," Lachlan said. "But to many the gargoyle is just scary. You know how it is. Humans can make anything evil."

Micky nodded. "By virtue of our ignorance."

"Can we move on?" Tom asked as she shone his flashlight over the walls and floor. "This place is giving me the creeps."

They proceeded deep into the interior like explorers on a jungle expedition, an adventure promised around every corner, topped with a healthy slice of danger. In an action adventure novel Micky would enjoy the edge-of-your-seat feeling. In this case it tightened her nerves into ready-to-snap status.

Before she could surround herself in positive thoughts, a malignant feeling built inside her like hurricane. Maybe the ancient one lurked nearby. She stopped in her tracks. "I feel something very strange."

Jared started to reach for her, his lips parted as if to ask a question. Before he spoke, the flashlights went out and solid darkness overtook them.

She gasped, her heart ramming into overdrive. A wall of night seemed to surround her and she put out her hand in the general direction of Jared.

Why didn't anyone speak? She hadn't even heard an exclamation from anyone.

As she stood stock still with building horror, a new terror unleashed upon her.

"Jared?"

No answer.

"Jared!"

No answer.

She was alone.

Chapter Fifteen

ഇ

Jared reached out for Micky as she disappeared, her form blinking out like a light bulb. His heart leapt into his throat, his fear staggering. "No!"

Gilda screamed and Tom wrapped her in his arms. Lachlan also encompassed Erin in his embrace. Everyone spoke at once.

As a million voices pounded in his head, Jared thought he would never take another breath without the agony of seeing Micky disappear returning to him over and over. For this was the embodiment of every nightmare he'd suffered. His love stripped from him, never to be seen again.

His heart stilled, anguish ripping through him. He turned in a circle, his gaze searching every portion of the darkness for the woman he loved.

"Shut up!" Ronan's voice tore through the commotion. "Everyone be quiet."

"I am here," the ancient one's voice said.

Jared took an involuntary step forward the disembodied voice. "Where is she? What have you done with her, you sick bastard?"

A chuckle rustled through the tunnel, and chills of illness and disgust rolled through Jared's body. "I've done nothing." The voice didn't sound as confident. "Something else has taken her. I am here for Dasoria."

Rage boiled inside Jared. Gathering his hands into fists he readied for a fight. "If that isn't the biggest crock of shit I've ever heard. What did you do with her? I swear to God, if you've hurt her—"

"Leave off!" Ronan grabbed Jared's arm. "Leave off!"

Jared yanked his arm out of Ronan's grip. "No!"

Ronan glared, and Jared saw for the first time the full force of Ronan's startling eyes. Golden but ringed with red fury, the vampire's gaze and tight expression would have sent fear through Jared at any other time. Now Jared challenged Ronan in his mind, his desire to find Micky more powerful and his love stronger than any trepidation.

If this asshole fucking vampire hurts her, I swear to God you're the first one I'm coming after.

Ronan's glare eased, the fire in his eyes simmering rather than leaping like flames from a fire pit. *We'll find her.*

Sorley's voice came into Jared's head. *Listen to Ronan. He knows of what he speaks. If you want her back, you must listen.*

Shaking, Jared allowed the gut-wrenching rage to seep from him. Ronan was right, whether Jared wanted to admit it or not. Without control they couldn't expect a victory.

Ronan held his hands out, his gesture like a plea. "Places. Move into place. Now!"

Everyone took their assigned spots. Jared took Tom's hand, Tom took Gilda's. Gilda linked fingers with Erin and Lachlan clasped Erin's other hand. Lachlan took Sorley's hand and last but not least Sorley took Jared's hand.

Ronan readied his weapon. The click as he took off the safety sounded loud in Jared's ears.

The circle was linked.

* * * * *

Micky froze. Her mind whirled, unable to register what happened to her friends.

Silence enveloped the tunnel. An eerie ambiance occupied the area, one with hard, sharp edges. Damp soil and decay touched Micky's sense of smell, reminding her again of Edgar's premature burial story. A *drip, drip* noise rapped at her ears like Chinese water torture. Like a beast waiting, crouched in the bushes, the tunnels seemed to breathe in and out, in and out. Expanding and contracting, the walls moaned. She heard it now as well as felt it.

Then she understood. The place was alive.

"I am here," the walls rasped. "I am more than you know and everything you fear. I am the darkness in every soul, the hate in every word, the midnight upon every day."

An answer ran through her head, a pitiful recognition. She was in the presence of the greatest evil. The one malevolence ruling all evil. Iniquity arrived on the back of many forms, insidious and treacherous.

This monster overruled even the ancient one.

Quaking shook her belly, tight adrenaline spiking through her system like electricity. Loneliness and yawning despair rose like entities from a putrid grave, begging her to give into the dark.

How many times did she dream this scenario in one form or another? Alone and afraid, she would wander a wasteland. Climb mountains and call for anyone, anyone at all to speak. Amble down hallways to discover no one lived here anymore. Abandoned and alone, she would scream out in her nightmare. As shivered with cold, she whispered in her mind, hoping for a semblance of contact with the man she loved.

Jared, where are you?

A deep rasping came from the walls. "He is not here, and neither are the others. We are alone."

Her hands felt damp and hot, and she brushed her fingers off on her jeans. "Ancient one?"

"The ancient one deals with the others. I deal with you."

"Oh my God."

"There is no god or goddess who would help you now."

She hesitated, her chaotic feelings trampling reasonableness. "Where are we?"

"You are within your nightmares."

"Who are you?"

"I am everything and nothing. The blackness and the light. I come in all forms and in nothing. I am birthed from the horrible thought-forms of many. I am created from hate."

Thought forms. Could this entity be an elemental brought on by the events this tunnel witnessed over time? "Are you helping the ancient one?"

Another rasping, grating breath filled the darkness. "The ancient one helps me."

Confusion gave way to comprehension. While they'd believed the ancient one was the being they needed to worry about, something far worse evolved.

"Join me," the walls said. "Join with me and become a part of me."

She clutched her fists together and turned in a slow circle, eyeballing the walls of this tunnel as they moved in and out. "I was a part of something until you took me away."

The walls groaned and now she could hear a heartbeat thudding in her ears. "I saved you from the torture your friends will endure. Now you will stay with me. We will become one as I have become one with many others."

"Stop it." Her voice went taut with strain. "Damn you. I don't want to be here. If I have to die to resist you, I will!"

Worry for Jared and the others made her panic launch upward like a missile.

In that moment she almost succumbed, swallowed up in the maw of an unforgiving, ravenous monster. Insanity lurked inside this evil, waiting for her to lose all control.

Then something inside Micky whispered.

Resistresistresit.

Rage tore up through her throat. "What have you done with my friends? Answer me!"

Again she felt an icy breath upon her neck, and she whirled to see nothing there. Heart pounding, she backed away from the unseen presence. She would have backed against a wall, then remembered the entire tunnel respired with evil life. If she leaned against the wall she feared *it* would absorb her. Digest her like a flesh-eating plant.

A dark laugh echoed, this one far worse than anything she'd heard coming from the ancient one.

Stark fear could have sent her running. Instead courage swelled inside Micky, giving her the strength to elude madness.

She fought the evil with her wits, her desire to survive, her love for Jared.

She found her voice. "Did you kill the young couple in the tunnel?"

"In every small way I help evil. The ancient one is a part of me. I'm within and without, a natural part of the world. Where there is good, I am there to bring evil."

To her surprise, the creature's answers made sense in a foul way. "Then you helped the ancient one to kill all those other people. The ancient one feeds off your evil. It made him stronger."

"Yes. As all evil beings do."

"You made him stronger than he would have been if he hadn't come here to rest and hide."

"Yes."

Tension eased from Micky as she learned more about this enemy. She took a deep breath and tried to stop her entire body from shaking. Curiosity overran some anxiety. "What are you?"

Darkness pressed in on her vision as the tunnel grew dimmer. Despite her enhanced ability to see in the dark, the place grew dusky. "I am humanity's worst fears and nightmares."

Not good enough. "Who are you?" she asked yet again.

"I am that which cannot be named."

Again the entity's statements made a weird sort of sense. "Why are you here?"

"I have existed since the world came into being. I am the antithesis of good."

"Pure evil," she whispered. When the entity said nothing she continued. "Why can I hear you?"

A long, drawn in breath touched her hearing, then the inevitable releasing of breath. "Among humans you are extraordinary. Now touched by the vampire you are more. You always have and always will know, hear, see, and feel more than most. There are others like you, vampire and not, who can know, hear, see, and feel me."

"What if I don't want to stay with you?"

"You have no choice, if I wish to keep you."

"How can I convince you to let me go?"

"You cannot."

Seconds ticked, and again she could hear everything. Water trickling somewhere, the earth shifting, the patter of mice running. But the voice said nothing.

"Return me to my friends."

"No."

A strange idea came to her. "Are you the shadow people?"

"Some shadows are part of me. Others are not."

Aggravated, she pressed for more answers. "The shadows that have surrounded me since I was a child. Are they a part of you?"

"No."

Relief sparked new hope inside Micky, and another revelation came. "Did you come here because this town has so much evil inside it?"

"I was here before the town. I will be here when the town no longer is."

Tears filled her eyes as frustration, fear, and a yearning desire to save Jared and her friends from the ancient one pierced her soul.

"Where am I?" she asked

"You are on a different plane from that which you existed moments ago."

Confusion warred with a weird sense of understanding. "You mean I'm in another tunnel?"

"You are in the same tunnel on a different dimension. Layers upon layers of dimension reside in this world. You see only part of it. You sometimes see your shadows."

"They exist on a different plane?"

"They are a part of your world for only a flicker of time. This is when you see them."

"I don't want to stay in your dimension."

Silence greeted her, and then the answer came to her out of the darkness and terror.

Somehow she'd stepped into the evil's pathway and became stuck in this element. She must leave it by sheer will. Whether she made it out of this situation alive was entirely up to her.

Paralyzed by indecision, she didn't move. What could she do?

"Come with me," the dark voice asked. "And we will watch the night for eternity."

She knew then the time had arrived. Now or never.

Shadows, please help me. As Micky's insides trembled with exhaustion, she wanted to sink down and rest but knew she didn't dare.

For several seconds a comforting feeling encompassed her, as if some benevolent presence attempted to surround her but then fell back.

She closed her eyes and imaged the shadows she'd known all her life surrounding her, but this time in an attempt to rescue.

Please shadows help me.

A vicious blast of wind roared through the caverns, ripping past her face and whistling in her ears like a freight train. She put her hands of her ears, crying out in reaction. Strange voices whispered, tickling her hearing with their feathery voices.

Helpherhelpherhelpher.

"No!" The tunnel echoed with a fierce cry of evil, guttural and sharp. "You shall not save her!"

Seconds later the wind disappeared, as if the shadows tried and failed.

As her body shivered in reaction, she had one thought.

Perhaps love alone could save her.

Jared, please hear me. Jared I love you!

* * * * *

As the group formed the circle, Jared felt a phantom pressure yanking at his grip, trying to tear his hands away from the others. A wind gathered speed, pressing against their bodies and buffeting from all sides.

"It's trying to separate us!" Gilda cried.

Lachlan's voice rang out. "Hold on!"

Ronan closed his eyes. "At Sorley's instruction everyone must invoke the white light! Spread it to the center of the circle and beyond you to encompass the room."

"Never!" the ancient one's voice came in a shriek.

Jared closed his eyes as well, ready to do everything he must to retrieve Micky and conquer the ancient vampire. As the power again tried to pull his hands away from the others', he drew in a deep breath and remembered what Ronan and Sorley taught the group earlier in the day. He felt the rush of white and gold light swim over him, a protective aura. It spread around him like a blanket, warming him until the glow seemed to pulsate from the center of his forehead. He felt the light increase until it extended way beyond him. Within seconds he felt the auras of all the others reach out and touch his.

One more time the force tried to pull his hands away from the others. He gritted his teeth.

Erin called out. "Hang on! Don't anyone let go!"

Sorley added his instruction. "On my mark, on the count of three, invoke the white light! One, two, three!"

Jared imagined the light streaming from his forehead and joining in the center with the others to form a blazing white circle.

A growl came from the air; it surrounded them all, the loud noise bouncing off the walls. Jared thought he heard a cry of anguish from Ronan, but he didn't dare open his eyes. Seconds later a gun shot rang out, and Jared flinched at the loud retort. Tom and Soley both jerked, their hands tightening around Jared's.

"Don't open your eyes!" Ronan's voice sounded harsh, almost in pain. "Don't let go!"

Alarm raced through Jared as he struggled to hold the white light in his mind. Shoving back the fear attempting to overwhelm him, he kept his grip locked with Tom and Sorley. Slowly power rippled through his fingers and suddenly the white flowed between them all, around the circle by way of their linked arms. Confidence pushed back his fear. They could do this. *They could.*

In his mind's eye Jared thought he saw, for a flash of a second, the horrible gargoyle head Micky must have seen.

A shot rang out.

A long, anguished cry pierced Jared's ears.

It echoed and unfolded, growing louder until Jared almost ripped his hands away from the others. Something told him it wasn't quite over. He had to hold on.

The cry faded, slow and sure until it disappeared all together.

Silence invaded, almost as unnerving as the horrible cries echoing through the tunnels moments earlier.

Ronan's voice came, this time rasping and weak. "Open your eyes. It is over, at least for now."

Jared complied, his grip loosening but not releasing. Around him the tunnel remained dark, but with his enhanced vision he could see the others standing near him. They looked as dazed as he felt, unsure and worried. Ronan sat against one wall of the tunnel, his face even more pale and his eyes almost glassy with what looked like pain. Gilda kept her hand linked with her husband, and Erin had buried her face in Lachlan's chest.

"You can let go now." Sorley wrestled his hand from Jared's grip. Sorley headed toward Ronan. "You all right?"

Ronan stood with help from his friend. "I'm perfect." He lifted the weapon and looked at it. "Trusty little thing, this. Plugged the bastard again."

As everyone released each other, Jared couldn't relinquish all his concern. "We've still got to find Micky." Another horrid thought came to mind. "What if he took her with him?"

Ronan shook his head. "I don't think so. Something else is going on here."

Slow panic crept up on Jared. He covered his eyes with his hand for a moment, weariness mixing with a cold, hard pit that seemed to grow in his stomach minute by minute.

Erin looked up, but Lachlan kept his arms around her. "We'll find her, Jared."

"How?" Tom asked.

Gilda smiled, and for a second Jared wondered what in the hell she could possibly be happy about at a time like this.

"I think I can help there," Gilda said. "There's one thing I didn't tell any of you because I didn't think of it before. I've developed a very strange ability since the ancient one bit me. I'm like a human blood hound. I can see into other dimensions. Earlier, when Micky just disappeared, I thought I could see where she'd gone. But then we were caught up in trying to fight the ancient one."

Ronan walked to the center of the group. "Then let's get on with it and see if we can find her. I've heard of this ability to see completely into dimensions, but unfortunately I don't have it and neither does Sorley."

"But you're vampires," Tom said with disbelief.

Sorley grunted. "Aye. But that doesn't mean we can do everything. We saw the shadow people, we can see ghosts."

"We've got to get her back," Jared said, desperation making his voice harsh. "I'll go to hell to get Micky back."

Ronan clapped on hand on Jared's shoulder and in uncharacteristic support he gave a squeeze. "We'll find her, old man. Sure, and if you can hang on to your faith a bit longer."

Gilda pulled her hat down farther on her head and closed her eyes. "I'll try now."

Jared prayed with all his being they could find her soon. In his mind he felt a feathery touch and he flinched. "Oh God."

"What's wrong?" Lachlan asked.

Jared shook his head. "It feels like...like someone's mind brushed up against mine." He speared Gilda with a look. "Was that you?"

Gilda said nothing, her eyes still closed. Jared heard the sound in his mind again, and he rejoiced.

Jared. Please hear me, Jared. I love you.

A half sob, half groan of relief left his lips and he placed one hand against the tunnel wall for support. "Oh God. I heard Micky. She's alive."

* * * * *

Exhaustion spilled over Micky as she forced her legs to hold her up. She couldn't lean up against the walls, afraid of their breathing, their obvious organic life. "Must stay awake."

Shadow people whispered to her, their voices strengthening. Their dark forms flitted around her like whispers on the night. Their entreaties, though not always recognizable as words she could understand, bolstered her to life. One theme repeated in her mind, the only reassurance she possessed.

Savehersavehersave her.

Beyond their insistence, she didn't hear the evil voice.

She experienced the blackness like a lead weight around her neck, dragging her into the deepness beyond. Her heart and soul yearned for clarity through the stained, horrible muck.

More than anything she wanted to see the man she loved. She ached to have Jared's arms around her and to tell him she loved him more than anything in heaven or earth. When she reached him he would know how much he meant to her if it took a hundred years for her to explain.

Desperate, she allowed her mind to reach out. *Jared, hear me. I love you more than anything. Please find me. Please.*

Micky thought she heard something tickling at her mind, like a timid inquiry. She reached for the sound, amplified it in her mind. Another voice? More cautious than the whisperings of the shadow people, the voice filtered into her awareness.

Micky? Micky is that you?

This time the female tone sounded somewhat familiar.

She put her energy into replying back. *Erin?*

It's Gilda. I can hear you and see you in a tunnel. Where are you?

Relief slammed through Micky. *In some sort of dimensional warp or alternate plane. I don't know how I got here.*

Hold on, we'll get you out.

Renewed energy made her open her eyes as she looked around at the walls of the tunnel. Although the walls undulated with the smallest of motions, she thought maybe the evil's hold on her weakened.

"I'm going to get out of here," she whispered with dawning joy.

"No!" the voice came out of the dark, banging against her ears and assaulting her. "You shall not leave!"

Voices once again converged, but this time they seemed all around the tunnel and not just inside her head.

Helpherhelpherhelpher.

Then she heard the one voice most dear to her. Jared. *Micky, I'm here. We're going to get you out of there, baby. Hold on and concentrate on us. We're going to link hands. Imagine us all reaching out for you. Imagine the shadow people helping you.*

With everything within her, Micky answered. *Yes. Jared, I love you.*

I love you, too.

Now was the time to assert her resolve.

She allowed relaxation to take over her muscles as she closed her eyes, her heart thumping with a steady but calm beat.

She would prevail.

In seconds she felt a warm glow surrounding and heating her body. Coldness receded and in her mind's eye she envisioned her friends holding hands. Every voice mixed with the shadow people's consistent call.

Wewillsaveherwewillsaveherwewillsaveher.

Wind picked up, swirling dust. Generating speed, the force buffeted against her until it blew with gale force. She put her hands out and up and braced her feet apart.

Breathing rapidly, she kept her eyes closed and hoped for the best. "I'm free from you!"

"No!" The evil voice vented its frustration, crying out louder the more she resisted its pull. "You will not resist me."

"I am my own!"

Her feet left the ground and before she could scream in alarm, the vision of her friends helping her faded and blinked out.

Seconds or maybe minutes went by. Blanketed like a person in a sensory deprivation chamber, she knew nothing but her own breathing and the rushing wind.

A popping sound made her jerk and all her senses returned.

Micky heard urgent voices nearby, and hard, powerful arms surrounded her.

"We did it!" Gilda's triumphant voice called out.

Laugher, mixed with cries of joy, came to Micky's ears.

"Is she all right?" Erin asked.

"She looks so pale." Lachlan said.

"Takes a few moments to come out of a dimensional slip," Sorley said.

"Micky." Jared's voice, rough with emotion, penetrated the fog in her mind. His arms tightened around her, then his fingers brushed her forehead and cheek with infinite tenderness. "Micky. Come on, wake up. Damn it, talk to me."

Joy made her struggle to obey. She succeeded and opened her eyes. Jared's eyes shimmered with tears, and she realized he sat on the ground with her clasped in his arms.

He smiled and tears fell on his cheeks. He closed his eyes and threw his head back. "Thank you, God."

"It's good to be back," she said with a dry, husky voice.

"Welcome to reality," Sorley said. "Such as it is."

Surrounded by the smiling faces of her friends, Micky released all fright. As Jared picked her up in his arms and they started to leave the tunnel, she thought she saw shadows flickering a short distance away. She smiled.

"What is it?" Jared asked.

"I think the shadow people are still here with me."

"Is that bad?" he asked.

"No. It's a good thing. A very good thing."

* * * * *

When they returned to the surface and back to the house, they discovered they'd spent much more time in the tunnels then they expected. To Micky it seemed time had sped forward at a furious pace, their reality altered in more ways than one. Night had descended.

Micky and Jared headed upstairs immediately; they wanted showers to cleanse away the dirt and the feeling they'd been touched by evil. They bathed together, and although she loved the touch of his hands coasting over her, and sensual stirrings touched her body, they knew sexual fulfillment would wait until later when they both rested. For the time being they cherished feelings of safety and contentment as they rinsed horror from their hearts and minds.

As they toweled dry and put on fresh clothing, Micky said, "I didn't know if I was going to see you again."

Jared pulled a sweatshirt over his head. "I know. I felt the same way."

She reached out and he tugged her into his arms. His lips touched her forehead as he pressed tender kisses over her skin. "For a minute there I thought I'd lost you forever." He buried his face in her hair and drew her even closer to him. "God, how I love you. And if we didn't need to get downstairs and discuss what happens next, I'd lay you down on that bed and make serious love to you."

"Mmm. That sounds nice." She sighed in happiness as warm arousal stirred in her belly. She pulled back far enough to see the fire flickering in his eyes.

"Where do we go from here?" he asked.

"One day at a time, I think."

"This vampire thing isn't over."

"No."

"Are you in it for the long haul? Do you want to stay in Pine Forest and fight for this inn?"

She looked up into his eyes and wondered. Her thoughts came with force. *What about you? If we stay together, we have to compromise.*

He nodded. *I'll quit the Denver police force if I have to, if you want to stay here in Pine Forest and make a go of this inn.*

Really?

Really.

I don't know, Jared. After the ancient one is gone forever, I think I'd like to move to Denver with you. The big city might be safer.

He chuckled. "We'll talk about it later. Let's get some of that food. This psychic shit seems to burn up a lot of calories."

She laughed, and it felt good way down deep where it should. Her heart lightened as if several burdens lifted from her shoulders.

After they settled at the dining room table with everyone else, Micky asked, "What happens next?"

No one answered right away. The chandelier above the big table threw soft light on their wary faces.

In each and every face she saw a new truth. They would stay banded together in their mission to rid the earth of the ancient one, no matter how long it took. Micky believed they would remain friends forever by virtue of mutual understanding and respect. Who could blame them after all they'd experienced together?

As Micky looked from one to the other, she noted their expressions. Exhaustion lined their faces, dark circles under the eyes and a slight downturn to the lips. Gilda looked the most refreshed of them all. Perhaps her vital participation in the situation revived her spirit. She'd already thanked Gilda more than once for finding her in the other dimension.

Sorley was the first one to speak up. He winked. "I say we have a party to celebrate."

Ronan pushed back from the table and crossed his arms. "Sounds like a good idea. But I think the mortals are a little used up. We should give them some time to rest."

Lachlan also moved back from the table. "The ancient one isn't coming back for at least a few days."

A few days. Micky felt the warning all through her.

"How do we know he isn't gone forever?" Micky asked.

Ronan started to speak, then a slightly pained expression crossed his face. "I'll know when the bastard is dead."

"And so will feckin' I," Sorley said.

Micky smiled at his twisted sentence structure. "How long do you believe we have, then?"

Sorley shrugged. "Nothin' is for certain."

Erin sighed and shifted her fingers through her hair. The short strands stood up in a bit of a mess, but she didn't seem to care. "Ronan, didn't you tell us that Halloween might be his most powerful time?"

Ronan's mouth curved with a cruelly handsome grin. "We took a little of the piss out of him, that's to be sure. But he will come back unless..."

When the vampire's voice faded off, Gilda put down her fork and leaned forward. "What?"

Ronan stood and went to the window, looking out into the darkness. "Unless I do as Yusuf said and as the seer said I must."

Sorley turned around in his chair and peered at the other vampire. "Sure, and I didn't really hear what I thought I just heard."

Ronan didn't give his friend a customary glare. Instead he continued to gaze into the night. "I was wrong when I refused to follow with the plan Yusef set out for me. There isn't an alternative."

When Jared smiled, Micky sensed that although he understood the gravity of the situation, Jared took a bit of pleasure from hearing Ronan admit to being wrong.

"Explain this to me again." Tom lifted his glass of water and took a deep sip. "You have to find a woman and do what again?"

Ronan's voice, when it came, rumbled sure and hard from his throat. "I must find a woman who is willing to pretend she wants me. To give the illusion of love."

"I don't understand why that would conquer the ancient one," Gilda said.

"No one does," Lachlan said.

Sorley gulped back a shot glass of whiskey. "No one's tried it to find out if it would work. It has something to do with immortals falling in love with mortals."

"But it must be tried," Ronan said. "Whether I like it or not. I don't see any other solution."

"There's got to be someone out there who would be willing," Micky said without thinking how it would sound.

Ronan's gaze flared with an almost painfully bright intensity. "I can make *any* woman willing. I've taken many women to bed over the centuries. It is a part of me that is no different than the ancient one." Ronan headed toward the door that led to the foyer, his strides sure and certain. "I'm taking a walk. I may not be back for several hours."

With that he left the room. Micky stood up and crossed to the window that looked out onto the driveway. "I don't think I handled that very well."

Jared rose and stood beside her, his arm going around her shoulders. He squeezed gently. "He'll get over it."

"He'll sleep it off in a graveyard, if I know him," Sorley said.

After a short silence, Erin spoke. "We're in this all together, I hope."

Affirmatives went up around the room.

Micky knew the race to save Pine Forest from the ancient one was just beginning.

The End

Why an electronic book?

We live in the Information Age—an exciting time in the history of human civilization, in which technology rules supreme and continues to progress in leaps and bounds every minute of every day. For a multitude of reasons, more and more avid literary fans are opting to purchase e-books instead of paper books. The question from those not yet initiated into the world of electronic reading is simply: *Why?*

1. *Price.* An electronic title at Ellora's Cave Publishing and Cerridwen Press runs anywhere from 40% to 75% less than the cover price of the exact same title in paperback format. Why? Basic mathematics and cost. It is less expensive to publish an e-book (no paper and printing, no warehousing and shipping) than it is to publish a paperback, so the savings are passed along to the consumer.

2. *Space.* Running out of room in your house for your books? That is one worry you will never have with electronic books. For a low one-time cost, you can purchase a handheld device specifically designed for e-reading. Many e-readers have large, convenient screens for viewing. Better yet, hundreds of titles can be stored within your new library—on a single microchip. There are a variety of e-readers from different manufacturers. You can also read e-books on your PC or laptop computer. (Please note that Ellora's Cave does not endorse any specific brands.

You can check our websites at www.ellorascave.com or www.cerridwenpress.com for information we make available to new consumers.)

3. *Mobility.* Because your new e-library consists of only a microchip within a small, easily transportable e-reader, your entire cache of books can be taken with you wherever you go.

4. *Personal Viewing Preferences.* Are the words you are currently reading too small? Too large? Too… ANNOYING? Paperback books cannot be modified according to personal preferences, but e-books can.

5. *Instant Gratification.* Is it the middle of the night and all the bookstores near you are closed? Are you tired of waiting days, sometimes weeks, for bookstores to ship the novels you bought? Ellora's Cave Publishing sells instantaneous downloads twenty-four hours a day, seven days a week, every day of the year. Our webstore is never closed. Our e-book delivery system is 100% automated, meaning your order is filled as soon as you pay for it.

Those are a few of the top reasons why electronic books are replacing paperbacks for many avid readers.

As always, Ellora's Cave and Cerridwen Press welcome your questions and comments. We invite you to email us at Comments@ellorascave.com or write to us directly at Ellora's Cave Publishing Inc., 1056 Home Avenue, Akron, OH 44310-3502.

COMING TO A BOOKSTORE NEAR YOU!

ELLORA'S CAVE

Bestselling Authors Tour

UPDATES AVAILABLE AT
WWW.ELLORASCAVE.COM

Cerridwen, the Celtic Goddess of wisdom, was the muse who brought inspiration to story-tellers and those in the creative arts. Cerridwen Press encompasses the best and most innovative stories in all genres of today's fiction. Visit our site and discover the newest titles by talented authors who still get inspired - much like the ancient storytellers did, once upon a time.

CERRIDWEN PRESS

www.cerridwenpress.com

Discover for yourself why readers can't get enough
of the multiple award-winning publisher

Ellora's Cave.

Whether you prefer e-books or paperbacks,

be sure to visit EC on the web at
www.ellorascave.com

for an erotic reading experience that will leave you
breathless.

3697431

Made in the USA